# JAZZ TOWN

a novel

by

Beth Lyon Barnett

ISBN: 13: 978-1477645857
      10: 1477645853

Published by: Prairie Acres Press
Prairie Village, Kansas
USA

# DEDICATION

*TO GLENN*
*for his love and relentless encouragement*

"Jazz is a good barometer of freedom. In its beginnings, the United States spawned certain ideals of freedom and independence through which, eventually, jazz was evolved, and the music is so free that many people say it is the only unhampered, unhindered expression of complete freedom yet produced in this country." *Duke Ellington*

# ACKNOWLEDGEMENTS

All my life I've heard tales about Kansas City, Missouri and its beginnings. As a writer I found such fertile background material irresistible. The story is a figment of my imagination but it would have been impossible to write without reference to real people who lived during that incredible era. Still, I might not have undertaken the task without the encouragement of the members of the Kansas City Writers Group, including Robert Chrisman and Karin Frank who read and critiqued my early efforts. Many others have read the book and made helpful suggestions. Thanks to Leon Brady, the well known percussionist, and Linda Richter, co-founder of Kansas City Youth Jazz, Inc., herself a musician and my persevering cheerleader, for their priceless knowledge and advice. In the long run, however, it was the e-pub group, Write Brain Trust, that helped me bring the novel to fruition. Special thanks to C.M. Lance and Norm Ledgin, both acclaimed authors, for beyond patient tech support, and incredible editing. Thanks to Maril Crabtree for her help and imaginative suggestions, and thanks to my creative daughter Lynn Barnett for her constant support and encouragement.

# CONTENTS

# CHAPTER ONE

## KANSAS CITY, MISSOURI
## 1916
## REBECCA

No one sees me slip out of the house. Seething with anger, I have to get away from my father. I throw on my new beaver coat, a gift from him to celebrate my sixteenth birthday, and keep in the shadows until I reach the street. In a rage I hurry toward town. When I can no longer see my house, I slow my pace and try to think.

This is America. Fathers can't just give away their daughters. Yet mine has done exactly that, betrothed me to a man thirty-six years my senior.

Worse still, I know him. He set my arm once. My father told me that Kurt Adler had been educated at the Heidelberg Medical Academy. In fact I've heard my father and his German Jewish friends brag about it. It means nothing to me.

I won't do it. I'll run away. I'll kill myself.

Night closes in as I pass the haberdashery, then the grocery store, and finally the dress shop, now dark and locked up tight. At least my father promised to put off the wedding until my eighteenth birthday. I have two years to figure something out.

As I near the center of Kansas City, the streets become well lit. Hordes of people bustle by, huddled together against the cold.

One thing father taught me never to do: go anywhere without mad money. I clutch my purse to my chest.

I hear lively music coming from the noisy bars. I jump back as two men fight their way out of one of them. Immediately, a crowd gathers and the excitement escalates. Blood spatters as fists meet faces.

The men knock each other down but people pick them up and shove them back together. Caught in the melee, exhilaration pulses through my body.

Someone grabs my arm and jerks me out of the mob. My father? In spite of my caution, has he caught me? I turn and look instead at the grinning face of Jimmy Galeno.

Relief floods over me, and then anger.

"Hey" I yell. "Let go of me."

"Not on your life. I'm saving a damsel in distress." He laughs. "What are you doing here anyway?"

I know Jimmy from school and I don't like him."Leave me alone."

"Is that any way to talk to a knight in shining armor?" he jokes, steering me to a quieter spot. "Explain yourself."

"Go to hell." I jerk away.

"Aw, come on, Rebecca." He sounds contrite. "There's gotta be some reason you're out wandering the streets at this time of night. You can tell me."

I look closer at him, surprised that I've never before noticed his Italian good looks. That prompts me to remember my father ranting that the Galenos are Cosa Nostra, Sicilians who kill people. A tremor races through my body. Maybe I can get him to murder my father.

"You won't believe it if I tell you." My rage returns. Weeping bitter tears, I relate the events of the evening.

"So," I say, wiping my eyes with my fingers, "I decided to take a walk and figure out what to do. Then those two men began hitting each other, the best and only real fight I've ever seen. Took my mind off my troubles."

"Wait long enough and there'll be another, but we can find better things to do." He takes my hand and steers me down an alley toward the rear door of a bar.

" Let's go inside where it's warm. My old man owns this place. Would you like a drink?"

I smile, thinking my father doesn't even allow me to taste the dinner wine.

"Something hot would be nice."

He takes me into a back room furnished with a red leather couch, a roll top desk, and an oriental rug. While he goes to get our drinks, I shrug out of my coat, fluff up my hair, and sit. I hear the noise from the bar, yet this place feels cozy and warm.

Jimmy returns with mugs of steaming hot cocoa, sweet and delicious. One swallow warms me through and through.

"Good, huh?" he said.

"Yum."

We talk of school. I remind him of the time I broke my arm when he tripped me while skating on the frozen pond.

"Doctor Adler, the man my father wants me to marry, set it," I tell Jimmy, "so in fact, this whole awful mess is your fault."

He laughs, strands of dark hair falling over his forehead. I've never before observed his long dark lashes or his gentle, soulful eyes. He takes my empty mug and goes to get a refill. I lean my head back, the room spinning pleasantly. When Jimmy returns, he sits next to me and places the steaming mug to my lips.

"Here, drink some more of this and all your problems will melt away," he whispers.

I close my eyes and sip the warm chocolate, the foam coating my upper lip. But my tongue doesn't lick away the bubbles. His does, and then I feel his mouth on mine, buttery soft and moist. I moan a little and move closer to him. His hand slips to my breast. and then I feel his lips on the bare skin of my neck.

I know I should make him stop, but the things he does feel so good. The manly, sweet smell of him intoxicates me. Gently he draws my sweater over my head and lays me down, his body over mine. I can feel his hardness pressing against me. His tongue traces the outline of my mouth, tasting, exploring, caressing. Still I don't resist. His fingers touch me everywhere, and when at last, he pushes himself inside me, I give a little cry and then moan with pleasure.

I remember the door bursting open and a tall, heavy set man with a cigar sticking out of his mouth standing over me, eyes sweeping my half-naked body.

Jimmy jumps up. "Dad, I . . . "

"Who is she?" the man asks.

"Just someone I know from school."

"Name? What's her name?"

"Rebecca. Rebecca Stern."

"A yid, Jimmy? Jesus Christ. Don't we have enough trouble without you screwing a yid?"

By now, I've grabbed my fur coat and covered myself. The dreamy state has worn off, and I huddle in the corner of the couch, terrified.

"Get dressed," he tells me. "And you." He looks at Jimmy. "Sober her up and get her out of here." He tosses car keys on the desk. "Now." With a shake of his head, he turns and leaves.

I struggle into my sweater and straighten my clothes.

Jimmy pulls up his pants, jams in his shirt and buckles his belt. "Don't mind him. He always sounds like that. Come on. I'll take you home."

Groggy and giddy, I tiptoe into my father's house feeling somehow triumphant. Safe in my room, I strip off my clothes and fling myself into bed, flush with my newly acquired independence.

The next day I awoke with a splitting headache and sheets stained with blood. I rolled over and moaned with only the vaguest memories of the flightiness and the dark-haired boy who had had his way with me.

# CHAPTER TWO

## KANSAS CITY, MISSOURI
## 1918
### SUSIE MAE

I have a picture in my mind of that red-haired little boy growing up here at Oakbridge, his eyes getting sadder and sadder. Oh, he's not really mine. I'm just the colored second girl, but I think of him as my own, and why not? I raised him, me and my brother John Charles.

Though his mama named him after herself, I expect most of you know him as Pete, but when folks ask us about him, we don't say much. He's Massah Stern to us, but that's because we're just the hired help.

I remember the day he was born. His papa, Doctor Kurt, stood at the foot of the bed awaiting his arrival. His mama, Rebecca, lay in what she called her glow, panting and crying.

Her labor had started around ten the previous morning. I'd just brought her breakfast on a silver tray – tea, toast, and a soft-boiled egg in a silver cup so she could crack off the top and spoon it out. I had set the tray in front of her as usual when she sat straight up in bed, grabbed her huge belly, and let out a gasp.

"Damn," she said. "I think the little monster just kicked me. Felt more like a cramp. Whew." She flopped back on her satin pillow and rested a bit, eyes closed. Then she reached for her napkin.

I puttered around the bedroom waiting for her to crack her egg and tell me I'd cooked it too long or not long enough. She buttered her toast and tapped the knife on her egg, and right then it happened again. "This doesn't feel right, Susie Mae," she said. "Do you suppose something's wrong?"

Though I'm only seventeen, I'd watched my mother birth three little ones, so I knew a lot more about such things than my eighteen year-old mistress. "Could be that baby is trying to tell you something," I said, hoping not to scare her.

Her eyes opened wide. She flung aside her breakfast tray and hoisted herself up, upsetting her juice and the vase of asters I'd picked from the garden."You mean now?" she said. "Right now? You think it's starting?"

"Yessum. I do," I answered, grabbing a towel and dabbing at the mess she'd made. "If not today, soon."

"Well hell-fire, Susie Mae. Don't just stand there. Do something."

"Now Miss Becka, you just relax. Babies don't come all that sudden. Takes a while afore they decides to leave that nice warm spot in your belly and take a peek outside."

"What do you know? You've never had a baby and . . . Oh – oh. He did it again. Don't argue with me, Susie Mae. Get my husband, you hear? And hurry."

Twenty-four hours later, she brushed feebly at her dark mop of damp hair and glared through tears at Doctor Kurt. "What kind of monster are you? Why don't you give me something to help?"

"There, there, sweetheart. It's not that bad is it? It's so much better for the baby if you don't have an anesthetic."

"You idiot. Cut the damn thing out of me or I'll surely die. Pleeease." Worn to a frazzle, her modesty long gone, she clasped my hand and whispered, "Help me, Susie Mae. I can't do this anymore." She screamed as the pains returned.

"Don't be silly, my darling," he told her soothingly, his hand on her belly. "You're almost there. Just a few more good pushes and you'll be holding our baby in your arms. That's a good girl. Bend your knees up. Susie Mae will help you. Higher. Just a little higher. I can see its head."

"You bastard," Miss Becka shrieked and bore down again with clenched teeth.

"A small episiotomy and it will be over," he said, unwrapping a knife he'd brought with him.

I watched him enlarge the birth opening. Then, he looked at her over her legs, her face contorted with pain. He ordered her to give one more good shove. "That'll do it. Here it comes," he cried triumphantly.

He guided the child out. As the baby slipped into his hands, Doctor Kurt gave a sudden sharp intake of breath. I looked up with alarm. Then a smile swept across his face.

Doctor Kurt grasped the infant by the heels and turned him upside down, thwacking him once on the bottom. The baby gasped and then added his own cries to the sobs of his mother. I couldn't help but think that the first thing that baby heard as he entered the world was his mother's shrill voice.

After cutting the cord and tying it with a piece of string, the doctor gently wrapped the little one in a soft yellow receiving blanket and carried him to the head of the bed. "Look Rebecca. We have a beautiful, perfect little boy." He placed the child in my mistress's arms.

Too weary to do more, she took the howling child and turned her head to look at him. Though still wet with the juices of his birth, he stopped crying and stared back at her with eyes as blue as cornflowers and sprouts of red hair.

"I'm so glad he's out," She sighed, sweat and tears covering her face.

Doctor Kurt laughed. "Now you can have your pain medicine," he said as he stuck a needle in her arm and then handed the empty syringe to me. After that, he moved between her legs to finish up. By the time he had done, both mother and child slept.

He moved to the washstand and cleaned himself. "I'm going to the library to tell my father the good news," he told me. "Take the boy and bathe him. Then bring him downstairs to us."

Nodding, I lifted the baby carefully from his mama's arms and held him for the first time. The sweetness of him caught at my heart. As I stood cooing and making silly noises people do around babies, Doctor Kurt took one last peek, grinned, and left, closing the door behind him. I sat myself down in the rocker, unwrapped the blanket, and looked the little one over real good. I uncurled his tiny fists.

My goodness," I told him."You gots the longest fingers I ever did see." I checked out the rest of him looking for birthmarks or moles, making sure he had all his male parts even though I guessed his father had already done that. Then, I poured out a fresh bowl of warm water and bathed his little self from the top of his head to the tips of his toes. He never cried but moved his arms and legs as though he liked getting clean. I dried him and dressed him in clothing from the layette his mama had bought, a soft, thin white shirt and snowy diaper so big it went around him twice. "Don't you worry none, little baby. Afore you know it, you'll have growed in and out of these things." I wrapped him in a fresh cotton blanket with blue embroidery around the edges, and carried him to the chair by the window. Cuddling him close, I rocked him to sleep, a bit of the noon sun on his fire-red hair. I knew right then that he would be mine to care for.

# CHAPTER THREE

## KANSAS CITY, MISSOURI
## 1918
### JOHN CHARLES

Massah Stern's first cry sounded like the screech of an owl, but it rang like music to my ears. Most of the night the house had echoed with Miss Rebecca's pain, but Susie Mae said first babies always come hard. Our Mama Leticia had seemed to pop out each new child like a prune pit, but what did I know of such things?

Before long, here came Doctor Kurt, grinning as wide as the big bend in the river. He hurried into the library where we waited, Mister Max and I. "Father," he announced, sticking his chest out, "I have a son, healthy and fine. Could you hear him cry?"

Mister Max nodded, his smile matching his son's. "We surely did. Sounded like a banshee."

Doctor Kurt collapsed into his brown leather chair. "He's a buster all right. Let out a lusty holler with his very first breath. Freshen my father's drink, John Charles. Bring me one and pour one for yourself so we may all welcome him properly."

"Yessuh," I answered, busying myself at the bar. "Imagine that. We got ourselves a chile in the house. Now ain't that somethin'."

Doctor Kurt brushed at his thick crop of hair, graying now, though I could still see dark around the edges. When I had first arrived at the big house, he and Mister Max looked alike except for their coloring, the doctor dark and tanned, his father pale with carroty red hair thinning. Back then, both stood six feet tall with broad shoulders, wide-set eyes, square jaws, full lower lips, and neatly trimmed mustaches. Up close, you could see Mister Max had pale blue eyes. Doctor Kurt's were dark like chocolate, but I reckon the two men looked as much alike as a father and son ought. The doctor hadn't changed much, older maybe, but Mister Max, he hadn't fared as well. After the fall from his horse, the bottom half of him seemed to shrivel and wither like an autumn leaf. The meat on his bones disappeared. His cheeks sank in, and the freckles on his hands that Miss Molly, rest her soul, called sugar spots melted together. Yet through it all, his mind stayed good and I could tell that a bit of the old fire remained.

"Got a name yet?" he asked.

"Rebecca has said all along if the baby is a boy, she wants to name him Stern," Doctor Kurt said.

"Hum," Mr. Max said.

"Don't be critical. Gentiles do it all the time."

"I like Hans Stern. Good business man."

"You like his money," Doctor Kurt laughed and his father laughed with him. "What would you say to a middle name of Peter after your father?"

Mr. Max nodded. They clinked glasses and toasted the new baby.

Then a stillness fell. The grandfather clock in the hall chimed the half hour, and a bird twittered in the garden.

"First, prep school. Then Harvard," Doctor Kurt finally said. "Later, medical school or perhaps the study of law."

"And what if he doesn't want to be like either of us?" Mister Max asked, his glass unsteady in his hand.

"As the twig is bent, so the tree's inclined," Doctor Kurt said, and I remembered him saying that 'cause of my part in bending that little twig.

## Beth Lyon Barnett

Truth be known, life might have been a whole lot easier for Massah Stern if Doctor Kurt hadn't saved my life and brung me to work at Oakbridge Estate, but destiny had other plans.

The badness began when my father came home one wintery night, drunker and meaner than usual. He plunked his big self down on the porch chair with his half empty bottle in his hand and hollered for Susie Mae. "Get yo puny self out here."

At fifteen, my sister had the body of a young willow tree and skin the color of fresh brewed coffee. Her eyes flashed and sparked with spunk, but sometimes that very thing got her in trouble.

Mama gave us all chores. Susie Mae had to help our daddy remove his big rubber boots and take them out back to wash off the filth and blood. Though she'd done it a million times, she hated it. For some reason, on that very night, she decided she'd had enough. When our daddy called to her from the porch, she pretended not to hear even though our shack had tinder-thin walls, a small cracker box of a place that housed all seven of us yet barely kept the weather at bay. It had begun to snow. The wind swirled around Daddy causing wet snowflakes to dampen his clothes and melt on his face. He yelled for her once, twice, three times, and when she didn't come, he stood up and thundered indoors, bloody boots and all. Mama screamed for him to get his nasty self off her clean floor.

"Shut up, Leticia," he bellowed.

Just then, Susie Mae streaked by him on the way out the door. With one quick motion, Daddy grabbed her arm and hauled her out on the porch. I'd been sitting on our faded old sofa minding the young 'uns when the commotion started, so I saw it all.

"I ain't cleaning your mucky boots no more," my sister told him, "no matter what."

Whack. He smacked her. "You'll do as I say," our daddy roared.

She tried to pull away, but the more she resisted the angrier he got.

"Let her be, James," Mama said calmly from her place at the stove.

But the rage and the alcohol overtook him. He hit her again.

I'd suffered the blows of those huge hands myself a time or two and I knew the pain they caused. I couldn't just sit by and let my sister take a whupping though it would have been better if I'd stayed sat. Instead, I jumped off the sofa and rushed past Mama, not understanding why she kept stirring her pot of 'tater soup that away.

"Stay out of it, John Charles," she called after me, but I couldn't do that. Even at sixteen, big and strong as I'd grown, I couldn't match my father's bulging muscles. Foolishly, I came between him and his daughter. He stopped beating her and turned all his anger on me, pummeling me unconscious. Later, after he'd gone off to drink with his buddies, Mama, Susie Mae and the young 'uns dragged me to German Hospital, one of only two hospitals in town where white folks would treat niggers. Mama had mopped floors for a spell at the other hospital, General Number 2, where she said she wouldn't take her dead dog because of the crowded, nasty conditions. Definitely no place for her oldest son beaten half to death.

Susie Mae said blood oozed from my ears and nose, and that my lips looked like thick chunks of fresh-cut pork liver. I would surely have died if Doctor Kurt hadn't been there. He poked, and punched, and told my mama blood had collected under the lining of my brain.

"If I don't relieve the pressure, he'll die."

"How you gonna do that?" she asked, near hysterical.

He told her he'd take me to surgery, and shave off my hair, and drill a hole in my head. Then, he'd cut open the tough tissue that covered my brain, and let out the blood. "After that I'll put in a small drain tube and close him up."

Susie Mae said he didn't exactly say it in a cruel way, but you could tell he meant no nonsense. She said Mama nodded and bit her lip. Doctor Kurt told her not to fret. He'd do the best he could and walked off rubbing his hands together.

I woke up in a hospital bed, my head throbbing like a sledgehammer banging on a rail. Soon a man dressed in white came to peer down at me. I might have thought I'd died and that a young God with hair the color of ink had come to lift me to heaven had it not been for my pain. He spoke to me, and I felt the prick of a needle in my arm. I blurred away and drifted in and out of sleep for the next few days. At last I woke up enough to realize God was Doctor Kurt. He told me I'd soon be up and about, "a big, strapping boy like you."

Sure enough, my body healed quickly. One day Doctor Kurt came into the ward where I lay and asked me if I felt like leaving the hospital. By then, I'd been up and about and had begun to find some strength in my arms and legs.

"Yessuh," I answered. "I'm feelin' a right sight better than I did."

He sat himself down on the side of my bed and said, "So now what, John Charles?"

"Whatcha mean?" I asked.

"Where will you go?"

"Guess I jest hafta git on home. Don' want 'ta, long as my daddy's there, but I ain't got nowheres else to go. 'Sides, my mama and the girls'll needs me to take care of them."

"Fat lot of good you did the last time you tried that," Doctor Kurt said, laughing. Then he wrinkled his brow and bit his lip.

"Not that it's any of my business, but you shouldn't go back there to live. Next time your father will kill you for sure. Isn't there someone else you could live with, an aunt or uncle perhaps?"

I scratched my bandaged head. "No, suh," I said. "I guess not. My oldest sister Bertha, her young'un, and her boyfriend, Emmett, only have a small place. My mother's sister, Bessie, she's been beggin' to come stay at our place, but my mama says we ain't got room enough for one more livin' thing. My daddy – his family all went north. Don't even know where."

The doctor tugged at his thick mustache and I knew he had something on his mind.

"Tell you what. I need a good houseman. I'm newly married with a young wife who expects the house to be magically clean. What do you say, you come live at Oakbridge and help my housekeeper Hilda with chores and the heavy work. I'll give you the room over the carriage house, your meals, and pay you fifty cents a week to boot."

Even though my mouth still ached from the bruising I'd gotten, I grinned at him as best I could. "Yessuh. I'd like that jest fine and my family could surely use the money."

But then I got to thinking again, and even though our daddy had almost kilt me, I loved him and tried to explain his actions to Doctor Kurt.

"Ya see, suh," I started, "it's de booze that does it. Gets some money and first thing he do is get hisself a bottle. Says he gots to get the stink 'a that ol' packin' house out 'un his nose. But then the booze makes him crazy. That's when he whups us."

Just saying it out loud made me sit straight up in bed. "What mus' I do 'bout my sisters? I can't jest up an' leave 'em alone with him. Why, out'n me to whup, he'll beat de young' uns to death."

Doctor Kurt waved off my worries. "Just leave it to me. I'll call the police. If your father dares touch any of the girls again my friends at the precinct will see to it that he ends up in the penitentiary in Jeff City splitting rocks."

"Uh huh," I nodded, skeptically.

"What's your father's name?" he asked.

"James, suh. James Washington, but people calls him Pigmeat."

"Pigmeat?"

"Yessuh. That's cuz he works at the Union Slaughter House. His job is to cut open the hogs hung upside down. Takes a big strong man to do that."

I leaned back on my pillow and closed my eyes, seeing once more the look on Susie Mae's face when our daddy smacked her. I didn't want to go back home neither. Could I trust the doctor to do as he said?

"I believes I'll give it a try, suh," I told him solemnly.

"Good. Then it's settled. I'll go sign the release papers and then give you a ride to my house. You'd do well to listen to my housekeeper, Hilda. She'll teach you how to be a fine houseman and feed you well in the bargain."

My mama brought me the clothes I arrived in, all mended and scrubbed clean. Weak and wobbly, I put them on, and Miss Jenny, the colored nurse, came to help me out. Next thing I knew, Doctor Kurt put me into his fancy black Cadillac with its yellow-spoked tires and off we went to Oakbridge. Mama grinned real big, and she and Miss Jenny waved us off from the steps of German Hospital.

Poor Hilda. She pretty nearly fainted when she first saw me, an oversized colored boy with enormous hands and feet, swollen black eyes, and a white bandage around his sorry head, but she set right about making me chicken noodle soup. She had been with Mr. Max and Miss Molly, Doctor Kurt's parents, since they first moved into Oakbridge, but Miss Molly passed before I got here.

Miss Hilda told me about the day she'd had her hair pulled back in a tight bun, her in her high top, black button boots polished to a glow, when the agency sent her to interview with Miss Molly. She'd heard about this house she went on, newly built and huge, but not nearly so big as the palace where she'd lived in St. Petersburg.

She spoke with an accent, but I understood the word palace. My eyes nearly popped out of my head. "You lived where?" I gasped.

"Russia," she said. "I'm German born but moved with my parents to St. Petersburg as a child."

She went on to tell me she'd been one of a great number of servants that worked in the Tsar's household. One of her friends had relatives in America and she decided to come here. Her friend asked Hilda to tag along. When they got to New York, they couldn't find no family, nor could they speak a word of English.

"Some man found us wandering the streets," she said, "two big, blond girls carrying bundles of all they possessed in the world and too young to be afraid."

He joked with them, laughed at their speech, fed them, and put them on a train full of women headed to Colorado. Hilda and her friend thought they'd find work out west, but then they learned they were being shipped to a mining town where the men wanted strong girls to marry. Outraged, they slipped off the train in the City of Kansas. They found a place where kind women helped refugees find jobs. Hilda was sent to Oakbridge because Mister Max understood German, his father having come from Hamburg.

"Mistress Molly spoke only English," Hilda told me, "but a kinder woman you never met." Her eyes got dreamy. "I can see her yet, sitting at the piano in the parlor, playing Mozart and Brahms, her silk skirt spread out about her. A real beauty, flowing curls as dark as the midnight sky. It's her portrait you see over the fireplace in the parlor."

She looked at me thoughtfully. "You know, we need to do something about the way you talk, too. I can hardly understand a word you say."

Over time, the bandage came off and my strength returned. Sure enough, someone arranged for me to go to school at night, while during the day Hilda taught me how to wax floors, shine windows, and polish silver. I kept the car sparkling clean.

I didn't like animals that much, but Mister Max loved horses. He had a barn full, and hired hands to care for them. As for me, I learned how to drive Doctor Kurt's big black Cadillac. Hilda saw to it that I served the drinks and the table proper. My days were long but full, and I made up my mind I'd be the best houseman in town.

One night, soon after I moved in to a little room atop the carriage house, Susie Mae came banging on the door. "Hush up there," I told her, "or you'll wake up my boss man. "

"Can't help it, John Charles," she said. "I got bad news." She sat on the only chair and sobbed. The kerosene lamp cast an eerie shadow on her chocolate skin. "Our daddy's dead."

"What?" I cried, sinking to the bed.

"A couple of days ago, a policeman went looking for Daddy at the slaughterhouse. Said he weren't gonna go into no slippery, smelly slaughtering place jest to talk to some fool who'd been beating up on his pickaninnies. The plant foreman said Pigmeat weren't there anyways, that they closed at eight on Saturdays. The policeman left muttering no wonder everyone who worked in the slaughterhouse drank considering how it stank.

"Mama knew our daddy'd gone drinkin' with the other workers, trying to rid themselves of their miseries. By late that night, Mama started to worry but wouldn't send any of us girls out in the dark."

She paused, and right then I started to say I should've been there, but Susie Mae put her finger to her lips to hush me up as she went on.

"I sat up with her, me on the kitchen chair, her huddled in her rocker by the fire not saying much. It scared me half silly thinking he might come home mean and drunk and beat her or maybe all us. Then I worried he wouldn't come home and what would we do?

Sometime during the night, I fell asleep, my head on the table. Near dawn I woke with a start. Something made a loud thump on the front porch. The fire had burned down to near out and Mama, wrapped in her blanket, got up and went to the door. Next thing I know, she's screaming and dragging his big, lifeless self inside the house." Her black eyes opened wide. "He'd been beat to death,

John Charles," she whispered, "his head so swelled up I couldn't tell if'n it was him or not."

A big silence filled my tiny room. "Maybe if I'd been there..." I murmured and let my voice fall.

"Don't take on now," Susie Mae said. "It wouldn't a done no good. Anyways, Mama says you should stay here and work hard 'cause we needs the money."

I thought on that all the next day. That evening as I served the men folks their evening cocktails, I asked Doctor Kurt if I might speak with him in private.

"Anything you have to say you can say in front of my father," he snapped, not at his best after a hard day in surgery.

"My father got killed yesterday," I began.

"Sorry to hear that. I suppose you want time off to go to the funeral," Doctor Kurt said.

"Yes suh, but . . ." I stammered.

"Out with it, man."

"I gots to go to the slaughterhouse and get a job so's I can care for my mama and the young uns," I said, forgetting my newly acquired good English.

Doctor Kurt nodded but Mr. Max said, "Don't do anything foolish. If you go back to the slaughterhouse you'll end up just like Pigmeat. You must stay here. Keep working and learning. Before long you'll be making enough money to care for your family. Until then we'll help, won't we, Kurt?"

The doctor stared wide-eyed at his father for a moment before saying, "Of course. Take a day or two off. Go to the funeral and then come back."

After the funeral, Hilda came to call on Mama Leticia. She asked could Mama do laundry, and Leticia asked who did Hilda think kept all these chillen in clean clothes.

From then on, every Monday, I took Mama all the dirty sheets and towels and shirts and sundries from Oakbridge and every Friday I'd pick them up, all fresh and done to a T. Doctor

## Beth Lyon Barnett

Kurt raised my pay some, and hired Susie Mae as Oakbridge's first second girl. was to keep the rooms on the second floor clean, change linens, wait on the ladies and take care of any babies that might come along. 'Course Susie Mae did much more than that.

# CHAPTER FOUR

## KANSAS CITY, MISSOURI
## OCTOBER, 1918
### MAX ADLER

As we sat there, Kurt and I, sipping our drinks and congratulating ourselves on the arrival of a new heir, there came a soft knock on the door. Susie Mae entered with a tiny bundle. She carried the baby to his father, but Kurt motioned to me. Before I could say no, she placed my grandchild in my arms. Trying to still the tremor in my hands, I peered down at the little face, his eyes closed in slumber, his rosy lips already twitching with hunger. When I moved the blanket just a tad so I could see his full countenance, I felt a shockwave ricochet through my body. "My God," I heard myself whisper. "He looks just like your brother Frankie."

"I thought that before he'd drawn his first breath," my son said. "Could be his twin, don't you think?"

I nodded, numbly and couldn't help the painful thoughts that jolted my brain. The infant began making noisy sucking sounds, and Kurt came and took him from me. "You can't give this baby what he needs right now, Grandpa. I hope his mother can," he said, and then after a moment added, "and will. Come, Susie Mae. Let's go find out."

## Beth Lyon Barnett

*Grandpa,* I thought. *How my Molly would have loved to hear that.* John Charles stirred the fire a bit and asked if I needed anything. I shook my head and closed my eyes.

I loved Oakbridge. I commissioned the house to be built of native stone and lumber for Molly. It rambled over the hilltop and reached toward the sky. My work as an attorney for many of Kansas City's most important men kept me busy and sometimes harried. I found myself in a powerful position even though I was an American-born Jew of German descent. I tried to blend in with the Gentiles, some of whom held anti-Semitic views. I worked hard and felt beholden to no man. Returning to the serenity of home and into the welcoming arms of my lovely wife served to renew my energy and revitalize my spirits.

Now, with Molly gone and my body failing, I worked hard to keep my mind sharp. I read every scrap of news I could get, including *The Wall Street Journal,* though it arrived by train a week late. City Council members continued to call for my professional advice. I enjoyed a close relationship with a select few of my old cronies, though that still didn't included membership in their country clubs. Yet the peace and serenity of the Oakbridge gardens served to bring good fellowship and a crackling fire fueled our friendships. On such occasions John Charles carried me down the winding staircase. He sat me in a chair and tucked a blanket around my now withered and useless legs.

I heard the rumble of distant thunder, and it caused me to hark back to the winter of 1860, the day Molly and I arrived in the City of Kansas. How well I remember handing her off the riverboat and wondering aloud if we'd made a wise choice. In my mind, I could see the streets of the untamed frontier town frozen in deep mud ruts. Indians huddled against dirty store fronts under greasy blankets. Bearded men in heavy leather coats hurried about their business. Horses stamped their feet and snorted smoky breath through flared nostrils.

Later, settled into drafty accommodations at the Gillis Hotel, we assessed our circumstances, a far cry indeed from the proper and sophisticated Washington we'd just left. I could hear Molly's voice imitate Senator Benton's deep baritone as she bravely pulled her shawl close about herself. "Never mind the weather. You are moving to the city of the future."

"Now don't you worry," I told her. "We'll have a look around, and if we don't like what we see, we'll just head right back to Washington."

"Oh, Max." she cried, her dark eyes flashing and her chestnut curls spilling out from beneath her bonnet. "Where's your pioneering spirit? What would your father say?"

"He might concede that we made a bit of a hasty decision."

"Nonsense. Your parents blazed new trails of their own, and I'll not be outdone by the likes of them. Here we are and here we'll stay. Besides, I clearly recall the senator saying his golden town between two rivers has a clearly magnificent future with vast and wonderful opportunities for a smart, young lawyer. He may have exaggerated about everything else but not about the brilliant young man I married."

I remembered telling her that she could go back home, that I could travel back and forth even though it would mean we would see less of each other. She shook her head violently.

"Well, then," I said, "if you're determined to stay, we must find a place to live."

"Big enough for my piano, I hope," she said.

I laughed out loud and hugged her close.

The next day I began to look for a house. Walking through the slush on Main Street, I spotted a college friend, Will Lykins, and gave him a shout. He turned and ran toward me with a big grin on his face.

"Well I'll be damned," he cried wrapping me in a bear hug. "You really did come. I wouldn't have believed it." He broke into a hearty laugh. "Have time for lunch?"

He steered me to a nearby hotel. We entered a plush dining room with wood paneling and Negro waiters in spotless white jackets. "My office," he said jokingly.

I smiled.

"Well, not really, but a quiet place with great food."

We had a drink and talked. "Growing up in the shadow of a famous man isn't easy, is it?" he asked. He too had a prominent father.

"I need to make my own way," I answered, "and for starters, I must find a place to live for my wife and myself."

"I can help you with a house," Willie said when I mentioned perhaps a room in Westport. "My father owns some nice properties, though I don't know how a Baptist minister will feel about renting to a northern Jewish boy."

"About the same as a northern Jewish boy will feel about renting from a southern Baptist minister, I presume," I said.

"Perhaps he's more moderate now since being elected mayor. After lunch, we'll go see."

That's how I, a young lawyer fresh from the East, came to know the once Bible-thumping southern preacher and sometimes doctor, Johnston Lykins, and through him other men with great interest in the territory. In fact, most of them hailed from the south and strongly favored slavery.

I vehemently opposed thralldom, so it surprised no one that in spite of my glowing charm, they looked at me with a jaundiced eye. After all, my father, a Federal Court judge, had lent his considerable influence to John Quincy Adams in protest against the gag rule, an ingenious method used by southern politicians to table any petition presented to Congress that mentioned the word "slavery."

Besides, even though I had flaming red hair and a straight nose, I'd been born a Jew. Due however to my father's political connections and a dearth of good attorneys in the territory, they came to me, and found I could be trusted to represent their interests fairly.

The growth and success of Kansas City became important to the financial achievements of us all. Above everything else, I made it my business to understand the needs of this little town on the edge of the Kansas prairie.

Slowly over the next ten years, I gained the respect of the town leaders. I made frequent trips back east to confer with my father and meet with influential congressmen and senators, some of whom I'd known since childhood.

On my own I found a small house near the river but with room in the parlor for Molly's Steinway. Other German Jewish families had settled nearby and perhaps because of our similar ancestry, Molly and I felt comfortable and welcome. Still, I knew that if I hoped to succeed in this town, I needed to blend in. I'd never been a very religious man. Molly wanted to attend High Holy Day services, Rosh Hashanah and Yom Kippur, but the closest synagogue was miles away in Leavenworth, Kansas. We decided to wait until we had a temple of our own.

One spring, Molly and I returned with the children to Washington for a visit. My father and my mother, ever the gracious hostess, welcomed us with open arms. Kurt and little Frank took to their grandparents right away. Kurt haunted my father's library, and Frankie enjoyed my mother's tales of her German childhood.

One evening James Carroll came to call. A judge of the Children's Court in Baltimore, he and father shared many interests. I jumped up to greet him.

"Good evening, sir," I said, grasping his arm and shaking his hand warmly.

"Good evening, my boy." A smile lit his weathered face.

After a brief chat, my mother retired to the parlor, and Molly put the children to bed. We men lit our cigars and settled down to discuss current trends. Judge Carroll sat on the board of the Baltimore and Ohio Railroad.

"You know," he said, turning to me, "you should think seriously about trying to bring a railroad to Kansas City. Perhaps you are just the person to do it."

"Me?" I asked, surprised.

"Well, Max. Let's look at the facts. Some town along the Missouri River will do it. Why not the City of Kansas?

"Impossible," I answered, visualizing the limestone bluffs that lined the muddy shores.

"Nothing's impossible. A railroading friend of mine, Senator Ross of Kansas, told me he is urging the bridge be built at Leavenworth."

"Really," I mused, my interest piqued.

"Believe me, a bridge will be built," the Judge said, "and the town that secures it will become the crossroads of the country. Competition will be fierce. Reflect for a moment on the livestock that will be shipped from west to east and south to north, the number of people who will travel across the country. Why," he said with a faraway look in his eyes, "your town could end up being the busiest depot in the nation. "

His words shook me to my core. I understood he knew of what he spoke, but it would require much work. Suddenly I realized, for the good of the town, that the bridge must be built at Kansas City. I would need to marshal my forces

I always loved a challenge. Even though I knew it would mean leaving my family for travel, I vowed to succeed. I met with my friend and fellow attorney Robert Van Horn, a congressman who told me he already had an interest in bringing the railroads to Kansas City. In addition, he owned The *Kansas City Journal Post*, an influential daily newspaper that could help sway public opinion

We had no trouble enlisting the aid of the Irishman Charles Kearney, himself a railroad man, and Kersey Coates, a fellow with a knack for business. As excitement built, others joined us. While

Robert took on the task of convincing our local population, I and the others made numerous trips to Washington.

We lobbied senators and congressmen alike. A hard-fought battle ensued, but we came out victorious. Congress passed a bill providing for the construction of the bridge across the Missouri River at Broadway Avenue. Angrily, the Leavenworth delegation withdrew their proposal.

Next we persuaded The Hannibal and St. Joseph Railroad to build the bridge. My friend Octave Chanute designed a fine structure that could swing open in just minutes to facilitate river traffic.

In February of 1866, as Kurt turned seven and Frankie three, work began. During the next three years, all of Kansas City shook with daily explosions of dynamite to tunnel a pathway through the limestone to the river. We watched as the bridge took shape, rising from the northern bluffs to span the Missouri River for hundreds of feet, making landfall within our city limits.

"What shall we call it?" Tom Swope said one evening when we gathered for drinks and dinner.

"Why not The Hannibal Bridge," I suggested. "Remember the Carthaginian general who had a vision of uniting his country? Well, that's what we have accomplished. Also," I added with a shrug and a sly grin, "The Hannibal and St Joseph Railroad will cross it."

For a moment all sat blankly silent and then they burst into laughter. "Excellent and very apt indeed," Will Lykins said, rocking back in his chair. "Are we agreed?"

What an opening day celebration we had that July third in 1869: hot air balloons, food, drink, and dancing in the streets. I wanted to bring Kurt but he wouldn't come with me, for by then we had lost our Frankie.

Both Molly and Kurt suffered terribly at the loss, each in their own way. Guilt rested heavily upon my shoulders and the child's death disturbed me deeply, but I had urgent business obligations to fulfill.

We buried Frankie in the newly opened Elmwood Cemetery even though it had not yet been incorporated. Our friends and neighbors came to comfort us. The women brought covered dishes and fresh fruits to our house. Molly could do no more that sit at the parlor window and weep. A deep depression blanketed my beloved, smothering her in isolation and loneliness. Her piano went untouched while she sat for hours on end staring out at the street. Meals went uncooked; words went unspoken.

One evening I found her in his room, Frankie's favorite toy train in her hand. "Oh, dearest one," I said softly, enfolding her in my arms. "How can I tell you how I feel?"

"You don't have to say it, Max. I am so sorry. My guilt overwhelms me."

"Your guilt? What are you talking about?"

Her large brown eyes swam in pools of tears as she whispered, "I killed him. But for me, he would still be alive."

I felt her tremble as I held her tight against my breast. "No one could have done more."

"If I'd sent for the doctor in St. Louis early on?" she sobbed. "Then maybe our baby would still be alive."

I soothed her gently. "I think often, what if I'd been here, but even then it wouldn't have mattered, Molly. You and Kurt did all anyone could do."

Right then I decided we all needed to get away from this neighborhood and the bitter memories. Though I could easily have run for office, I'd built quite a nice law practice. In addition, I had delved a bit into real estate, bought cheap bottom land that turned quickly into stockyards and factory sites. As a result of my endeavors, I found myself a man of considerable means.

I wondered about moving farther south, away from the river. Others like Tom Swope and Kersey Coates had already done that, traveling to town in their fine carriages. One afternoon, as we three met with John McCoy at his general store to discuss properties, I said I thought a move might be good for Molly. "How's she doing?" Tom asked, his voice tinged with kindness.

"Not well," I answered, "nor is my older boy."

"Maybe Johnston Lykins could have helped," Kersey said pensively, "but then, probably not. Even as a practicing physician, he fell far short." He smiled and then became quickly serious.

I patted his shoulder. "I doubt I'd have thought to call him even if I'd been home," I said. "Anyway, I've been thinking. It might be best to move my family away from where it all happened."

"There's good land right here in Westport," John said but I had my sights on some hilly land I'd heard about.

Some days later, I drove my horse and buggy out to have a look around. I couldn't get over the beauty that lay just beyond town. Small creeks and streams made patchwork quilts of rolling fields and hilly forests. Of course, no one knew what direction the city would take, but I felt buying a chunk of land to the west could turn out to be a wise investment.

At one point, I came upon wagon ruts that crossed a little creek and continued up a gentle slope through a stand of elms and oaks. I decided to follow along. The tracks came to an end at a clearing where stood a small house, behind which stretched farmland as far as the eye could see. Summer had arrived, hot and humid, but a gentle breeze rustled the young corn and tickled the leaves of the trees. Right then, I knew I must have this property.

The next evening Mayor Lykins and his wife hosted a party at their mansion on Twelfth Street and invited many of the town's most prominent citizens. I felt honored to be included, but Molly, still mourning the loss of our child, couldn't bring herself to get dressed in her finery, so I went alone. When I ran into Tom Swope I told him I'd seen a bit of land I liked.

"Where?" he asked, taking a bite of cheese he'd grabbed from the tray passed by a colored waiter.

I took a piece of paper from my jacket and pointed to the spot. "There, on the fringe of the city near the state line. Kansas is but a stone's throw away. I'd want a quarter section or so. What do you think?"

He studied the map and chewed thoughtfully. "How much are they asking?"

I told him and he responded with a nod. "Reasonable, I'd say." We both saw his wife motioning to him. "Offer them half and buy double," he said slapping me on the back and hurrying off.

Following his advice, I closed on the deal and hired one of my clients, a southern architect named Andrew Nelson, to design a house with a winding staircase and a big, airy room for Molly's piano. Instead of a structure made of wood and colonnades, he suggested we use Kansas limestone which, though abundant, had to be hauled a good distance to the site. Andrew built a sturdy oak bridge that spanned the creek. For lack of a better way to direct workmen to the construction, he told them to look for the oak bridge. Soon they and everyone referred to the property as Oakbridge.

Molly began to rally and take a real interest in the house, but not Kurt. He continued to hide away, sullen and silent. Finally one day, I called him into the parlor.

"Sit down, son. It's time we talked."

Kurt chose the ladder-back chair and faced me, lips tight, chin tucked in, dark eyes raised defiantly.

"I understand your sorrow, Kurt, but you are making your mother and me very unhappy. You won't talk to us. You mope around or go off alone. You must realize we lost one son. That's enough. We don't want to lose another. What is it? Why do you act this way?"

"You should have been here," he glowered. "That stupid old doctor didn't know anything. I tried to say something but they pushed me away. Maybe if you'd been here . . ." Then he raised his eyes to mine. "He's dead, Father, and it's your fault."

Oh, the wrenching feeling I had in my heart as he spoke. Perhaps what he said held some truth, but I couldn't – I wouldn't accept that. Instead, I shook my head sadly.

"You're old enough to understand that Doctor Weiner did the best he could, as did you and your mother. Nobody wanted Frankie to die. It happened. Some things just do."

I stood and grasped my son in my arms.

"I'm so sorry, boy." Tears coursed down my cheeks.

"Sorry I couldn't be here. Sorry Frankie died. Sorry for us all. We have suffered a terrible loss, but I want you to know this. I'm so proud you are my son. Had I been here, I wouldn't have done anything different. You acted like a man. You went for the doctor. You helped your mother. You even sent the telegram. Yes. I know about that."

I reached down and pulled the child to his feet, holding him for the first time in ages.

He stood like a wooden soldier, stiff and unyielding. "What can I do to make it up to you?" I asked. "What is it you want?"

"I want to be a doctor," he said.

"Then a doctor you shall be. I shall arrange for you to go off to the finest medical school in the world, the University of Heidelberg in Germany."

"I'd like that," he answered with the first bit of enthusiasm I'd seen in him for a long while. "When may I go?"

"As soon as you are old enough. You must study hard and learn German."

Time and the promise of an education abroad seemed to soften his heart, but mine never healed, so heavy a burden of guilt I felt. Some years later, after my Molly passed away, I arranged for a concert grand piano to be delivered to the local school in her memory, but the pain and loss of her never eased. Now, thanks to a higher power, perhaps I would get a second chance. A new Frankie had been born.

# CHAPTER FIVE

## KANSAS CITY
## 1918
## KURT

So many emotions whirled though my mind as I carried my newborn son upstairs: joy, pride, relief, and finally sorrow. One could hardly fail to notice his resemblance to Frankie, my long dead brother.

Frankie had arrived in the winter of my fourth year. When my mother placed the squirming bundle in my arms for the first time, I peered down at his tiny apple-cheeked face and giggled. "He's got big ears, a button nose, and red hair like Papa. How come I didn't get red hair, Mother?"

"Because, silly, you look like me."

She had shiny black hair that curled softly around her clear, smooth skin. Her wide, brown eyes sparkled when she looked at me and now Frankie. In spite of the twinge of jealousy that ricocheted through my mind, I brushed at the soft fuzz on top of Frankie's head. He screwed up his mouth in a funny, toothless grin.

"Gas," my mother said, but I knew different. I already felt an iron bond between us.

He grew into a carefree, happy-go-lucky boy with nary an evil or mean thought. His laughter rang through the gardens, his impishness a constant source of fun. I was the dark one, serious and studious, sensitive and stubborn. He loved everything and everybody with a gentleness that made all he touched special. Even my friends enjoyed having Frankie tag along.

As the years went by, I learned to accept our father's odd hours and sudden trips. Even when he came home, he spent most of his time in his office. Once in awhile I'd say something about it to Mother, but she would just pooh-pooh me and tell me most other children didn't have a father nearly as important as mine.

I spent long days traipsing around thecity park to find insects and snakes to dissect. At first Frankie thought finding the creatures a wonderful game, but when he found out what I did with them, he sobbed and stopped helping me.

That summer had been a carefree time for us. I took to pithing frogs, which for me consisted of taking out their guts and examining them under the little microscope I'd gotten for Christmas. Frankie thought that gruesome and fled outdoors to play.

The date August first, 1868 would forever be etched into my memory. With work proceeding on the Hannibal Bridge, my father had rushed off to Washington . . . "one more emergency," he said as he swung out the door, document-stuffed briefcase in his hand.

After lunch that golden day, I asked my mother if I could go with my friends to River Park near our house. Frankie swiveled his head anxiously between us and we both laughed at the silly, pleading look on his face. "Okay. He can come," I said.

Mother dabbed at her moist brow and nodded, knowing that many of his little friends would be there under the watchful eyes of their German nurses.

With my little brother dancing stupidly along, his freckled face glowing with pride, we older boys walked down the tree-shaded paths and flopped lazily under the cottonwood trees.

Upstream we could hear occasional loud booms as workmen blasted out the limestone bluffs. We took out our pocketknives for a game of mumbly peg, and though we didn't let Frankie play, we allowed him to keep score, which he did with continual editorial comments.

I handled the knife well, and after one of my particularly good throws, Frankie cried out, "Yeah," and then jumped around, arms and legs askew, his missing lower front teeth making his grin all the more silly. Everyone held their sides laughing. I shook my head and rolled my eyes skyward. Finally he went off to play with his friends.

After he'd gone we older boys lounged in the shade and watched the girls, whispering about their big titties and bragging about the ones we'd kissed, though I doubt any of us had. After awhile, I began to miss Frankie. I looked toward the river but didn't see him, so I stood up, stretched, and ambled toward the playground. I asked one of the kids if he'd seen Frankie.

"Yes." he answered. "He's here somewhere."

I scanned the landscape, calling his name. I felt a wave of relief when finally I heard him answer. I followed the sound of his voice to a willow tree where I found him lying in the shade curled up with his hands around his knees. "You got me all worried, Frankie. Are you all right?"

"I don't feel so good."

"What's the matter, sport?"

"I gotta throw up," which he promptly did.

I held his head, and after he'd finished, his eyes clouded with tears, strange because Frankie seldom cried. "I wanna go home."

"Sure," I told him. "Climb on. I'll carry you."

"I can walk," he said, sighing.

"Aw, come on. I'll give you a free ride."

My mother said the heat probably made him sick. She put him on the settee in the parlor and told him to rest. She'd go make him a tall glass of lemonade.

Frankie groaned.

Mother patted his cheek and said he'd feel better soon. Then she told me to leave and let him sleep, but I didn't do that. I sat on the ladder-back chair and stared at him, thinking he looked pale, his freckles standing out against his white cheeks.

Mother brought back the lemonade. She set the glass on the table by the settee. "He'll be all right, honey," she said. "It's probably just something he ate. You know how he is, always getting into things he shouldn't."

I pulled a piece of peppermint from my pocket and gave it to her. "Maybe this'll help," I said, and went outside to sit on the porch.

Toward evening, Frankie managed a few swallows of soup before pushing the spoon away. I picked up his favorite storybook and read to him. Mother let me stay up later than usual, hoping the sleeping porch adjoining our rooms would cool off some before we went to bed.

Around midnight, I woke with a start and glanced over at Frankie. He sat doubled up on the edge of the bed, gasping with pain. "Mommy," he sobbed. "Mommy."

"Okay, buddy. Don't move. I'll get her."

"My tummy hurts," he sobbed.

I hurried to my parent's bedroom where my mother met me at the door, wrapping her dressing gown around her. "Is that Frankie I hear?" she said, her voice tired, her brow creased with worry.

For the first time, I felt real fear. Tugging at her hand, I cried, "Hurry up, Mother. He looks awfully sick."

We ran down the hall and onto the sleeping porch. A cool breeze came through the screens, but Frankie sat bathed in sweat, his face fire engine red. "What is it, baby?" Mother murmured, kissing his forehead. "You're burning up." She turned to me saying, "I wish your father was here. I think maybe Doctor Weiner should see Frankie, but I can't leave you here alone with him."

"I'll go. I'm not afraid of the dark. Besides, it isn't far. Please, Mother," I pleaded. "Send me."

She hesitated, searching for another way, but distraught, she nodded. "All right. Get your clothes on and hurry. Try to run all the way, dear."

"Don't worry. I can do it," I said. I quickly pulled on my pants and shoes, drew a shirt over my head and rushed down the stairs. Our front door, which we never locked unless father left town, cost me precious moments as I groped to find the key. We kept it in the drawer of the hall chest, but it had slid toward the back, and in my haste I missed it, found it, fumbled with the lock, and finally got the door open. Then I took off running down the walk to the moonlit street lined with familiar houses.

I turned north at the corner and raced past the grocery store and the pharmacy, running so hard my breath came in short, hard gasps. Five blocks later, I saw the doctor's house, standing behind a white picket fence with a sign nailed to the gate. GUS WEINER, MD.

The City Hall clock struck twelve just as I screamed the doctor's name and  raced up the porch steps to pound with all my might on his door. Up above, he poked his head out the open window. "Yes? Yes? What is it? Don't you know it's the middle of the night? You'll wake the dead."

"It's my brother, sir," I yelled back. "My mother says he's bad and for you to hurry."

"All right. All right. No need to holler," he called, his gray hair in disarray. "Just let me get my clothes on and I'll be right down."

Soon he appeared and motioned me to follow. Bent with a curved spine, he limped out back to hitch up his horse and buggy. "Get in, boy, and tell me about it."

As best I could, I told how Frankie got sick at the river but seemed better at home before waking up in pain an hour or so ago.

"Well, don't you worry, child. You did the right thing, coming to get me. We'll have him fixed up in no time."

When we got home, Frankie looked worse. Whimpering softly on the bed, he peered up at the doctor and groaned. Mother stood to let the doctor sit by his side, her face frightened and pinched.

"What is it?" she asked, her voice edging close to panic.

Heaving a sigh, Doctor Weiner slowly lowered himself to the bed, causing it to creak and sag. "*Ach du lieber, mein kind,*" the doctor said. "To call me out of my bed in the middle of the night for a bellyache. Did you eat too many green apples today, Frank?"

"No, sir. Not a one," came the weak reply.

"Where do you hurt, boy," he asked as he probed with gentle fingers.

Frankie screamed in pain, and the little bit of soup he'd eaten shot out of his mouth onto the bed sheets. Mother grabbed a towel to mop it up.

"You see," the doctor said. "Something he ate. A good physic will fix him up like new."

But I saw a drop of blood staining the sheet amidst the vomit. "Doctor Gus. Look," I said, pulling on his sleeve.

"Yes, yes," he said, nodding. "Just something he ate."

"Shush," Mother said to me, her finger to her lips.

"But Mother . . ."

"Be quiet, Kurt."

Helplessly, I turned away, sure of what I'd seen.

The doctor asked me to bring him his bag. As I handed it to him, he said, "So, Kurt, do you want to be a doctor when you grow up, eh?"

I shrugged.

"Well, now," he continued, "look closely and you will see a classic upset stomach. Nothing unusual here at all." He tousled Frankie's hair and smiled reassuringly.

"I want you," he told Mother, "to give him this medicine right away. It will clean him out good. By tomorrow he'll be fit as a fiddle. Isn't that right, Frankie?" He handed her a bottle of dark fluid that I eyed suspiciously. Rising to leave, the doctor patted his little patient's hand. "Soon, you'll be ready to eat more green apples."

A flicker of a smile crossed Mother's lips. "Show the doctor to the door, will you, Kurt? And thank you so much for your trouble, Gus. I'll go get a spoon."

When I returned after letting the doctor out, I watched as Frankie, too weak to resist the bitter medicine Mother placed in his mouth, swallowed it. His empty stomach seemed to accept the substance. Mother wanted me to go to bed. "He'll be fine now," she whispered. "I'll stay with him. You try and get back to sleep," She kissed me softly and told me what a brave boy I'd been.

But I couldn't leave until I knew Frankie was all right. "I'll just stay here in case you need me," I said, and curled up in the chair by the window.

As I now know, the mixture Doctor Gus prescribed coursed its way through his body. Mother sat by him the rest of the night. She continued to bathe him with a cool cloth and soothe his whimpers, convinced he'd be fine as soon as the medicine worked.

Dawn brought the first glimmers of sun and a refreshing breath of air to the sleeping porch. I must have dozed, but when I awoke I went to Frankie's bedside. Mother had lain down next to him and fallen asleep, her head next to his. His skin looked like alabaster, and deep circles surrounded his pale blue eyes, open and staring at me as though unseeing.

"Mommy," I whispered, scared out of my wits, "he looks awful. Maybe I should go back and get Doctor Gus."

She roused herself through her exhaustion but had no patience with the ramblings of a twelve year-old. "No, darling. You heard what the doctor said. As soon as the medicine works, Frankie will be fine. Now, go get dressed. I'll be down later to fix you something to eat."

Just as I reached the door, Frankie screamed with pain. "I can't hold it, Mother. I can't hold it," with which he let go his bowels.

Mother had been expecting this and at first seemed relieved, until she pulled back the sheet and saw the blood and pus. Horrified, she yelled at me to run get the doctor. When we returned, we saw that she had tried to clean him up. She held him in her lap and sang softly to him, but poor Frankie lay limp in her arms, his bodily fluids running out of him and down my mother's leg onto the floor.

"Get out," Doctor Gus told me. "Let us do our work." Very quietly, he closed the door behind me.

I wandered aimlessly around the house. I saw Mother run up and down the stairs with ice and more sheets. I wanted her to stop and talk to me, but I knew Frankie needed her. I thought of my father and wished he were here. Suddenly, I knew what I had to do. I slipped out of the house and ran to the telegraph office, sobbing all the way.

I startled Harry Stein when I burst through the door. "Whoa there, boy. What's the matter?" he asked, concern spreading over his long, thin countenance.

"It's Frankie, sir. He's real sick. My mother wants my father to come. I don't have any money to pay, sir, but we need to send a telegram."

"Well, now. Don't you worry about that for one minute. Just write down what you want to say and I'll get it out quicker than a wink."

I grabbed the pencil and the yellow paper he pushed in my direction and wrote, "Dear Max: Frankie very ill. Come home. Love, Molly." The telegrapher glanced at what I'd written, flashed me a look of concern and hurried to his transmitter. I stayed long enough to hear the first few clicks of the key and then ran back home. Let them be mad at me, I thought. I don't care.

Upstairs on the sleeping porch I watched helplessly from the doorway as Frankie roused himself now and then and mumbled something I couldn't hear. My mother would whisper, "Hush, baby. Doctor Gus is here. Lie still. You'll be better soon." I saw her press her lips to his brow and push back his damp curls.

At noon, Frankie suddenly opened his eyes and said, "Mama."

She turned to the doctor. "Can't you do something?"

The doctor just shook his head, his pockmarked face full of worry. "He needs an operation, but I can't do it."

"Why not?"

"I'm an old man, Molly, and I don't have the right instruments. I'd kill him for sure. I've thought about getting someone else, but they've gone down south to help with the cholera epidemic. I know of a man in St Louis but. . ." He left the sentence unfinished. "Besides," he said, shaking his head sadly, "it's too late. I think his appendix has burst. All we can do now is give him more laudanum to ease the pain and pray."

Mother bent forward and laid her cheek next to Frank. "Oh, God," she prayed. "Don't take my baby."

My brother slipped into unconsciousness. Mama smoothed the covers over his tortured little body as the elderly doctor, gray with fatigue, stood by. I eased into the room. Together we listened to the shallow breaths come further and further apart until finally, he breathed no more. Long moments passed. Only the ticking of the hall clock could be heard. The trembling old man stepped to the bed, closed Frankie's empty eyes, and pulled the sheet over his small face.

Mother watched in disbelief,. She reached to remove the sheet but Doctor Gus gently pulled her away.

"It's over," he said sadly. "He's gone."

"No," she wailed and slipped to the floor.

The funeral had to wait until my father got home. The service took place in the parlor of our house. We sat on the sofa staring at Frankie's small casket while the young, round-faced rabbi spoke.

When it came time, I mumbled along stoically, using the Hebrew words I knew. "*Shema Yisroel adonai eloheinu adonai echad.* Hear, Oh Israel, The Lord our God, The Lord is One.*"*

Our poor little Frankie became one of the first occupants of Elmwood Cemetery, forty-three lovely acres in the heart of Kansas City. Though it hadn't yet been formally organized, my father's friend, George Kessler, a landscape architect, suggested we bury Frankie there.

We stood by his open grave with bowed heads while the rabbi recited the Kaddish.

"The departed whom we now remember has entered into the peace of life eternal."

*His name is Frank Adler,* I mouthed.

"He still lives on earth in the acts of goodness he performed and in the hearts of those who cherish their memory."

*He didn't live long enough to perform many acts of goodness.*

"May the beauty of his life abide among us as a loving benediction."

I swallowed thickly as the little coffin disappeared into a deep hole.

"May the Father of peace send peace to all who mourn, and comfort all the bereaved among us."

My mother leaned against my father, sobbing. My father dabbed his wet cheeks with a crisp, white handkerchief, but I didn't cry. My grief had turned to anger: at the doctor, at my mother, and most of all, at my father. In my grieving mind, I believed if he had been there, he could have done something.

At first, I resented moving to Oakbridge. It meant leaving my friends and my old neighborhood, but I soon came to realize that life in the country offered a solitary quiet. My mother busied herself with furnishing the new house, placing her beloved piano in the drawing room. Sometimes, as I walked the hills alone, I could hear her playing as she did before Frankie died, but she spent much of her time at a child's orphanage run by nuns.

Father, who now fancied himself a country gentleman, purchased several horses and a herd of cattle. He begged me to join him, but I refused, preferring to brood with my books and my microscope.

As soon as I grew old enough, my father sent me off to the University of Heidelberg in Baden-Württemberg, Germany, to study. On my own for the first time, I got a taste of the prejudice that caused my grandfather to immigrate to the United States. I sensed waves of anti-Semitism sweeping through the university, but I held myself aloof, concentrating instead upon my studies. I was required to take a course called the History of Science. Professor Leo Konisberger, a charismatic teacher, convinced me I had chosen the correct field of endeavor.

One summer I traveled to Paris on holiday. While there, I met William Keen, a young Army doctor who had served as a surgeon during the Civil War. The study of the brain held particular fascination for him, and his pioneering brain surgery led to his fame in later years. We became friends, and in fact, had we not, I would never have known how to diagnose and treat John Charles.

In addition to his surgical skills, William had a compassion about him that I lacked. Yet I loved surgery, particularly of the chest and abdomen. I made them my specialty, studying all I could learn of the organs that resided therein. No one would ever die of a ruptured appendix on my account. And while I worked inside an obese patient's belly, I had no compunction about removing great quantities of adipose tissue, "fat" to the layman. Sometimes, to their amazement, my grossly overweight patients would come out of surgery weighing thirty pounds less than when they went in.

Upon attaining my medical degree, I returned to Kansas City eager to begin practicing. Since the opening of the Hannibal Bridge, the population had surpassed a hundred thousand, and I found that doctors were in short supply.

I am very good at what I do, the best. My reputation quickly grew to reflect that. Furthermore, I freely admit that I enjoy the prestige that comes with saving lives.

Yet here, in my own home town, I found that Jewish doctors were welcome on the staffs of few if any local hospitals. Outraged, I called upon my father. He enlisted the help of his wealthy German friends, Jews and non-Jews alike. They bought a house in town, named it German Hospital, and welcomed all doctors except Negroes, of course, who were thought to have inferior brains. Four nurses came to us from the Sisters of the Third Order of St. Francis. I stayed in town to be near the hospital, visiting Oakbridge only when invited or to check up on my parents.

My mother loved to entertain their friends with small dinner parties. She had always been a good cook and asked me to join them upon occasion. "You know my son the Doctor?" she would say. It was at just such an event that I first noticed she appeared unwell, her usual energy flagging.

"Have you lost weight?" I asked her, in a private moment.

"Thankfully," she answered. "I've grown plump on the good food your father's tenants raise here at Oakbridge."

But the next time I visited, she seemed even thinner. After dinner that night when the guests had departed, I questioned her again. In spite of the resentment I still felt toward her regarding Frankie's death, I loved her as any son loves his mother. Her lack of vigor concerned me.

"I've probably caught something from the children at the orphanage," she said. "It will be gone soon enough."

"Let's have a look," I said.

"You are my son, not my doctor."

"Just let me listen to your chest."

"No. Go take care of sick people."

I knew I shouldn't care for my own family – too much emotion involved – so I shrugged, secretly a little glad that she would be someone else's problem.

To help her with the household duties, Father had retained the services of a German immigrant, a woman named Hilda. Big and strong, she seemed competent to handle the chores, a good addition to Oakbridge.

Months went by before I visited again. My practice grew and my skills as a surgeon seemed in constant demand. The next time I dropped by Oakbridge, my father took me aside and told me about a cough that seemed to plagued my mother.

"Why didn't you notify me sooner?" I asked.

"She wouldn't hear of it," he said.

This time, my mother's pallor truly alarmed me, and when she tried unsuccessfully to hide her bloody sputum in her handkerchief, I unhappily suspected I knew the cause of her distress.

I called my partner, Sam Seligsohn. He examined her and confirmed my diagnosis. It wasn't long before my mother took to her bed, weak and coughing up quantities of blood. We knew the end was near. Sadly, even if she had allowed me to treat her, I could only have suggested she go to a sanitarium in Switzerland. I explained to my stricken father that there was no cure. She died of phthisis . . . tuberculosis. . . which she no doubt contracted from the orphanage children.

With great sorrow, we buried her next to Frankie's tiny grave, and though my father didn't ask, I bought a good horse and buggy and moved back to Oakbridge.

Many things happened in the year 1918: I bought a car; I performed my first skull surgery, and I married Rebecca.

Ah, my Rebecca. So beautiful, so charming, so difficult. How well I remember the day Hans Stern came to my office, not as a patient, I soon learned, but to broker a marriage. Though not a big man, he cut a fine figure, straight and slim.

"Becka's mother died of influenza, as you well know, eleven years ago this spring, and you can't imagine how difficult it is to raise a daughter alone," he began. "I'm afraid I've spoiled her outrageously, but never mind. She's as smart as she is beautiful."

He tapped his cheek thoughtfully. "A trifle headstrong to be sure and perhaps a bit self-centered, but a worldly man such as yourself should have no trouble training her to your liking. A well-established gentleman would be well served by a young, attractive wife, who comes," he added softly, "with a substantial dowry."

The matchmaking didn't surprise me, but the obvious disparity in our ages did. At fifty-two, I gave little thought to marriage since I had an endless supply of bright, pretty young nurses to fulfill my carnal needs. At the same time, I recognized the custom of arranged marriages.

I had been approached many times before, but until now no offer had tempted me. Yet just the week before, I had seen Rebecca Stern at a social event and remember thinking, *What a beauty.* Gowned in pale green satin, she had jet-black hair that hung girlishly across her shoulders, accenting her delicious-looking breasts. Around her waist a dark velvet ribbon accented her slimness and perfectly proportioned hips. I noticed her thick-lashed deep blue eyes and full mouth as she glanced at me.

Intrigued, I accepted Hans Stern's invitation to dinner the following Sunday. I arrived in time for a drink and a few tasty hors d'oeuvres. Rebecca looked fetching in a modest white dress and sat quietly by her father's side as we discussed politics. She knew little of the war raging in Europe. I'd stayed out of that conflict to care for my ill and aging parents.

"Probably a wise decision," she volunteered.

At first, I thought of it as a game. I discussed it with Sam, who had married his childhood sweetheart while still in medical school. Their son, almost as old as Rebecca, would soon be off to Harvard. "Do you think I'm crazy?" I asked Sam.

"Lord, no. I've been telling you for years you need a wife. What more could you ask for? A young, pretty girl that can bear lots of children. And Jewish." He clapped me on the back and laughed.

One day I spotted a dainty bottle of perfume and on a whim, bought it for her. She seemed pleased and I continued the practice over time with lace hankies, porcelain figurines, and a picture frame painted with pink and blue flowers. Two years flew by. Though we spoke little of marriage, I presented her with a suitable gift, a sparkling diamond and emerald necklace.

"Oh,Kurt," she gasped, her cheeks flushed with excitement. "It's beautiful. Wherever did you get such a lovely thing? Here, help me put it on."

"It belonged to my mother," I told her, fastening the clasp, kissing a spot on her neck, and feeling my desire rise. "It's your engagement gift."

Barely hearing me, she fled, hair flying, to the hall mirror where she turned this way and that to see the three-quarter-inch cabochon green stones, surrounded and separated by tiny diamonds, encircling her neck. Then she rushed back to me and throwing her arms around me, kissed me on my lips. "I love it," she cried.

Our wedding took place at Oakbridge the day after her eighteenth birthday. My father had no trouble at all persuading Hans Stern that our country place better accommodated the hundreds of invited guests than his town house. He presented me with the money he had promised. I didn't need it, of course, but I accepted it graciously and put it into various stocks and bonds. Better still, he gave me a full-length portrait of Rebecca in her wedding gown, done by a local artist. When I exclaimed at its beauty, he agreed, saying, "And not nearly as expensive as you might think."

That picture, framed in gold, now hung on the wall above the stairs, and I stared at it as I carried my son to his mother. The artist had caught a mischievous look in her eyes and the creaminess of her silk gown as it flowed like honey over her slim body. At her throat she wore my mother's diamond and emerald necklace and on her finger the diamond and platinum ring I'd given her. I felt overwhelmed with my love for her and the gift she had now given me, the infant in my arms. I looked at his tiny face and beheld my dreams wrapped up in my little brother reincarnate.

# CHAPTER SIX

## KANSAS CITY, MISSOURI
## 1918
## REBECCA

I've heard that one forgets the pain of childbirth, but I never shall. Nor shall I forget that Kurt withheld any relief medication until after the baby came. Then, at last, he deemed it appropriate to give me a shot and tell me we had a son. Tired to the point of exhaustion, I drifted off. I dreamt I lay in Jimmy Galeno's arms. He whispered in my ear and brushed my hair from my face. He kissed my neck and massaged my breast. He lifted my blouse and placed his lips on my nipple, sucking it to erection and causing my loins to contract with desire. But then his lovemaking no longer felt good. In my dream, he tugged at me noisily and though I tried to push him away, his hands stopped me. I cried out and woke to see Kurt standing over me.

"Your son is hungry," he said, holding the baby's mouth to my breast. You must sit up a bit and help him. Don't worry. I'll stay in case you fall asleep."

Groggily, I pushed the child away and stared down at the tiny face. I felt him squirm in his blanket, his mouth searching for my nipple. Even wrinkly and frowning, he looked strangely familiar and a softness came into my heart. Yet, I didn't want the shape of my pretty breasts altered. "No," I said. "I told you before I don't want to breast feed. Give him a bottle."

48

"Don't be stubborn, Rebecca. Nursing is far better for him," Kurt insisted.

I shook my head.

"Won't you just try?"

"No. Can't you see I'm tired? Every bone in my body aches."

Before I slept, I heard Kurt whisper, "See if you can find him a wet nurse, Susie Mae. I don't think she'll do it."

When finally I woke, a new day had dawned. I found myself alone. Was it really over, the nightmare of my pregnancy? I felt my stomach: not totally flat, but the squirming mound was gone.

I pushed myself to a sitting position and gasped with pain from the stitches between my legs. Struggling to reach my bedside mirror, I saw that sometime during the last twelve hours, Susie Mae had seen to my needs. She cleaned me, placed me in a soft, satin nightgown, and brushed my hair. Even so, I looked pale and gaunt.

What a disastrous condition this baby has left me in. I might never get my beautiful figure back. If Kurt thinks for one moment that I will allow my baby to stretch my already sore and swollen breasts out of shape, he is sadly mistaken.

A soft rap came on the door and Susie Mae stuck her shiny face around the side, saw me stare back at her, and quietly entered. "How you feel, Miss Becka?" she asked, plumping up my pillow and straightening my covers.

"Like I've been trampled by a herd of horses."

"You hungry?"

"Maybe a little. Some tea would be nice." My stomach rumbled. "And some thick strips of bacon, very crisp, and eggs over easy, toast with butter and currant jelly. Don't forget I like the tea good and hot."

"Yessum," she said sweetly. "I'll tell Hilda." She paused by the door and looked back at me. "You wants to see yo baby?" she asked.

"He's all right isn't he?"

"Oh, yessum. He's happy and well fed. I found a wet nurse for him jest like Doctor Kurt told me."

I felt a tingle of relief and then a twinge of jealousy. "Who?" I asked.

A tiny smile crossed her lips. "My older sister. She birthed her chile six months ago. She a regular cow, she is."

"Your sister?" I asked in disbelief.

"Yessum. He took to her right away."

I frowned and I think she read my thoughts.

"Don't you worry none. He won't turn dark. Lots a white ladies get Negroes to wet nurse their young' uns. "

I looked at her coloring and thought of Neosha, my father's maid.

I barely remember my mother. I knew her name, Gertrude, but my father and friends that came bringing food and flowers called her Trudy. The nurses were nice to me but shooed me outside to play as they ministered to her needs. I can see her to this day lying wasted and thin in her bed. Sometimes I'd sit beside her and beg her to play. "Perhaps tomorrow, Becka," she'd say, her voice barely a whisper. Sometimes, she'd brush my dark curls with her thin, shaking hand.

On a cool spring afternoon of my kindergarten year my father led me to my mother's bed. He sat beside her as she slept and took me on his lap."

She dying, *Liebchen*," he said as tears trickled down his cheeks. I'd never seen him weep before. "Soon she will leave us forever."

But I didn't cry, for by then it seemed to me she was already gone.

Neosha lived in the little room behind the kitchen. My father told me not to go there but I paid him no heed. When I needed someone to comfort me, I'd crawl into her lap and rest my head on her ample bosom. She'd rock me and hum until I'd fall asleep. The day of the funeral, she dressed me in my white silk party dress with a blue satin sash and pulled little white gloves upon my hands. I stood beside my father. Two men lowered my mother's casket into the ground. I heard the sobs of others but I shed no tears. I thought only of how glad I would be to take off those silly gloves.

Susie Mae's voice broke my reverie. "It ain't too late for you to nurse him yo'self," she said. "He's beautiful, Miss Becka."

"No, no. It's all right." I answered. "Just see that his needs are met. Now get me my breakfast." I leaned back and closed my eyes as Susie Mae quietly slipped out the door.

Why couldn't things have stayed the way they were, just Papa and me and Neosha, plump and jolly with laughing eyes and a pleasant face? She always wore a clean white uniform and comfortable white shoes with the holes cut out the sides through which her bunions protruded. She comforted me when I was hurt and folded me into her arms when I needed holding. I told her things I never told anyone else, least of all my father. He spent so much time at his business, he hardly knew I existed.

Two years after my mother's death, he began dating Erika Grumbach, a tall, skinny, angular woman he'd hired as his secretary five years before. One night she came for dinner. She wore her black hair pulled back tight in a bun, a high-necked white shirt with puffed out sleeves, and tiny pearl buttons down the middle, a black skirt, and black shoes with laces. She had emigrated from Germany. She spoke broken English to me and German to my father. I couldn't understand them when they spoke to each other.

I shrank inside myself as she made herself comfortable in my mother's chair. Neosha served her first. That upset me because, since my mother's death, I'd been the lady of the house. We had chicken and mashed potatoes. She took both drumsticks, my favorite. I hated her and prayed she'd choke on them. My father smiled and urged me to eat my salad. Erika said vegetables helped a girl's figure. I spit out the lettuce.

Every day Neosha walked me to the big stone house on Elm Street, Mrs. Vandersloop's School for Young Ladies. In the afternoon, she would come to take me home. Sometimes I'd skipped ahead and sometimes I held her hand.

During the summer, I'd cool off in Mrs. Vandersloop's backyard pool. In winter, when the water in the public park pond froze, I'd put on my small fur coat with a muff to match and skate with the my best friend, Sybil Grossman. She made me laugh with her jokes and tricks.

In that way time slipped by, and before I knew it I had my thirteenth birthday and Neosha waved goodbye to me as I headed off alone to the neighborhood school. It seemed more private than public since most of the kids came from wealthy families. All through those years Sybil and I tittered about our studies and classmates, but I confided my deepest secret to Neosha. I had met a boy.

"Skinny as a beanpole," I told her, "with red hair and freckles."

"Don't sound like much," she said, but I told her he had two redeeming features: a gentle, sweet mouth, and a special gift for playing the piano. I didn't tell her that I listened to the boy practice at school or that I had never heard such beautiful music.

"He in your class?" she asked, turning away from the sink to look at me with a half-scrubbed potato in her hand.

"Not in all of them," I hedged.

Actually, that afternoon I had leaned against the door where he practiced. The music stopped, and when he came out I only just managed to avoid an awkward fall. Though his surprise equaled mine, he smiled and shyly asked, "Are you all right?"

Embarrassed and flustered, I rattled off something that sounded like an apology and tried to explain that I enjoyed his music.

"Me?" he gasped. "You like hearing me play?"

"I do," I answered, my eyes meeting his.

He blushed, his cheeks turning red. "I rarely have an audience, except for my mother. Come in." He touched my hand.

I'd never been in the music studio, couldn't carry a tune and until now, had no exposure to music. I don't know what drew me to him, perhaps that he lowered his eyes when he spoke yet dared to touch me. A big piano stood at the far end of the room, the lid raised. I looked inside at the rows of strings and felt hammers.

"Beautiful, isn't it?" he said. "A famous lawyer in town donated it to the school in honor of his wife, but they only haul it out for special occasions like graduation. I'm glad, because I get to use it whenever I like."

"Will you play for me?" I asked.

"Sure. Come sit next to me. What would you like to hear?"

I sat on his left, my leg brushing his. "Whatever you'd like."

"How about a Chopin polonaise?" he asked.

"That sounds swell."

He placed his long, beautiful fingers on the keys and began. Before long, the piano seemed to become an extension of his body. I had been to band concerts in the park and even taken a required music appreciation course, but nothing compared to the vibrant strains that this boy drew from that instrument.

It seemed like we floated in a musical bubble, the sounds captivating me, quieting my breath. I had never felt so close to anyone. He played just for me: wild raucous pieces, slow drifting melodies, hushed, soft tunes. I couldn't take my eyes off him, my heart melting like butter. Albert was the antithesis of everything and everyone I'd ever known.

Before we parted that day, I knew his name and that he lived in the Russian neighborhood.

"He promised to play for me every day," I bragged to Neosha. Her face clouded in a frown. "You too young to have a boyfriend," she told me.

"He's not my boyfriend," I replied testily, "and you better not tell my father."

"Well, now, Miss Becka. I don't know about that."

My hands flew to my hips, and I narrowed my eyes. "I mean it, Neosha. Don't forget. You're not my mother."

"I ain't likely to forget that," she said with a grunt and turned back to the sink.

As time went by, Albert's and my friendship grew. He invited me home to meet his mother, a kind gentle woman who gave piano lessons to the neighborhood children. I noticed a beautiful ring on her finger, a sparkling diamond surrounded by sapphire baguettes. I asked Albert about it. He told me it had belonged to his father's mother, an engagement ring that bespoke of better times.

I thought him the kindest, nicest person I'd ever known. What did I care about his Russian heritage? We would meet after school and stroll together, sharing thoughts and dreams. When I'd get angry, he'd joke and make me laugh, and when I'd cry, he'd comfort me and make me smile. I called him Bertie and told him he could call me Becka. Becka and Bertie. I liked that.

He played hundreds of private concerts just for me. Sometimes I watched him and wondered how he made his fingers move so fast. Other times I would stand by the piano and let the music wash over me, enveloping me in an ocean of sound waves.

On a frosty, fall day, we huddled together on the stone wall watching boys practice for the Friday night football game and spoke of the upcoming fall concert.

"I've never asked a girl," he told me. "I'll be playing, of course. I'll get you the best seat in the auditorium and take you out for ice cream after."

"Ice cream? Let's go for dinner? I'll pay."

"I couldn't let you do that," he said. "Never mind."

54

"Oh, Bertie. Can't you take a joke? Of course I'd love to do it." I snuggled against his arm but he pulled away.

A football landed at our feet. One of the red-shirted players, Jimmy Galeno, ran over to retrieve it. As captain of the football team, he'd become accustomed to all the girls swooning over him. Sybil said Sicily produced some real good lookers. As he reached for the ball, he swept me with his eyes, a hint of a smile on his lips. "Helloo Rebecca," he chortled. "Prefer the pansy type, do you?"

His words stung and infuriated me. "Shut up, Jimmy. Go play with your little friends."

He laughed and turned to Albert. "Wanna come play with me and my little friends, pansy boy?" he grinned, nodding toward the others.

Albert shook his head.

"Why are you are so mean, Jimmy Galeno?" I said. "Come on, Bertie. Let's go."

"Do we have a problem here?" one of boys wearing a red shirt asked. They all looked so big in their football uniforms.

Jimmy's face went serious and he stared at me. Then, he swept up the ball. "Naw," he said. "Leave 'em alone."

But his friends weren't done yet. One of them pulled Albert off the wall. They formed a circle and began pushing him back and forth. "Come on, BERTIE. Come on," they mimicked me.

That really made me mad. "Hey, you bums," I said. "Go pick on someone your own size!"

I guess Jimmy had had enough because he said something I couldn't hear and they all followed him back to the playing field.

"Are you all right, Bertie?" I asked.

He stood up and brushed himself off. "Don't call me that anymore," he said and walked away.

"Is that the thanks I get for saving your life?" I called after him, surprised and hurt.

He turned around. "I don't need you to defend me, Rebecca. I can take care of myself."

For the next few days, I avoided Albert. I didn't go to the studio and I didn't wait around after school for him. When I told Neosha about it, she said, "You should be glad he ain't no sissy, Miss Becka. Besides, you papa'd have a fit, you seein' that boy."

"I'm not 'seeing' anyone. Why do you always exaggerate?" I cried. "He's just a friend." But her words made me realize Papa would indeed have a fit over Albert, which of course made me more determined than ever to see him.

I broke my arm my first year in high school. It happened in such a silly way. Sybil and I had gone ice-skating. I remember I wore my new purple velvet outfit with the ermine collar. Mr. Hanstrom from the city had come to stoke a fire for us in the big, black metal drum, and the boys had already started their Saturday hockey game. Sybil always dawdled putting on her skates, so I went out on the ice without her. Jimmy Galeno broke away from his game and skated toward me. He slid to a stop, rudely spraying ice on my new coat.

My face grew hot with anger, the kind Albert tried to make me control. "Damn you," I said, brushing at my clothes. "Look what you've done."

He swept his cap from his head, freeing his crop of black wavy hair, bent low and said, "Oops. So sorry. Do you want to skate with me?"

"Not even if you were the Pope," I sneered.

He just smiled, wiggled his finger at me, and skated back to his friends.

Furious, I spun around, tripped, and went sprawling. I heard a crack and felt the pain shoot up my arm. I started to cry. The boys stopped playing hockey and watched as Sybil got Mr. Hanstrom to help me up. He drove me to German Hospital. The doctor, Kurt Adler, set my arm. Later Papa wanted to know what happened, so I told him about Jimmy Galeno, which turned out to be a big mistake.

"Galeno," he said. "I know the family. Sicilian bunch. Mafioso. Do business with them. "

"Why, if you don't like them?" I asked.

"No choice. Do business with them or they shut you down. Big bunch of crooks. I won't have you exposed to that element."

"He's not the only person in my class," I said, trying out a snotty tone of voice I learned at school. "There's Sybil and Henrietta and Albert, of course."

"Albert who?" he said, shark-like.

"Rapinsky," I answered, wishing I'd just kept my mouth shut. "He plays the piano."

Papa slapped his hand against his forehead and rolled his eyes, "*Oy gevalt*. A Russian musician yet. Your poor dead mother would roll over in her grave."

"No, she wouldn't, Papa," I said. "She'd like him." But it was too late.

He rubbed his chin. "Maybe I should send you back east to a finishing school."

"No. Please." *How did things get this far?*

"Then again, maybe not. That's very expensive, but something must be done. Perhaps I can find another solution." Suddenly, I noticed his face light up and he smacked the table with his hand. "As a matter of fact, I think maybe I've hit upon the perfect plan." He stood up and grinned. "Yes, sir. I think I know just the answer."

Weeks went by before I learned what he meant. By then, I'd gotten the cast off my arm. One night, as Papa and I sat down to dinner, I saw the strangest look on his face. Neosha brought in the roast and set it before him. Funny how certain things stand out in your mind. I watched him pick up the knife and begin sharpening it on the honing steel just as he had done a hundred times before. Slowly, he leaned forward and began to carve the meat.

"I have a surprise for you," he said, not looking at me. Neosha returned with the gravy.

Generally, I love surprises, but something about his demeanor made we wary. "Oh?"

"Yes, dear Rebecca. A good father takes care of his daughter, and so today, I finished making arrangements for your betrothal." He returned to his carving.

Stunned, I gasped and sat speechless, not quite grasping his words. "My *what?*"

"Your marriage," he said nonchalantly as he placed a piece of meat on a plate, slathered it with rich, dark gravy, and handed it to Neosha . He grinned with satisfaction.

I went to pieces.

"Papa," I cried. "Are you crazy?" Neosha placed the plate in front of me, but I pushed it away.

He slammed his fist on the table and gravy jumped onto the white damask cloth. "Don't you ever talk to me like that. You'll do as I say."

I glared back, flabbergasted. "But Papa," I persisted. "You don't understand. This is America, not the old country. People here don't arrange marriages for their daughters."

"Well, I do," he said simply.

I glowered at him. "Can I at least ask who the lucky bridegroom will be?"

"Did I forget to tell you that? His name is Kurt Adler."

"The doctor?" I shrieked. "He's old." The horror of it hit me, and I began to cry.

"Rebecca," he said, "this is not a subject for discussion. You will marry the day you turn eighteen. That's the end of it. Now eat your dinner."

"I'll never eat again," I replied, hurling my dinner plate across the room.

He leapt out of his chair before the plate hit the floor. He grabbed my arm, jerked me up and turned me over his knee.

"In this house, you do as I say." He pulled up my skirt and brought his hand down repeatedly on my bottom. Then, he dumped me off his lap and stood.

"Now clean up your mess and go to your room."

Shocked and sobbing, I got up and brushed myself off.

"I hate you!" I screamed, and ran upstairs. I flung myself on the bed, banging my fists into my pillows. Neosha came later to soothe me and bring me dinner, but I yelled at her to go away. Later that night, when I heard my father snoring, I slipped out of the house and ended up with Jimmy Galeno.

I awoke the next morning wondering what I had done. I rolled over and moaned with memories of pleasure and shame. God. How could I ever go back to school? How could I face Jimmy Galeno? With pouty lips, I stared out the window. Snow fell from a gray sky. Each gust of wind sent clouds of giant flakes swirling past the panes of glass and around the bare tree limbs. I tried not to think of Doctor Kurt but I saw his wild mane of hair, his thick, unruly eyebrows and his nose, humped in the middle, nesting like an egg over his great bushy mustache.

I didn't see Jimmy Galeno that day or the next, and when we ran into each other he acted like nothing had happened.

The years slipped by. Before I knew it the time came for graduation and my eighteenth birthday. Albert learned he'd won a scholarship to The Conservatory in Vienna.

We spent one final evening together, the night of our senior prom. We danced every dance, rebuffing Jimmy and the other boys when they tried to cut in, and later strolled for the last time to our secret glen in the park. I knew that what I felt for him could never be. We came from different worlds and my fate was sealed. We watched the young leaves flutter in the moonlight, reminisced, wondered about our futures. Dawn came, casting soft shadows over the downy turf where we lay glumly, side by side, not touching.

"Our time together grows short," he murmured.

"I know," I said and turned toward him, wanting to memorize every feature of his face. Almost without realizing it, I drew close and kissed him, my tongue tracing the outline of his mouth in much the same way Jimmy Galeno's had done to mine.

Albert didn't resist nor did he protest when I undid his shirt and pressed my breasts against him. I felt his manhood and guided him into my secret place. When at last he spilled his seed I cried out with pleasure. Kissing and holding each other close, we stayed there until the apricot glow of sunlight peeked between the limbs of the trees.

The next day he left, and a week later I married Kurt. My father, now relieved of me, asked Erika to marry him. I learned she had never bothered to become a citizen – perhaps because she knew she would one day become my father's wife. She breathed, however, a visible sigh of relief and haughtily moved all her stuff into my mother's house. I fumed.

Kurt and I spent a few weeks on the east coast touring and visiting his old classmates. I endured his lovemaking but loved shopping in expensive boutiques and dining in the finest restaurants. At last we sailed from New York on the British luxury liner *Mauretania*. I flitted around the huge ship exploring its exquisitely appointed areas and staring at the red gold of the grand ballroom. The crossing would take six days, and I intended to enjoy every minute.

Our first class accommodations thrilled me. Dressed in light seersucker, I luxuriated in the warm sun. I promenaded around the deck pretending Kurt was my father and when he went back to our room to rest, I arranged myself on one of the canvas deck chairs and enjoyed the attentions of fellow passengers.

That night, we dined at the captain's table. I picked at the French cuisine and took pleasure in compliments that flowed my way. I'd chosen one of my new designer gowns, an ice blue chiffon, and found myself whirling around the dance floor with first one and then another handsome, young Naval officer to the music of The Royal Derby Band.

The third morning out, disaster struck. I arose early intending to take a walk around the deck before breakfast. Telling Kurt to hurry, I donned a breezy white dress and went to get a sweater from my drawer when I suffered the first of consecutive waves of nausea.

"Let's go," I heard Kurt say, but I could only lean against the chest with my head down, swallowing repeatedly as I tried not to throw up.

"What is it, darling? Tummy not too steady this morning?"

I didn't even bother to answer that stupid question.

"Don't let it worry you," he said, smiling. "Just a touch of seasickness, I'd say." He took my arm and guided me to the bed. "Lie down while I fix you a little something to settle your stomach." He picked up his satchel and took it to the bathroom where I heard the water running. He came back with a glass of foamy liquid and gave it to me to drink. "There's a good girl. Just rest now. You'll feel better soon. Do you want me to stay with you?"

I gagged on the drink, shook my head, and managed to motion him out the door.

Amazingly, within a few hours, I felt fine and had no further problem until we reached Liverpool where I had another bout of nausea. Kurt had gone to arrange for us to disembark. By the time he returned the sickness had gone.

We trained across England to Dover where we took the ferry to Calais, all the while planning to stop in London on the way back. The channel was rough and choppy. The medicine Kurt gave me did no good, and I huddled below deck, miserable.

"Not a very good sailor," my husband said, "but no matter. We'll land soon and you can rest before we board the train to Paris." We arrived on schedule at the Georges V Hotel where I curled up gratefully into the inviting quiet of the lovely cherry bed.

Kurt gave me a sleeping pill, tucked me in, kissed me in an affectionate manner, and left me to rest. The next morning, thank God, I awoke feeling refreshed with all signs of my illness gone.

I fell in love with Paris. While Kurt caught up with old friends, I joined the crowds at Notre Dame, wandering through the huge, musty church, marveling at its splendor. I strolled the Champs Élysées, soaking up the feel of the city, gawked at the Eiffel Tower, roamed the Louvre. Kurt took me to the Place Vêndome to shop and we dined with friends in a small, elegant restaurant. We visited the artists on the left bank, bought wine and long thin loaves of bread to take on idle afternoon picnics.

The last night, Kurt treated me to La Tour d'Argent, the elegant restaurant overlooking Notre Dame and the Seine. I felt ravenously hungry and ordered duck and drank wine from a glass a mere child of a waiter refilled after every sip. But when the first course arrived, a wave of nausea overwhelmed me. I bolted for the ladies room. After that, I begged to go home.

Kurt had wanted to visit his old school in Heidelberg but decided that might be too dangerous anyway, since the war had not yet ended. He turned in our luxury liner tickets and managed to book immediate passage on a returning hospital ship where he could be of some help and I could recover from what Kurt called my stomach infection in the semi-comfort of officers' quarters.

Once back in Kansas City, I went home to visit my father. Neosha took one look at me and said, "What's the matter, honey? You is so pale."

"I don't know. I'm just exhausted," I whined and fell into her arms. "No matter how much sleep I get, it's not enough."

Her round face broke into a wide grin. "You gonna have a baby, honey chile. Ole Neosha can tell."

"A baby. Oh, my God. No. Can that be?"

"You miss yore time?" she asked.

I knew I had, maybe twice, but I had attributed it to excitement and travel. Now I understood why blue veins had sprung up like winding city streets across my breasts and the bouts of nausea had continued. I was pregnant.

How could Kurt not have known? Yet his excitement knew no bounds. "A statement to the powers of the Adler men," he exclaimed, but I surely didn't want to become anybody's mother.

I thought of getting rid of it, even going to the extent of jumping up and down and taking long, arduous walks. I mentioned abortion to Sybil, but she said she'd heard you could die and I didn't want to go that far. So instead, my belly stretched out of shape. My face filled out, and my feet swelled.

"You've never looked more beautiful," Kurt told me. I felt huge and ugly. When the big day arrived, my dear husband wouldn't even give me something for pain. I truly thought I would die. After the baby came out, I just wanted to be left alone.

Susie Mae brought little Stern to me, all sweet-smelling and clean. As he slept peacefully in my arms, I got my first really good look at him. A more beautiful baby had never been born: carroty red hair, dark blue eyes like mine, long slender fingers. He looked exactly like Albert. I gawked, smiled, and kissed his cheek.

# CHAPTER SEVEN

## KANSAS CITY, MISSOURI
## 1924
### STERN

My first memories go back to the days when I tagged along after John Charles as he went about his chores. Dusting as he hummed, he paid little attention to me when I crawled up on the purple  cushion of the piano bench and touched a key with my finger. I found that by pressing different keys, I could make different sounds, the same sounds that John Charles hummed. Pretty soon, he looked up and grinned at me.

"That's right good, Massah Stern," he said bending to run his cloth over the brass andirons, "but I bet you can't play this one." He began to sing a familiar spiritual I'd heard him do before. At two or three years of age, I had to kneel on the bench to see the keyboard, but with studied concentration, I used my index finger to tap out the melody in the very key in which John Charles sang.

I remember him standing up with mock surprise and then singing along in his deep resonant voice as I played. Our music filled the room. After we'd finished, John Charles slapped his knee and laughed out loud.

"We make a good team don't we, Massah Stern?"

We heard my mother say, "So it would seem," and looked up to see her standing in the doorway.

"I need to go to my meeting, John Charles. Hurry and get the car. Susie Mae?" she called. "Come get Stern."

"Hum a tune, Mother," I asked.

"Don't bother me now, darling. Can't you see I'm in a rush?"

But I persisted. "Pleeze?" I begged.

"For heaven's sake, Stern. I'm already late. "

"Just one?" I whined.

"All right. All right. Just one." Impatiently, she dadi da'ed *Oh! Suzanna.*

I pecked out the song. She stopped short and turned, a stunned look on her face. "My goodness, dear. Where did you learn to do that?"

"I can do more," I said. A smile flicked across her face. "Sing another one."

She stared at me for a moment, her dark blue eyes filled with surprise. Then she glanced at her watch. "Oh my goodness. I really must go. I'm meeting Aunt Sybil for lunch and I'm already late. Hop down now and give me a kiss. Your nursemaid will be here in a minute."

Susie Mae came to take my hand and lead me away. Her starched, white dress crackled when she moved, and her shiny, black face beamed above her stiff collar. "I think we'll go see if we can find a cookie for this boy," she said, eyes twinkling.

"Take him to the garden," my mother said. "He's pale. A little fresh air will do him good."

"Yessum, we'll do jest that." She bent down and picked me up, whispering "cookie first" in my ear. Outside on the tire swing that John Charles had hung over the biggest limb of the elm tree, I screamed with excitement as she pushed me and twirled me around. Then, she stopped the tire dead still and put her finger to her lips.

"Listen," she'd say. "What do you hear?"

"Songs," I told her."

"Who's doin' the singing?" she whispered.

"That birdie." I pointed.

"Who else?" She lifted me out of the tire and we walked toward the creek.

I told her I heard the bees hovering over flowers, but actually, I heard much more. Water trickling over stones sounded like music to me as did the chirping of crickets and the rustle of the wind.

All those noises came together as melodies in my head, and sometimes those tunes came out through my fingers. I didn't know it then, but I was already composing music.

By age six, I could play the piano with both hands, simple little ditties that I'd heard or made up. My grandfather said I took after my grandmother, but no one took my musical games seriously until mother invited a group of women to tea, including Aunt Sybil. As a special treat, she asked Albert Rapinsky and his friend, a violinist, to play. To my surprise she let me sit on her lap and listen.

"Well for goodness sakes," Aunt Sybil whispered to my mother. "I've never noticed it before, but Stern's hair is almost the exact same color as Albert's. It makes them look alike."

My mother gave me an extra little squeeze and said, "Yes, don't they?"

The music enchanted me. The beauty of it brought tears to my eyes. I sat listening for many moments, carried away, until a sound from the violin made me cover my ears and cry out. Shocked and embarrassed, my mother shushed me, put me down, and sent me to my room.

When at last she told Susie Mae to fetch me, my mother and her friend, Mister Rapinsky, sat waiting in the parlor, a look of displeasure on her face.

"Well now, young man," the pianist said kindly, "What do you suppose got into you?"

I shrugged and stared at my shoes.

"I think you've been rude enough for one day. Now answer Albert," my mother said.

Tears clouded my eyes. "I liked hearing you play," I told him, "but then something made my ears jangle, and I felt like throwing up."

He smiled. "I think I know what bothered you, but I need you to help me prove it. Will you do that? Will you play a little piano game with me?"

I glanced at my mother, who nodded.

We went to the piano where he seated himself and told me to turn around and not to peek. "I am going to play two notes and you must tell me which is higher." He touched the keys and I said, "That's easy. The first is the highest."

Then he instructed me to turn around and watch. "Let's say this key is middle C and is number one and so on up to high C. Do you understand?"

I nodded.

"Now turn away again and tell me what number keys I play."

"Four, eight, five."

He seemed to get excited and hit three more keys, but he didn't fool me. He'd struck a black key between two and three. Then he played three notes together, and I knew them too. I looked up at my mother who stood by the piano watching.

"How does he do that?" she said, surprised. "What does it mean?"

"He has a good ear," he said. "Probably perfect pitch. I have it, though sometimes it isn't a blessing. I also heard the violin slip out of tune. Most people wouldn't notice it, but for those of us who do, it sounds like chalk on a blackboard."

My mother stared at him, her lips curling into a pleased smile. "My word. What do we do now, Albert?"

"If he were mine, I'd probably see to it that he got piano lessons," he said.

My mother started to say something, but I interrupted.

"I can already play," I cried and climbed up next to him. Before anyone could stop me, I drummed out the song my mother had sung, *Oh! Suzanna.*

Mr. Rapinsky clapped his hands. "I think, Becka, you need to find a good teacher for our little maestro here. I might know just such a person. "

"How about you?" she asked, a funny look on her face.

"Oh, no. I'm not a teacher. Besides, I leave on tour in a week. I shan't be back for a year or more."

"I didn't really mean it," my mother said, though her voice didn't sound that way. "You've become quite famous, I know. I see your name in the paper often. Actually," she said, brightening, "Kurt and I have tickets to your concert Saturday evening. Perhaps you'll dine with us later."

The person Mr. Rapinsky suggested, Madame du Preé, caused me no end of trouble. I thought she looked like a high-stepping rooster I'd seen at the state fair. She walked with her chest puffed out and her pointy chin tucked in close to her long, skinny neck.

Her black hair, pulled tightly into a bun, pulled her eyes squinty, and she sucked her lips together in one, stern vertical line. She always wore black, both skirt and jacket, and a hat with a red feather that bobbed up and down over her ear. The first day she came to our house, I hid behind my mother's back.

"Don't do that, Stern," she reprimanded me. "Shake hands like a gentleman. Pay attention and do as you're told." To Madame, she said, "I hope you don't expect me to sit and listen."

"Of course not," my teacher answered primly. "Most children apply themselves better when their parents are not in the room. The lesson will last precisely one hour, after which I may wish to speak with you. Are we clear?"

I watched in wonder as my mother nodded and left the room. No one ever talked to Mama like that. Madame swept over to the piano and glared disapprovingly at the long fringes dangling from the purple bench cover.

Without hesitation, she walked into the library, plucked two fat books off a shelf, and brought them back into the parlor and placed them on the bench. Then she grabbed me under my arms and lifted me into position before the keys.

She placed my hands on the keyboard, shook her head, put me down, and retrieved another book. Back on the bench I went, and this time she studied my position, placed my fingers on the keys, and nodded. "Voilà."

She pulled up a chair on which she sat ramrod straight, one pointed shoe slightly ahead of the other. The whole time I took lessons from her, I never saw her in any other pose.

"First you must learn to sit properly," she instructed. She pulled back my shoulders and poked a sharp finger into my back.

"I can play a tune," I told her proudly. "Do you want to hear it?"

"No, and furthermore, I don't want you to pick out any more songs. You will develop bad habits."

She positioned my hands in a curve, wrists slightly elevated, fingers resting gently on the keys.

"Do not let your wrists fall." She jabbed her sharp thumb nail into my palm.

"You must practice your scales every day until you gain strength and dexterity. Then, perhaps you may play your little tune for me. So. Are you ready?"

Even though her breath smelled like rotten cabbage and her heavy perfume made me nauseous, I couldn't wait to begin. At first I used only one hand, then both. Over and over, I struck the keys, five notes up and five notes down, until I could do it moving only my fingers.

Next she taught me how to cross my thumb under my palm and continue up the scale. "I didn't know I could do that," I cried, thrilled.

Before the first lesson ended, she delighted me with my very own piano book, *Easy Little Exercises for Little Fingers*. It contained big black notes placed on particular lines. Madame explained their meaning and their position on the keyboard. Before I knew it, I discovered I could read the music all by myself.

My teacher circled the first page with a sharp red pencil. "Your assignment for the week," she said. "Next time, if you do well, we will continue." She stood and ordered me to get my mother.

I found Mama doing her nails. "Nervy thing, isn't she. I hope it went well," she said. "Well, come along. We'll see what she wants."

"I asked to speak with you, Mrs. Adler, so that we understand each other from the beginning."

"I think that sounds like a good idea."

"I am not at all sure Stern is ready for lessons. You must realize that the study of piano requires much practice. A pupil needs maturity to learn proper form. Stern is very young, five is he?"

"He's six and quite mature," Mother said.

"Just because he has a good ear is no guarantee that he will be able to play well. One has little to do with the other."

My mother smiled. "Mr. Rapinsky disagrees," she said in her nicest voice, "and he recommended you, after all. I'm sure you will be able to justify his confidence."

"We shall see about that." A tension filled the air. "You should know I do have misgivings. However, I am willing to try if you are." She looked at me. "Stern must be made to practice every day, one half hour at first and later an hour. And most importantly, he must not be allowed to pick out tunes by ear."

"You hear that, Stern?" I could tell my mother's patience wore thin.

"There will be plenty of time for that later." Madame took a deep breath. "I may appear very strict but if he is gifted, as Albert seems to think, he must be molded properly. If not, we shall know soon enough."

Later, after Madame had gone, I sat down at the piano and thumped out a song I'd recently heard.

"That doesn't sound like your lesson," Mother called from a distant part of the house. I dutifully played a scale, but I secretly liked that she listened.

At first I enjoyed playing scales and lessons from my new book. Sometimes John Charles would bring Grandpa Max to listen, but soon I became bored with *Easy Little Exercises for Little Fingers*. Tunes ran around in my head until they had to come out.

My mother reprimanded me if she heard me fooling around, but more frequently, my mother or my grandfather would ask me to play a familiar song or two for company. I discovered I loved entertaining an audience.

One blustery spring day Madame du Prée gave me my first real piece, a little Bach minuet. She made me read the music and work out the melody, note by note.

"I have placed tiny numbers above the notes," she told me. "They are to tell you which finger to use. Use only those I've written."

Why, I wondered and looked out the window at the puffy white clouds.

"Pay attention, young man," she said, placing her hand on my head and turning it back to the music. "This week we will learn the right hand only. Next week we will add the left hand."

But of course, I couldn't do that. Long before my next lesson, I had memorized the piece and added my own base harmony. It sounded fine to me, and I played it again and again. My grandfather smilingly shook his head, and if my mother knew the difference, she didn't say.

The next time Madame came, she asked me to show her what I had learned. Dutifully, I played the right hand but then, in a moment of exuberance, I added my innovative left hand.

She reacted in a way I didn't expect. She yanked my hands from the piano and banged the lid down.

71

"I told you to play just the right hand and only the notes you read. Now look what you've done. Trash. That's what you play. Trash. Get your mother this instant."

Sobbing, I raced around the house trying to find her. I burst into the kitchen where Hilda and Susie Mae sat peeling potatoes. John Charles gaped from the butler's pantry. "Where's my mother?" I cried. "I need her right away."

Startled, Susie Mae jumped up and pulled me to her. "What's the matter, baby? You s'posed to be taking you're lesson, ain't you?"

"She's really, really mad at me," I whimpered, "and wants to see my mother." As Susie Mae soothed me and told me my mama had gone out, John Charles slipped from the room.

Afraid to go back to the parlor alone, I begged my nursemaid to come with me, jerking on her arm with desperation. She pulled back, making up all kinds of excuses and saying, "It's not my place. Go on, now. You a big boy. Just tell her your mama ain't at home. You can do that, can't you?"

Then I saw John Charles come down the steps carrying my grandfather. In the parlor, Madame stood by the piano rapidly tapping her foot. Wordlessly, John Charles placed Grandpa carefully in a chair and drew a robe about his legs. "I've come to hear my grandson play," Grandpa said simply.

"I have stopped the lesson," Madame answered, chin up, nose in the air.

"And why is that?" he said with an arched eyebrow.

"Because he refuses to read the notes. He thinks his way is better than the composer."

"Is that right?" he asked me.

"No, sir," I answered, hanging my head. "It's just that sometimes my ears tell me what to play."

Madame du Prée got more flustered. I could tell because her foot went even faster than ever. "He plays drivel, that's what he does. Bach would roll in his grave."

My grandfather chuckled. "Maybe Bach also played drivel as a child," he said, "but here now. Do stop that tapping and sit. You are making me nervous. I'm sure if we calm down, we can reach a satisfactory solution."

Glaring at me, she took a seat. "I wonder, Madame," Grandpa asked, "how many six year-olds you teach?"

"He," she pointed at me, "grâce à Dieu, is the only one."

"Does he have some talent?" Grandpa said.

"I have no idea. Albert Rapinsky seems to think he does."

Grandpa leaned his head back against his chair.

"You know," he said in a way I recognized when he talked of Grandma, "my dear Molly and I loved the symphony. The City of Kansas had none and we missed it greatly, but my darling loved to play the piano and so we kept up our interest in the classics. She played until her illness took away her energy, but oh, how she loved her music."

He looked toward me. "She would be so proud of you, Stern. Now tell me. Do you want to continue?"

"Oh yes, Grandpa," I said. "I love to play."

"Well, then, perhaps I can help. What if I listened as he practices his assignments each day? Would that be satisfactory?"

Madame sighed heavily. "I don't know, Mr. Adler. You would have to be quite discerning. He is very clever."

"Let's give it a try anyway. Stern will be seven in the fall. I propose we give him until then. If he does no better, then the lessons stop." He looked at me questioningly.

I nodded and Madame agreed, albeit with what appeared to be great reluctance. I believed even then she could see the end in sight.

After that, every afternoon at exactly four o'clock, John Charles carried Grandpa to the parlor where, settled comfortably in his chair, he listened to me play.

One afternoon, my father, who usually left for the hospital before I awoke and returned after dark, burst into the parlor in a fit of rage.

"Have you lost your mind?" he roared at my grandfather. "Here you've worked all your life, made a fortune, built a hospital, funded a museum, and now you're sitting every day listening to a six year old play the piano?"

"So?" Grandpa answered, "I believe the child has talent."

"Posh," my father said, and turned his back.

"It's not impossible." Grandpa said, sounding very irritated. "Your own mother played beautifully. Who knows? Perhaps if Frankie had lived, he would have been musically inclined too."

Papa whipped around to face his father. "That's just your guilt showing. He never showed the slightest interest in the piano."

"How would you know? He was only six . . . " My grandfather 's voice dwindled away.

"Why don't you just admit you're bored. Go back to your reading or call up your crony friends, but for heaven's sake, stop encouraging Stern. I want my boy to grow up to be something."

Grandpa shrank in his chair. "I don't see that I'm doing the child any harm, Kurt."

"Fine," Father said with an anger I didn't understand. "It's certainly more than you ever did for Frankie or me." With that, he stormed out of the room.

I could tell he hurt Grandpa's feelings, and I worried that the lesson-listening would stop, but sure enough, the next afternoon at four, there he sat, waiting for me to begin.

Sometimes he'd say things like, "Don't play so fast, my boy. It's not a horse race you know," or, "Are you tired today? Your wrists sag. Ah ha. Yes. That's much better."

Over time, I began to improve, but I still couldn't resist playing anything and everything I heard. Once in awhile, my improvisations spilled over into my lessons, by accident or on purpose. Eventually, Madame du Prée had enough.

"I am a traditionalist," she told my mother. "I simply cannot put up with such reckless, sloppy playing. It is useless to continue. Perhaps you can find someone else. Convey my regards to your father-in-law. Tell him we both tried . . . and failed. *Au revoir.*" She swept out the door.

My father seemed greatly relieved. "At last," he said. "Someone with a grain of sense in her head. That should put an end to this piano nonsense. Now we will all just forget it."

My mother nodded, but I later learned she had no intention of doing so, for she harbored a secret even I didn't know.

# CHAPTER EIGHT

## KANSAS CITY, MISSOURI
## 1928
### STERN

Behind our house stood an old elm tree with a trunk so big even John Charles couldn't reach his arms around it. He had hung an old tire from one of its branches. I loved to sit in that tire and pump myself into high arcs. Sometimes I could even catch a glimpse of the creek beyond the fence.

At night I'd dream about that swing. I would float out of the tire and drift like a balloon over the earth, then I'd pick up speed and begin a dizzy spiral down toward the empty concrete wading pool below. Faster and faster I'd go, hearing my own screams and awakening just before I crashed.

Shaking, my cheeks wet with tears, I'd open my eyes to find Susie Mae there to comfort me. She always said the same thing. "There, there now, sweet chile. You is all right, safe here in your own little bed. No, don't tell me. It's bad luck to say a dream before breakfast," and then she would stay with me until I'd drift off to sleep.

One morning I asked John Charles if he ever had bad dreams.

"Course I do, but nothing like my sister Bertha's chile Ramsey. Why, he tells the worst tales about his dreams."

"Susie Mae says it's bad luck . . . "

"I know. To say your dreams before breakfast, but he do it anyway." He laughed and said, "One of these days, I'll just carry him out here. I reckon you and him'd get along fine."

Ramsey Patterson leaped into my life like a young colt, his gangly arms and legs poking out of his clean shirt and pants. He had shiny black skin and short, curly hair that glistened in the sun.

Sometimes, when he got excited, his brown eyes would open so wide you could see the whites all the way around. Other times they would crinkle together into slits, and tears of laughter would spill out onto his long black lashes. He had the biggest, whitest teeth I'd ever seen.

He always arrived with his head crammed full of games and fun things to do. I didn't know that as infants we had shared the same breast milk – only that he was six months older. We were best friends from the start, playing and sharing secrets together.

My mother said she didn't like me spending so much time with "that little Negro child" and she should tell John Charles to quit bringing him, but I begged her not to do that. She said she'd think about. She must have forgotten, because the day the piano lessons ended, John Charles had brought Ramsey.

I ran out the back door to tell them the good news, and Ramsey said, "'Bout time ya showed up, ya ole coot. I been waitin' for ya a month of Sundays." He threw back his head and laughed, those big buck teeth gleaming.

"Bet you didn't play your scales good." He rolled his eyes and fell backwards into the half filled wading pool they'd been cleaning.

"I guess not," I told him, kicking off my shoes and jumping in with him. "Madame isn't coming back any more."

"Whatcha mean, boy?" John Charles asked with alarm.

"My teacher left. She said I wouldn't amount to anything and that they'd better get someone else."

Ramsey started to say something but John Charles tossed him a warning look and said he better quit clowning around and get back to work.

"Can I help? I'm all wet anyway."

John Charles told me to get a brush and start scrubbing, but before long Ramsey and I collapsed into the water, splashing and giggling. Hilda appeared on the back porch with sandwiches and a pitcher of lemonade. She set them down on the table and put her hands on her hips. "Look at you two. Go right inside and take off those wet clothes before you catch your death."

"Oh, Hilda," I said. "We're fine."

She brushed a trailing gray hair from her face and shook her head disapprovingly. "So? Well then, all of you come get your lunch. John Charles? Why do you let them play in the pool with their clothes on?"

"Didn't see no harm, Miss Hilda," he answered. "They'll dry off before you know it."

"Don't forget to bring that tray in when you're done," she said.

Ramsey and I took our sandwiches and went to our hideout under the thick tangle of lilac and spirea branches, while John Charles sat on the porch steps enjoying the shade.

Safe inside our makeshift clubhouse, I confided a secret to my friend. "I'm glad Madame quit."

"I thought you wanted to be a piano player when you grow up."

"My father wants me to be a doctor like him."

"He must be a good one. I've heard John Charles tell a thousand times how your pa saved his life. "

"But I don't want to be a doctor," I told him.

"Maybe you can be both. Now you take me, for instance. I'm gonna be a fireman AND a policeman." He laughed. I thought him very brave.

We heard a familiar whistle and crawled out of the bushes to greet two neighbor boys that lived in a house down the lane. The oldest, Louie, taller than me with close-set eyes and long blond hair, came swaggering into the yard. Luke, his pudgy little brother, yelled, "Wait till you see what I found."

"Be quiet, stupid," Louie growled. "Do you want the whole world to know?"

Luke shrank into his fat self and hid the brown paper sack he carried behind his back.

Later, I wished I'd never said what I did. Then the whole thing might not have happened. But curiosity got the best of me and I asked, "What have you got?"

"It's a gun," Luke whispered.

Louie grabbed a handful of his brother's flaxen hair and yanked. "I'm gonna kill you with it if you don't shut up," he growled. "Give it here."

Luke dropped the bag and a small, silver pistol fell out. Ramsey's eyes got round as dollars. "Lawd a mercy. Where'd you get that?"

Louie snorted, pushed Luke away, and swept up the gun. "The little squirt found it in my pa's handkerchief drawer," he said. "I guess you might as well have a look if you want."

"Is it real?" I asked.

"You bet your boots it is."

I shied away, but Ramsey stepped right up and took the gun from the palm of his hand. He grasped it between his thumb and forefinger.

"Jesus. Don't you know anything?" Louie scoffed. "Here's how you hold it." He grabbed the weapon, put it in his right hand, positioned his finger on the trigger, and pointed it straight at me.

"Hey. Don't point that thing," Ramsey yelled. "You crazy or something?"

"It ain't loaded, stupid."

"How do you know?"

"Well just gather round, children. I'll show you."

I glanced in the direction of the driveway where I could see John Charles washing the car.

"See?" Louie explained as we huddled together under the old elm tree. "That's where the bullets go and there ain't any in there now, are they?" He pointed to the empty chambers. "Hey. Wanna play war?"

We played the game often near a shallow stream that ran through the pasture beyond the gate. Hedge apple trees and young willows grew on either side. Squirrels, cottontails, frogs, and snakes made it an ideal hunting ground but we played Yankees and Rebels. Ramsey and I were the Yankees. We'd make imaginary guns out of our thumbs and index fingers and yell "bang" every time we thought we saw the Rebels, Louie and Luke. They did the same.

Louie fondled the gun. "We can pretend even if we don't have any bullets."

"Yeah, but you're the only one with a gun," I reminded him.

"That's okay. We'll take turns, but I get to go first 'cause it's my pa's gun."

"I found it," Luke whined.

"Then you're next. Come on. You and me'll go across the creek."

We raced out the back gate and took up our positions in the field while the brothers crossed the creek on jutting rocks. Ramsey and I spread out. "You ready?" I yelled.

"Ready," Luke called back, and we all began quietly prowling the banks of the stream. From across the way, I heard Luke yell, "Pow. Pow."

Ramsey raised up, pointed his finger and pretended to shoot back. I saw a flash and I heard a bang. Ramsey fell to the ground.

"Quit your clowning," I told him. He didn't answer. "Are you all right? You'd better be fooling." Frightened, I raced over to him.

"Help me," he whimpered, his hand to his eye. That's when I saw the blood ooze through his fingers.

# CHAPTER NINE

## KANSAS CITY, MISSOURI
## 1928
### JOHN CHARLES

I'd almost done washing Doctor Adler's new Ford when I heard the pop of a gun down where the boys played. "Oh Lawd," I cried and took off toward the creek at a full gallop. I caught sight of Stern yelling at me to hurry. "It's Ramsey. He's been shot."

Louie just stood there, a gun hanging loosely from his fingers. As I drew near I heard him say, "It wasn't loaded. I checked it. You saw me do it."

Luke stood frozen, mouth agape. "Is he dead?"

"Stand back, all of you," I said as I knelt down by Ramsey. "Hold on, boy. You're gonna be just fine."

Louie threw the gun at Luke. "It's all your fault. If you hadn't found it, this wouldn't have happened. You killed him," he screamed.

"No, I didn't," Luke bawled, rubbing his arm where the gun had hit him. "You did."

"Hush up, both of you. Go on home. I gotta get this boy to the doctor." I scooped him up and took him back to the car, talking to him all the time, telling him he'd be all right. I laid him in the back, jumped into the driver's seat, and screeched out of the drive. I drove as fast as I dared, all the time hoping Doctor Adler might be able to do something. When we arrived at the hospital, I parked out in front and opened the back door. There, huddled on the floor next to him, sat Stern holding Ramsey's hand. I had been so rattled I hadn't paid him no never mind.

We must have made a strange-looking threesome, rushing into the hospital calling for someone to find Doctor Adler. They led us to a room with a white curtain around it, and I laid Ramsey down just as the doctor arrived. He shooed us out, ordering me to go get the child's mama, and then take Stern home. I got back to the hospital just in time to hear Doctor Kurt break the news to Bertha. She gasped as he said, "I couldn't save it. The bullet destroyed his eye, but with any luck, that's all he'll lose."

"My baby. My poor baby. I wants to be with him. Can I see him now? He needs his mama."

We got her settled with Ramsey, who lolled, still drowsy from the anesthetic, and I drove Doctor Kurt home. On the way, I told him as best I could what happened. Back at Oakbridge, we went together to look for Massah Stern. We found him in his room staring out the window at the old elm tree, its branches greening up with young leaves. He hadn't changed his clothes, and I could see the blood on his shirt where he had cradled his friend's head.

"I'm at fault, Papa," he said when he saw his father. His eyes clouded with tears. "I shouldn't have asked to see the gun. That's what started it all."

"What happened?" Doctor Kurt asked, and slowly the whole story spilled out the child's mouth punctuated by sorrowful sounds.

He'll be fine, won't he ,Papa?" Stern finally asked, worry lines creasing his young brow.

"If you call living with only one eye fine," Doctor Adler said.

Massah Stern stared at his fingers for the longest time before slowly raising his head to look at his father.'"You're mad at me, aren't you?"

"No, Stern. Just disappointed. You knew better than to play with guns."

"But it didn't have any bullets in it, Papa. We checked."

"You didn't do a very good job of that, did you?"

"I guess not." For a moment the boy stayed silent. Then he asked, "Can he still be a policeman or a fireman when he grows up?"

"Probably not," his father answered.

"Is that true, John Charles?" Stern asked.

I didn't want to come between father and son, but I had to answer truthfully. "Yessuh. It's true all right, but don't you fret none. He's alive, and lucky for him, the Lord done gave us two of most everything so's if we lose one, we still got us a spare. Ramsey's got a good spare eye so he won't be blind, and thank God for that. Ain't that right, doctor?"

"Ramsey will just have to rethink what he wants to be when he grows up, and you, my boy, should begin thinking about that, too." He stood staring at his own hands, flexing his fingers. "Perhaps it's just as well that this nonsense with the piano is over. Now you can start to concentrate on your books. You can be a doctor like me or a lawyer like your grandfather. You must study hard so you will be able to go to Harvard or Yale."

"Can I go see him?" Massah Stern said in a soft voice.

"Did you hear a word of what I said?" Doctor Kurt yelled.

I saw Miss Rebecca standing in the doorway. How long she had been standing there I didn't know.

"Perhaps John Charles will bring him out to play after he recovers," she said, and it pleased me to hear that, but Doctor Kurt shook his head. "In the meantime, we'll have to see about another piano teacher."

Doctor Kurt threw up his hands and walked out of the room. "We can talk about that later," Miss Rebecca called after him."

84

She turned back to Massah Stern. "Right now, young man, you could use a bath. John Charles, call Susie Mae. Dinner will be ready soon. Perhaps we should all wash up."

After she'd gone, Stern rubbed his eyes and looked at me. "I'm going to be Ramsey's friend forever. I promise."

"I know you will, Massah Stern," I answered. "I know you will."

From then on, the accident weighed heavy on my heart. Maybe it wouldn't have happened if only I'd kept a better eye on them boys. I swore to make it up to Ramsey. Lord knows I never meant to make matters worse for Doctor Kurt, but that's the way it turned out.

# CHAPTER TEN

## KANSAS CITY, MISSOURI
## 1928
### MAX ADLER

I saw him peeking around my door and lifted my hand to motion him in. Head held low and lips turned downward, Stern crept to my bedside and climbed up next to me, nestling his head against my chest. "Ramsey got shot," he told me.

"I heard all about it, child. Don't blame yourself."

"I'm so sad. He can't be a policeman now," he said. He pronounced policeman like Ramsey did: po-lees-man.

"I suppose that's so." We cuddled together. His warm little body pressed close to mine and I gently patted his back. For a time, neither of us spoke. Then Stern murmured, "Papa doesn't want me to play the piano anymore."

"Why is that?" I asked.

"So I'll be smart like the other boys and go to Harvard."

"You are smart already."

He looked up at me and shrugged. "Besides, Madame du Prée quit."

"Does that mean you can't play anymore?"

He lifted his head off my chest."No. I guess not."

"Then what does it mean?" I asked, teasing his brain into action.

His little face brightened. "I guess it means I can play anything I want."

I had to laugh. "Then what's the problem?"

"I still need a teacher, don't you think?"

I nodded. "Yes. I do."

He pursed his lips and wrinkled his brow.

"Would you practice every day?" I said.

"Could you help me?" he asked.

I gave that some thought. "I guess so, though I'm not much good on the piano. Let's see what we can do. I'll call my friend Nigel Biddle. He owns the piano store downtown. Maybe he knows someone who would like to have a smart, seven-year-old, redheaded boy for a student. What do you say to that?"

Stern answered by throwing his arms around my neck. "I love you, Grandpa. Now can we read some more of King Arthur?"

We had begun the story several weeks ago and managed to read a few pages every day. "Run get the book, Sir Stern of Oakbridge," I ordered in my commanding Knight of the Roundtable deep voice. "Let's see. Where were we?"

Later that day, I rang up Biddle's Music Company and spoke to the owner.

"He's quite young," I told Nigel, "but when he hears something once, he can play it again. Is there anyone you might recommend who could teach and not thwart him?"

"Let me think about it, Max. It would be a shame for Molly's beautiful Steinway to go unused."

"Yes. She would hate that. How she loved her piano, but you know, I never heard her pick out songs like that boy does. You can name just about anything, and if the boy's heard it once, he can play it. Molly needed the sheet music to do that. Are you still there, Nigel?"

He paused so long I thought perhaps he had hung up. These newfangled dial telephones still mystified me. Then I heard him back on the line.

"Yes I'm here. Just thinking. I may know someone, but I'd like to talk to the man first. Let him know what he would be getting himself into," he said, but I could hear him chuckle.

"Certainly. I understand." I found myself getting excited. "So. I'll wait to hear from you." I hung up feeling more alive than I had felt in days.

A week went by before Nigel Biddle called back. "I think my man will do it, but he wants to meet the child before he says a definite yes. Jonas Parker is his name. Would Monday at four be a good time?"

My hopes soared. "I'll arrange it," I answered, hardly able to contain myself. "Thanks, old friend."

"Don't thank me yet, Max. Let's see if it works out first." I could hear him chuckle as he leaned back in his squeaking chair and hung up.

The following Monday, Stern and I sat in the parlor waiting. As the clock struck four, the bell rang, and John Charles went to answer it. We heard the door open, and then a loud hoot and a holler.

"Whatcha doin' here, boy?" an unfamiliar voice shouted.

"Lawd a Mercy. I works here. We is surely off the beaten path for the likes of you, ain't we?" A long silence followed as I imagined the two of them staring at each other. Then John Charles cried out, "Oh, no. It can't be. You ain't de new piano teacher we been expectin', is you?" When John Charles got excited, he reverted to his old way of speaking.

Stern couldn't stand it. He ran to the door. "Who is it?" I heard him ask.

"This here brother plays the meanest piano and blows the loudest horn of anybody in these parts, Massah Stern," I heard John Charles tell him.

"That's right. I do. And maybe I'se gonna be your teacher. Is your grandpappy about?"

"Yes, sir. He's waiting to meet you in the parlor."

He filled the room with his voice and his body, the biggest man I'd ever seen – not fat you understand, but large. He had big arms, big legs. Everything about him was oversized, even his eyes that seemed to dance, and his lips that covered most of the bottom half of his face when he smiled. And heart. We discovered his heart carried so much love it's a wonder it didn't burst.

"This is Jonas Parker, Mr. Adler," John Charles said, "but folks here about call him Whale."

That needed no explaining.

The man reached out a ham-like hand. "It's an honor, suh," he said.

I hid my curiosity by pointing to the piano. "Can you play that thing?" I asked.

"Whooie," he hooted. "Ain't that a beaut. How's it sound, I wonder?"

"Well, why don't you try it out and see?" I said.

Jonas ran his fingers in chords up and down the keyboard. He pulled up Molly's old bench and sat, his body spilling over the sides. He patted the Steinway with a reverent gesture, caressing the shining keys.

As Stern hovered nearby, Whale's big fingers rested momentarily on the keyboard. Then music filled the parlor. I'd never heard anything like it. Stern danced around the room, caught up in the joyous rhythms and tunes. John Charles stood by the piano swaying back and forth, and I drummed my fingers on my legs, just as I'd done when Molly played.

Abruptly, Stern stopped dancing and ran to the piano. "I can do that," he cried.

"Sho you can. You jest situate yoself next to me, and we'll do it together."

Whale began to sing, booming out the words in a deep, rich voice, while the boy picked up the jazzy melody and banged happily on the treble keys. Time flew by as we all lost ourselves in the toetapping music.

But then a voice rose above us all. Kurt stood in the doorway, an astonished-looking Rebecca behind him. "Father," he yelled. "What the hell is going on here?"

The music stopped. A deafening silence followed. Stern reacted first. He jumped down off the bench and ran to his father. "Papa. Isn't he wonderful?"

But Kurt pushed the boy away. He pointed his finger at me. "You did this, didn't you? Is this your idea of a joke?"

I resented his disrespectful manner but tried to remain calm. "No, no joke. Jonas Parker, meet my son, Doctor Kurt Adler, and Mrs. Adler. Mr. Parker has agreed to teach Stern to play the piano."

"What?" Kurt stared at me with anger-filled eyes. "Now look here. We've been all through this. My wife told me Madame du Prée said the child was hopeless and that's the end of it. He's seven years old, for God's sake, the age when boys need fresh air and sunshine. Why," he directed his fury at his son, "aren't you outside playing? Have you no friends?"

"You mean any that don't carry guns?" Rebecca said, her voice icy.

*Uh oh*, I thought.

But Jonas came to the rescue. With a relaxed air he pushed his titanic body off the piano bench and walked toward the feuding adults.

"Pleased to meetcha," he said, directing his comments to Kurt. "The strangest thing, suh. Me and John Charles been friends all our lives, and I never knew where he worked. Now I puts it altogether 'cause it's thanks to you he's still with us, ain't it? Lucky man to be workin' for you and your missus. You and Mistah Max here been our heroes forever down in nigger town."

Kurt changed his tone. "Now, look here, Parker. I really do think this whole thing has been blown out of proportion. I can't for the life of me imagine why you would want to waste your time with a child, and I certainly don't envision my son spending hours practicing scales. Fact of the matter is, I don't care if he can play a note. I'd rather see him concentrate on something more productive, like his reading, for instance."

"Well, suh," Jonas grinned, his two front gold teeth gleaming, "Lemme put it this away. Your boy and I jest hit it off real good. I certainly do agree that every young chile needs his schooling, but I thinks he'll have plenty of time for that. I figures a few hours on the eighty-eights couldn't do no harm. Might keep him and his grandpa happy."

Kurt pursed his lips and glared.

"What could it possibly hurt?" Becka said. "Why don't you go have a drink? I'll take care of this."

I glanced at Rebecca, then back at my glowering son. "If you really think so little of your time," he said to Whale, "I guess I won't stop you, but just so you know. I think it's a monumental waste of money. He'll get bored just like he did with Madame du Preé, and you'll end up with no job and nothing to show for it."

He glanced at me and headed for the library. "More piano lessons, for God's sake," I heard him mumble as he closed the door behind him.

John Charles breathed an audible sigh of relief. Rebecca smiled, a graceful, manicured finger to her mouth. Then, she looked at the colored man and said, "You do know, Mr. Parker . . .."

"Whale," he corrected her

". . .that Madame du Prée quit."

"Yessum. I heard. Don't know the lady, but she probably had her reasons."

Rebecca nodded and wiped the corner of her mouth daintily with her lace handkerchief.

"I ain't never taught no one before," Whale told her, "but like I said, me and the little fellah seems to get along, and I'm willin' to give it a try." He smiled, a grin that went from one ear to the other.

Now that the air had cleared, I proceeded with the business at hand. I motioned for John Charles to lean down so I could whisper, "What do you know about this man? Is he honest?"

"Yes, suh," he whispered back. "He's as honest as he is big."

He stood up and addressed us all. "Jonas' mama used to take him to choir practice and make him sit there and listen, like it or not. That's where he learned to play. Taught himself, and before long, he played the organ at all the services. In fact I remember him picking out tunes just like Massah Stern does. The boy will sure enough be safe with Whale."

"Picking out tunes seems to be one of the problems," I reminded everyone in the room. "Can you teach him to play real music? Chopin and Mozart?"

Jonas just smiled. "Why, he's already playin' real music, suh. I can teach him to read notes if that's what you mean."

Rebecca nodded with satisfaction. "Good. Now if you'll excuse me, I have an important engagement. Mr. Adler will take care of the financial arrangements, won't you Father? I really must rush along."

"That'll be fine, ma'am. Just fine," Jonas Parker said.

And so Stern had a new teacher. Later that week Rebecca reported a conversation she had had with her friend Albert Rapinsky.

"When I told him I'd hired Jonas Parker, he clapped his hands with surprise and said, 'Not Whale Parker, per chance?' I told him the same, and he said he knew him well. They had played together only the previous evening.

"Apparently this Whale person plays regularly at the Moonlight Club," she told me. "Once when Kurt was working, I went there with Sybil and Herb, but he must not have been there or I'd surely remember. Albert says he is truly a genius, and he can't imagine how I convinced him to come and teach Stern."

That she took the credit for finding Whale Parker got my dander up, but I had neither the strength or the desire to argue about it. Another matter troubled me more – the anger and the disappointment I had seen on Kurt's face. I meant to talk to him about it. Did this have something to do with Frankie?

Even though they physically resembled one another, Kurt's son had a very different nature than his brother. I saw Stern as sensitive, imaginative, and quite possibly gifted; not at all like the raucous little boy his uncle had been. In that instant, I saw troubled waters ahead.

# CHAPTER ELEVEN

## KANSAS CITY, MISSOURI
## 1928
### REBECCA

My heart bled for Stern the day that little colored boy got shot. On my way to my boudoir, I passed his room. I saw him sitting pensively on the window seat, his arms around his drawn up legs. He looked tired and sad. An odd feeling of *déjà vu* came over me. I had seen that same look before. Something in the eyes or the downward turn of the mouth. Albert.

At times I regretted not spending more time with Stern, but as the wife of a socially prominent physician, my obligations and community work kept me busy. Still,I trusted Susie Mae to watch over him. Now it seemed I needed to have words with her, to demand she be more vigilant.

I often found myself staring at Stern, watching the way he walked, listening to his voice. The more I studied him the more sure I became. I could find nothing of Kurt in him. My son had indeed inherited my deep blue eyes. His, too, turned violet with emotion. True, he had red hair but that proved nothing. So did Albert.

One day, sunk deep in my perfumed bath, my hair piled high on my head, I reviewed the ramifications of my suspicions. I knew I held a bomb in my hand, but for what good? If I told Kurt, what would he do? Throw me out? Maybe. In some ways I wouldn't have minded that. I wrinkled my nose at the thought of how his touch and wet kisses disgusted me. Yet I loved the social position his name and wealth brought.

My father's own success and wealth didn't hold a candle to the Adler family. Besides, he and Erika had a life of their own. She came from the old school, one not to my liking, and even though I took Stern to see them once in awhile, they became less and less a part of my life. After Neosha passed away, I quit going all together.

Was there a way, I wondered, that I could tell for sure? I thought about it as I washed my arms, absently scooping up a handful of bubbles and floating them into the air. I stepped from my bath and wrapped a warm pink towel around my body. Dressing leisurely, I wandered downstairs to the library.

The dark room seemed cold and foreboding in the morning light. I drew aside the heavy maroon velvet drapes and threw open the floor to ceiling windows so that garden air and sunlight streamed in. The stale odors dissipated, and in their place a freshness filled the room.

I rang the bell cord for John Charles and ordered coffee and sweets. When he returned with the tray I told him to take Susie Mae and Stern to River Park for a picnic.

"Yessum," he said, with a trifle of hesitancy.

"Don't worry about Mr. Max. Hilda and I will see to his needs while you're away."

After they'd gone, I wandered around the room. I picked up a book, laid it down, ran my fingers over the mantel testing for dust. Absently, I seated myself behind the desk. Kurt's leather chair swallowed me.

I pulled open the top drawer. My husband's ledgers took up the major portion of the interior, all neatly arranged along with an address book, pencils, and pens. I withdrew a financial record book and thumbed through it, noting with resentment my meager weekly allowance. But then I came upon something of great interest, pages of securities listed in Kurt's scrawling handwriting: my dowry.

I spent most of the morning studying that book, making notes to myself in case I needed them for future reference. Finally I replaced the ledger.

From another drawer I retrieved an address book. A photograph fell out, a picture of a small boy seated on a chair, one leg drawn up under him. The photographer had touched up the child's picture with pastels, red-gold hair, and pink cheeks. He wore a pale blue sailor suit with white stripes and white high-top shoes. He looked like Max: a broad forehead, wide eyes, full mouth. He had his mother's doe-like brown eyes and sweet smile.

In my mind I pictured my own son's small, straight nose, thin face, high cheekbones, blue eyes, and mouth shaped exactly like Albert's. I turned the photo over. Someone had written in flowing German script, Frank Koenig Adler, age six.

Stern's red hair had deluded Kurt and Max into thinking Stern looked like Frankie. In truth, the two boys looked nothing alike. I felt emancipated, no longer indebted to a husband years older and his musty, oppressive family house. I had a weapon.

I chose to defy Kurt the day Jonas Parker entered our lives. By now I knew Stern's talent came from Albert. That they already liked each other thrilled me no end. Kurt's refusal to acknowledge Stern's ability angered me. Still, I truly wondered why Whale Parker would choose to teach so young a boy.

His answer stunned me. " 'Pears he's got quite a talent, ma'am, " he said.

"Really?" I responded. "Whatever do you mean?"

"Why, he can play a tune even if he hears it only once."

Just like his father, I thought, secretly delighted. If I had not been convinced before, I now knew for sure. My child most definitely carried Albert's genes, not Kurt's.

"Now looky here," Whale said. Playing with only his index finger, Jonas Parker drummed out *Yankee Doodle* on the piano. When he'd finished, he nudged my son and grinned.

"Your turn," he said, and Stern played exactly the same notes.

Max clapped his hands. "Never seen anything like it," he explained. "Why even your Grandma, bless her heart, couldn't play that."

Stern giggled. "It's easy, Grandpa. Just listen to this," and he proceeded to play the song again, but this time added some harmony with his left hand.

That day, I vowed to do what I could to help him use the gift bestowed on him by his real father. I trembled at the thought of Kurt ever finding out what I now knew to be true.

Yet somehow, my discovery made my life easier. I had become the custodian of a powerful secret. I no longer had to carry on a romantic pretense with my husband. With my social position secure, my private life became my own.

The next morning, I arranged for Susie Mae and John Charles to move my things into the southern suite, three lovely rooms with a dressing room and bath of its own.

"I won't allow it," Kurt roared, when he found he out what I had done. Just as I'd anticipated, a terrible argument ensued, but even though his fierce temper scared me, I stood firm.

"There, there," I soothed him, slipping out of my little girl mode and assuming the more mature role I'd never been able to muster.

"However am I to maintain my looks if I can't get my beauty sleep, what with your snoring loud enough to wake the dead?" I patted the age spots on his hand and kissed his receding hairline. "Never fear, my darling. Nothing has changed. You can visit whenever you like."

That night, long after the rest of the household had retired, he came to me, knocking discreetly and entering with a hangdog expression, the smell of desire emanating from every pore in his body.

Keeping in mind the matter of my estate, I had prepared for the occasion placing fresh, ivory colored satin sheets on the bed and wore my most seductive nighttime attire. In the glow of flickering candles, I beckoned him to join me and handed him a flute of his favorite champagne.

As we sipped the wine, his eyes caressed my body. "Perhaps," he said, appreciating the seductive atmosphere I'd created, "having separate bedrooms is not such a bad idea after all."

He spoke loving words and I let him make love to me but not before I teased him with my mouth to the crest of desire. Finally I allowed him to gratify himself, after which he fell back sated and content.

I didn't want him to fall asleep in my bed before I accomplished what I'd set out to do. Waiting only for a few minutes to pass, I snuggled my naked body next to his and whispered softly, " I think, darling, it is time I had my own money."

"Hum?" he sighed. "But you know nothing of such things." He waved his fingers in the air.

"You could teach me," I said, kissing him lightly on the cheek.

He yawned. "We'll discuss it tomorrow."

"No. Tonight."

I think my tone surprised him. The mood broken, he sat up and turned on the bedside light. "All right. What is it you want?"

"I want a checking account and a bigger monthly income. . . "

"You'll spend it all in a day." A smirk distorted his mouth.

". . . and the dowry money my father gave you."

His eyes narrowed. "Why would you want that? Are you thinking of leaving me?"

I patted his arm and put on my most charming smile. "Of course not, but I am a modern woman, old enough to handle my own estate. You know, of course, that my father plans on taking Erika back to Germany to live," I said, but thinking to myself, *so I won't be able to tap him any more for a little extra cash.*

"It is not a good time, my dear. The country is on the brink of depression. Even here at Oakbridge, my father has begun to sell off much of the land and livestock. Have you not noticed?"

"Why would I? I don't pay attention to his animals and he doesn't take me into his confidence."

"I understand but I wish you would follow my advice and leave things be. You know nothing of stocks and bonds."

I ducked my head with a coy smile. "Your friend Ben Rosen, who owns First National, has offered to help me."

"You've spoken to him already?"

"Yes."

"And he thinks this is a good idea?" Kurt appeared incredulous.

I flounced out of bed, threw on my robe, and grabbed my hairbrush. I began furiously running it through my hair.

"Why would you ask such a question? Do you think I'm too stupid to manage my own affairs? Pay the bills?"

"No. Of course not. It's just that you have no experience."

"How could I when you do it all and give me only a pittance now and then."

Kurt sighed. "I'll speak to him in the morning, if that's what you want."

I turned to face him, my hands on my hips. "I think you don't understand. I want what is rightfully mine, the dowry my father paid you. I believe I've paid you a thousand times over for my father's stupidity."

He sat on the edge of the bed, hair rumpled, and stared at me with tired eyes. "Have I treated you badly?" he asked.

"No. Of course not."

"Then what . . .?" He didn't finish. "I guess I'll never understand you, but I love you."

He pushed himself to standing. "I've got an early morning surgery," he said, "after which I'll call Ben." Huffing, he yanked his robe around himself, gathered up his pajamas, and retreated to his own suite.

Life continued much as before with a few notable exceptions. I got my dowry. I called Gertrude Rosen and invited her to lunch. We sat over wine and chicken salads at the Trianon Room of the Muehlebach Hotel while she gave me a quick lesson in the stock market: what stocks paid the most dividends, what seemed to do well.

She gave me the name of her stock broker, and when I called him, he surprised me by offering to double and triple my investments by loaning me more. That made me very suspicious. With so much to learn I decided to wait until I felt more confident in my own abilities. I turned my dowry into cash, secretly had a wall safe installed in my bedroom, bought a Matisse to hang over it, and locked my money safely away.

As I settled into the role of the matriarch of Oakbridge, I began the makeover of the house. June brought good weather and seemed the perfect month to start. I spent vast amounts of Adler money redecorating and remodeling, transforming that stuffy estate into the jewel of Kansas City.

And finally Albert returned from Europe.

# CHAPTER TWELVE

## KANSAS CITY, MISSOURI
## 1929
### ALBERT

I had no friends until Becka. Painfully shy, tall and lanky, I spent most of my time in one of the school studios that contained a Steinway piano. Miraculously, someone kept it properly tuned, good for my sensitive ears.

We had a piano at home, of course, an upright my father bought. He died a week before my fifth birthday, and my mother taught piano to numerous Jewish children for a paltry sum. Yet somehow she managed to keep a roof over our heads and food on the table.

Often, she sat me on her lap and placed my fingers on the keyboard. She laughed when I banged, and began to teach me to play. One day I picked out a familiar tune, and from that moment on I became her life and her obsession.

Though she didn't hear music the way I did and could never afford to upgrade the instrument, she taught me technique, thirds and fourths and fifths, arpeggios, cadence, and chromatics. Were it not for her, I would never have become a concert pianist – her and Becka.

She was the prettiest girl in our class. She made me, a homely kid with my kinky red hair and freckles, feel special. Some people called her stuck up. Her spoiled manner and arrogant ways bothered me not at all. She seemed to enjoy hearing me play and encouraged me to work hard. As my best friend, she defended me against brutes like Jimmy Galeno, and I loved her almost as much as I loved my music.

Our assignation, however, the week before her marriage, bound us in ways I could never foresee. That event, though not of my choosing, cemented my affections for her, even if in a special kind of way.

An amazing woman, Becka assumed the role of civic leader quite well. She served as an asset to her husband, hosting dinner parties and representing the respected Adler name. She saw to it that I spent time with Stern, and he became an integral part of my life.

Perhaps she could have brushed up on her parenting skills, but one can't be all things to all people. His amazing musical talent, inherited no doubt from his paternal grandmother, delighted me, the common interest bringing us even closer.

When I returned from Paris, I had wonderful news to tell Becka. As it turned out, my report would have to wait. She invited me for tea, and of course I asked, "How are the music lessons coming? Has he done well under the tutelage of Madame du Preé?"

"That didn't work out too well," Becka said. "Actually, she and Stern didn't get along. We found a new teacher, someone you've probably never heard of."

"Oh? Who?"

"Parker is his name. Jonas Parker."

I could hardly believe my ears."Not Whale Parker by any chance?" I exclaimed.

"Do you know him?"

"I do. I saw him only last night. He plays at The Moonlight Club. A genius. A true genius. I can't imagine how you lured him to Oakbridge."

"Father Max did," she said. "To tell the truth, Albert, I've been dreading this moment. I can hardly wait for you to see Stern, but I'm not at all sure I want you to hear him play."

"Why is that?"

"Jonas has made certain he plays classical music, but he only does it to please his grandfather and me, and he certainly doesn't play like you did as a child. In fact I have begun to doubt I did a good thing, hiring Jonas Parker. Stern and Ramsey spend hours together. Jonas gave Ramsey an old trumpet and is teaching him to play too. You should hear the noise."

I had to laugh. "That's what boys do," I said.

"I wish Stern would spend more time practicing the classics, but what can I do?"

"Where is the little scamp?" I asked. "You can't deny me the pleasure of seeing him any longer."

John Charles entered, carrying a tray of hors d'oeuvres. "Just put them here and see if you can find the boys," she told him.

Soon after, the clatter of little feet announced the boys running into the parlor. Ramsey bowed, worn trumpet clutched to his chest, and Stern pumped my hand.

"You have eyes just like your mother," I said.

"And hair the color of his father," Becka added.

She misspoke, I thought. She meant Grandfather.

Stern ignored us both. "Would you like to hear our new act?" he asked.

Becka looked toward the ceiling.

"Of course," I said, unable to keep from staring at Ramsey's black patch.

The child touched his face. "Got shot with a gun," he explained. "Blowed out my eye."

"Oh, my goodness. How awful. Does it bother you?"

"Sometimes. Makes me look kind of funny."

I patted Ramsey's cheek. "Distinguished, I'd say. Can you play that thing?" I pointed to his horn.

"Sho I can."

I sat down in the wingback chair and crossed my legs. "All right then. I'm ready. Let the concert begin."

Becka groaned.

Stern leaned against the edge of the bench so his feet could reach the pedals.

Ramsey stood next to him, horn at the ready. He moistened his lips with his tongue and gave a nod. "One, a two, a one, two, three."

They began to play *Old Folks at Home*. It had a quick, even rhythm, eight to the bar, just the way I'd expect Whale Parker to interpret it. Though the boys started off playing the same tune, as they got into it, Stern bounced around, sometimes standing, sometimes pressing a pedal, and Ramsey, cheeks filled like two helium balloons, depressed the valves and blew away. He didn't always hit the right note, and neither did Stern, but it didn't matter. Stephen Foster might not agree, but I thought they thumped out a lovely, harmonious tune.

Becka watched for my reaction and looked faint when I smiled with approval. The boys ended with a loud finale. I clapped and went to the piano. "Wonderful, boys. Wonderful. Did Whale teach you that?"

"Most of it, suh," Ramsey said.

"But we added our own bit," Stern added.

I sat on the bench next to Stern and pulled Ramsey to my lap. "Gentlemen," I said, being very serious. "Always play like you did today, what you feel in your hearts. Next time you see Whale Parker you tell him I said he's got himself two peas in a pod."

Stern threw his arms around me. I hugged him back, and I have no words to express how good that felt.

Rebecca stood beside me. She bent down smiling, and whispered in my ear, "He is so like you."

I laughed. "Even better. I never played like that. You owe Jonas Parker a debt of gratitude. He is bringing out the best in the boys."

A thought suddenly occurred to me. "Would you like to hear him?" I asked her. "There's a new, young musician in town by the name of Benny Moten, a pianist like Whale. They will be performing the whole week at Club Reno. I'd be honored to take you and Kurt."

I admit I loved the nightlife in Kansas City: great music, sometimes great ragtime, and great jazz musicians, better even than Paris.

She clapped her hands. "I'd love it. Tonight?"

"What about tonight?" Kurt Adler roared from the doorway.

"We've just been invited to go clubbing," Rebecca said. "Sounds like fun."

"Sorry you missed it, my friend. The boys have just given us a great show."

"I heard it clear down to the bridge." His angry tone of voice surprised me.

"Too busy to say hello?" he said to Stern.

The boy ran to his father, but Kurt pushed him away. "You missed your chance," he said.

Tears sprang to the child's eyes but Kurt turned his attention to his wife."What were you two saying about tonight?" he asked.

"Albert has offered to take us to Club Reno. I'd love to go," Rebecca said.

"Yes. Do come," I chimed in. "Meet me at the Savoy. We'll dine together and then go listen to Jonas Parker."

Kurt stared at me, amazed. "I hear that mad man play every time my son touches the piano."

I laughed, but Kurt cut me off. "You go. Have fun. I have important work to do." He stormed into the library and slammed the door.

Becka glared after him as the little boys crept from the room. "Crabby old man. He doesn't understand," she raged, but then she sighed. "Don't mind him. He's just tired."

Secretly, I was glad we could dine alone. I hadn't yet gotten to tell her my news.

The booth I chose afforded me a clear view of the door. I watched for her, admiring the clean, white table linen, shining flatware, and twinkling crystal. Now and then a stranger would pass and nod or smile at me with recognition.

I rose when I saw Becka enter and took her hand. She wore a soft blue dress trimmed in mink, her dark hair mostly contained in a bejeweled cloche. Her cheeks glowed with excitement, and her violet eyes sparkled.

We chatted over wine, and as our pre-ordered dinner arrived, I told her of my most recent success in Paris, a Rachmaninoff concert I was asked to perform at St. Ephrem, a lovely church in the heart of the city.

"I'm so proud of you, my dear," she said, reaching for my hands. She held them in hers and kissed my fingers. "His are so like yours," she murmured, looking up into my eyes.

"What?" I asked, confused. "Who?"

"Stern. He has hands just like yours."

"He's a fine lad. Reminds me of myself as a boy," I said.

"He should," she said. "He's yours, you know."

Her words stunned me. "How can that be?" My mind whirred. "You don't think . . .?"

"Yes, I do."

"But we didn't . . . "

"Of course we did. Don't you remember?"

I nodded. A long silence followed. "Does anyone else know?"

She shook her head. "Nor will they unless it proves to our advantage."

"No. No." I tried to keep my voice down. "You must never tell. That would prove disastrous for us all."

She frowned, her dark eyebrows knitting together. "Why is that?"

"Because, my dear Becka," I searched for the right words, "the boy has a father."

"Not really. Kurt hates him."

'No father hates his own child," I said, my tone low and harsh.

"And therein lies the tale," she answered.

"But he will provide him with everything he could possibly need. Besides, how could we ever explain what we did? A childish escapade?"

She half closed her eyes and took a slow sip of her wine. "It was sweet, pure love, my dear."

"No," I protested. "I mean love in a friendship sort of way." I picked up my fork and teased my salad. "Surely you must know that what we did was a charade."

She looked stunned. "A charade? Is that what you think?"

"No. Of course not. A poor choice of words, but you must try to understand." I lowered my voice. "I've met someone in Paris."

She said not a word, but the tears began to flow. She reached into her beaded purse and pulled out a perfumed handkerchief. She dabbed at her eyes.

"All this time I thought you loved me."

"I do," I said, exasperated and full of angst. "Please don't make me explain. We will always be best friends, but this other person. He is the one with whom I want to share the rest of my life."

"He?" she whispered, a questioning look in her eyes.

I nodded with a smile meant to reassure her. Instead, her eyes went wide, and she covered her mouth with her hand. She stood and motioned to the maître d'.

"Call me a cab," she said, her cheeks flushed and glistening.

"Please," I begged, "don't go."

But Benny Moten and Whale Parker would have to wait. Rebecca left me there, and it would be some time before we would see each other again.

# CHAPTER THIRTEEN

## KANSAS CITY, MISSOURI
## 1929
## STERN

I loved Whale from the start. I even practiced hard between lessons. Everyone liked my music except my father, so I never went near the piano before he left in the morning or after he came home at night.

Sometimes Hilda pretended the noise bothered her but then I'd catch her out of the corner of my eye, swaying along as she went about her daily chore. Susie Mae, who hovered over me, found more than enough excuses to come listen.

And then there was Grandpa. Even though we could see him growing more frail with each passing day, John Charles carried him to the parlor, placed him in a chair close to me, and tucked a blanket around his legs.

He relished the classical pieces. I liked to play Mozart because he began composing as a child, just like me, light and lyrical to my ear. Grandpa would lean his head back against the chair and close his eyes.

If I hit what he thought might be a wrong note, his eyes would pop open and he'd look at me with a hint of question. Then I'd replay the part, and he'd smile, praise me, and tell me how much I reminded him of my grandmother.

I dedicated the first piece I composed to Grandpa. A ragtime fugue, it tripped along over three and one half sheets. I called it *The King Max Court.* He loved it.

As soon as Papa left for the hospital each morning, I ran to the parlor and began fiddling with the piano, not because I had to, but because I wanted to, couldn't stop myself, couldn't resist.

Sometimes I'd begin playing and wouldn't stop until hunger drove me to the kitchen. Always attentive to my needs, Susie Mae brought me milk and cookies, but Mama found out and said crumbs would attract ants.

Over time, I learned to read music with all its nuances and signs. One day, Whale brought a shiny gold horn, and at the end of the lesson, played it for me. I sang and laughed so joyously that even my grandpa joined in. I knew our music made him feel good. But I missed Ramsey.

"When will he be well enough to come back?" I asked John Charles as he went about his cleaning.

"Don't rightly know," he said. "Your papa told us maybe someday he'd get the boy a glass eye and put it right in where the old one used to be."

"You know what, John Charles? If Ramsey had a horn like Whale's we could play together."

John Charles looked up from his dusting, an eyebrow raised.

"Now ain't that an idea," he said. "Just you let me think on it, Massah Stern."

"Why do you call me Massah, John Charles? I'm not your master."

"Cause your papa told me to," he answered.

"Well, I don't like it. I want you to call me by my name like you do Ramsey. Will you?"

"I don't know, Massah Stern. I wouldn't want to disrespect your papa."

"How about when no grownups are around? How about just then?" I asked.

John Charles smiled his lopsided grin and nodded. "All right . . . Stern." He rolled my name off his tongue, and it didn't sound right. "But its gotta be a secret."

I nodded. "Now, about a horn for Ramsey . . ." I prodded.

"I'll talk to Whale," he said. "See if'n he can help."

Every day I asked John Charles about Ramsey until he finally told me to quit pestering him. Then, seven days later, while I sat at the piano figuring out a new tune, I heard squawks and screeches coming from the kitchen. The racket got closer and closer, until there in the archway stood Ramsey, a black patch covering his missing eye, his lips glued to the mouthpiece of a silver horn.

"Wow," I cried. "Where'd you get that?"

Rolling his good eye and grinning so big his brand new permanent front teeth seemed way too big, he handed the horn to me.

"Whale give it to me. He told me he used to play it, but now that he had a new one, he didn't need this no more  He told me it's a cornet but most people call it a trumpet. Then he said he'd teach me how to play it if I wanted."

We walked to the piano and sat down next to each other, our eyes never leaving the horn. "What'd you tell him?" I asked, holding my breath.

He just stared at me, straight faced and serious.

"Well?"

He looked down at the horn, then back at me.

"I told him yes, fool." He burst out laughing. "You want to try it?"

Relieved and slightly miffed, I took the trumpet and put it to my lips. I blew, but nothing much came out. "Wonder how it works?" I muttered.

"Whale says you push those little buttons and blow a certain way to make different sounds. He says if we both learn to play the same pieces, you on the piano and me on the horn, we could play together. Sound like fun?"

I stared at him and nodded. "Does it hurt? Your eye I mean?"

"Where it used to be? Naw."

"Not at all?"

"Naw. Sometimes it itches, but it don't hurt."

"Even when you poke at it?"

"Especially when I poke at it. Why? You planning on poking me?"

"Aw, gee. No."

He laughed, but I still felt like him losing his eye was my fault. I tried not to think about the empty place under the round back patch. "Guess you know you'll always be my best friend."

Ramsey grinned, his teeth gleaming. "It's okay. I don't want to be a policeman no more. My mama says she's glad of that."

"My grandpa says there are plenty of other things you can be."

"Yeah. Mama, too."

I perked up. "Maybe we can start a band. Want to hear what I can play?"

"Sure."

"Whale brought me a book full of pieces his old piano teacher wrote. I'll show you." I hopped off the bench and raised the lid to get the music.

*"School of Ragtime, An Instruction Book by Scott Joplin,"* Ramsey read. "It looks pretty hard."

I shook my head. "Whale says his teacher made it easy for beginners like me. Listen."

Ramsey stuck his horn under his arm and began marching around the room. Then he lifted the trumpet to his lips and blew. Susie Mae came rushing into the parlor. "Lord a mercy," she cried. "Y'all gonna wake Mistah Max."

Month after month Ramsey practiced, all the time getting better and better until one day sweet, clear notes emerged from that old, beat-up trumpet. "I'll be jiggered," I heard John Charles say, a smile bright on his face.

In no time at all Ramsey and I got the hang of playing together. Sometimes I'd start a song he hadn't heard, and then I would bet him he couldn't learn it. Of course he always did.

Occasionally, he'd play one I didn't know, minstrel type songs sung at his church like *Camp Town Races*. We'd play it and John Charles would sing, *Gwine to run all night!, Gwine' to run all day! I bet my money on de bob-tailed nag, Somebody bet on de bay*, and sometimes Grandpa and Susie Mae would join in. Hours would drift by as we practiced, giggled, made mistakes.

That's when I first started arranging. I would change keys just for the fun of it, and Ramsey would look at me strangely and change keys too. Sometimes I'd move the bridge around, though I'm not sure I knew what a bridge was, and Ramsey would follow along.

If I liked the sounds, I'd write them down so we could play them for Whale later. He laughed and said that was the difference between arranging and improvising.

I remember one particular day. My mother came home looking tired and out of sorts. Late afternoon shadows had crept across the parlor floor. John Charles turned on a light next to my grandfather's chair.

Ramsey and I had just figured out how to play a few bars of *Maple Leaf Rag*, an upbeat Scott Joplin piece in my book. Mother stood in the doorway listening, and I saw the weariness seem to seep out of her body. Suddenly she began to dance. We finished as much as we knew and then clapped.She flushed and ran from the room.

As time went by, Ramsey and I learned the terms for the world of music we explored. What real musicians called improvisation we called fooling around. Without realizing it, we had begun to jam.

We attended different schools, I to John Keats, an all white elementary school south of town, and he to Abraham Lincoln, where the colored children went.

After Ramsey got shot, Luke and I became arch enemies. As soon as school started in the fall, Luke rushed to tell everyone that I'd been the one to shoot Ramsey. Some of the kids didn't believe him, but Luke, a year older and much bigger than I, threatened anyone who stuck up for me with extinction. The first day back at school, he picked a fight with me on the playground, and though I did the best I could, he ground me into the dirt.

"That's for the lickin' my father give me after your old man tattled. You breathe a word of this, and next time, I'll kill you."

Then he started calling me names, and soon I became Stern the Fern to everyone in my class.

Once in awhile Ann Oppenheimer, a squarish block of a girl with amber eyes and a chipped front tooth, would ask me to play for her, but the only piano, an old upright in the kindergarten room, sounded tinny and out of tune. Sometimes she dragged me in there, but before long the kids started calling us sweeties, so I stopped.

I must have been an odd looking duck, with curly red hair, shoulders slumped, shuffling from one place to another. If I got A's they dubbed me smarty pants. Anything less disappointed my father. I hated school.

The best part of the day for me began when John Charles came to get me and we went and picked up Ramsey in darky town. Back at Oakbridge we could play our instruments until time for Father to arrive home.

On the days when Mother entertained her lady friends or Grandpa had visitors, Ramsey wasn't allowed to come and I had to study in my room.

Sometimes Grandpa let me join him and his friends in the library where conversation grew lively, and blue cigar smoke permeated the air. Old, portly Mr. Van Horn, white beard trimmed to a perfect point, often joked about the deal my grandfather and he had pulled off getting the Hannibal bridge for Kansas City.

Though everyone had heard the story a hundred times, they told it over and over, slapping their knees and laughing out loud.

Mr. Volker, never one to talk much, smiled quietly and tugged at his own neatly trimmed mustache. I once overheard him talking to Grandpa about ways to give away some of his money. I thought that rather odd, but Grandpa told me Mr. Volker was a shrewd businessman who had made a fortune. Now, with Grandpa's legal help, he wished to do more. "Could he give some to me?" I asked. Grandpa smiled and said no, I didn't need any of Mr. Volker's money.

Both Mr. Van Horn and Mr. Volker were Germans like my grandfather, but not Jewish, which didn't seem to matter since they had been good friends for many years. When they and other men came to visit, they spoke of old times and about their plans for the city or their businesses, and to seek my grandfather's advice.

At the beginning of the summer, my mother's friend Albert Rapinsky came to call. I remember that day because when my father came home, I didn't jump up to greet him. After that, my father refused to speak to me for days. I hated that punishment worst of all.

And then, my grandfather took ill. Although in my memory he had always been frail, this sickness seemed different. He came less often to the parlor, and John Charles made many more trips up and down the stairs carrying juice and tea and Hilda's marrowbone soup. Thus began my grandfather's final illness.

"Pneumonia," my father declared. "Contagious as hell, so stay out of his room. And keep away from that damn piano. He needs peace and quiet."

During the following days, the house took on an unusual somberness. Ramsey came once but Hilda shooed him away. Susie Mae opened the door to Grandpa's friends who went silently to his room and then stole solemnly away.

Toward the end, my father kept a vigil, ministering to my grandfather or pacing the hall outside his room. My mother supervised meals and assisted with the steady stream of guests who had come to bid farewell.

Late one night, I tiptoed into my grandfather's room and went to his bed. I had been with him earlier, but in the dim light of the bedside lamp, I saw how painfully thin he had grown, blue veins visible through thin skin.

"Come sit," he said, his voice a whisper.

I climbed up on the bed, snuggling close as I'd so often done in the past. "Time for one of our serious talks."

With my head nestled against his chest, I could almost hear him wheezing.

"Of course you already know you are the last Adler. It falls to you to keep our proud name alive." He coughed, little bursts of dryness that made his chest heave.

"I know," I said, not exactly sure what that meant.

"Thank goodness you have inherited your father's brain and your grandmother's love of music. I charge you Sir Stern, Royal Knight of Oakbridge, to be strong and make me proud."

Somewhere he found the strength to clasp my face between his white hands and pulled my cheek to his lips. "If only I had made time to spend with your father as I have with you, maybe ..." he let his voice drift off. He kissed my forehead. "Now go. I'm spent."

I slipped off the bed. "I'll come back tomorrow. We can finish King Arthur," I said, but I don't think he heard me.

# CHAPTER FOURTEEN

## KANSAS CITY, MISSOURI
## 1929
### REBECCA

I arrived home late in the afternoon, tired, my head aching, and needing to rest. We had plans to attend the Rosenthal's formal dinner party that evening, but soon enough I learned there would be no party for us.

As I passed by the parlor, I saw Stern, his little legs dangling from the piano bench, his small body hunched over the keyboard. Ramsey sat next to him, his trumpet hanging from one hand, the other placed lightly on Stern's shoulder.

"What's the matter?" I said.

Stern climbed down off the stool, and in an unaccustomed display of emotion, ran to me. He threw his arms around my waist and buried his head on my jacket. I knelt down and raised his chin. "Stern? What is it?"

His words came out in chunks punctuated by sobs. "It's Grandpa Max. I did so want us to finish reading King Arthur." He could barely go on. "But he wouldn't wake up. I ran to get John Charles. And then . . . " he looked at me, his eyes swimming in tears, ". . . John Charles said my grandpa had gone to heaven." Stern crumbled in my arms.

"Oh, honey," I said holding him close.

Kurt took care of the funeral arrangements with Rabbi Mayerberg. The Temple B'nai Jehudah on Linwood and Flora filled quickly with Max's old friends and ours. Kurt knew many more people than I. He pointed out the politician, Tom Pendergast, whispering that prohibition be damned, Boss Pendergast kept liquor flowing in Kansas City in spite of the law.

After the service, I stood by Kurt's side as people passed through a line to offer condolences. Tom Pendergast shook Kurt's hand and acknowledged me with a smile saying, "You ever need anything, just ask. This town owes Max Adler more than it can ever repay."

Kurt and I rode to Elmwood Cemetery in a hearse with Stern sitting stoic and silent between us. John Charles brought Susie Mae and Hilda in Kurt's car. We stood as Rabbi Mayerberg spoke the Hebrew words.

Several hefty men lowered Max's coffin into the ground next to Molly and Frank. Kurt gathered dirt on the back side of the shovel, a Jewish custom that demonstrates reluctance to say a final goodbye, and threw it onto the casket. Others did the same until only Stern and I remained.

I deferred, unable to face the task, but Stern wiped his tears and stepped up to the edge of the grave. He bent, scooped up a handful of earth, and sprinkled it onto the casket below. I choked up when he said, "I'll miss you, Grandpa."

Back at Oakbridge, I oversaw a beautiful reception. Kurt took possession of his father's belongings and directed John Charles to distribute Max's clothes to the needy. After that, the door to Father Max's room remained closed, though from time to time I saw Stern in there, sitting in the old chair, reading King Arthur.

I must admit, I didn't realize how much Father Max's death would impact my life. I did know, however, that with him gone I remained the last vestige of hope for Stern and his music.

I had had little time to consider Albert's confession, though at first, I'd been stunned. How had I not known, I wondered, or at least suspected that he had homosexual tendencies?

Still, as I reassessed the situation, I realized it made little difference in my life. Marriage to Albert had never been an option. Being a sensible woman, I could see no reason why we shouldn't continue our friendship. I called and told him so. He sounded grateful and much relieved.

As to Stern, I saw a satisfying way to defy my husband by allowing Jonas Parker to continue. Besides, I had many other things to occupy me: servants to supervise, supplies to order, meals to plan, and social functions to arrange.

In the beginning, Kurt's visits to my bed came with some regularity. However, when his late hours and frequent emergency calls caused me to complain, his padding the halls diminished to an occasional few, and finally to none at all. In return, I faithfully portrayed my role as charming and gracious young wife. As I sharpened my skills, Kurt seemed to appreciate the new me.

March howled in with a final heavy, wet snowstorm. I bid John Charles light a fire in the library fireplace so that by the time Kurt arrived home from the hospital, the logs had turned to glowing embers. As he settled himself in his worn, leather chair, I said, "You look exhausted. What is it?"

"Nothing you'd understand," he replied.

"Tell me anyway. Don't treat me like a child."

"How can I expect you to advise me?"

"Try me," I said, hands folded quietly in my lap.

He raised an eyebrow. "All right. I suppose you've heard the stock market crashed the day after my father passed away."

"Of course," I said. "A person would have to be blind not to know about the stock market crash. It's in all the papers."

"Businesses are closing. People have been thrown out of work. Many of my patients can no longer afford medical care. Long lines of people wait at food pantries for a piece of bread." He looked at me, his eyes red with fatigue. "Is there something you can do about that?"

His tone was facetious, and I wasn't sure how all this would affect my life, but I answered, "Maybe. What do you suggest?"

"You might consider volunteering, at the hospital perhaps."

I thought about that long after we'd finished our drinks and gone to our separate rooms. In the morning I called my friend Sybil.

"I've started working at the dispensary," she said. "They are desperate for volunteers." She went on to explain that the small clinic had been opened to help the poor, many of whom were impoverished Eastern European Jews.

"Whatever would I do?" I asked.

"Make bandages, screen patients, help with the children. I go there on Tuesdays. They have so many in need and not nearly enough help. This blasted stock market thing has made matters much worse for everyone. The dispensary operates on donations and they can't afford to hire more people. Come with me and meet the director? She might give you a better insight into the problems we face."

Distasteful as it sounded, I agreed.

From the outside the dispensary looked like any other single-story building in the northeast part of town, but inside, crowds of people milled about. Some found chairs. Others slouched against the wall. Still more paced aimlessly up and down the halls.

Young women, their faces pinched with fatigue, cradled their infants. Toddlers clung to their mothers' skirts. Old men with nasty stains on their pants leaned heavily on canes and stared at the floor.

An unnatural stillness permeated the building. I heard muffled voices, words spoken in languages I couldn't understand. When a child's cry penetrated the quiet, sympathetic looks crossed a few faces. Others remained unemotional, detached.

The place reeked of unpleasant odors. It helped to breathe though my mouth, but those smells remained in my nose long after

I returned home. Curious eyes followed me as I glided toward the office. I felt overdressed in my simple blue suit.

"Who are all these people?" I asked Janet Weinstein, the clinic supervisor.

"Mostly poor Jewish refugees. Relatives and friends have helped them escape the persecutions of their countries, Hungary, Russia, Poland, and brought them to Kansas City, but life here brings many difficulties. They don't speak English. They have trouble getting jobs. They can't find proper housing, and though they expected some religious prejudice, they didn't expect it from other Jews."

I sensed she meant me and my body went rigid with indignation. "I'm not prejudiced," I said.

"Of course you are. What you call being Jewish bears little resemblance to them. Do you worship on the Sabbath? Do you go to services, cover your head, sit apart from your husband? Do you keep kosher? Will your son have a Bar Mitzvah?"

"No, no, and no, but that doesn't make me prejudiced."

She sighed, her shoulders slumping. "Never mind. If you and more of your friends will volunteer, it would be greatly appreciated. We need people to care for the children while their parents are being seen, someone to staff the front desk and direct folks where to go, help patients fill out forms, and there is always filing to do."

The thought of performing any of those duties except the last disgusted me, but I said "yes," and went home to call up my social set. Many of them must have been frustrated nurses and all were as bored with their lives as I.

We formed an auxiliary and ordered fashionable uniforms from New York. We elected committee chairwomen and soon found ourselves volunteering several hours a week. We elected officers. I became the first president. After that, I performed my duties from the comfort of my parlor. I delegated many of my responsibilities to snooty Kate Roth, the newly elected vice-president. Her husband Henry had made a fortune in the milling business. Kate found the work exciting and worthwhile.

At the end of the first year I gave a luncheon for our rapidly growing auxiliary. Everyone loved coming to Oakbridge, not only because of the complete renovation I'd supervised, but because Hilda made delicious delicacies that Susie Mae and John Charles served on the exquisite china and crystal once owned by Kurt's mother Molly.

One day, as the servants cleared away the plates, I stood and tapped my goblet for silence. I thanked the group for coming, and for making the project a success. People like to hear their own name mentioned, so I talked about everyone, rewarding each with a framed paper certificate that included a gold seal. "Because of you," I said, "Janet Weinstein tells me things have never run better. All the doctors can see additional patients."

The ladies applauded.

"However," I continued, "they still need equipment and supplies, and that requires money."

I took a sip of water and waited until the murmur had died down. "As you know, the dispensary charges only what the patients can afford. Although the United Jewish Charities provides funding each year, there is never enough. At times, patients need hospitalization, and since most of them have no money, they must be sent to Memorial where conditions are, to be frank, awful. If we go out and raise enough money, Janet Weinstein will be able to send those people to German Hospital."

"You mean Research," Sybil corrected.

I nodded, having forgotten momentarily that because of the awful war we'd fought against Germany, the hospital board of directors thought it prudent to change the name from German to Research.

"Well, Rebecca," one of the ladies grumbled. "I'm not at all sure we want those refugees in our hospital. I mean, won't they bring their germs and diseases with them?" She looked around the room and added, "After all, that's where our doctor sends us when the need requires."

Shocked, I said, "Adeline Aaron, I'm surprised at you. Do you think for one minute that Kurt would sponsor this idea if he thought it might put us at risk? Besides, we're talking about other Jews. We simply can't turn our backs on them."

A buzz went through the group and Sybil spoke up. "Becka has a point. Those poor folks have suffered enough, what with the pogroms and prejudices they received in their homelands. As Americans we should welcome them to our town and help them all we can, even if they are not our kind."

Heads nodded. "In that case," I said, "I propose we appoint a committee to look into the possibilities of raising funds through a charitable event, a ball perhaps." Everyone liked that idea.

In addition to the clinic, I decided Kurt would also like me to volunteer for the Library Literary Club and the Kansas City Art Society. Before long, a Jewish settlement house requested I become a member of their board of directors. I accepted, even offering to teach English to the growing number of immigrants, but found myself singularly unqualified for that task.

"They don't even try to assimilate," I complained to Janet one day while visiting her at the health center. "I asked several seemingly intelligent couples to dinner at Oakbridge, and guess what? They refused. Now why do you suppose they did that?"

"Simple." She shook her head at if to say I should already know the answer. "You don't keep kosher, and they prefer not to embarrass you or themselves."

"Well, for heaven's sake. Somebody ought to tell them those stupid dietary laws are old fashioned and unnecessary."

"Becka," she sighed. "Listen to yourself. You can't tell people that. They finally make it to the land of the free and what do they find? Narrow-minded people like you."

I bristled. "I am *not* narrow-minded. Perhaps you can explain to me how in the world those people expect to be accepted if they are determined to set themselves apart?" I glanced out the office door just as a young man with the long side curls walked by. "Take him for instance," I whispered. "He needs to cut his hair, shave off that beard and buy some decent clothes. Instead, he insists on looking. . . well . . . different."

Janet closed the door mumbling, "and vive la différence." She plopped in her chair and stared out the window. "Well, let's see. You and your friends live in fine houses with your prominent and successful husbands. You own lots of jewelry, and cars, and all that money can buy, but I don't see any of you belonging to Red Cedar Country Club. Why's that?"

She was referring to a posh Gentile country club. "Because we have our own country club. We'd much rather associate with our friends than people we hardly know."

"That's not the real reason," she scoffed, "and you know it. The truth? R triple C doesn't allow Jews. Neither does The Downtown Club nor The Merry Fox Hunt Club. And while we're on the subject, how many of your rich, Jewish daughters are presented at the spring debutante party?" She waited for my response, and when I didn't have an answer she said, "That's right. None. So you see, you're not much better off than that guy out there with his curling sideburns, which are called *payos*, just so you know."

Seething, I drew in a deep breath. "Well. At least we try to fit in. We eat what everyone else eats. We send our children to religious school on Sunday. We wear modern clothing. Kurt and I have a lot of non-Jewish friends, some quite close. One lovely gentleman has already told us he intends to sponsor us for membership at R triple C."

Janet blew air out the side of her mouth and glanced skyward. "Great. For your sake, I hope it happens," she said. "At any rate, don't worry about these new immigrants. With a little help, they'll manage."

"All right," I said chewing on my lip and watching a wasp bounce off the windowpane.

"Let them keep to themselves." I rose and straightened my dress with my hands. "I must go. I'm already late to my next meeting."

Janet waved weakly, shook her head, and watched me leave.

Conner Watson II, President of The American Legion, had decided a classical chamber music quartet would be good for Kansas City. Generally speaking, whatever that large, austere gentleman with the perfect white hair wanted, he got. Today it was money.

I hurriedly took my seat in the library conference room and flashed my apology for being late smile at him, as other board members, my good friends and wives of prominent businessmen, acknowledged my arrival.

As I glanced at them with their perfectly coiffed blond hair, straight noses, and high cheekbones, I heard Janet's voice ringing in my ear.

*Are we really good friends?* I thought. Now and then, we lunched together but we rarely had intimate dinners, meeting mostly at fund raisers, school meetings, and grand events. And during the summer, they and their families went off to their cottages in the Hamptons while mine stayed home and my son played with a little colored boy.

"Don't you agree, Rebecca?" I heard Mr. Watson bellow.

I shook my head to clear away my thoughts. "I'm sorry. What were you saying?"

He gave me his most ingratiating smile. "And how much will you and the good doctor ante up?"

"I'm not at all sure my husband would be interested in a chamber music quartet," I said, meeting his vapid eyes with mine, "but you must ask him yourself."

"That I will," he answered, "at a dinner I'm planning. I hope you will attend."

"I'll check my datebook," I said, but the nasty little seed of doubt that Janet had planted in my head began to take root. We often attended parties at the private clubs that flourished in Kansas City, but only as guests, not members. *Why,* I wondered, and meant to speak with Kurt about that this very evening.

# CHAPTER FIFTEEN

## KANSAS CITY, MISSOURI
## 1929
## KURT

As exasperating, irritating, and demanding as Becka is, I adore her. She frustrates me to distraction, but then when I gaze upon her beauty or hold her in my arms, she enchants me. I knew when I married her it would be like bringing up a spoiled child, but her beauty and intelligence overwhelmed me.

Now here we are ten years later, and she still infuriates and charms me. Much sooner than I expected, she gave me not only a son, but the reincarnation of the brother I lost. What a gift. I foisted maternal responsibilities upon her too soon, and I claim fault for her leaving the child's upbringing to the maid. Now I must repair that, and soon enough I will.

Still, my lovely girl is becoming a woman. She graces our home, and at the end of the day I relish walking in the front door to be greeted by her. Take for instance last evening. I arrived home at nine o'clock, exhausted. I thought only of retiring to my room and falling into bed. Though I hate to admit it, Rebecca did the correct thing by separating our sleeping quarters. I miss her but we both rest better. Our infrequent lovemaking becomes a mysterious tryst.

My beauty greeted me at the door, wrapped in a stunning pink satin negligee, and offered me my favorite scotch and a bit of cheese on a cracker. "Poor darling," she said, and led me to my leather chair in the library. A cozy fire glowed in the fireplace. She instructed John Charles to bring me a bowl of delicious oxtail soup, and chattered away until I began to revive. Who could ask for more?

I half listened to her babbling about inconsequential things until I heard her say, ". . . and I simply don't understand why we aren't invited to become members at R triple C. Do you?"

"'You mean the country club?" I asked.

"Yes. Of course. After all, we *too* are listed in the Kansas City Social Register."

"What brought this up?"

She relayed her conversation with the hapless supervisor of the clinic. It remained for me to explain to her the depth of anti-Semitism that follows the Jews.

"I don't understand. We are as rich or richer than they," she said, "and in some cases, better educated and better dressed. What is it about us that they hate?"

"Aside from the Christian propaganda that the Jews killed Jesus?" I asked with more than a hint of sarcasm.

"Yes."

"I believe," I told her in all seriousness, "that there is a need for one human to elevate himself above another. Embattled white men came to this country to free themselves from political and religious persecution. Once liberated, they killed the Indians and made slaves out of Negroes. Bigotry is handed down from one generation to the next, intolerance perpetuating racism." I sipped my scotch.

Rebecca sat opposite me in thoughtful silence.

"Fifty years ago, the Adlers immigrated to this country," I continued. "They knew anti-Semitism would follow them, so they decided the best course of action would be to try and assimilate. They didn't exactly turn their backs on Judaism. They modified it so that they might  fit in."

Anger flashed in Becka's eyes. "Makes sense to me."

"Me, too." I yawned.

"But the rest of the world didn't buy it, did they?"

"It seems not. Anyway, that's the lecture for tonight. I must get some rest or I'll fall asleep in someone's bloody abdomen tomorrow. Goodnight, my love."

"Wait," she cried. "I'm not done yet."

"But I am." I stumbled off to bed.

Sometimes I worried about Rebecca and wondered if that dirty little kike Albert, with his arrogant ways and perfect pitch, hadn't managed to steal my son from me, and perhaps my wife as well. Hell. I should have suspected him long ago, but coming upon them huddled together around the piano was proof enough.

I must say Stern's birth fulfilled my wildest dreams. Even though his coloring reminded me of Frankie, I didn't expect him to be a carbon copy. I only hoped he'd be a normal boy. The day the little Negro child got shot, I thought Stern could have behaved more appropriately. He knew better than to play with guns. I did what I could to save the injured boy's eye and stormed over to the offender's house to confront his parents. I'd never met the family. They lived on Oakbridge property in a rundown shack. The farmer, a sharecropper, appeared overwhelmed with anger when I told him what prompted my visit. He assured me his son's punishment would be swift and thorough, and there would be no such incident again.

My father built Oakbridge for my mother and he managed the care and maintenance of the grounds. Though it had been my home for many years, I knew few of the people that tended the fields and the livestock. I spent my time treating illnesses.

Now in my sixty-eighth year, I had a thriving medical and surgical practice at German Hospital, an institution financed almost entirely by my father and his German friends, amongst them William Volker. The ridiculous war in Europe had caused much angst over the hospital's name, and I appealed to Volker and others on the board of directors to change the name to Research, which in due course they did.

I enjoyed surgery. It allowed me to remove myself from personal involvement and thus concentrate on the mechanics of the human body. This in turn often required me to stay late at the hospital, not an ideal circumstance with a beautiful young wife to satisfy. Nevertheless, I did my best.

I admit Stern disappointed me. He seemed to lack the carefree boyishness one would expect of a lad his age. Instead, he turned to that damned piano. It began when Albert decided Stern had perfect pitch. I didn't know what that meant, but to my wife it seemed to imply a highly unusual quality.

I gave in and allowed her to hire a piano teacher for the boy, but within a year, that experiment failed. I naively thought that would be the end of it. Of course it was only the beginning.

The day I learned my father hired Jonas Parker to continue teaching Stern, I blew up. Even Rebecca seemed to approve. What in the world crossed her mind?

In an effort to turn things around, I invited Stern to accompany me on my hospital rounds. Maybe if he saw my professional world it would jar him into reality, but at the first sight of blood he felt faint.

While I finished seeing my patients, I had him wait in my office, and when I returned, I found him sitting behind my desk being entertained with coin tricks by one of my gangster patients, John Lazia.

John had once worked for my father's law firm where he had demonstrated more than a spark of intelligence. However, that didn't save him from the influences of the Mafia. To my father's disappointment, John chose a career opposite to the law.

I first treated him in the emergency room for multiple cuts and bruises obtained in a particularly violent clash with a teenage gang of thugs. He'd been my patient ever since.

"Fine boy you have here," he said, flipping the coin to Stern.

I nodded, noting John's thinning hair and pinch nose glasses. "Yes, but not cut out for medicine," I said, eyeing my boy.

"I wouldn't be either. All that blood and gore? Ugh." He laughed and Stern laughed with him.

"What can I do for you today?" I asked, angered by the interchange. "You look fit as a fiddle."

"Stomach's been bothering me," he confessed. "I was hoping you could fix me up."

"Let me call my man to take the boy home, and we'll have a look."

"Good. Have him stop by my car. I brought you a gift, a case of your favorite." He winked. In spite of prohibition he kept me well supplied.

After that unsuccessful excursion with Stern, I found little excuse to be with him. I realized we had nothing in common. Rather than hugging him, I wanted to shake him. He cast his eyes down when addressing me or avoided me altogether. What had I done to deserve such a son?


No matter how much you prepare for death, it creeps up and steals away those for whom you care. I loved my father though I'd never been able to rid myself of the bitterness of Frankie's death. It ate at my soul. Because of Stern's close resemblance to Frankie, my father showered him with attention, far more that he'd ever shown me.

That's why, I figured out, he encouraged Stern's interest in the piano, a career path that he must have known could lead nowhere. His decision drove us further apart.

At least he recognized I had no interest in farms and livestock. Before he died, he sold off all but a few acres. Did he see the depression coming? I suspect so.

A flawless business man to the end, he turned his profits into gold, thus securing his assets and mine. The stock market crashed on October 29th, 1929, the day after his death. Perhaps now I could finally forgive him.

The invitation to a Christmas party from John and Maria Lazia arrived at the perfect time. In observation of my father's death, Rebecca and I had been cooped up together too long. She needed to get out, and I needed to get back to my practice.

Becka jumped for joy when I told her we could go. She took the occasion to do her favorite thing: shop. She hurried off to Harzfeld's and selected an extravagant gown in gold lamé.

I must admit when I saw her dressed and wearing her diamond and emerald necklace, she looked stunningly beautiful. I puffed up with pride.

Snow fell in big, soft flakes the night John Charles dropped us off at the Park Central Hotel on Armour Boulevard. The Lazias' lavishly furnished apartment had deep-set windows and high ceilings. It smelled of pine branches. A glittering Christmas tree dominated the living room, surrounded by gift-wrapped packages.

A servant took my wife's ermine coat, and John, decked out in a black tuxedo, ushered us to the bar. He shook my hand, his eyes roaming appreciatively over my wife's body. "You lucky devil," he whispered as we shook hands.

"What are you drinking? I imagine there are a lot of people here you haven't met. We hoped Tom and Caroline Pendergast would come, but they are such homebodies. Marie tells me they hate all parties except their own." Johnny laughed, his voice booming. "But you know this gentleman," he said, throwing his arm around Tom Bash's shoulders.

"Of course," I said. "How are you, Tom?"

A county lawman, Sheriff Bash topped six feet and looked every inch a cowboy. He lived on a nearby farm, and had once invited my father and me to hunt there.

"Fine, Doc. I'm still waiting for you to take me up on my invitation."

I smiled, knowing I'd never go, and introduced him to Rebecca. He eyed her lecherously, but she knew how to handle such situations. She fingered her necklace, teasing his eyes from her breasts, and cooed, "Lovely, isn't it? A gift from my husband."

"Indeed," he said, a pink flush coloring his cheeks.

Just at that moment, Maria Lazia joined us. She and Rebecca knew each other from The Young Women's Democratic Organization. They chatted briefly, and Maria whirled away to welcome more guests. Rebecca and I mingled, visiting casually with people we knew slightly or not at all.

As the evening wore on, we drank champagne and dined on delicious hors d'oeuvres. I piled my plate high at the buffet table while Becka picked daintily. Then we found our seats next to my old friend, Herb Woolf. He owned a racehorse farm, so it didn't take much to imagine that he and John were horseracing buddies. Otherwise, we appeared to be the only Jews there.

After a flaming dessert, Becka and I got separated. People were starting to leave when I spotted her off in a corner engaged in convivial conversation with a dark-haired young man she obviously knew. I admit I felt a stab of jealousy.

"Oh darling," she said, as I approached. "I lost you in the crowd. Meet Jimmy Galeno. We've known each other for years."

# CHAPTER SIXTEEN

## KANSAS CITY, MISSOURI
## 1932
### SUSIE MAE

A whole lot of things changed after Mr. Max passed. John Charles didn't have no reason to light the fire in the parlor anymore. Doctor Kurt hardly ever came home. We saw less of Miss Rebecca, though she tried to have dinner with Massah Stern now and then, but usually he ate in the kitchen with us.

Ramsey, he come most every day. Them two boys surely could whip up a music storm in the parlor, and even though Oakbridge stood a long way from our closest neighbor, I worried that someone might grumble.

Whale kept up the lessons and I began to hear a difference. Massah Stern tole me the names of the composers and soon I knew the likes of Mozart, Beethoven, and Bach. My chile's fingers sprang across the keyboard, sometimes moving so fast I could hardly see, and other times, ripplin' like water on the pond. It was a sight to behold. I could tell he missed his granddaddy and we hired help tried to keep him company, but it weren't the same.

Ramsey and Stern was fourteen now and growin' like weeds. They'd been jivin' all afternoon when I heard the front door slam shut. I hurried from the kitchen to the parlor where the late summer sun came through the open window and tiny specks of dust danced in the air.

"Afternoon, Doctor," I says, a little out of breath.

"Afternoon, Susie Mae," he says, never taking his eyes off his boy. "Mrs. Adler home?"

"No, suh," I answers. "We don't s'pect her 'til after five. I'll just go tell Hilda you're here so's she can start dinner."

He didn't pay me no mind. He walked into the parlor and pointed a finger at John Charles's nephew. "Run along, Ramsey. And Stern," he says, "Go to your room and start packing. Tomorrow you leave for Hollings."

"What?" Stern gasped. "No. I don't want to go to military school."

"You will do as I say. Susie Mae will help you pack." He went to the piano, banged down the lid, walked into the library, and shut the door.

Ramsey, his eyes big as saucers, skedaddled. Stern sat on the piano bench lookin' like he'd been whopped in the stomach, tears in his eyes. "I won't go," he mumbled. "He can't make me."

"Run on," I whispered. "I'll be up soon."

"Mama won't let him send me away, will she, Susie Mae?" he sobbed, his whole face sagging.

"Can't rightly say, honey," I said, but I knew the answer to that, and so did he.

# CHAPTER SEVENTEEN

## KANSAS CITY MISSOURI
## 1932
## REBECCA

I knew something was amiss when Susie Mae met me at the door. "Evenin', ma'am," she said, wringing her hands. "Doctor Kurt says for you to go to the library as soon as you gets home."

"He's home? What's happened? Everyone all right?"

"Yessum."

"Then what?"

She looked down at her shoes and mumbled that I'd best find out for myself.

*Uh oh.* I handed her my coat and went to the library.

My husband sat in his leather chair, a glass in his hand, a medical book open on his lap. He looked up and motioned me to enter. "Come in, Rebecca. Want one of these?" He held up his scotch.

"No, but I'd be glad to freshen yours." I took his glass. "What brings you home at this time of day? Are you planning to stay for dinner?"

"Actually, I thought we might go out, just the two of us. I have something I'd like to discuss with you."

"Oh, dear. I'm afraid that's not possible. The library board meets this evening. I promised I'd be there. Another time perhaps?"

He scowled. "That will be too late. Obviously you haven't seen Stern yet."

"No. Why? "

He peered at me over his drink. "I've enrolled him at Hollings," he answered.

I caught my breath. "Why? What's he done?"

"It's not punishment, Rebecca. It's for his own good. He is totally out of control, undisciplined, and disobedient. If we don't do this now he will grow up a worthless, no good bum playing piano in some local honky-tonk or worse. I won't have it."

"He'll hate that school."

"He'll get used to it. Besides, it will be good for him. My God. Just look at him. He's soft, sloppy, and shiftless. He fiddles around with that damn piano all day. It's not normal. I'm sorry I ever let him take a lesson."

"Don't be silly. He loves his music. Besides, all that practicing is hard work."

"Posh," he grumbled and closed his book.

"You have to admit his grades are excellent."

"I do, but he needs discipline. He gets none of that here. A year or two at Hollings will make a man of him."

The leather groaned as he heaved himself out of his chair, put the book on the desk, and walked to the window. A few clouds covered the sun, but not a breath of air stirred the early summer heat.

I bristled. "He's a good boy. You know that as well as I. What brought all this on, anyway? Are you afraid your son might truly be an artist?"

"Don't be ridiculous. If you mean would I choose a different path for him than playing the piano in a bar? Absolutely."

I wondered if Stern's real father would agree but remained silent.

"Today's little episode just made my point."

"What did he do?" I asked.

"Stern shows total disregard for my wishes."

"What are you talking about?"

He turned to face me, arms hanging at his side, and then slumped against his desk. In that moment, I thought how old he looked. Deep wrinkles etched his face and his hair had turned completely gray.

"I can't count the number of times I have told the boy to stop the racket."

Crotchety old man, I thought.

"Yesterday I came home early to pick up some papers. I could hear the commotion from as far away as the bridge. I caught your friend Albert here along with Ramsey and his confounded horn. That boy is as much a nuisance as Stern. I won't have it any longer. From now on, the piano remains closed."

When he mentioned Albert, I started to speak, but he held up his hand.

"Don't, Rebecca. Surely you can see you are the cause of it all. Sometimes I wonder if you even know you have a son. Where were you yesterday and today? At one of your social functions? Who supervises Stern? The colored girl? And what business did Albert have here?" He glowered at me.

"I don't notice you spending much time with him," I shot back.

"At least I've tried, but apparently he'd rather be with your old boyfriend."

I let that pass. I didn't think I should tell him just then that "my old boyfriend" was, in fact, the real father of the subject of our conversation.

"Neither of us has done a very good job," I conceded, "but Susie Mae has always looked after his needs."

He shook his head. "Need I say more?"

Tears sprang to my eyes. Whether from anger, frustration, or sorrow, I didn't know. I sank to a chair. "The house will be so quiet without him."

"You'll barely notice."

"Do they have a piano at Hollings?"

"I certainly hope not," he laughed.

"When?" I asked.

"Don't worry. I've taken care of everything. I've called the headmaster, gotten him enrolled, made arrangements to take him tomorrow."

"Tomorrow?" I wailed.

"The sooner the better," he said.

I recognized this as an argument I couldn't win, and I remembered something about better to lose the battle and win the war. I changed my tactics. "All right," I said, unknowingly sealing Stern's fate forever.

Kurt's eyes softened. He stood tall, shoulders straight, and placed his finger under my chin. Suddenly, his demeanor too had changed.

"You're looking especially lovely this afternoon, my dear," he said huskily. "I don't suppose you could skip the library meeting tonight?"

I hesitated, weighing my options. A few months at Hollings wouldn't hurt Stern and would give me a chance to work something out. Living with this man had its challenges at best but without the aggravation of my gifted son to constantly plague him, perhaps I could change his mind. "What library meeting?" I answered.

He raised me to my feet, arms encircling me, and bent to kiss my neck, my ear, my lips. I wondered if he could feel my derision.

"After you attend to the boy, come join me for a drink. Then, I'll take you to the Rendezvous for dinner." My favorite place, he knew.

I slipped from his arms and went to Stern, grateful for the time to think. I found the boy sobbing on the bed, Susie Mae hovering nearby. "I won't go," he said when he saw me. "He can't make me."

Motioning for the servant to leave us, I stared down at him. "Yes, he can."

"Isn't there something you can do?" he cried.

I shook my head.

"I knew it. You don't love me," he moaned.

I sat on the bed next to him, smoothing his silk bedcover and thinking of the rough army blanket he'd have to get used to.

"Of course I do, but you must be strong and give me some time to work on this. Now stop all this silliness." I wiped his tears and hugged him. "It won't be so bad."

I tried to sound cheerful."There will be lots of other boys, and you'll get such a good education. I'm going to phone tomorrow and be sure they have a piano you can use. Try and be brave."

I rose to leave but then remembered Albert. "What was he doing here?" I asked.

"He found an old sheet of ragtime music Scott Joplin wrote. He said he thought it might be valuable someday and wanted me to have it."

"How nice. Who is Scott Joplin?"

"You've never heard of Scott Joplin?" he groaned. "He's just about the greatest ragtime musician who ever lived. He wrote *Maple Leaf Rag*."

"Oh," I murmured, wondering what Albert would think of military school.

# CHAPTER EIGHTEEN

## KANSAS CITY, MISSOURI
## 1932
## STERN

That night the brewing storm matched my mood exactly. Why did my father hate me? Because I didn't want to be a doctor? Once or twice he took me on rounds, but the smells and sights of sick people made me queasy.

And my mother? Did she agree to Hollings? I thought not, but she could do nothing. I sat thinking of her, the lilies of the valley smell of her lingering in my room. I did so enjoy our moments together. Sometimes she told me about her childhood, how her father came from Hamburg, Germany and started making furniture.

"It was all he knew how to do," she said. "Jews in the old country weren't allowed to own a business. If they got lucky, they learned a trade, but even then they were paid very little. As soon as he could, he came to the United States. He began to make beautiful wooden chairs. The rich ladies bought them for their fine homes. Soon he added other pieces to his collection and a nice little business developed."

"Then why did he leave?" I asked.

"He never got used to this country. After my mother died, he and Erika spoke only German to each other. I never liked her."

I remember the bitterness in her voice when she said, "As soon as he got rid of me, he sold the business, they married, and returned to Hamburg."

That's what my father is doing, I thought, my mood sullen. Getting rid of me.

As I watched the black thunderheads rumble past my window, I saw Ramsey frantically waving his arms under the swaying branches of the mimosa tree. I knew what he wanted. I shook my head, afraid. A bolt of lightning blistered the sky and rain began to fall.

Pretending to pray, he put his hands together and sank to his knees. Then he jumped up and marched up and down, his wet face grim. Military school, boys in uniforms acting like soldiers with guns. I hated guns.

Running away never entered my head, but now, could I do it? I stared at Ramsey, waiting for me in the rain. I wanted to be brave like him. Yes. I could.

I grabbed a jacket, took a quick look up and down the hall, ran down the stairs and out the front door. I didn't stop, just streaked toward Ramsey waiting at the base of the old oak bridge.

The rain came down harder, but he grinned, clapped me on the back, and said. "You made it, ya ole coot. Let's go."

"Where?" I panted.

"Town," he said. "Welcome to my world."

# CHAPTER NINETEEN

## KANSAS CITY, MISSOURI
## 1932
## RAMSEY

My brain churned. I couldn't take him home for fear my mama would tell, so I headed for the coal yard. It was a long way, maybe the farthest Stern had ever been, but I had a plan. I knew about a little-used lineman's shack near the Union Station. I'd hid there myself from time to time.

It took us an hour or more, stayin' in the shadows. I didn't notice anyone followin' us but I didn't want to take any chances either. If I'd been by myself, I'd have hooked a ride on a streetcar but Stern, he'd never done such, so we walked and ran 'til we got where we was goin'. Wet to the bone, we hurried inside while the storm passed over.

"There's some matches on the table," I said, " but don't light 'em. Never can tell who's out there. Gimme your jacket and get out of those wet clothes. They'll be dry by mornin'."

"You're not going to leave me here, are you?" he said.

"If I don't show up at home, they'll suspect something. You'll be okay. There's a blanket yonder. I've slept on it plenty of times. I'll come back first thing in the mornin'. . . " I paused, seeing the look of panic in his eyes, ". . . with breakfast. Then, we'll figure out what to do."

He stared at me with a look that said he hated the idea, but okay.

My mama worked for the Winthrops. She cleaned mostly, but on occasion served dinner parties at night. Emmett, her boyfriend, hated her being gone at night and took it out on me, but by the time I got home, Mama and Emmett were in bed.

I didn't hold much with the boyfriend. He worked off and on at a fur plant, and most of the time smelled like a skunk, which I thought he was. I tried to stay out of his way 'cause he didn't like me neither and smacked me every chance he got.

Mama had left ham hocks and beans on the table. My stomach growled with hunger, and I knew Stern must have felt the same. I saved back some of the meat. It tasted a little like bacon. Stern had never eaten nigger food, but I figured he'd be so hungry he wouldn't know the difference.

Mama was up and about when I woke. "Where 'd you get to last night?" she asked.

"Oakbridge," I told her, "until Doctor Kurt kicked me out."

"You misbehave? I'll tan you good I hear you misbehaved out there."

"No, Ma. Me and Stern just played our tunes like usual. He come stormin' in and told me to leave.

She shook her head. "I better not hear anything different," she warned me. "Now eat yore breakfast." She put down a plate of grits and gravy.

"I gotta get Emmett up and ready for work. You better hurry or they'll be missin' you at the dime store. Emmett," she yelled. "Get yore lazy ass out a bed." She headed to the bedroom.

Long ago, Ma had sewed me an eye-patch. It itched but I wore it every day so's people wouldn't have to look at the hole in my head. I put it on, shoved an orange and a couple of slices of bread into the paper bag where I'd hid the ham hocks, and hurried out.

When I got back to the coal yard, the door stood open. *Oh God*, I thought. *He's been caught.* Just then, here he came, swingin' around the side of the shack, his red hair shinin' in the sun.

"Had to take a whiz," he said as we went inside,"and I'm starving."

I handed him the paper sack.

He laid the food on the table "What is this stuff?" He pointed to the ham hocks with white beans clingin' to them.

"Never you mind. Just eat." As I watched him stuff the food in his mouth I told him, "We got business to do. First off, we gotta do something about your hair. They'd spot you a mile away, and . . . " I said, thinkin' out loud . . ."I believe I know just what that might be." I went outside and gathered up a handful of coal dust.

"Oh no you don't," he said, leaping back. "You're not puttin' that stuff in my hair. Can't I wear a cap?"

"We ain't got a cap. And another thing. You gotta have a different name 'cause everyone's gonna be lookin' for you. You got any ideas?"

He rolled his eyes upward, cogitatin'.

"How about Peter? That's my middle name."

"Pete it is," I grinned and rubbed the coal dust in his hair. It didn't look half bad. I got it on his face and clothes too, but for what I had in mind, he looked good. It had come to me in the middle of the night, a place we could go where no one would find him.

I looked out the window. To my surprise, I saw a big, fat, uniformed yard guard walkin' the rails west of the station. I'd had trouble with him before. He banged his billy club against the boxcar doors and stooped down to look for hobos underneath. "Uh oh," I murmured. "Trouble."

Pete peered over my shoulder.

"He'll check here next. We gotta get goin'." I eased open the door. "Don't you worry none. Just do what I do," I whispered and slipped out the door, but Pete hung back.

*Oh no. What's he doin'?* "Come on," I called softly. I pressed myself against the wall and watched the guard walk west down the track. I went back for Pete.

"You gotta do what I tell you or it's off to military school for you," I said in a stern voice. I grabbed Pete's arm and took off runnin' but by then it was too late.

Wavin' his club, the guard loped toward us yellin', "Come back here, you damn niggers."

Like jackrabbits, we leaped over rain puddles and raced down the tracks. Dartin' behind the caboose of a Union Pacific train, we circled back under the bridge.

I glanced over my shoulder. Nothin'. Thinkin' we lost him, I slowed to a walk, but then I heard a sound that made my blood turn cold.

Rat a tat, tat, tat. Pop, pop, pop.

"What was that?" Pete asked.

"Gunfire," I answered, pickin' up the pace.

"They shooting at us?" Pete panted, his face gone white.

I could hear sirens coming. "Nah," I said, tryin' to sound sure, "but we gotta get outta here."

We ran down the brick street that led to the stockyards. Hundreds of cows milled inside the dirty wooden enclosures. The smell made our eyes water, but I dragged Pete through those pens, swivelin' in and out amongst the critters.

All of a sudden a colored cowboy loomed above us. As his horse shied, he yanked hard on the reins, a stream of dirty words comin' out of his mouth. I waved as Pete and I hightailed it out of there.

We could hear the police cars wailin' in the distance, huntin' for us, I reasoned, but I'd grown up in these parts and knew dozens of places to hide. No one would find us now.

We slipped into the backdoor of an empty warehouse. The sirens stopped, and I figured we'd shook 'em for good.

Pete sank against the brick wall and slid down, pale and exhausted. I wiped a hole in a dirty window and peeked out. "We done good. I think we're safe."

"I don't think I like your plan," Pete said.

"Very funny," I answered.

We rested a bit and then I took him through the back alleys to Thirteenth Street and Miss Sissy's whorehouse.

Her real name was Cecelia D'Angelo. She'd saved my butt a time or two. Once, several years ago, I ran afoul of her brother Tony. He owned a fruit and vegetable stall on Third Street. I often swiped an apple or two, but this time, instead of yellin' at me, he chased me near to the river. He had me by the scruff of the neck fixin' to whup me when she come along.

"Now ain't that the cutest little nigger," she said. "What's the matter with you anyway. You can't beat up a half-blind darky. Let him go."

"He's a thief," Tony said, taking a swing at my head. "He deserves a good lickin'."

"What'd he take?"

"It ain't what he took. It's the principle of the thing," he told her.

"I'll pay you. Just turn him loose."

Tony let go of me and she yanked me to her side. "You. Patch. Tell him you won't steal from him anymore." That's what she called me. Patch. "I won't steal no more."

"There. You see?" She patted my cheek.

Tony shook his head.

I followed her home where she handed me a broom. "You owe me your life, ya little beggar. Keep this place clean and I'll let you live."

'Course I'd grown a mite since then but I done such a good job she decided to pay me a penny or two, and I been workin' there ever since. I couldn't tell my mama I worked at a whorehouse so I made up someplace presentable: the dime store.

On the way to Miss Sissy's, I pointed out the sights. No one paid us no mind, two dirty  street chillin. Most of the clubs were shut until later, but we peeked in and saw the fancy decorations, mirrors, and tables loaded with chairs turned upside down.

When we passed the Starlight Club I said, "You should just hear the music that comes out of there."

A big sign stood in the window advertisin' The Webster Five and showed a picture of Negro musicians with their instruments.

About noon we knocked on Miss Sissy's back door. Veronica, a Negro girl who acted as a maid when she wasn't hookin', opened the door. I'd taken pains to ingratiate myself to her."It's Patch," she called over her shoulder.

Miss Sissy nodded. She sat at the kitchen table, a cup of coffee in one hand, her head leanin' in the other. She made a stab at closin' her robe but not enough to cover her boobs. I'd seen all that stuff before but Pete's eyebrows shot up. "Who's your friend?" Miss Sissy asked.

"This here's Pete," I said.

"Why'd you bring him?" She tended to be grouchy at this hour of the day.

"I been thinkin'," I said. "You know how houses like ours have entertainers?" I used *ours* like I owned the place. "Well, Pete is a real good piano player. You should hear him. I betcha me and him could draw in a good crowd."

"Not interested," she said.

"No really, Miss Sissy. You should give us a try. I swear I wouldn't steer you wrong. "

"Yeah? What do you do? Dance a jig?" She laughed, a harsh sound followed by a phlegmy cough. She tried to focus on Pete. "He white?" she asked.

"Yessum."

"In trouble?"

"Yes 'um."

"I thought so. No deal." She pointed toward the door.

Pete stuck out his lower lip. "They're dead," he said. "My parents, I mean. They're dead. I ran away from an orphanage. In Leavenworth," he added.

"An orphanage?"

"Oh yes, ma'am. A horrible one right next to the prison."

"Really? How old are you?"

"Sixteen, ma'am."

"Liar."

"And he's about to hit a growin' streak," I butted in.

"You got a name?"

"Uh . . . Pete," he said. "I see you have a nice piano in the parlor. Would you like to hear me play?"

"No." She pressed her fingers to her temples like she was tryin' to rub away an ache.

Her brother Tony burst through the door, all breathless and pantin'. "Did you hear what happened? There's been a shootout at Union Station."

My ears perked up.

Sissy looked at him. "No kidding?"

"I heard two feds brought a prisoner from Little Rock on the train. A couple of city cops met the train ready to drive the con to the Leavenworth prison, but some guys with machine guns tried to bust him loose."

"Anybody get killed?"she asked.

He shrugged.

Now I understood all the gunfire."I thought they was shootin' at us," I cried, punchin' Pete on the shoulder. His mouth fell open. We fell on the floor, hootin'. Sissy wanted to know what was so damn funny.

"Long story," I gasped.

"All right, you two. Get cleaned up and then we'll see."

"Where's the bathroom?" Pete asked, but Sissy pointed to the door with her thumb.

Veronica handed him a bar of soap. "Things are different in the city," I told him when we was outside. "Niggers can't use the indoor facilities." This last I said snooty-like.

"But she knows I'm not a . . ." he began, but I shrugged and handed him the hose.

He took off his clothes and shook out the soot. Then he scrubbed the coal dust out of his hair and washed his face till it turned pink.

While Pete rinsed off, I went upstairs and knocked on Miss June's door. I knew it might be a little early but I needed her help. I'd run errands and such for her, so she liked me. Sometimes she gave me candy and sips of scotch, and she told me I'd soon be old enough for her. More important, I'd seen her dye her own hair black.

She opened her door, half dressed, and smiled at me. "Why, Patch. Sweetie Pie. Whatcha doing here?"

"I needs a favor." I told her.

"I won't get in any trouble, will I?" she asked.

"No, ma'am." I told her what I wanted her to do.

She shrugged. "Might be kind of fun. Bring him up and I'll give it a try."

# CHAPTER TWENTY

## KANSAS CITY, MISSOURI
## 1932
## JOHN CHARLES

The first I knew of it, Susie Mae came running into the kitchen to tell us Doctor Kurt planned to send Massah Stern away. "Military school," she said.

I could hardly believe my ears. "Why he gonna do that?" I asked.

"'Cause he and Ramsey make such a racket," she said.

Just 'cause them two boys whooped it up didn't seem a reason to send him away, but what did I know? When Massah Stern didn't come down for dinner, Doctor Kurt told me to go get him, but Miss Rebecca said to leave him be.

The next morning, at breakfast, Doctor Kurt seemed brighter than I'd seen him in a long time. He smiled when I brought him the paper and his morning coffee. He told me we would be going into the country.

"Gas up the Cadillac, John Charles," he said. "Then wait for Stern and me out front."

I took off my white jacket and hurried on to get gasoline. When I returned, Doctor Kurt told me Massah Stern had run off.

"Damn!" he said. "I should have seen this coming."

"None of us did," Miss Rebecca said, her voice quivery, "but you'll find him, won't you, John Charles?"

"I'll try, ma'am," I said. "Where must I look?"

"Anywhere you think he might be," she said.

I hurried out back where the boys played: behind the wading pool, across the field past where Ramsey had been shot, behind the row of old cottonwood trees.

I scoured the brown cornfield, jumped the creek, and ran down the lane to the sharecropper's house. Breathless, I asked had they seen him, but they shrugged and said he'd show up when he got hungry.

Before I got back to the manor, the doctor called the police. I searched the house, all Massah Stern's favorite spots, but found neither hide nor hair of him.

"Take the car and go into town," my boss man ordered. "Maybe he's at your nephew's house."

I too figured, rightly or wrongly, they must be together, so I went first to my sister Bertha's. Emmett let me in. "Ain't seen 'em," he said when I asked after Ramsey, "but he's been here all right. Et my ham hocks, the little bastard."

"What time?" I asked, somewhat encouraged.

"Don' know, John Charles. You'd have to ask Bertha."

The sky had cleared off during the night and the sun shined bright as I drove to the Winthrop's house on Ward Parkway. If Bertha had seen the boys, it would have been late last night or early this morning because she had to be at work by six, and that meant catching the five a.m. bus. I knew the place because I'd helped her serve a party a time or two.

She opened the back door, a look of surprise on her face. "Whatcha doin' here, boy? Somethin' bad happen?"

I told her Massah Stern had run off.

She said she hadn't seen him, and Ramsey seemed like his normal self, but she'd keep an eye out. She poured me a cup of coffee and we talked in low voices so as not to disturb the lady of the house.

"I don't know where Ramsey goes. He brings me money and says he works at the dime store, but I knows better," she whispered.

I left thinking maybe Whale could help. I tried his house but found no one at home. It dawned on me maybe he went to church but Preacher Emmanuel said he hadn't seen Whale since he'd played the organ for Sunday service.

"You might try one of the honky-tonks. He likes to play with those jazz musicians."

I thanked the preacher and put my thinking cap on. Where might a fella be at eleven o'clock in the morning–maybe at the 627 Union building on Highland Street?

I knew about the place because two years ago, they'd held a band contest there to raise money for fixing it up. Every nigger with money in his pocket went to hear the likes of Benny Moten and George E. Lee try to outplay each other – eight bands in all. Don't you know that was something to see?

Sure enough, that's where I found Whale, playing tunes with Euday Bowman. Long ago, Euday had tried to hop a train and lost one of his legs, but it didn't bother his piano playing none.

I could hear Whale's trumpet from the street. They switched and started to play Euday's *12th Street Rag*. I'd never met Euday in person though I'd saved my pennies to buy his recordings. He was in his thirties with thinning hair and a pointy chin. It pleased me that he shook my hand.

I told him I worked for a doctor. He said he'd come to town to see somebody about his leg, or rather the stump that was painin' him.

When I told Whale about Stern running off, he said, "Can't say as I blame him. If'n it'd been me, I'd a done it a long time ago."

"Why's that?" I asked him.

"I ain't saying," he answered, like he knew somethin' I didn't know.

"I did that once myself," Euday said. "Ended up right here in Kansas City playing piano in a whorehouse."

Whale puckered his fat lips and stared at Euday. "Whorehouse, huh?" He turned to me and said, "Let me see what I can turn up, John Charles."

When I got back to Oakbridge, Doctor Kurt had me drive him to the hospital. A police car and an ambulance pulled in ahead of us. Doctor Kurt jumped out of the car and rushed inside. The police said there'd been a shooting at the Union Station and a prisoner got killed.

Later on, I heard that Doctor Kurt had saved the life of one of the policemen. The next morning as I brought in the newspaper, I saw a big, black headline: **Union Station Massacre.**

It took Whale less than twenty four hours to find the missing boys. "At Miss Sissy's," he said, "Safe and sound."

When I told Doctor Kurt, he said, "Don't breathe a word of this to anyone."

"Not even Miss Rebecca?" I asked.

"Especially not Miss Rebecca," he said.

So I didn't.

# CHAPTER TWENTY ONE

## KANSAS CITY, MISSOURI
## 1932
## PETE

I cleaned up the best I could and slumped down on the back steps, wishing I was back at Oakbridge in my nice, warm bed. I wondered if my mother missed me. The last twenty four hours had whizzed by in a blur, but my hunger and anxiety were real.

Patch – that's what Ramsey said I had to call him now – came out and sat next to me.

"What are we doing here anyway?" I asked. "Maybe I should just go home."

"Whoa up there, boy," Patch said, putting his arm around my shoulders. "I know how you feel, but it's gonna all work out. I got a plan."

"Oh no. Not another plan," I said, and had to laugh.

"First," he told me, "Veronica has bacon and eggs frying."

The thought of it made my stomach growl.

"After we eat, I'm gonna take you upstairs to Miss June. She'll dye your hair black."

"What?" I cried. "Oh, no you don't. If that's your plan, forget it."

"Okay," he said with a sideways glance, "but military school, here you come."

I collapsed. "There's got to be a better way," I groaned.

"There ain't, so get used to it. Then you and me is gonna do some jammin' for the head lady. We gonna knock her dead. She'll love us. We're gonna draw customers like flies. Look, Pete," he emphasized my new name, "This place is kinda off the beaten path, if you know what I mean. We make enough good, loud music, it'll draw folks in."

I guessed I didn't have much of a choice. Besides, the thought of playing for an audience kind of excited me. Patch left me with Miss June while he ran home to get his horn.

She looked to be about my mother's age though not nearly as pretty. "What a shame to have to dye that beautiful head of hair," she said as she eyed me up and down, "but okay. Let's get at it. Take your clothes off, honey."

I shook my head.

"You don't want black stain all over your clothes, do you? Here. Have a drag off this. It'll calm your nerves." She shoved a glowing, wrinkled cigarette between my lips. "Suck it in and hold it. Oops. Don't cough. You'll get use to it. There you go. Feel better?"

I felt dizzy, and my throat burned.

"Now don't be embarrassed. I'm used to men undressing in front of me."

I took another puff, knocked the ash off, and pulled my shirt over my head.

She laughed and led me to a basin. Just then, we heard a commotion in the hall.

"What's going on out there?" I asked, looking toward the door.

"None of our business," Miss June said, pulling my head over the sink and squirting stuff on my hair.

Outside Miss June's room I heard Miss Sissy say, "Careful now. Get another towel. He's bleeding pretty bad."

"Where you taking him?" I recognized Tony's voice.

"Anita's room. She'll know what to do."

I heard a man groan. A door opened and closed, and after that, things got quiet. Miss June continued working on me.

Someone screamed, loud and piercing. It scared me and I jumped, splattering black water on the walls. Miss June mopped it up.

"Don't worry," she said. "Miss Anita'll take care of it."

She towel dried my hair and handed me a mirror. "What do you think?"

I hardly recognized myself. I turned the mirror this way and that, admiring my sleek, black curls. "I kind of like it."

"Not bad," she crowed. "See there? I even touched up your eyebrows. Now you go lay down on my bed while I wash your clothes and make them presentable."

My head felt funny, and bed sounded good. It smelled sweet, like lavender, and made me think of my mother.

When I awoke, I saw Patch whispering to Miss June. He glanced at me.

"Have a nice nap?" He winked. "Miss June thinks we ought to dress up."

I rubbed at my eyes.

"Black hats, red shirts, black pants, a little makeup. Wanna give it a try?"

"No," I said.

"Now you sit down right over here," Miss June ordered. She lit a candle and leaned a cork into the flame. Then shaking it to cool it off, she began to rub it on my face.

"Hey," I yelled.

"Guess you don't need any of this, Patch honey," she said, ignoring me.

He gave her a crooked smile.

"Don't worry, baby doll. Blackface is all the rage. No one will recognize you now, not even your mammy."

Miss June collected clothes from the other ladies that we could use as costumes: shirts, vests of different colors, black pants and the like.

All dressed up, we went downstairs to what Miss Sissy called the entertainment room. It contained a sofa or two, nice chairs, tables, and the bar plus the upright piano. The ladies, dolled up in fancy gowns that left little to my imagination, stood around talking to one another. "Waiting for their customers," Patch whispered. I wasn't sure what that meant.

"I had to dig around, but I finally got the bullet out," I heard Miss Anita say.

"Lucky it was only a shoulder wound."

"How about that. Pretty Boy Floyd right here in this house," Miss June said, "and I didn't even get to see him."

"Shush," Miss Sissy said, nodding at us. I arranged myself at the piano, trying to keep my hands from shaking. Patch stood by my side. Miss Sissy gave us the go ahead.

"All right boys. Let's hear what you can do . . . and it better be good."

I began with a little Mozart fugue, but Miss Sissy shook her head and rolled her eyes. I switched to *12$^{th}$ Street Rag*. Patch came alive, his horn nearly drowning out the piano. The ladies perked up.

We didn't have much of a repertoire. When we'd gone through the songs we knew, I started fingering whatever came into my head. We played like we did at Oakbridge. Whale called it jammin' but we called it messin' around.

I guess we did okay because Miss Sissy danced over to the front door and opened it wide. First one man and then another arrived.

Soon, the room hummed with people drinking, and talking, and rubbing up against each other. Now and again, a gentleman came over and dropped a few coins in the jar Miss Sissy put on the piano.

That first night we played the same pieces over and over again, but nobody seemed to mind. Once, when we slipped out back to pee, I asked Patch, "Who's Pretty Boy Floyd?"

"Tony says he's a gangster from Chicago. He's the one got shot today at Union Station."

We played until midnight – not my usual bedtime – and my fingers ached and quit working. Patch went home and Miss Sissy found me a bed in the storage room off the kitchen. I collapsed, exhausted.

Over the next year, I grew to love performing. All the songs that had been rattling around in my head poured out. Sometimes I wrote them down, but most often I just stored them in my brain. I even began jotting down lyrics as I thought of them.

Miss Sissy treated me well as did all the other ladies except Miss Anita. I got on her wrong side that first night when I accidentally brushed up against her, smearing black cork on her white dress.

"Get away from me, you dirty nigger," she spat.

I shrank from her and mumbled, "I'm not a nigger."

She brought her face down to mine, and I could see the wrinkle lines in her face through the layers of makeup.

"Oh? What are you then?"

"Jewish," popped out of my mouth.

"Worse,"she snarled, and whacked me on the head.

Miss Sissy let me use the indoor facilities. She took money out of the jar in payment for my bed and board, and told me to stay out of Anita's way.

I couldn't help but notice the way the ladies teased the men, kissing and stroking them, all the while letting the men pat their fannies and pinch their breasts, but when I mentioned it to Patch, he said, "You don't know nothin,' do ya? See 'em go upstairs together? They gonna have sex. That's how the ladies make their livin' here."

"You mean they get paid for doing it?" I asked.

He giggled. "'Course they do, ya ole coot."

I felt the blood rise to my face knowing that my education in such matters had been sadly lacking.

Eventually my hair grew out but no one suggested dyeing it again, and our costumes got too small. One day Miss Sissy gave us some of our tip money and told us to go to a rummage sale and get clothes that fit.

Patch had a better idea. He went through his family's pile of hand-me-downs and found some pants and shirts that sufficed. We found a better use for the money.

I thought we needed to increase our inventory of songs. "Got any ideas how we can do that?" I asked Patch.

"You can keep making up tunes," he answered.

"That's not good enough."

"Sure it is, but the nightclubs in town don't close 'til morning. When we get off, we can pay them a visit. We could start with the Starlight Club. They jam all night. For a bottle of beer or two, we can listen as long as we like." That's where the money came in handy.

We left Miss Sissy's at two in the morning. By then, the summer heat had abated, though humidity steamed off the streets. We changed out of our costumes and I'd washed the cork off my face, but we knew we'd have to be creative to find a way in.

A black sign with mile high yellow letters announced the presence of Fats Waller. "Who's he?" I asked.

Patch shrugged. "That's what we come to find out," he said.

We went around back. A door opened and a Negro came out the kitchen door dragging a bag of trash. He set the bag down and stepped around the side of the building for a cigarette. Snake-like, we slithered into the nightclub.

The kitchen hummed with traffic: cooks sweating at the stoves, dishes rattling, waitresses yelling. Music burst through the swinging doors that led to the restaurant. With all the hustle and bustle, no one paid any attention to us.

We slipped through the swinging doors and found ourselves a table at the back of the room. A colored waiter appeared, looked at us askance, and over the noise, asked us what we wanted. "Water," I said.

"You old enough?" he laughed.

Patch kicked me under the table and said, "He means beer." He laid fifty cents on the table and with a breezy air said, "Keep the change."

The waiter grinned, picked up the money, and hurried off.

This place jumped with jazzy music. Lights flooded the stage. We saw Fats Waller on piano, and a trumpet, a sax, a base and drums.

No wonder they called him Fats. He was a big man, dark-skinned and buggy-eyed, but the words that came out of his mouth left me breathless. I picked up a sound I'd been experimenting with. I called it a third because I used three fingers of my left hand, but it had a minor sound that I liked. Fats Waller must have liked it too because he used it a lot.

He sang smooth, catchy melodies the way I wanted mine to work. And he mugged to the audience, making them laugh.

People crowded the dance floor. Those not dancing sat at cloth-covered tables, keeping time with their hands, eating, and drinking.

Two nicely dressed men strolled by our table and I heard one say, "Lucky we could get that guy to stop here on his way to Cincinnati."

"Yah. He wrote a piece last night that I bought off him for thirty-five dollars," the other said.

"Wish I could get thirty five dollars for something I wrote," I whispered to Patch.

The waiter returned with our beer. We picked up the bottles and inched our way closer to the stage. I could see Fats' hands flying over the keyboard, his left hand strong and pounding a four beat pulse. I concentrated on memorizing the sounds.

The tune we heard stuck in my head. I worked it out at Miss Sissy's the next night. My voice was changing but I tried to sing it anyway.

Every honey bee fills with jealousy, When they see you out with me, I don't blame them, Goodness knows . . .

Miss Sissy stuck her fingers in her ears, so I quit singing but continued playing the song.

During the next few weeks, we snuck past the guys at Dante's Inferno. We had no trouble getting in, but we didn't stay long.

Right up there on the stage, playing the piano with George E. Lee's band, was my mother's friend, Albert Rapinksy. Speechless, I poked Patch. "What's he doing here?"

"Don't know but we ain't staying to find out."

George E. Lee didn't stay long either because it turned out he ended up joining Benny Moten's band right after we saw him.

We hid behind some curtains at Club Reno on 12th Street where Andy Kirk and His Twelve Clouds of Joy packed 'em in. Their real draw was a pianist named Mary Lou Williams. She played an unbelievable eighty-eight.

More importantly, we found out she did the band's arrangements and I thought they were so good, I tried to copy them. That night, a club bouncer spotted us so we had to leave, but I went back time and again.

At first, Mary Lou ignored me ("Who is that white kid keeps pestering me?") but when she found out I played piano at Miss Sissy's whorehouse, she befriended me and let me in on some of her arranging secrets.

Like me, she had perfect pitch and had been playing the piano for as long as she could remember. Through her, I got to meet Bud Tate, a young saxophone player, Shorty Baker on trumpet who she unfortunately married later though they never got along, and Ben Thigpen, the band drummer. Turned out, everyone one in this business knew everyone else and switching bands was like changing toothbrushes.

When Whale Parker first introduced me to Scott Joplin's music, he called it "ragged time." Later I learned Benny Moten also played hot ragtime music. Even though it was pretty old-fashioned, it had a bouncy essence that Miss Sissy loved. When I banged it out, she'd grab a partner and dance around the room.

One evening she mentioned she had it in mind to slip over to The Cherry Blossom, a nightclub where the waitresses dressed in Japanese kimonos. Benny Moten and his band were playing there. She invited a boyfriend, got all dolled up, and off she went.

The next night, after we got through playing, Patch and I decided we had to go too, where for the first time, we got to hear Walter Page on his double bass.

When his time came to solo, he had the room hopping with four feels, quarter notes that sounded a little like walking feet. He'd had a hot group of his own once, The Blue Devils, but they'd fallen apart. "It happens," Patch said.

In 1920, two years after my birth, the government prohibited the sale of liquor in the United States, but that never seemed to affect anyone in Kansas City. Miss Sissy and all the houses and clubs served alcohol. Boss Tom Pendergast saw to that. Gambling parlors, dens of gangster activity and iniquity, served liquor free to anyone who played.

On our trips to various nightclubs, Patch and I often ran into people we'd met at Miss Sissy's, men like Joey "the Pig" Gambini who had big, thick lips, bushy black eyebrows, and a mole with a hair sticking out right under his nose.

Miss Sissy's ladies loved him because he laughed a lot and tipped generously. He even bought drinks for Patch and me and left C-notes in our bottle, which Miss Sissy grabbed and split with us.

In December Patch and I went back to The Crystal Palace. On our way there, we stopped by Uncle Moses' lunch wagon, all decked out with stringy Christmas lights.

Patch loved the stuffed hog maw and chitlins, pigs' innards if truth be known, but the smell turned my stomach. I opted for a chicken sandwich which cost a dime and a five cent bottle of beer.

Outside The Crystal Palace, we ran smack dab into Joey the Pig. It had started to snow, big flakes that melted on your clothes and made the street shine.

"If it ain't my two favorite musicians," he said, making the first part of musicians sound like a mooing cow. "Come on in and get warm."

Patch stalled. "I don't think I'm allowed," he stammered.

"A course you are. This here is my place and if I say you can come in, you can come in."

Dwarfed by his size, we found ourselves shoved up the back steps. Pig gave a signal rap. The door magically opened to a noisy, crowded room full of people shooting craps, playing blackjack, and betting on numbers around the roulette table.

"Go on in, boys, and have yourselves a time. Anyone give you trouble, you just tell 'em I said it's okay." He slapped us on our backs and disappeared.

I had never gambled but I'm a quick learner. It took me no time at all to lose all the money in my pocket. Patch did better. He didn't fool around with card games and little marbles circling a wheel. He headed straight for the crap tables. Before long he had a crowd of folks surrounding him.

Joey the Pig sent over rounds of scotch, and we downed them like we'd been drinking all our lives. Patch swung back his arm and let go those dice like flying birds. More and more men began betting with him. By the time he'd made twelve passes in a row, the crowd went crazy.

But Patch had consumed a lot of liquor, and to say he was drunk might be a bit of an understatement. As he hauled back to throw number thirteen, a tall, thin man with an ugly mouth-to-ear scar went all in.

"Four's the point," called the dealer, and with all his chips on the table, Patch let fly. The dice bounced against the far end of the table and rolled around until they finally came to rest.

"Seven," said the dealer and despite the groans, began to pull in all the chips on the pass line. Scarface stood there stunned, his face turning an ugly shade of red.

I patted Patch consolingly, and we staggered toward the door. That's when I heard Scarface yell, "Who the hell let that nigger in here anyway?" and I saw the glint of a silver blade flash in his hand.

Everything went dead quite. Joey the Pig came walking out of the pit, flanked by four of his brawny employees. He stopped in front of Scarface and put a hand on his shoulder.

"They're friends of mine, Buster. I was just having a little fun with 'em. Go get yourself a drink on the house. I'll take care of it."

"Buster" appraised the four goons, curled his lips, folded up his switchblade and turned away. Joey the Pig's hoods helped us to the snow-covered street, slipped us some money, and told us to have a good night. The cold air felt good, and leaning on each other, we stumbled home feeling lucky to be alive.

Local 627 opened our eyes to real jam sessions. The union helped establish some sort of pay scale, but most Negro musicians belonged so they would be protected from bad booking agents.

I couldn't join, but they let me in the building anyway. We got to know guys like singing bartender Big Joe Turner and piano playing buddy Pete Johnson. Young guys, Hot Lips Page, one of Benny Moten's trumpet players, and Lester Young on sax, jived to the beat.

Patch fell in love with that kind of music and began improvising on his own. Of course it didn't sound like The Webster Five or the Barley Brothers, but Miss Sissy's ladies didn't complain, so we added it to our repertoire. We didn't know it then, but it was all about to come to an end.

# CHAPTER TWENTY TWO

## KANSAS CITY, MISSOURI
## 1932
### REBECCA

Susie Mae woke me with gentle shakes that dreadful June morning to tell me she couldn't find Stern. "Now don't you worry none," she said. "He probably jest visitin' with my sister's boy Ramsey. Doctor Kurt – he already sent John Charles to fetch him."

By the time the police arrived, we knew for sure that Stern had run away. Cruelly, they made it sound like a typical runaway case. After all, no body had been found. Their declaration didn't make me feel any better, and I paced all day, wondering where he would go and how he would survive. After all, he'd hardly been alone for a minute of his life.

Nerves stretched taut, I couldn't sit around and do nothing. I called the mothers of Stern's few school friends, but no one had seen him. I searched his room for any clues, noticing only that his jacket was gone. Alone in my suite, I called Albert. "Kurt and his damned military school," I sobbed.

"We'll find him," Albert said. "With that head of red hair, he can't have gotten far."

"This is all your fault," I screamed at Kurt, but strangely, neither he nor John Charles seemed overly concerned. "Don't worry," my husband said. "He'll turn up."

Having a child simply disappear is a chilling experience. Not knowing what to look for, I had John Charles drive me through the streets of downtown Kansas City and into the countryside looking for any signs at all. When I tried to sleep at night, I'd see my child wandering the streets, hungry and cold, or lying in a fallow field, bloodied and dead.

I spoke to Sybil daily, and though she could offer nothing but sympathy, she did allow me an outlet for my emotions. Finally one day she suggested we go to lunch. I went gladly, tired of sitting in that dusty, old house playing wife to that dusty, old man. Over cocktails, we discussed Stern's disappearance and what I should do next. She encouraged me to get back in the swing of things, join some boards, redecorate Oakbridge.

Our sandwiches arrived, lettuce and mayonnaise seeping out the sides just as we liked them. "Have you seen Sam lately?" Sybil asked, meaning Kurt's partner.

"Not since he and Serena returned from New York," I answered. "Why?"

"He's grown a mustache, Rebecca. It's a scream. All waxed and curled at the ends. And I caught a glimpse of him last week wearing a fancy bowler hat and carrying a gold-headed cane. He must think he's hot stuff."

I laughed. "Probably got them in New York. But really, Sybil, he's a nice guy," I said.

"I know, but still . . ." Her voice trailed off and she got a faraway look in her eyes. "Never mind. Let's finish our lunch and go to Harzfeld's. I hear they have a divine new collection," she said.

Sig Harzfeld met us at the door. An old friend of Kurt's, he was only slightly taller than I with an endearing round face, a sparkle in his eyes, and sparse white strands of hair combed over his balding head. He kissed my cheek and asked if we'd found Stern yet. I told him no. He said not to worry. Even he had thought of running away once long ago.

As he ushered us to the designer section, he assured me Stern would soon tire of fending for himself. Miss Harrison, our personal shopper, came to greet us and show us the things she'd picked out for us to try.

One look at the beautiful new Schiaparelli collection and I succumbed. Sybil, who'd put on weight, didn't look nearly as good as I in the colorful suits and gowns. Black had become passé, so I bought tweed suits and pullover sweaters. The new Chanel gowns dripped with beads and bangles. Fur-trimmed collars and cuffs were in style. I had a hard time deciding what to buy. We staggered, giggling, to Sybil's car with our bags and packages.

Following Sybil's advice, I hired the most expensive decorator in town, and before long the house rang with the sounds of workmen's hammers and saws. We replaced the ugly drapery with light, airy curtains, peach-colored, to blend with the pale green of the walls.

We bought new furniture or had the old reupholstered, moved the piano to the corner between the windows, and bought new lamps and end tables. I purchased a Persian rug for the dining room, woven with colors that matched the re-covered Victorian chairs and pineapple print wallpaper. All the bills went to Kurt.

It took time, but I found the results so pleasing that I wanted our friends to see. A dinner party would be just the thing. I invited Gertrude Rosen and her banker husband Ben, Kurt's partner Doctor Sam and his wife Serena Seligsohn, and of course Sybil and Herbert Hirsch.

I took great pains to plan things to perfection and suffered great disappointment when Sybil called to say she had a terrible cold and was going straight to bed. "Don't worry," she sniffled. "Herb's coming."

Herbert designed and manufactured children's clothing in a brick building close to the river. He had laughing brown eyes, a large Roman nose, and a sparkling sense of humor. Sybil met him at a Zeta Beta Tau fraternity party at the University of Missouri in

Columbia and immediately fell in love. She had gone to Stevens, a nearby two year finishing school, and as soon as Herbert graduated from MU, they married. I likened him to a big brother and could count on him being the life of the party.

Grain broker Henry Roth and his pretentious, stuffy wife Kate came. We went way back, having grown up in the same neighborhood. They had a son, Martin, the same age as Stern. He went to a private school.

I never liked Henry. Overweight and thick featured, he usually greeted me with sloppy kisses, inappropriate pats, and peers down my dress, but I invited them anyway since they were part of our crowd. Kate surprised me by trying to help us find Stern. They still lived in the old neighborhood and she placed pictures of Stern in all the local stores in hopes that someone would recognize him. I, of course, had hardly forgotten about him, but planning the gala formal affair helped to take my mind off my troubles.

As usual I instructed Hilda to hire reliable help to assist with the serving. I inspected the polished silver to be sure it achieved the highest degree of luster and laid out my best china and crystal. After much contemplation, I chose to wear a low-cut formal dress in pale green and my beautiful diamond and emerald necklace.

The guests arrived at seven. Everyone looked lovely, the women in gowns and the men in black tie and tails. Henry asked about Stern, but Kurt assured him that no news was good news. "He'll show up eventually."

Susie Mae passed hors d'oeuvres while we drank our cocktails. I delighted in showing off our redecorated house, soaking up the compliments. John Charles, looking fine in black tie and white serving jacket, announced dinner. Taking Serena's arm, Kurt led the way to the dining room. All found their places by the little Dresden nameplates next to damask napkins.

Two gleaming candelabra containing tall tapers lit the table. The burning candles illuminated the gardenias floating in crystal bowls. My guests, enchanted by my lavish settings, continued their conversations in subdued tones.

Susie Mae and the rotund colored waitress Hilda had hired began the meal with soup, served in elegant bone china bowls. Although she was properly dressed in a black uniform and white apron, something about her made me nervous. To my dismay, I noticed her thumb sticking into the bowl of soup she served to Ben Rosen. Right then I should have dismissed her. Instead I looked furtively at my guests, hoping no one else saw.

On cue, John Charles came through the kitchen door carrying a silver tray heaped with slices of juicy tenderloin which he passed to each guest. Following right behind him came the extra waitress with the gravy boat.

All went well until the maid got to Kurt's partner, Doctor Sam, his newly acquired mustache waxed to perfection. Suddenly he startled everyone by crying out and jumping out of his chair. I saw gravy running down his bald head, his glasses, his neck, and dripping in rivulets across his shoulders onto the pleats of his white dress shirt. The maid juggled the near-empty gravy boat. I jumped up and rushed to grab it, thinking of my new oriental rug.

"Lord have mercy," Sam complained, making the mess worse by brushing at his shirt. "Could someone get me a towel?"

The maid turned and ran to the kitchen. My guests sat in stunned silence. Then, to my embarrassment, Kurt pointed at Sam and burst into gales of laughter. In an instant, everyone else did likewise.

Sam was a sight, gravy dripping off the handlebars of his mustache. Ben the banker laughed so hard his face turned red. Prim and proper Kate's mascara ran as she dabbed at tears and doubled over.

Furious, I steamed into the kitchen. The stupid waitress had ruined my dinner party.

John Charles raced past me with wet tea towels. Susie Mae stood paralyzed holding a silver bowl of crusty baked potatoes.

Hilda hurriedly took the gravy boat from my hand. The hired colored woman leaned quivering over the sink.

"Where did you find that woman?" I hissed at Hilda.

"I had trouble finding someone for tonight, so I called Miss Sybil and she said she'd send someone over."

The hired maid shook.

A bell began to ring in my brain. "You. Do I know you? Have you been here before?"

She nodded her head violently and I moved toward the sink, ready to seize her. "Turn around this min . . .."

Hilda interrupted me. "I'll send her away, ma'am. Should we pay her the regular?"

"Not one dime," I answered.

The maid whirled to face me.

"Not even a dime, Rebecca?" she howled.

And then it registered. "Sybil Grossman Hirsh. You fiend. Look at you. Where did you get that makeup?"

I shook my head in disbelief and collapsed onto the kitchen chair.

My friend couldn't contain herself.

"I thought this party would need a little livening up, and I was right. Have you ever seen anything funnier than dignified Sam Seligsohn jumping up and down? Serves him right, acting all fancy. Oh Lord. This is the best one I've ever pulled."

I turned a suspicious eye on my servants.

"You. All of you. You were in on this, weren't you?"

Sybil jumped to their defense. "Of course they were, but don't blame them. This was my doing. Come on, let's join the party." Arm in arm, we returned to the dining room. When my guests recognized Sybil, they broke into more peals of laughter. Sybil pointed a blackened finger at her husband. "Even you didn't recognize me."

"Yes, I did," he lied, his chin tucked down on his chest.

Everyone began talking at once.

"Bring a chair, John Charles. It seems we have another guest."

Sam, clothed now in one of Kurt's smoking jackets, found it in his heart to be forgiving. John Charles and Susie Mae continued serving the delicious dinner, and the party went on.

"Rebecca," said Sam's wife, Serena. "I've been admiring all the new decorating. I especially like how the draperies pick up the color in the chairs. I would never have thought of doing that. I don't suppose you'd be willing to share the name of your decorator, would you?"

I smiled mysteriously. "Of course, though it will cost you," I said.

"How much?" she asked Kurt.

"I don't know. I haven't seen the bills yet." Everyone chortled.

Later on, I saw Kurt in deep conversation with boring Henry Roth. When they saw me looking at them, they turned and walked out on the terrace. What could that pretentious fool have to say that so interested my husband?

After everyone had gone home, I asked Kurt. "Nothing important," he answered. "I'll take care of it."

"Take care of what?" I persisted.

"Let's go into the library and have a nightcap," he suggested.

"It's something about Stern, isn't it?"

"Yes, partly." He poured two little glasses of sherry.

I swung around to face him. "What is it?"

"Henry thinks he saw him."

"Oh?" I felt faint. "Where? Is he all right?"

He waved his hand in the air. "He's fine." He gulped his drink and lowered his eyes.

"I have a confession to make, Becka. I've known where he's been all along."

"What?" An angry lump began to rise in my throat.

He looked tired as he poured himself another drink. "We need to talk about something else." He sank into his chair. "How much did all this cost?"

"What? The party? I don't know. Tell me about Stern," I insisted. "You've known all along where he was and you didn't tell me?"

"Oh, that. Yes." He raised the glass to his lips and took a big swallow. "I mean all this redecorating. How much did it cost?"

"You'll get the bill from the decorator. What does it matter? I want to know about my son."

"I told you. Stern is in good health." He stood up, set his glass down, and went to the door.

"Nice party, Becka," he said.

"Kurt, wait."

"I'm going to bed, Rebecca," he said. "You should, too."

Fuming, I bit my lip, wondering why I stayed with him. He infuriated me. I paced the library floor, so mad I could hardly catch my breath.

The next morning, sleepless, I heard Kurt's footsteps on the stair and rushed after him. Leaning over the banister, I screamed, "Where are you going?"

"To get our son."

"Wait. I'm coming with you," I said, following him.

"No. You're not," he said.

By the time Kurt got home, I had worked myself into a real tizzy. "So? Where is he?"

"He's gone," he reported.

"What do you mean, gone?"

Finally, the whole story came out: how Stern had spent the last six months playing a piano in a house of prostitution, how Jonas Parker had found Stern at Miss Sissy's, how he'd told John Charles who'd told Kurt, how Kurt knew Miss Sissy from way back and trusted her to look after my son.

"Why didn't she get in touch with me?" I asked. "What kind of a woman hides a fourteen year old boy and doesn't even tell his mother?"

"She did it because I asked her to."

"This is all your fault. You and your damned military school."

"Calm down, Rebecca. Sissy took good care of the boys."

"Boys? How many boys does she 'take care of?'"

"Just Stern and Ramsey. I thought it was a good way for Stern to get some real life experience. Unfortunately, they must have known the jig was up. They've run off again."

My anger overwhelmed me. I lost control and slapped him as hard as I could.

The shock transformed him. His face turned red, all calmness gone. He grabbed my arm and threw me into the chair. Age hadn't diminished his strength.

"Don't you ever do that again," he spat.

Tears flooded my eyes. "You son of a bitch," I sobbed. "He didn't turn out the way you wanted him to, did he? You've always held that against him."

He rubbed his face where a red welt rose. "What are you talking about, Becka? I have always wanted what was best for him. He's my son."

I wanted to hurt him. I couldn't stop myself.

"That's where you're wrong," I said. "He's not your son. He's Albert's son."

He stared at me, speechless. "Albert's? That can't be." He looked at me intensely for what seemed a very long time. Finally he said, "You delude yourself, my dear."

Soothing his cheek, he turned to leave. "Try to pull yourself together. We have some serious talking to do when I return."

"I'm done talking," I called after him, wishing him dead.

# CHAPTER TWENTY THREE

## KANSAS CITY MISSOURI
## 1933
### KURT

Maybe I should have gone after Stern the minute John Charles told me where to find him, but in that instant I chose another course. Though both angry and relieved, I also felt a degree of pride that Stern had mustered enough courage to run away.

As it happened, I'd known Sissy D'Angelo and her "girls" for years, ever since one of them had carelessly gotten pregnant. I called her immediately.

"The redhead is your kid?" she laughed. "Well, I'll be damned. The faker. He had me believing his parents were dead. Yes, he's here, and his little nigger friend, too."

"Are they all right?" I asked.

"Oh, sure. I'm thinking of putting them to work."

"Really. Doing what?" I asked, suspicious as to what two young boys would do in a whore house.

"Playing piano and horn, you chary old fart. I think they may have a pretty good act. I'm calling them Two Peas in a Pod. Pretty cute, huh?"

I decided Sissy D'Angelo's place might be a better solution to Stern's problems than military school. Give him a taste of the life he'd chosen. "Are you certain?" I asked her.

"Yeah. Sure."

"I'll pay you," I told her. "Whatever you want."

"You're a good guy, doc," she said. "I'll send you a bill. Take care."

I didn't tell Rebecca. She would have had a fit. The night of her dinner party, however, I knew my little game was over. On one of his whorehouse visits, Henry Roth had spotted Stern.

"I have a favorite girl there," he confided. "Anita. You ought to give her a try. She is round as a berry, voluptuous, tight in the right places," he winked, "and savage, just the way I like 'em. I've been there a few times but never noticed the entertainers. Too much else to look at."

He disgusted me, but he said he had something more important to discuss and guided me out onto the terrace. "Beautiful night," he said.

"A little too chilly for me," I answered, buttoning my dinner jacket. "What's so important, Henry?"

"Oh, nothing much. Just wondered how you're faring in the stock market."

"Could be worse," I said, "but I'll have to rein in Rebecca. "How about you?"

"Not so good." Worry lines flitted crossed his face. "Kate doesn't know it yet, but we may have to take Martin out of private school. And her seeing all this beautiful redecorating," he flung an arm toward the living room, "doesn't help."

He said that through clenched teeth, but then he smiled and slapped me on the back.

"Come on. You look like you're freezing. Let's go back inside, and don't worry. I won't tell anybody about Stern. Thing is, you can bet if I've seen him, others have too."

I knew he was right. I had to tell Rebecca and I had to bring him home. But the next day, when I got to Sissy's, she met me at the door.

"You're too late, honey. They've flown the coop."

"Where could they have gone?" I asked. She had no idea but she gave me Billy Joe Blanchett's card.

"Try him," she said. "In the meantime, have a cup with me. We can talk about old times."

The tantalizing smell of freshly brewed coffee persuaded me and I agreed to stay for a bit. A radio shaped like a cathedral played softly. I told Sissy that Henry Roth had seen Stern. She laughed and said she knew him well.

"He loves to squeeze Anita's fat butt."

My ears perked up when I heard the announcer say, "Looks like another of Kansas City's prominent businessmen has ended his own life after reportedly losing a fortune in the stock market."

I held up my finger to listen. Both Sissy and I gasped when we heard Henry's name. It was eerie. We had just been talking about him. Shaken, I set my cup down, sloshing coffee on myself, and reached for Sissy's telephone to call Sam, my partner.

"You heard it on the radio?" he said, his voice thick. "How awful but yes; Henry jumped from the top of one of his grain elevators."

I sat trying to compose myself. Then I laid fifty dollars on the table and left.

Fresh worries sprung into my head as I thought of Rebecca's dowry. I had given it to her as she wished. Now I wondered if any of it was left. My father had managed to hold on to the Adler money, though the estate had not come through entirely unscathed, but I thought I should discuss that, too, with Becka.

I went home to change my clothes and tell her Stern had run away again. I knew she would be angry, but was totally unprepared for the slap she delivered, much less the venom that spewed from her mouth.

Of course her vengeful declaration about Stern's origin was pure nonsense but I knew that in her present state of mind, further talk would be useless. I would deal with her later. John Charles had laid out a fresh suit which I quickly donned. Then, he drove me to the hospital.

I finished two surgeries, an appendectomy and a gallbladder removal. Resting at my office desk, I stared at Billy Joe Blanchett's card. I picked up the phone and dialed his number.

# CHAPTER TWENTY FOUR

## KANSAS CITY, MISSOURI
## 1934
### PETE

I remember when Miss Sissy introduced us to Billy Joe Blanchett. I overheard him tell her that when he stopped by the Wee Willie Club to check on his clients, JoJo March and his Jazz Band, big Dan Tarantella came up to his table and suggested he drop by Miss Sissy's and catch her new talent.

"I thought he meant girls," he told Miss Sissy with a lecherous grin. "Imagine my surprise when I heard a piano and a horn duo riffing in the living room."

He glanced at us, me dressed in blackface and Patch wearing a red thing over his eye.

"I don't think they need dressing up," he told her. "They're good. Really good." Then he asked her to introduce him to us, and I saw Miss Sissy wink at him and chuck him under the chin.

She brought him over during our break and told him she'd named us Two Peas in a Pod. "Now, don't you go stealing them. You hear?"

"Hello, boys," he said. "How old are you?"

Patch squinted his eyes and asked, "He a cop?"

"Nah. He's an booking agent," she explained. "Be nice now, children. He's a good man to know."

She walked away, and he said, "How old did you say you were?"

"Sixteen, if it's any of your business." That's what Patch told everybody.

"I sure do enjoy hearing you play. Where'd you learn improv like that?"

I toed the floor. "Aw, we just fool around," I said.

Patch cocked his head all uppity like he does. "An agent, huh? What's your schtick?" he said in street Yiddish.

"You Jewish?" the guy asked.

Patch giggled.

"I find places for good entertainers to play, mostly members of TOBA," Billy Joe said.

"TOBA?" I repeated.

"Theater Owners Booking Association."

"You take a cut?" Patch wanted to know.

"Sure I do. I don't scout clubs for free."

"We got a place to play," I said.

"You might not need me now but maybe later, when you get a little older."

He winked. We knew he didn't buy the sixteen bit even though we'd both grown. He gave us his card with his name and number on it.

"Call me," he said, and he wandered off to find himself a lady.

As time went by, my thoughts of home came less often, though once I did sneak back to Oakbridge and hide in the trees to watch who came and went.

I saw the car swing down the driveway with John Charles at the wheel, my mother in the back seat. I hid so as not to get caught, but a longing rose in my chest and I fought back the tears. For an instant I thought I might jump out and surprise them, but then I remembered why I'd run away. That kept me glued out of sight.

It didn't take long for Patch and me to fall into the house routine, sleep until midday, do our cleaning chores, practice, take a little time off to roam the city, then race back to dress up in the outfits our ladies made for us, and play until one or two in the morning.

Finally, I talked Miss June out of the blackface. It played havoc with my skin, which broke out in pimples. The days turned into weeks and the weeks into months.

One evening, Miss June rubbed my shoulders as I played. She patted me on the cheek and then pulled my face closer and looked at me real hard.

"Pete, my boy," she said, "I do believe you need a shave. Maybe the time has come for me to teach you a few things. What do you say?"

I knew what she meant and wanted more than anything to take her up on it, but I gulped and sputtered, and she walked away laughing.

Sure enough, the next day, when I looked in the mirror, I saw hairs over my lips and sticking out of my chin. Also, I had to crouch down to see in the mirror. I made up my mind I'd take Miss June up on her offer.

The very thought made things happen in my crotch. I'd seen how the customers treated our ladies, some nice as pie, others not so good. That night, as Patch and I headed outside for a break, I caught sight of Miss June bending over a seated customer as she served him a drink.

She all but fell out of her low-cut red dress, but when he reached up to touch her, she shook her finger at him and grinned mischievously, saying something I couldn't hear. She saw me staring at her and mouthed "later." I nodded, trying hard to control the thing in my pants.

"Quit your drooling and come on," Patch sniggered. "Looks like you gonna get your cherry popped, ya ole coot." He propelled me toward the door whispering, "I found us a couple of jays," street talk for marijuana. "You want yours now or later?"

"Maybe later," I whispered back, thinking Miss June and I could share.

That night, when I went into Miss June's room, I didn't know what to expect. The bed looked clean and inviting, turned down like Susie Mae did back home. In the dim light Miss June sat in her slipper chair, her robe covering only the parts of her body I most wanted to see.

"Come in, honey bunch," she said. "I've been waiting for you." I went to her, all but panting, but she put up her hand.

"Now just a minute, sweetie. First thing we gotta do is negotiate," she said.

"Huh?" I murmured.

"You don't think I do this for free, do you, sugar?" She stuck out her lower lip in a delicious pout.

"Uh, no. I guess not. I didn't bring any money, but I've got a joint. Will that do?"

She laughed. "I guess it will have to. I love doing firsties anyway, so tonight's on the house."

Patch had gotten some True Gold marijuana, a high quality, strong grass that made everything seem vivid and more real. We lit up and shared drags. Miss June went to the bed and motioned me to follow.

"Take off your clothes, honey," she said, much like the first time she'd told me that, but this time it didn't sound the same. She reached up and unbuttoned my pants.

That's all it took. I threw my head back and came in uncontrollable spurts, panting and trying not to cry out. Weak and embarrassed, I murmured apologies and headed for the door.

She called me back. "It's all right, baby cakes. Now that we got that out of the way, we can get down to business." She wiped up the spots I'd made and patted the bed.

I undressed and lay down beside her. She brushed at my hair and told me we never should have dyed it. She said she thought I had the bluest eyes she'd ever seen, and that she'd never been with a man who had only one chest hair before.

She used her hands to fondle me, her tongue to excite me, her month to torment me. Suddenly, her age made no difference. She knew her trade and she taught it to me.

We fooled around 'til dawn. Then she kicked me out. "That's it, little buddy. From now on you pay like the grownups. Now run along. I gotta rest up for my regulars."

As she curled up around her pillow, I crept down to my little room and fell exhausted on the bed. I didn't hear a thing until Patch came to wake me for dinner.

"Have fun?" he asked.

I grinned and nodded.

That night we played as usual but I saw someone that changed everything. Miss Anita sat at the far end of the bar with Martin Roth's father. He saw me too. "Patch," I whispered. "I know that guy."

"Which one?"

"The fat, balding guy at the bar."

"The one buying Anita a drink?"

"That's him. My parents and him are friends. I know his son."

Patch made a face. "After a little nooky. Look at him, all over her butt and her acting like she likes it. Oh, oh. That's it. She's taking him upstairs. "

I rolled my eyes, wondering why anyone would want to be with Anita.

"Do you think he saw you?"

"I'm sure of it."

Miss Sissy swished by. "What are you two gabbing about? Pay attention. This isn't break time."

I played louder and Patch put his horn to his lips, but before he did, he said, "Don't worry. Anita'll have him tied to the bed most of the night."

I told Patch, "I can't stay here. We have to move on."

"Where we gonna go?" he whined. I knew he didn't want to give up this spot. Then I remembered Billy Joe Blanchett.

We played small towns in Missouri, Oklahoma, and Arkansas. Sometimes things went well and sometimes they didn't. Dusty Miller, the band leader, owned the bus, and I hated riding in that old rattletrap thing. On hot summer days we smothered with the windows closed rather than breathe in all the dust from country roads. In winter we huddled together trying to keep warm.

I got used to sleeping on the damn bus since no hotel would allow Negroes. But with practice, we found we played well together. Dusty let me do some arranging and he even added some of my compositions to our repertoire. *Working for a Living* and *High Time Jazz* seemed to go over big.

I was fifteen years old and life was good.

# CHAPTER TWENTY FIVE

## LITTLE ROCK, ARKANSAS
## 1934
### PATCH

I didn't want to leave Miss Sissy's. I truly didn't, but Pete insisted we run down Billy Joe Blanchett that very night. We found him puffin' on a big black cigar, listenin' to Cookie Crocker play a mean saxophone at The Jungle Club.

"Hello, boys," Billy Joe said, like he'd just seen us yesterday. "What are you up to?"

When Pete told him our troubles, he yawned and said he thought he could help us out. He had a bus leavin' in the mornin' to go on tour down south.

"You game for a little travel?" he asked.

"How much we get paid?" I asked.

"Well, let's see. Minimum is twenty five cents an hour. That's for play time only. Travel time doesn't count."

"Not enough. We gotta eat," I griped.

"You play four hours, you get a buck," he said. "Take it or leave it."

"We'll take it," Pete said over my loud protests. "What do we have to do?"

"You play wherever I book the band: Joplin, Carthage, Springfield, Little Rock. Travel by day. Play by night. Bus leaves at six in the morning. Tenth and Main," Billy Joe said.

And just like that, we had us a new job.

I ran home to tell my mama that I wouldn't be around for a bit, but she'd gone to bed so I left her a note sayin' not to worry, I'd be fine. I grabbed a few of my shirts and an extra pair of pants plus a spare mouthpiece for my horn. By the time I got back to Miss Sissy's, Pete was ready to go.

The bus didn't look like what I'd expected. It was a piece of junk with paint peelin' off the sides and a cracked windshield. Sleepy guys draped themselves over the torn, fake leather seats. Instrument cases filled the aisle and nets hangin' over the seats. What didn't fit inside got tied to the roof.

We climbed over bodies to find a place in the back. Someone opened a window and a welcome breeze took some of the stink out of the bus. We got ourselves settled, more or less. The driver, a big, fat man named Lester, cranked up the engine, and away we went.

Everyone but me and Pete slept, don't ask me how. With all the bouncin' and rattlin', my bones ached and my ears rang. I was never so glad as when we stopped at a roadside park.

We'd already passed one with a sign that read **NO DOGS OR NEGROES** but at last we came to a coloreds only Jim Crow park. We'd been travelin' all mornin' and I had to pee somethin' fierce.

Everyone else had brought their own lunch, and now ambled over to picnic tables to eat. Pete and I relieved ourselves and then sprawled unhappily in the shade of an elm tree.

"Hey you kids," a tall, skinny guy called. "Come sit with us. You got names?"

That's how we met Lawrence "Big Lips" Hayman: trombone. He introduced us to Marty Roach, who played tenor saxophone, Beefy Barton, clarinet and only a few years older than us, and Max Furman, one of two drummers in the group. They shared their sandwiches. "We go by Two Peas in a Pod," Pete told 'em.

"Hey. That's a good one," Beefy said. "They's ten of us. How about we call ourselves Ten Peas in a Pod?"

"You idiot," Big Lips said, poppin' Beefy on the head. "Your name don't start with no P. 'Sides, Dusty wouldn't like that."

"Who's Dusty?" I asked.

"Our leader."

Dusty Miller had a knack of pullin' a bunch of oddball musicians into a band and makin' what came out sound good. Plus, he played a mean trombone. We found out he paid us, made the rules, and meant what he said.

"Ever any trouble, we leave town," he told us. "Meet at the bus at 10 AM. I'll tell you where. Anyone late gets left," he said.

Our first engagement was at the Masonic Hall in Joplin. A sign out in front said in large letters,

DUSTY MILLER AND HIS JAZZ BAND TONIGHT. Bring your partner and dance to the best music this side of Kansas City.

Lord have mercy. Seein' that sign, I had flip flops in my stomach. Billy Joe arranged for us to bed down in a flea bitten flop house across the railroad tracks.

Most of the guys had played with Dusty before, but his piano player had quit and he needed one real bad. Late that afternoon, we got together in the hall to practice.

As everyone milled around, Pete sat down at the little upright and began to make his magic. Before long, the boys picked up their instruments and we was off to the races.

Over time, we learned the band's staples: "I Wish I Could Shimmy Like My Sister Kate," "Royal Garden Blues," "It's Right Here For You," and such like that. Pete began doin' our arrangements and before long, Dusty had us both playin' every night, me on second trumpet.

As hard as it was, life didn't get really tough until we got to Little Rock, Arkansas. By that time, we'd left Marty Roach, down with pneumonia, in Springfield. Buddy Fisher, who played soprano sax, joined us.

One night, we played on an outdoor bandstand, the lights shinin' down on us, air sweet with the smell of marijuana. Our instruments gleamed and Pete's red hair stood out amongst all us nappy headed guys. The crowd seemed right friendly at first, dancin' and singin' along.

A wispy, blond white girl jumped up on the stage, grabbed the mike and began to croon alone to "Jazz Baby" in a surprisingly deep, throaty voice.

*My daddy was a rag-time trombone player.*
*My mammy was a rag-time cabaret-er.*
*They met one day at a tango tea.*
*There was a syncopated wedding*
*And then came me.*
*Folks think the way I walk is a fad,*
*But it's just a birthday present from my mammy and dad.*
*'Cause I'm a Jazz Baby.*
*I wanna be jazzin' all the time.*

She flashed a big grin at Pete, and he shyly smiled back. Then one big bruiser in the front row shouted somethin' ugly at Pete.

Pete turned his head and the guy says, "Yea. I mean you. You one of them white niggers I hear'd about?"

Pete shrugged him off and kept playin'. Blondy kept singin'.

*There's something in the tone of a saxophone*
*That makes me do a little wiggle all my own.*
*'Cause I'm a Jazz Baby.*

Big Bruiser yelled, "What are you doin' up there makin' out with this nice little white girl? We don't cotton to no niggers makin' out with our white girls."

Pete yelled back, "If you got eyes in your head you can tell I'm not a . . ." but before he can finish, this guy and his friends were up on the stage yankin' Pete to his feet.

I guess you can figure out what happened next. The place went nuts. Understand, I'm a pretty good street fighter, but when you get blindsided, what can you do?

I ran over to help Pete, and a couple of big lugs plowed into me. The audience turned real ugly. Fights sprang up everywhere. Dusty got most of the band off the stage, all except me and Big Lips, who stood his ground and swung at anyone who came at him.

Pete, he's not much of a fighter, which is fine because fightin' is not good for the hands of a piano player. Just before the lights went out, someone pulled a knife on Big Lips and cut him bad. He lay on the stage bleedin' until the police came. When people heard the sirens, they trampled each other tryin' to get away.

The police carted Big Lips off, and I lost track of Pete. I didn't find out until later that the white girl with the voice had managed to get him out of there.

Lucky for me and some of the other guys, we ended up in jail instead of swingin' at the end of a rope. Dusty came to bail us out the next day.

"Where's Pete?" he asked.

"Don't know," I said.

"We're leaving," he told me.

"You can't go without him."

"Go find him then," he said. "We leave at 10."

I ran all over Little Rock lookin' for him, but finally gave up and headed back to the bus. I raised all kinds of hell. Then, just before Lester cranked her up, here came Pete and the girl, hand in hand, runnin' as fast as their legs would carry them. Pete tried to load her on the bus, but Dusty blocked the way.

"She can't come," he told Pete.

"Then neither will I," Pete answered.

"This ain't no place for a white woman. They'd lynch us all."

If there was one thing I'd learned about Pete, he had a stubborn streak. "Okay, "he said, his cheeks flamin'. "I guess we stay here."

I had hung back until then, but even though I truly didn't want to stay in Little Rock, I couldn't leave my best friend."Me too," I said, a lot braver than I felt.

Dusty changed his tone. "Now look fellas," he pleaded. "Don't do this to me. We got a good thing going here. You understand, don't you, honey?" he said to the girl. "What's your name, darlin'"?"

"Margene," she answered, all soft and husky.

"Well, Margene, tell them. We're in the south now and white folks don't cotton none to coloreds."

"Pete isn't a colored," she said, tilting up her chin with a defiant look.

For the first time, Pete looked at me.

I stared back.

His deep blue eyes lingered for a moment on mine and then swept up and down the girl's fine figure. Finally, he took a deep breath and said, "Go home, Margene. I'll catch up with you later."

He stepped on the bus and pulled the door closed. Right away, Lester fired up the engine and away we went, leavin' Margene standin' in a cloud of dust.

# CHAPTER TWENTY SIX

## NEW ORLEANS, LOUISIANA
## 1934
### PETE

We played towns on the Mississippi Delta, ending up in Memphis at Christmas time. It may seem strange but I found myself bitterly homesick, I guess because I remember it as the one time of year we felt like a family.

A big, tall tree would mysteriously appear in the parlor. John Charles would go to the basement and bring up the Christmas tree decorations: delicate glass Santas, tiny houses, dogs and cats brought from Germany by my grandparents, and colorful ropes of beads. My mother bought boxes of silver aluminum strands. I wanted to throw them on the tree, but my mother showed me how to put them on the limbs one piece at a time.

We had an annual Christmas Eve party, packing our house with people, some I didn't even know. Guests said they could smell the food clear down to the oak bridge. The dining room table sagged with turkey, ham, brisket, cranberries, hot rolls, spaghetti, pickles, olives and a medley of desserts.

My father didn't seem to mind when my mother sat me at the piano and told me to play Christmas carols. Aunt Sybil and Uncle Herbert, always the first to arrive, would stand beside me and sing. Soon everyone joined in.

A big bowl filled with champagne punch and surrounded by glasses sat in the entryway. John Charles offered a cup to everyone who entered, but soon folks refilled their own. When I was small, I'd go around picking up people's punch cups and draining the remains. Long before the party ended, I'd fall down drunk somewhere, and had to be carried to bed.

"You ain't even Christian," Dusty scolded me, that first year when I couldn't hold back the tears, but by the second Christmas, I'd gotten used to being away from home. In fact, I loved playing gigs on the holidays.

Soon after we'd finished playing an engagement in Nashville, Patch and I heard Louie Armstrong on the radio. He mesmerized us with his rendition of Hoagy Carmichael's "Lazy River."

"Man, I can do that," Patch screeched, meaning the trumpet part, but I was fascinated by the vocalization. He wasn't just singing the words to the song. He stuck in meaningless sounds and tones that added to the interest of the melody; strange, but I loved it.

I knew I couldn't sing like that, but I knew who could: the girl I'd met in Little Rock.

Meanwhile, Patch continued taking lessons on the clarinet from Beefy Barton. We could hear ourselves getting better and better, and some nights we'd just sit around and improvise for free. November found us in tiny Mansfield, Louisiana, just south of Shreveport.

The next day we headed for New Orleans. By now we knew lots of musicians just like ourselves, guys who loved to play but had a hard time making any money at it. I couldn't wait to get to the big city and meet up with the greats I'd heard about, musicians like Armstrong and Tony Jackson, a piano player Dusty said remembered every tune he'd ever heard.

Billy Joe Blanchett booked a gig for us in Storyville, the red light district.

"That's where all the big-time jazz players hang out," he told us. He didn't say that most of them had gone up north to escape Jim Crow.

"Too many can'ts for them," Beefy Barton said. "Can't walk on the same side of the street as whites, can't kiss your wife in public, can't look at no white woman less'un you lookin' to get lynched, and a thousand more."

We also heard that the booking association, TOBA, really stood for Tough On Black Asses, because the traveling was hard and the pay no good, but we already knew that. Prohibition had ended, so clubs didn't need small bands to draw in customers any longer, and the depression took its toll on peoples' spending money.

I heard all those things and more. "Maybe that's what we ought to do," I said to Patch, "head up north." But we didn't, not just then at any rate.

Storyville felt like Miss Sissy's, only bigger. Cheap cribs – that's what they called the houses of prostitution – flourished, as did the fancier ones up on Basin Street. Our group played in a dance hall near the railroad station. It offered easy access for tourists and lonely salesmen.

We played crowd pleasers like "Cake Walk Babies" and "Tain't Nobody's Bizness." People loved it, clapping their hands and stamping their feet. Now and then we'd each get a chance to play solos. Patch, on his newly learned clarinet, always wowed them, especially when he imitated George Gershwin's *Rhapsody in Blue*.

After hours, some of our boys caroused at black brothels. Patch and I preferred to prowl the French quarter. It was dangerous for us to be seen together, colored and white. Jim Crow said a Negro couldn't even shake hands with a white man, but we found certain places we could meet up and jam.

Here's something I didn't expect. I couldn't get that pretty little blond girl with the big husky voice out of my mind. What I did with Miss June I had ended up doing with Margene. The night of the riot, she hustled me to her tiny apartment just a block off Little Rock's Main Street.

She didn't have much furniture – a chair, a table, and a small icebox from which she pulled a couple of beers. We sat on her bed, which backed up to the open window where a breeze made the curtains flutter. She told me she loved music, that she worked at a local bar with a quartet, and that once in awhile they'd let her sing. "Maybe I could be your vocalist," she said.

"Maybe," I answered, but I think she heard my doubt.

She'd stuck out her lower lip. "I'm twenty-one after all. I guess I can do what I want."

I didn't want to argue. I wanted to put my hands on her pointy little breasts and press my lips to hers like I'd seen Miss June and the others do to the men who came calling. But I just sat there, not saying anything, smelling her sweet scent, only brave enough to take her hand in mine.

She had gotten a really soft look in her eyes and told me not to be shy, that I wasn't her first. Lucky for me, Miss June had taught me what to do next, and though I'd only known Margene just that one night, I realized I wanted to spend the rest of my life with her. Crazy, huh?

The depression hit New Orleans bad. Some of the clubs closed. Bookings dried up. Dusty said we might have to move on, maybe split up.

Patch and I didn't think much of Billy Joe Blanchett. He drank too much and spent most of his time womanizing. One day, he pulled us aside and asked how we'd like to go it on our own. "Bill you as Two Peas in a Pod," he told us.

Patch said, "You know we ain't legal."

Billy Joe brushed his hand in the air. "Could have fooled me."

"Maybe yes. Maybe no," Patch said. "Let us think on it."

"And by the way," Billy Joe said, looking squarely at me. "Your daddy is looking for you."

"So what else is new?" I said.

"Only that he called me. Offered to pay to get you back. What do you think I ought to do?" he said, in his sleazy tone of voice.

I heard this guttural noise come from Patch's throat right before he hauled off and hit Billy Joe square in the nose. Billy Joe went down. Patch spat on him and walked away saying, "Figure it out, scum bum."

We had enough. We wanted to go home, and that was that.

# CHAPTER TWENTY SEVEN

## KANSAS CITY, MISSOURI
## 1934
## KURT

I wired five hundred dollars to Billy Joe Blanchett to pay his fee, and for train tickets home for the boys. The crook. I didn't know until they arrived home that they'd decided to come on their own. They rode the rails and managed to survive on what little they'd saved. I lost my five hundred dollars, but they arrived safe and sound.

I made up my mind to get along with Stern. He must have been shocked when I asked him to join me in the library for a drink before dinner each evening, but he came.

Little by little, we found we could communicate on some level. He told me about the towns they'd played and how danger lurked everywhere, especially for the Negros. I tried to stop comparing him to Frankie and began to accept him for himself, or at least who I thought he was. If he wanted to waste his time playing the piano, so be it. I wouldn't stand in his way, but I couldn't help trying now and then to change his mind.

I was in my office having just finished a difficult operation to remove malignant tumors from the intestines of a very ill patient. My telephone rang. It was my childhood friend, Bill Swartz. Some years ago, he married Harriet Wolfberg, his childhood sweetheart, and they moved to St. Joe, about sixty miles north of Kansas City where he started his own plumbing business.

He told me Harriet had taken suddenly very ill. He was worried and would I mind flying up there that afternoon?

"Are there no good doctors in St Joe?" I joked but his reply was terse.

"No. There aren't. None that I trust. Doctor Foster thinks it may be grippe, but the medicine he prescribed hasn't helped. In fact, she's worse. "

I glanced at *The Journal Post* laying on my desk. There was an article about a famous jazz pianist, someone I'd never heard of, playing in St. Joseph's only nightspot, The Liberty Club.

Perhaps this was providence, a perfect opportunity to get closer to my son.

"All right. Let me see if I can get a plane. I'll let you know."

I called Fairfax Airport. They had a Cessna DC-6 that I liked. It seated four and I could spread out a little. The plane and its pilot, Jimmy Daws, were available, and would be ready to go in an hour. Perfect.

I called Stern. Would he like to go with me? We would be home tomorrow. He said he was afraid to fly. I told him the pilot was excellent. He begged off. Another appointment.

I mentioned the jazz pianist, Jelly Roll Morton. He came alive. I could hear the excitement spring into his voice. He couldn't refuse. I told him to pack some clothes for us both and come with John Charles to pick me up.

I called Bill and told him I was on my way.

# CHAPTER TWENTY EIGHT

## KANSAS CITY, MISSOURI
## 1934
### REBECCA

As soon as I arrived home, John Charles told me Kurt and Stern had flown to St. Joe and planned to spend the night. I decided to call Albert and invite him for dinner. I had long since forgiven him his dalliance in Paris, and even if it wasn't an affair, I no longer cared.

He had felt the bitter sting of anti-Semitism in Europe, especially Germany, so he and his friend returned to the United States and to Kansas City, where he prepared for a new concert. I imagined strenuous rehearsals, so I thought a quiet evening would be a welcome relief.

I dressed carefully, choosing a blue silk gown the exact color of my eyes. It hung loosely to my ankles, yet mysteriously clung to my every curve. I did and redid my hair, first piling it on my head in dark, austere lines and finally, brushing it free to fall in gentle curls below my shoulders. I needed no rouge, my cheeks already flushed with excitement.

With the tip of my little finger, I added a touch of red to my lips and donned a necklace of graduated pearls. I surveyed myself in the full-length mirror, loving what Kurt's money provided. Tonight my friend Albert and I would be alone for the first time in months.

He arrived promptly at seven-thirty. When the doorbell rang, I waved John Charles away and opened the door to a blast of cold air and a swirl of falling snow. Albert shrugged out of his overcoat. He wore a European-cut dark suit, a starched white shirt, and a fashionable blue bow tie.

I thought him more handsome than ever. His hair, the exact color of Stern's, reminded me of our secret. As we strolled into the parlor, arm in arm, we discussed Stern's disappearance.

"I believe Kurt drove him away," I told him, my tone bitter.

"Surely not on purpose," Albert said. "He would never do such a thing."

"That shows how little you know," I said.

John Charles had prepared a tray of whisky and soda, and as I fixed us each a drink, Albert sat at the piano and began to softly play, the first time I'd heard it since Kurt had slammed the lid shut.

"You remind me of the old days," I said.

Albert blushed. Then he said, "You must meet Emil."

"Emil?"

"You'll love him, Rebecca. I never got to tell you about him. We met several years ago in Paris. I had been asked to perform with the symphony. Emil directed the music program at the Sorbonne, but that night, purely by chance, he took the place of the first violinist who had become ill. Oh, I know I'm rambling, but you understand. We hit it off immediately. After the concert, we went to a small restaurant and talked for hours. I think we both knew we had discovered something special."

He stopped playing and reached in his pocket to pull out a picture. "Here we are, standing in front of a *brasserie* on the Left Bank."

I stared down at the photograph: my dear Albert, tall, trim and handsome with his hair flying, and Emil, plump, bald, and grinning. "You both look so happy," I said.

"We are, Rebecca. He's not Jewish, you know, but what does it matter? We've been together a year now, and hardly a disagreement." He stopped, his face beaming.

"If it is ever safe again, you and Kurt must come and visit us in Paris. We had a lovely flat overlooking the Seine."

"I visited Paris on my honeymoon but felt sick most of the time. Then I discovered, much to my surprise, that I carried your son in my belly." I smiled. "I think often of our precious time together in the park."

"Ah yes. The park," he answered, his face coloring. "A cherished childhood moment."

I glowered at my engagement ring. "He knew all along where to find Stern."

Albert covered my hand with his. "He didn't tell you?"

"No. He knew I'd bring him home."

I raised my eyes to Albert's. "Kurt thinks Stern should stop the piano nonsense and go to Harvard."

Albert studied my face. "And what do you think?"

"I know he hates medicine. Still, I would be very proud if he became a lawyer or a concert pianist like you. But play in bars? No. How would that look? Kurt is right."

He nodded, his expression quizzical.

"I have a wonderful idea," he said, breaking the somber mood. "Let's have an evening on the town. Do you think Kurt would mind? First dinner and then The Moonlight Club. Maybe hearing some good jazz will change your mind."

"Yes. Yes," I squealed. "You have another drink while I put on something more suitable. I won't be long."

I ran to my boudoir where I donned a black crepe dress and replaced the pearls with my diamond and emerald necklace. Quickly, I brushed my hair and perched a matching hat with veil on top. I got my mink coat from the hall closet and we went out into the chilly night.

## Beth Lyon Barnett

We dined in a secluded nook at The Savoy, our table set with spotless table linen, shining crystal and polished silver. Waiters dressed in black jackets served us as we sipped frosty martinis and feasted on succulent, buttery lobsters. Time flew by, but when the River Market clock struck eleven, Albert motioned for the check and requested a cab.

There must have been ten clubs in the single block, but I heard The Moonlight Club before I saw it. Sounds of a rich baritone accompanied by the raucous beat of a piano, trumpets, and drums carried their way into the cab via an outdoor speaker. It reminded me of Stern and Ramsey.

Albert handed me from the cab, and we entered a crowded, dimly lit room, the noise assaulting my ears. Smoke snaked up the shafts of lights beamed at the stage.

A stocky young man dressed in a brown suit with a gold chain stretched from one vest pocket to the other, rushed to greet us.

"Maestro," he yelled, clapping Albert on the shoulder. He looked at me, gave an appreciative whistle, and extended a bearish hand. "And how do to you, ma'am."

Albert bent to introduce us over the din. "Meet the owner, my dear. George Dunbar, a friend of longstanding."

I had read frightening things about these kinds of nightclubs. In fact Sam Mayerberg, our Rabbi, had spoken harshly of them, but this man acted nice enough. He seemed quite friendly, taking my arm and steering me to our seats while he and Albert acknowledged friends on the right and the left.

"As soon as you called, I saved you the best table in the house."

I thought I saw Ben Rosen with someone besides his wife, but I lost them in the crowd.

"Now then," George said, motioning us to our table, "you two just have yourselves a fine time. I'll send Thomas," he pointed to a big Negro waiter, "right over to take your orders."

Then he leaned close to my ear and whispered, "I told Whale you were coming and he's as nervous as a cat on a hot tin roof."

"Whale?" I stuttered, and looked at Albert.

"Oh. Did I neglect to mention? Whale Parker is playing here tonight."

George waved at the mountainous piano player and pointed his index finger at the top of my head.

I waved my fingers, delicately.

He saw me and grinned.

George Dunbar bellowed with laughter and hurried off.

"Isn't this wonderful?" Albert said, his voice barely audible. "How about a scotch and soda?"

"Maybe I'd better stick with sherry."

"Don't be silly. You're with me. I'll take care of you." He nodded to the waiter and held up his hand.

I looked back at the table where I thought I'd seen Ben, but his table appeared empty.

"What is it, dear?" Albert asked over the swelling crescendo. "See someone you know?"

I shook my head, disappointed, thinking of the gossip I could have related to Sybil if only I'd caught Ben Rosen with a woman other than Gertrude.

We settled down and I began to get used to the noise. When the music jarred to a stop, I said, "How do you know all these people?"

"Birds of a feather," he answered. "You don't remember, but we went to school with quite a few of them."

Just then, all the lights went out except for one, a round white beam focused on the microphone. With a drum roll and the crowd cheering, Whale Parker entered the circle.

I stared, unable to believe that the enormous man dressed up in a tuxedo, starched white shirt, and black bow tie was the same person who had come to my house to teach my son how to play the piano. Nevertheless, there he stood, grinning and holding up his hands for silence.

"Good evening, ladies and gentlemen," he said, adjusting the squawking mike. "There are some special people in the audience that I'd like to introduce. Right down here in front is our own pride and joy, maestro Albert Rapinsky."

The spotlight swiveled around and fell on our table.

"And seated with him is the beautiful Mrs. Kurt Adler, daughter-in-law of Kansas City founder, Max Adler."

I smiled, embarrassed but pleased. "Let's give them a round of applause." Albert stood and graciously bowed.

The spotlight swung back to the stage. Whale pointed a big black finger. "I see six distinguished people, some of Big Tom's friends who need no introduction."

The spotlight came to rest on a group seated at a round table toward the back."Stand up, gentlemen."

Greeted by loud clapping. they reluctantly stood and waved, smoke swirling from their fat, black cigars. One turned toward me. He bowed slightly, grinned, and raised his glass.

"Jimmy Galeno," I whispered to Albert. "Do you recognize him?"

"I should. He bullied me, and you shook your finger at him and told him that I would be somebody someday, and he wouldn't. Well, you were only half right. Jimmy Galeno is definitely somebody now."

"I've only seen him once or twice since high school," I said, remembering the dinner at the Lazia's. "What does he do?"

"Whatever Tom Pendergast asks," he whispered.

"And now, ladies and gentlemen," Whale said, "Jake, Charlie, and I would like to play a little 'Fizz Water and Marmalade' for y'all after which we're gonna jam with a few fellas down from Chicago."

Cheers, loud shouts, and whistles followed.

"You feel like dancing, come on up. Feel like listening, that's okay too. Just have yo'selves a good time."

He waved, grinned widely and ambled across the stage to his piano, the spotlight following him.

"Hit it, boys," he called, and the contagious beat of their special brand of music issued forth.

We danced, Albert and I, twirling around the crowded dance floor until tall, slender Jimmy Galeno cut in, and I found myself in his arms.

"You grow more beautiful every time I see you, Rebecca," he said, his lips near my ear. He pulled me to him, so close I could feel his heart beat. My face went hot, but I didn't push him away. I felt his breath on my face.

"I see you're still hanging out with the piano player. So where is the good doctor?" he asked.

"St. Joe," I explained, the strong, masculine smell of him making me dizzy. "He and my son are on a mission of mercy."

"Does that explain the finery?" he said, sweeping my necklace and my low cut gown with his half closed eyes.

"Not really," I snapped. "I always dress like this. What's your excuse?" I pointed to the diamonds flashing on his fingers and his cuff links.

The music stopped, and Jimmy returned me to my table. He clapped Albert on the back with a hearty, "Hasn't changed a bit, has she, old man?"

Bowing to me, he found his way back to his friends.

Albert twisted his nose like he smelled something awful. "Stay away from him, Becka," he said. "He's bad medicine."

"Oh, Bertie," I laughed. "I do believe you're jealous."

His eyes followed Jimmy. "Those men he's with? I know who they are: criminals, bookies, racketeers, killers. You've heard of the Mafia?"

"How do you know them?" I asked, more serious now.

"I get around," he said. "Would you like another drink?"

The musicians bouncing around on the stage glanced now and then at the sheet music sprinkled on the floor at their feet, but as each took their turn playing solo, they referred to nothing.

Time sped by, and though it got late, we couldn't tear ourselves away. For now, we sat back and soaked up the easy syncopation and warm harmony.

It must have been close to three in the morning when Albert leaned forward and said, "I hate to do this, but I have rehearsal at ten and I'm not going to be worth a damn."

Outside, we huddled together against the cold wind while a doorman waved for a taxi.

"Well? What do you think? Did you like it?" Albert asked.

"You know I did," I answered, still feeling the throb of the music. "But I can't help wondering."

"What?"

"Why Stern would choose this over the comforts of Oakbridge."

"It gets in your blood," Albert said. "Whale taught Stern basic musical techniques, counterpoint, tempo, stuff like that. What difference does it make if his approach is more informal than Madame du Preé's."

I told him I loved Bach and Brahms.

He called me a musical snob.

I stuck out my tongue at him. "I am not. I enjoyed tonight."

Albert leaned back against the seat. "Then you must try to understand. The difference between jazz and the classics is simply in the length and intensity of the tones."

"Oh. So that's what I heard," I joked.

"And of course, there's the riff, Kansas City's own special brand of jamming," he continued, ignoring me.

"Which is?"

"When one instrument echoes another. Like when Whale played a melody and the trumpet repeated it. It's what kept you jumping all night," he teased.

"How do they memorize so many different songs?" I asked.

"They don't. They are making it up as they go alone. Everybody gets a turn, and when the leader thinks it's enough, he points to his head, everyone plays the melody one more time, and it's over."

The warmth of the cab and the late hour made me sleepy, but the minute we drove across the bridge, I knew something was wrong. A police car sat in front of my door.

# CHAPTER TWENTY NINE

## KANSAS CITY, MISSOURI
## 1934
## JOHN CHARLES

I most never have a hard time sleeping, but this night I kept waking up, staring at the clock and closing my eyes again. Finally, after three in the morning, I got up and peered out my carriage house window. A light snow covered the ground. A police car rumbled over the bridge. It drifted up the drive and stopped by the front door. I knew Doctor Kurt was gone so I pulled on my clothes and went to see what they wanted.

I entered the back door with my key and met Hilda struggling into her robe. "Who could that be at this time of night?" she grumbled.

"Go back to bed," I told her. "I'll get it."

Two police officers stood on the front steps. The yard lights still burned, meaning Miss Rebecca hadn't gotten home yet. "Can I help you?" I asked.

The older of the two asked if the doctor was home. Just then I saw the taxi cross over the bridge and pull up behind the police car. Mr. Rapinsky jumped out.

"Are you Doctor Adler?" one of policemen asked.

"No, no. I'm a friend of Mrs. Adler."

She stepped out and said, "What is it? Has something happened?"

"We're not sure, but the captain thought you ought to know."

"Know what?" Miss Rebecca steadied herself on Mr. Rapinsky's arm.

"Perhaps we should go inside," the younger officer suggested.

She nodded, and I scrambled to turn on the lights.

As Mr. Rapinsky guided Miss Rebecca to a parlor chair, he said, "I'm an old friend of the family. Mrs. Adler and I have been out to dinner." The policeman didn't say nothing so Mr. Rapinsky went on. "Doctor Adler and his son flew to St. Joe today."

The younger officer took off his hat and stuck it under his arm. "That's why we're here. We believe there's a plane down, sir, and we think it might be the doctor's."

My heart skipped a beat. My mistress paled.

"That's not possible," she said. "We've already told you. They're in St. Joe. They are not even due back until this morning. There must be some mistake."

Mr. Rapinsky patted Miss Rebecca's hand. "Calm down, my dear. They're just doing their job."

He turned to the officers. "The doctor and his son planned to stay over, so you see, it can't be them."

The older policeman nodded.

"I hope you're right, but our captain thinks they may have decided to fly home tonight. We haven't been able to verify that, but we called the airport which told us a pilot filed a flight plan from St. Joe to Kansas City at eleven p.m. Someone called the Jackson County Sheriff's office and said they heard a plane that sounded in trouble."

I had a bad feeling.

"We checked before coming here, ma'am." the younger officer said, looking at the floor. "The pilot was the same charter your husband hired to fly him to St. Joe."

"But that doesn't mean . . ."

"Thing is, the flight personnel in St. Joe reported seeing them: the pilot, who they knew, a woman, an older man, and a boy."

"Well, that proves it," Miss Rebecca said, sighing with relief. "There wasn't any woman with them."

"I hope you're right," he said.

Mr. Rapinsky didn't seem eased. "What's being done?" His tone scared me.

"We wanted to check with you, but now, the way things are . . ." he cleared his throat. . . "I think we'll take a run up there for a look-see. Maybe it isn't them after all," he said, his voice trailing off.

I don't know what got into me but I stepped forward and said, "I'd like to go with you, if it's all right."

The sergeant shook his head, but my mistress interrupted. "Yes, John Charles. Do go. I'd feel much better if you were along," so I hurried to get my coat.

I'd never ridden in a police car before. The younger man drove too fast for my likings, especially since the streets were slick. Once we got across the Missouri River, the road narrowed. It wound between Kansas City and St. Joseph through the rolling farmland.

At this time of the morning it snaked along, dark and deserted, lit only occasionally by the headlights of an on-coming car. Sometimes I strained to see the driver, wondering who would be out at this hour. Why weren't they home in bed?

As though reading my mind, the sergeant glanced around from the front seat and said, "Probably some farmer checking on his cows."

We drove slowly, wiping our breath from the windows to stare out into the darkness. I strained my ears to hear the crackly reports on the police radio. A cold north wind bore down, seeping into the car. The heater whirred on full blast.

Time crept by. The eerie shadows of crooked old barns rose on the horizon and then faded into the blackness as we drove past. Once we spotted a deer crossing the road. He paused to stare at us, his eyes aglow. Then, unhurried, he continued on, leaping a barbed wire fence that surrounded the barren field.

Finally the young officer slapped his hands on the steering wheel and pulled off to the side of the road. "I give up," he said. "We've been up and down this road for two hours now and we haven't seen a thing. I think we got bad information."

"I don't know," the sergeant said, yawning. "Sure seems that way."

Though a speck of hope came into my heart, I leaned forward and told them, "I got a feeling. I just got a feeling."

"What if he's right?" the older man murmured. "Let's keep going a little while longer. It'll be light soon, anyway."

We turned around, heading back south. I noticed a dark farmhouse we'd passed before, and I shifted my gaze off to the left. We'd been looking into the shadows for so long that at first, the flicker didn't register in my brain. Then, I saw it again and yelled, "STOP. Did you see that?"

"What? Where?"

"Over yonder. A light."

"Could have been inside the farmhouse."

"No. There it is again." I jumped out of the car and ran in the direction of the flash, the policemen hard on my heels. I could see the battered little plane more than half settled in the farm pond.

Crashing through the crust of ice, I shouted as loud as I could, "We've found you, Doctor Kurt. We're coming."

The landing lights, half under water, continued blinking on and off. We yanked at the cabin door, beating and kicking at the wreckage that held it shut. With a final jerk, we got it open, and I scrambled inside.

It was deathly quiet, the only sound a steady clicking. The sergeant shined his flashlight into the blackness, and what I saw made me gasp in horror: crumpled bodies everywhere. I inched forward, toward someone in a back seat, strangely positioned but alive. He shivered convulsively and opened his eyes. "Massah

Stern?" I cried, forgetting that he went by Pete now. "It's John Charles. We gotcha. You gonna be fine. You all right?"

The young policeman pushed me out of the way "Where do you hurt, son?"

"My head." he groaned, teeth chattering. "I think I banged my head. Thank God you're here. Father? Father?"

"Stay here," the policeman ordered me, "while I see to the others."

I soothed young Stern, feeling for broken bones. Thankfully, I felt none.

The policeman picked his way through rubble to the front of the plane. He found a woman lying between the two front passenger seats in six inches of icy water flipping the landing lights on and off. "It's all right, ma'am," he said softly. "You can stop. We're here. We've found you."

She seemed not to hear him 'cause she kept flicking the switch.

The officer turned his flashlight on the man in the pilot seat. In that small, crushed airplane, I could plainly see the pilot's crumpled body leaning forward, head twisted at a strange angle.

The policeman shined his flashlight into the man's eyes. "He's gone," he said, and turned his light on the last passenger. It was Doctor Kurt. The policeman gagged, crawled past me, and jumped out the door, retching.

I struggled up to be by Doctor Kurt's side.

"Don't you worry none, suh," I said. "We gonna get you out of here."

He moaned. *Praise the Lord*, I thought. He's still alive.

In the dim dawn, I could see his poor body hunched over, his head swollen and cracked like a broken pumpkin. Blood matted his hair and oozed out of jagged cuts in his face. I don't know nothin' about doctorin' but I touched his wrist and felt a fluttery pulse.

"Help me get him out of here," I called, trying to grab him under the arms.

The policeman yelled back at me. "Sarge went back to the car to radio for help and set out flares."

"I can carry him by myself," I yelled, despair clouding my brain.

"You'll kill him for sure. Let him rest where he is until more men arrive."

I heard Massah Stern say, "He's right, John Charles. Better to wait."

"Don't you worry none," I told him. "He's gonna be fine."

I knelt inside that poor, collapsed little plane and prayed, *Lord, please let the doctor live.*

The clicking sound continued, and I reached over and gently removed the woman's fingers from the switch.

She must have finally realized we'd come, because she closed her eyes and slept. I wanted to lift her from the water but dared not. She lay at a strange angle, and I could see the white bones of her leg sticking out through her stockings. Maybe the cold had numbed the pain, but I took off my coat and covered her.

At last I heard the wail of the sirens, and soon I could see the flashing red lights of the ambulances coming through the gray dawn. White uniformed attendants hurried across the frosted fields.

I heard myself crying out until someone slipped an arm over my shoulder and guided me out of the plane.

"It's all right now. We can handle it."

They bandaged Massah Stern's head, and we rode in the ambulance with Doctor Kurt. They let me hold Doctor Kurt's hand, and I fretted over the sound of his labored breathing.

Miss Rebecca and Mr. Rapinsky waited for us at Research Hospital. I heard someone say Doctor Kurt needed blood and hurried to offer mine, but they refused. Negro blood don't mix with white, they said.

Maybe not, but I can't help thinking – *If they'd used my blood, Doctor Kurt might still be alive.*

# CHAPTER THIRTY

## SAINT JOSEPH, MISSOURI
## 1934
## PETE

I still have nightmares about the crash. I told my father I didn't want to go, but when he said Jelly Roll Morton would be playing at a nightclub in St. Joe, I couldn't resist.

I had heard him play with the Red Hot Peppers on tour down south, with guys like Johnny and Baby Dodds. Patch thought Johnny played the best clarinet he'd ever heard and tried to imitate him for weeks. Meanwhile, I dreamed of someday having a band of my own with Baby Dodds as my drummer; he was that good.

But by now, Jelly Roll had hit a bad streak. I heard that he'd even taken to performing with a vaudeville act, but I didn't care. I loved his songs, his music, and his technique. I had to go.

The minute I saw that tiny airplane, I regretted saying yes and tried to back out. Father and Jimmy Daws, the pilot, laughed and shoved my six-foot, one hundred and thirty pound frame into one of the two back seats.

I almost lost it on takeoff, but once in the air, I felt better. As my stomach returned to its normal anatomical position, I began to think maybe this wouldn't be so bad. The hum of the engine somehow comforted me, and I began to enjoy the close up view of the sun dipping behind the clouds in the cold November sky.

Once or twice, my father turned to smile at me. I smiled back. Maybe we both felt a sense of camaraderie that had eluded us in the past.

When we landed, my heart went south, but the wheels touched the ground and we rolled smoothly to a stop. As we disembarked, my father said, "I hope I don't disappoint anyone, but I need to get back to Kansas City in time to do an early a.m. appendectomy."

He looked at the pilot. "Can we plan to head back around eleven?"

Jimmy said he'd check the weather and for us to check with him around ten. My father wrote down the number. Jimmy gave a mini salute and walked to a waiting car, where a chubby-faced woman waited. *Schmaltz gesicht*, Grandpa Stern would have called her. Fat Face.

Father's friend, Bill Swartz, had arranged for a car to pick us up and take us to the hospital. He waited for us in the lobby, looking haggard but glad we'd arrived, and rushed my father to his wife's bedside. I waited in the hall, leaning up against the wall.

A pretty young nurse walked by. Her slim figure and blond, bouncy hair reminded me of Margene. I followed her to the nurse's station and asked for a pencil and a piece of paper. She smiled and handed me a pad with the hospital insignia on it. She watched as I placed my elbows on the desk, drew bars across the page, and began marking in some notes.

"Are you a musician?" she asked.

"Uh huh. I play in a band," I mumbled, distracted.

"How wonderful," she said, all bubbly."I play the violin but I don't have much time for it."

A light came on over a door and she said, "Oops. See what I mean?"

I watched her cute little bottom wiggle as she hurried off, and that made me miss Margene all the more. I doodled a page of full and quarter notes in four/four time and jotted down a quick lyric:

*Lovely girl with golden hair,*
*I turn around and you are there.*
*You're my music, my light, my life anew*
*If it takes me forever I'm coming for you.*

"Hungry?" my father asked, standing over me.

I tore off the pages I'd written, stuffed them in my pocket, and bounced to my feet. "Starving. How's Mrs. Swartz?"

"Fine, fine. It's the flu," my father said.

Mr. Swartz took us to dinner at an old farmhouse with green shutters and a wraparound porch. A cold mist had begun to fall, and the steps glistened with moisture. Inside, a fire crackled in the fireplace. A few diners looked up from their meal and nodded to Mr. Swartz. He waved back and stopped to visit a minute with an elderly couple.

A waiter in a red vest showed us our seats. He returned with a basket of steamy, hot biscuits. "The feature of the day is Mary's meatloaf," he announced, "with mashed potatoes and gravy, though of course, we have other entrées as well. Shall I bring a menu?"

My father looked smitten, and the grin on Mr. Swartz's face widened.

"Meatloaf it is," he exclaimed, "and bring us a bottle of your best red wine." He turned to my father.

"Dinner's on me. My way of apologizing for dragging you up here."

"If it's as good as advertised, apology accepted," my dad said. He buttered a biscuit and popped it into his mouth.

"These are better than Hilda's, but don't tell anyone I said so."

I'd never seem my father like this, relaxed, friendly, and enjoying himself. Was it because I'd grown up or because, for this trip anyway, he'd stepped out of his parenting role? I didn't know, but I liked it.

Our wine came and we clinked glasses. "Cheers," my father said.

"*L'chaim*," answered Mr. Swartz, somewhat prophetically. "To life, my boy. To life."

Dinner hit the spot. My father and Mr. Swartz began to reminisce. They had lived next door to each other as children. They told me about pranks they had pulled on teachers and spoke softly of their first girlfriends.

Eventually the conversation turned to Frankie. Not until then did I know the full story. Mr. Swartz had been with father the day Frankie took sick.

"You," he said, turning to me, "are what I imagine Frankie would have looked like, if he had lived."

My father nodded, his eyes misty.

After dinner, Mr. Swartz went back to the hospital. We caught a cab to The Liberty Club where Jelly Roll Morton, his vocalist, and a juggler had contracted for one night. Twenty bucks got us a table.

I raised my eyebrows when my father ordered a scotch for himself and one for me, and then offered me a cigar.

*What's gotten into him?* I wondered, but pretended to be thrilled. I coughed on my first drag, not letting on that I'd been drinking and smoking for the past two years.

I doubt my father would have been so eager to take me to The Liberty Club had he known more about the star attraction. Just like me, Jelly Roll Morton had gotten his start playing in a whorehouse at the age of fourteen.

When you work in a place like that, sexual terminology becomes a part of your daily language. The lyrics he wrote were full of dirty words, and even his name was nigger talk for the private part of a woman. He'd pimped for girls, gambled, and played his way to fame, but now, at the age of forty-five, things weren't going too well. His black, curly hair had gone gray, and the famous diamond I'd seen in his front tooth was gone. Only his music hadn't changed.

His vocalist, a brown-skinned woman, could have been better, but the two other musicians, Zutty Singleton on drums and Nat Dominique, a trumpet player, complemented the piano. Zutty liked to brush the drums, a sound I admired.

I memorized their technique as they played "Jelly Roll Blues" and "Kansas City Stomp," both foot-tapping tunes. Then they did "Jazz Baby," the song Margene had sung in Little Rock. It brought tears to my eyes.

During intermission, I introduced myself to the man himself and told him I'd traveled with Dusty Miller. We found we had mutual friends, and when he asked what I liked to do best, I told him "compose," then showed him the piece I'd whipped up at the hospital. He took it to the piano and diddled it out before singing what little I'd written. He looked at me as though he was seeing me for the first time.

"How old are you?" He asked.

"Sixteen."

"'This ain't bad. Not bad at all. You needs to finish it," he said, "smooth it out, and it'll be good enough to record."

Radiating excitement, I returned to our table.

"What was that about?" my father asked.

I showed him my song and told him what Jelly Roll said. He glanced at my squiggles and shook his head with a shrug of disgust.

I sighed. Obviously nothing between us had changed.

The vocalist came waltzing over and asked if she could borrow me for a few minutes. She took me outside saying, "You look like you need this," and handed me a rolled cigarette.

"How'd you know?" I asked, grateful. I held it in my lungs as long as I could before slowly letting it out.

"I saw the look on your face," she said, cuddling up to me. "Never you mind, honey. Somebody loves you."

She pressed her big boobs against my chest. We stood there in the cold, huddled together, smoking and smooching.

It must have been pretty good stuff because by the time we went back inside, I felt much better. I went to the men's room, washed my face and stuck a mint in my mouth. My father ordered more drinks, and I sat back to endure the rest of the evening.

I was feeling no pain when he checked his watch and told me to go call Jimmy Daws. When I got back to our table, I told him we could leave.

"Good," he said. "A couple of hours of this racket is all I can take."

At ten thirty, as an icy haze swirled around our heads, we hailed a cab and headed back to the airport. Jimmy Daws had the plane gassed and ready to go. His girlfriend with the fat face stood next to him, dressed in a wool coat and plaid scarf.

"Mind if she comes along?" he asked.

My father shook his head. "Not a bit."

"Once we get off the ground, all this mist," Jimmy said, twirling his finger in the air, "will be gone. We're set."

The woman sat in back with me. I remember she held my hand on takeoff. When we leveled off, I could see the stars. Relieved, I leaned my head back, and fueled with scotch and weed, fell instantly asleep.

I thought I'd dreamt it when Jimmy's girlfriend screamed. The plane gave a violent shudder and nosed down. My stomach plummeted and my head banged the seat in front of me. That's the last thing I remember until I opened my eyes to darkness and silence.

I knew we'd crashed. I heard a cracking noise. I felt a sharp pain and put my hand to my head. It came away wet and sticky. My feet were in water. I remembered seeing the Missouri River when we'd left Kansas City that afternoon. *Had we crashed into the river?* Panicked, I began to shiver.

"Father?" I screamed. "Jimmy?" No answer.

The woman groaned. "You. Boy."

I sighed with relief. I wasn't alone. "Yes."

"Are you hurt?"

"Yes."

"How bad?"

"I don't know. You?"

She moaned. "Not so good."

I could hear her breathing. "Can you move?" she asked.

I made the effort to stand up but my head hit something. "No."

"Try again."

I took a deep breath and leaned forward. The plane lurched to the side.

The woman sobbed.

Cautiously, I sat back in my seat. The plane settled back.

She spoke again, in gasps. "Can . . . you . . . see anything. . . outside?"

"No." Water crept up my ankles.

"Maybe we're in the river," I said.

"I can see a cow," she answered.

I called out again for my father. He didn't answer.

She said, "One of us has to get help."

"If I move, the plane could sink."

"Please . . ."

I shifted my weight and the whole plane listed to the right. More water sloshed inside. "You see?" I cried.

"Okay," she groaned. I felt her body brush my leg as she slid to the floor.

"What are you doing?"

"Gotta get to the front," she groaned. Each movement made the plane rock.

I begged her to stop, but she didn't answer; just kept splattering around in the water. Then, I heard a clicking sound.

*The gas tank? Oh God. Are we going to blow up?* I lost consciousness. When I opened my eyes again, I saw John Charles.

# CHAPTER THIRTY ONE

## KANSAS CITY, MISSOURI
## 1934
### PATCH

Mama had already gone to work when John Charles called. I answered the phone, and he told me the news. There'd been a plane crash. Pete survived but Doctor Kurt was dead.

"Where? When?" I almost fell over with surprise.

But he didn't want to talk. Just said, "You best come quick. Pete's gonna need you now," and hung up.

I grabbed my eye-patch off the table and ran.

Oakbridge buzzed with activity. Cars lined the driveway. I didn't know all the people inside, but I saw Pete's mother in the library talkin' to the police. She looked pale and small.

Susie Mae sent me up the back stairs to Pete's room. I gave him our secret knock and could barely hear him say, "Come in."

I found him lyin' on top of his bed, his head bandaged. Outside, the wind had kicked up, and the branches of the old elm tree scraped against the window. I closed the curtain. Pete stared at the ceiling. I sat on the edge of the bed.

"You okay?" I asked.

"I got a headache. That's all."

"You was lucky," I said.

He looked at me, then closed his eyes.

"I was so scared," he whispered. "The sides crushed in and I could feel the ceiling on my head. There was water inside the plane. I thought we'd drown."

I patted his shoulder. "I understand," I said.

"But other people don't," he cried, rolling on his stomach. "I bet they think since I wasn't hurt bad, I should have gone for help. Even John Charles looks at me funny."

"You just imaginin' it," I said.

*The Kansas City Journal Post* carried the story of the plane accident on the front page. Hundreds of people came to the funeral to pay their respects.

I heard some folks whisper they wanted to see Rabbi Mayerberg 'cause someone had taken a pot shot at him for tryin' to run Boss Pendergast and his boys out of town.

I'd never been in a Jewish church before. No statues or crosses, just real pretty windows, row after row of wooden pews, and squares of light bulbs in the ceilin'.

I stood at the back with John Charles and Susie Mae. She kept dabbin' her eyes with her kerchief until it was soaked clean through. Hilda sat up front with the other white folks, but I could see her shoulders shakin'.

The Rabbi had a long face, fierce eyes, and a head of black hair that shook as he spoke. His boomin' voice carried clear to the back of the room.

"This fine man that we bury today," he said, "personified the courage of great Kansas Citians. Day and night he was at the beck and call of the ill, the rich, the poor, the good, the evil. He and his father before him helped build this town from a simple little landing on the Missouri River into a fine city worth fighting for, and we must continue that fight. We must rid ourselves of the vice that prevails."

Someone down front had a violent coughin' fit that stopped the sermon, and when the Rabbi continued, it was in a different way. He talked about Mrs. Adler, the doctor's dear, loving wife, and his fine son who had been with him in the crash but whom God had spared.

Everyone strained their necks to see Pete. A murmur went through the crowd, and that's when I began to get a whiff of somethin' bad. I heard the word *coward* drift in the air like a filmy, floatin' cottonwood seed. I took heed of it again as we skirted people's graves to get to the burial site next to Mr. Max.

"What's that people are sayin'?" I asked John Charles.

"Hush up there, Ramsey," he said."Just never you mind."

"Can't call him Ramsey no more," Whale Parker said, come to pay his respects. He and Mr. Pete are buildin' quite a followin'."

"I'll try and remember that," John Charles said sourly.

"You two boys still playin' together?" Whale asked me, hisself even bigger than I remembered.

"Why? You got something in mind?"

"Maybe." He pulled me to one side and lowered his voice.

"I know a place be willin' to hire Two Peas in a Pod if'n they'd be interested," he said. "Pays not great but better than nothin'. What do ya say?"

I had been hangin' out at the union blowin' my horn a little bit and waitin' to see what happened with Pete. Maybe this was it.

"I'll ask him?" I answered, thinkin' it might be just the thing to bring him out of his funk.

I waited a few days before I went back to Oakbridge. People still came acallin', and Mrs. Adler kept Hilda busy makin' food and Susie Mae and John Charles servin' drinks and pickin' up plates. The day was clear and cold, and Stern sat at the window. "Whatcha thinkin, ya ole coot?" I asked.

He turned, a sad smile on his face. "About Margene," he said. "I miss her so much. I want to see her."

"You try callin'?"

"She probably doesn't even remember me," he answered.

"Only one way to find out," I said.

After hemmin' and hawin', he finally got on the phone and called information.

"Margene Drew?" he asked.

They'd never heard of her, so he asked for the number of all the Drews in Little Rock. Even I heard the operator laugh before she disconnected him. He sagged and went back to starin' out the window.

"We need to go down there," I said.

"What? Are you kiddin'? After what happened? God, Patch. Don't you remember? They damned near killed us."

"Couldn't be no worse than bein' in a plane crash," I said. "Sides, ain't no other way we're gonna find her" . . . I poked him in the ribs . . . "that is, if you really want to."

His eyes lit up. "You bet I do. I can't get her out of my mind," but then he wilted. "How are we going to do that?"

"Drive. I bet your mama will let you borrow your papa's car if you ask her nice. I don't expect he'll be usin' it anymore."

I wasn't around when he asked her, but it must have been somethin' – him sayin' he could drive good enough – her sayin' he weren't old enough – him sayin' yes he was.

Christmas came and went and then the New Year. I guess they kept discussin', and then one fine spring day, she finally gave in. He said he told her he'd saved up some money and we'd stay with Margene.

"How we gonna do that, ya ole coot? We don't even know where she's at."

"I know, but I had to tell her something, so I told her Margene's folks had a big house and that I'd call her as soon as we got there."

It must have been okay because early the next mornin', he came by my mama's house and tooted the horn. We was off to Arkansas.

# CHAPTER THIRTY TWO

## KANSAS CITY, MISSOURI
## DECEMBER 1935
### REBECCA

Kurt's death hit me hard. Shocked, saddened, and bewildered, I struggled with my emotions through the next days and weeks.

Is anger a part of grieving? Though my life with Kurt had been mundane to say the least, I raged at him for putting his life and that of my son's at risk, and I deeply resented that he'd left me alone with a sixteen-year-old boy.

Stern had it in his head that he should have saved his father's life. Nothing I said could dissuade him. To make matters worse, he wanted to drive the Cadillac to Arkansas and find some girl he'd met.

He seemed so depressed that finally, in the spring, I relented. He and Ramsey would go together.

I never expected him to return with the girl, a thin sickly woman with a seven year old child. He wanted me to let them stay at Oakbridge, but how could I do that? I did offer to pay for the woman's hospital care and a place for her to rent, but Stern became unreasonable and drove off in a huff.

To make matters worse, my father exploded back into my life. Soon after the airplane crash, I wired my father and told him about the death of my husband. I didn't go into the details of Stern's head injury or the woman's broken leg, though she'd recovered enough to go back to St. Joe.

Given that my father and Erika preferred living in their beloved Germany, I didn't expect him to return to Kansas City, but I did think he might come for the funeral.

Instead, he wired back, "Am deeply sorrowed. *Mein Beileid.*" (I had to dig out the German dictionary to learn that meant Condolences.) "Letter to follow."

To my surprise, he wrote that he and Erika wanted to return to the United States. The Nazis frightened them. He had heard tales of violence against Jews, especially naturalized Americans.

He'd been to the U.S. Embassy a number of times trying to get a visa for Erika, who it seemed had never taken the time to become a citizen. Now, the state department appeared unwilling or powerless to help.

To make matters worse, he couldn't retrieve his assets from the Deutsche Bank. When he called to enlist the aid of a Jewish board member, he discovered the man had been relieved of his position and had subsequently disappeared.

"For heaven's sake," I grumbled to Sybil. "What in the world does he expect me to do about it?" I called Ben Rosen.

He invited me to lunch at the bank where he arranged for us to talk in private.

I arrived promptly at one the next afternoon, suitably dressed in a beige suit with white collar and cuffs. As I shrugged out of my mink, he ushered me into a small dining area where we could meet uninterrupted. After offering tea, a Negro waiter served lunch on bone china plates and then withdrew.

"The Jewish situation in Berlin has become quite serious, Rebecca," Ben began. "Your father and his wife are in great danger. Gertrude and I have already helped relatives leave, some moving to Switzerland, others coming here."

He spoke softly, as if not wishing to be overheard, even though we were alone.

"I'll see what I can do, but I'm afraid you can't count on me. With Kurt's estate in probate, do you have money you can send if it becomes necessary?" he asked.

I must explain that when Kurt released my dowry to me, I consulted Ben. He recommended I leave it invested, and I'm sure he thought I did that, but I knew nothing about the stock market, so instead I converted everything to cash until I could learn more. I bought a Matisse painting to cover the  safe I installed in my suite at Oakbridge.  I put it all in there.

 I frowned. "How much do you think he might need?"

"Five thousand, maybe."

That seemed like a lot, but I nodded.

Ben pursed his lips and stared into his teacup.

"I have one other thought," he said at last. "You could certainly use some help from Washington. Do you know anyone there?"

"If you mean because of Max's connections, no. I never got to know any of them well. Perhaps I should have."

"We have a newly elected senator from Missouri, a fella named Harry Truman. How about him?"

"I doubt he'd be much help. I hear his wife is anti-Semitic."

"Doesn't matter. He owes his election to Tom Pendergast. "

"Him I've met."

"Then he's who you must see."

Ben picked up a small silver bell from the table. Its pleasant tinkle brought the return of the Negro waiter along with a cake covered in thick chocolate icing. I graciously refused, pointing to my waistline.

Ben walked me to the elevator and waited until it glided to a stop. He leaned forward and brushed my cheek with his lips.

"Good luck," he said softly. A uniformed operator pulled back the heavy railed door and I stepped inside. The door clanged shut. As the operator pushed the brass handle forward, we floated down, and I watched Ben's legs recede. Outside, John Charles waited for me in the Cadillac sedan.

I already had a plan. Kurt was gone and John Lazia too, shot in a gangland murder right outside his house. I sent flowers and fruit to Maria, and when she wrote me a note of thanks I remembered that she knew the Pendergasts.

I hadn't kept up with the politics of our town but recalled meeting Tom Pendergast and knew his reputation. I called Maria and asked for her help. Could she put me in touch with Kansas City's political leader?

"Perhaps," she said. "He's a very busy man, you know."

"Of course, but I need to speak with him."

"Really?" I knew she was dying to know why.

"Private matter," I whispered.

"I think I can arrange it," she grumbled.

Tom Pendergast held court in a yellow brick building on the corner of 19th and Main not far from where I'd grown up. Everyone called him *The Boss*. Winter had arrived early, bringing with it the kind of sharp cold that turns your cheeks red.

I drove myself to his office and parked out front. I took the elevator to the second floor, joined by two men in dark suits. One tipped his hat. "Nice day," he said, his voice gravelly.

I nodded. He lowered his eyelids and muttered something in Italian. The other man smiled and bobbed his head. My dark hair curled around my face from under my modest felt cloche. I wore a soft blue silk suit with a scarf around my neck and carried a purse. I'd hoped to look stunning, and his gaze assured me I did.

"Going to see the boss?" he asked, a lecherous grin curling his lips.

"Cut it out, Petey, " Gravel Voice said. "His office is straight ahead. Can't miss it."

The elevator lurched to a stop. Ignoring four or five men loitering in the hall, I walked into the office where a fiftyish woman with graying hair and no makeup sat behind a desk, a telephone receiver pressed to her ear. She looked all business, her hair tied back in a bun.

"Good morning," I said, with more confidence than I felt. "I'm Mrs. Kurt Adler. I believe Mrs. Lazia called?"

"Yes. Of course," she answered. "The boss is in a meeting, but I'll tell him you're here."

She entered his office and I could hear his booming voice say, "Sure. Sure. Show her in."

He sat at his desk, a big, jowly man in a white shirt, dark vest, and gold cufflinks. Two men sat in chairs facing the desk. One must have weighed three hundred pounds. The other looked as though he needed a shave. A corner fan stirred up the musty air.

"Good day, Mr. Pendergast," I said, extending my gloved hand. "I'm . . . "

"I know who you are," he boomed. "Kurt Adler's wife. Call me Tom." He smiled, the lines around his gray eyes deepening. "Meet Charlie Carollo and Police Chief Higgins."

They both stood. Carollo heaved himself out of his chair.

"Doc took care of John Lazia," Tom told them.

"Good man, " Carollo huffed. "I was with him the night they gunned him down. Me and his wife barely made it out alive."

"How awful," I gasped, covering my mouth with my fingers.

"Maria's a nice lady." He picked up his hat. "Good to see you, Boss. Nice meeting you, Mrs. Doctor Adler."

"A pleasure, Mr. Carollo," I said.

They all laughed. "Nobody ever calls him that. He's just Charlie The Wop around here."

I blushed and The Wop said, "Now lookie here. We've embarrassed the lady. Come on, Higgins. Let's get out of their hair."

Tom leaned back in his chair. "I read about Doc," he said. "What a terrible thing, the plane crash. Terrible."

He retrieved a cup from his desk and held it up. "Coffee?" he asked. Without waiting for my response, he yelled, "Mabel. Bring Mrs. Adler a cup of coffee."

"With cream," I said.

He smiled, the lines deepening.

"With cream. And you, my dear. How are you doing? This must have come as shock."

I lowered my eyes. "Yes," I said, "but we've managed. I have a son, you know."

Mabel came with my coffee.

"I believe our boys are the same age. Do they know one another?"

"Perhaps," I answered, sipping my coffee. The phone rang. He answered, barked an order, and hung up. He pushed a mechanism on his desk and spoke into a microphone.

"Mabel," he yelled. "Find Pig Gambini and get him over here. " He turned to me. "Now what can I do for you?"

I told him about my father stuck in Berlin, and how my banker, Ben Rosen at the First National, suggested perhaps Senator Truman could help.

He chewed on his black cigar and popped his chair forward.

"Tell me again – how is it you know Maria Lazia?"

I squirmed, a bit uncomfortable. "Well as you know, my husband and John were friends. His wife and I met at the Young Women's Democrat meetings."

He smiled. "Ah yes. My wife belongs to that, but she doesn't go. Too busy with the children."

He frowned, his bushy eyebrows coming together, lower lip protruding.

"I'm sorry to hear about your father. Damn Nazis. Well, that's what we sent Harry up to Washington for, isn't it? To help our constituents?"

I nodded, giving him an appreciative look.

"Let me see what I can do."

"I'd be most grateful," I said.

The office door flew open and in breezed Jimmy Galeno.

"Sorry to interrupt," he said.

"Who let you in?" Pendergast roared. "Can't you see this is a private meeting?"

Jimmy looked at me and his face burst into a wide grin.

"Rebecca," he shouted. "How is it that you always show up in the least expected places?"

"Hello, Jimmy," I said, throaty and reserved.

"Friends?" Big Tom asked.

Jimmy grinned. "I wish."

I rose to leave, placing my coffee cup on Tom's desk.

"I think we've finished our chat. Thank you so much, Tom. You have been most kind."

He came around the desk and helped me on with my coat.

"Give me a few minutes with the boss and I'll buy you another cup of coffee," Jimmy said, his brown eyes gone liquid.

"Another time," I answered. I wanted to be with him in the worst way, but not like this. "Why don't you give me a call?"

"I'll do that."

"Pleasure to see you again, Madam. I'll take care of the matter," Tom said.

I raised my eyes in gratitude. In so doing, I glanced over his shoulder. Jimmy Galeno winked. My heart raced.

Tom Pendergast yelled, "MABEL. Get Truman on the phone."

# CHAPTER THIRTY THREE

## LITTLE ROCK, ARKANSAS
## 1935
### PETE

We found Margene, but not where we'd expected. Even though the 18th Amendment had been repealed, Arkansas remained dry. I figured Margene, with her great voice, must be singing with a band in a private club.

Patch and I drove my father's Cadillac. It had less than a thousand miles on it and still smelled new. I'd never driven it before, but after a few starts and jerks, I got the hang of it. Sitting in this car with its luxurious leather seats made us feel rich and famous.

We both let out "WOW. LOOK AT US" yells as we drove out of town headed for Little Rock. We left early so we could make the trip in one day, because we knew all too well how redneck Arkansas felt about us.

Patch's Aunt Bessie lived in Little Rock, though we hadn't known it the first time we'd been there. She worked as a hotel maid and had finally found a husband, Moses, a porter on the Union Pacific Railroad, She said we could stay with them as long as we didn't make a mess or eat too much.

I remember the first time our band bus drove through Arkansas. The narrow roads curved back and forth across the razorbacks, making me so car sick I threw up into a brown paper bag. Big Lips Hayman held my head and moved me to the back of the bus.

Driving myself seemed to make a difference, even though the road wound through forests of scrubby cedar, budding oak, and maple trees. A March chill caused us to open the windows a crack to breathe in the crispy cold air, while the car's heater kept our feet warm.

We stopped at busy filling stations a few times along the way. No one bothered us. Patch filled the tank so people maybe thought he worked there, while I went inside, bought us some candy, and paid in cash. I called Aunt Bessie from the outside pay phone and got directions. Patch slumped down in the front seat. We weren't taking any chances.

We got to Little Rock late. Uncle Moses greeted us outside the house in his undershirt and waved us into an alley out back.

"Don't want no fancy car parked on the street," he said as he covered my father's Caddy with a big, gray tarp, "else it won't be here in the morning."

Aunt Bessie waited inside, blinds drawn. She hugged Patch and offered us seats in the living room where little doilies sat on end tables and the wood floor gleamed. She'd prepared food for us, chitlins which smelled like rotten eggs, greens in thick bacon grease, and gooey yellow grits.

Patch gulped it all down, but they didn't have to worry about me eating too much. Aunt Bessie asked why we'd come such a long way, and Patch said to look for a friend to sing in our band, which was sort of true.

Moses had to be at work at four in the morning, so he went off to bed. Aunt Bessie gave us blankets and told us to sleep next to the wood stove.

She pointed to the indoor bathroom with pride, and gave us instructions on how to jiggle the chain to get the toilet to flush properly. I knew it made them nervous, having a white boy under their roof. Hopefully we wouldn't stay long.

The next morning I left Patch asleep on the floor, pulled the gray tarp off the Cadillac, and drove downtown. I went into the National Bank of Little Rock, reached in my pocket, and pulled out a ten-dollar bill. I asked the young lady teller to exchange it for nickels.

"Nickels?" she asked, her eyebrows bouncing up.

"Yes, ma'am," I answered, smiling.

She opened her drawer and rummaged around.

"Do you mind waiting a minute or two? I need to get a few more rolls."

Her soft, southern accent reminded me of why I'd come to Little Rock. When she returned, she placed the rolls under the bars and retrieved my ten dollar bill.

"Do you need a bag for them?" she asked with a tilt of her head.

"No, ma'am," I said and stuck the paper-bound rolls in my pockets. My pants sagged dangerously, but I made it out to the car and to the nearest phone booth.

My first call went to Billy Joe Blanchett. He told me Red Nichols and His Five Pennies were in town doing a gig at a private party.

"They might be your best bet. His soloist took sick and he's looking," he said.

I'd met Red, a white guy, on the circuit. He played a hot cornet and improvised well, but I thought he had a bad attitude. Still, I liked his style of jazz: sweet and low.

I ran him down at the Baker House Hotel. When I introduced myself, he said he remembered me.

"You still playing with Dusty Miller?" he asked.

"Naw. We broke up last year."

"It's a good thing. I don't mind jamming with the coloreds but . . . " he let the rest of the sentence dangle. "You looking for a job?" he asked.

"No," I said, uncomfortably brushing the hair out of my eyes. "I'm looking for a girl I once knew. Had a voice like an angel. I thought since your vocalist, Tony Sacco, took sick, she might be singing for you."

"What's her name?"

"Margene. Margene Drew. Blond, blue-eyed. Cute as a button."

"I had a girl come in a couple of days ago. Might a'been her. Called herself Margie. She had a good voice, but she looked like she'd been rode hard and put away wet. Know what I mean? Anyway, Eddie'll be back soon."

He stuck out his hand. "Sorry I can't be more help."

I thanked him and told him maybe we'd meet up again in Kansas City.

"Everyone meets up in Kansas City," he said.

I told Patch what Red Nichols had said about coloreds. He shrugged it off.

"They all likes jammin' with us but no one wants to mix."

Then I told him we might have a lead on Margene. Best we start calling.

There are a lot of Drews in Little Rock. Patch and I split up my nickels, found a couple of phone booths, and began calling. Neither of us had much luck.

"No Margene here."

"Nope."

"You got the wrong number."

We'd all but given up when I saw Patch begin to bounce around and point to the phone. "Margie?" he said. "You know someone named Margie?"

"Give me the phone," I said.

He shook his head.

"Wait a minute," he mouthed. Then into the phone, "You know where she's at? The hospital? What hospital?"

"GIVE ME THE DAMN PHONE," I demanded.

He handed it over.

"This is Pete Adler. I knew her several years ago. I'm wondering if this is the same girl."

There was a long pause and I thought maybe the person on the other end had hung up.

Then she said, "I 'spect so. She told me 'bout how you run off without her."

"Who is this?" I asked.

"Her mother, and if you want to see Margene, she's at St. Vincent's."

She banged down the phone.

# CHAPTER THIRTY FOUR

## KANSAS CITY, MISSOURI
## 1935
### JOHN CHARLES

So much happened right after Doctor Kurt passed. Massah Stern, Pete as we now called him, came home from Little Rock with a woman and her child. Miss Rebecca said they couldn't stay at Oakbridge. We didn't know it then, but her father and his wife were coming to live with us.

One day Miss Rebecca sent me to the train station to fetch them home. I didn't know them very well, having only seen them a few times before they went to Germany.

Fifteen years changes a body, but I managed to recognize Mr. Hans Stern, though he looked pale and thin. Mrs. Stern gathered up their belongings and spryly helped carry them to the car.

Miss Rebecca had a meeting that day. She instructed us what to do and told us she'd be home in time for dinner. Susie Mae and I got them settled in the suite that had once belonged to Doctor Kurt.

I felt painful pangs of sorrow as I placed Mr. Stern's things in the drawers. Susie Mae helped Mrs. Stern unpack, hanging her dresses in the closet and taking wrinkled items downstairs to press. We left them to their own devices until the cocktail hour.

Precisely at six the library bell that connected to the kitchen rang. Mr. Stern, looking some refreshed, asked for a scotch and soda, and Mrs. Stern followed me back to the kitchen and ordered Hilda to prepare her husband's dinner.

Bewildered, Hilda explained that Mrs. Adler had already ordered the evening meal, her father's favorite: roast beef with mashed potatoes and gravy.

"Oh my, no," said Mrs. Stern. "That will never do. His doctors in Germany ban all meat. For tonight, a simple salad will do."

Hilda was flummoxed. Dinner was in the oven, the meat cooking, the potatoes peeled and ready to boil. We didn't go against Miss Rebecca's wishes.

"I best wait for Mrs. Adler," she said.

"That will be quite unnecessary. From now on, I'll do the planning for my husband," Mrs. Stern said.

We three stood staring at one another, all of us seeing a storm brewing.

That evening, when Miss Rebecca came home, she embraced her father and told him she was glad he and Erika were safe. Stern, who'd been invited to dinner, hugged his grandparents and announced loudly that he was starved.

I served dinner as usual except that when it came time for the meat course, I placed a green lettuce and shredded carrot salad before Mr. Stern.

"What's this?" my mistress asked.

"Yes. What is that?" Mr. Stern said.

"Your dinner, of course," his wife answered. "You didn't think I'd let you off just because we've returned to America, did you? I ordered you a proper diet."

"You ordered?" Miss Rebecca said in a voice we all recognized. I tried to back pedal to the kitchen.

"One minute, John Charles. Take that with you," Miss Rebecca said, pointing to Mr. Stern's salad.

Mrs. Stern started to say something, but Miss Rebecca held up her hand.

"We should probably get this straight right now, Erika. This is my house. If there is something you want changed, consult me. Tonight's dinner used to be my father's favorite. I planned it especially to welcome him home, and it will be served exactly as I ordered.

She nodded to me. "Please continue, John Charles."

Stern bowed his head with a tiny grin and looked down. Mrs. Stern spoke to her husband in a language I didn't know, but I guess everyone heard her anger.

"And that will stop too," Miss Rebecca said. "It is just plain rude to speak German when you know we can't understand."

Mrs. Stern started to answer, but Mr. Stern said, "Be quiet, Erika."

Then to my mistress, he said, "You are right on both counts. Please forgive us. Erika only looks out for my best interests."

I brought the meat on a silver platter and set it in front of Mr. Stern. He stood, gripped the knife and steel, and briskly sharpened the blade.

"Feels just like the old days," he said, getting into the rhythm. He sliced the meat that Hilda had cooked to a juicy pink, and Susie Mae passed creamy mashed potatoes and green peas. I came along with thick brown gravy. Mrs. Stern seemed to pick at her food, but when I gathered the plates in preparation for serving the lemon pie, hers was empty.

That night, during the last course, the telephone rang. What with Doctor Kurt now gone, Miss Rebecca didn't allow disturbances during dinner. I went to the pantry and lifted the receiver.

An unfamiliar voice asked to speak to my mistress.

"She is unavailable, suh. May I take a message?"

He said, "Tell her Jimmy called," and the phone went dead.

# CHAPTER THIRTY FIVE

## KANSAS CITY, MISSOURI
## 1935
### REBECCA

For the past several months, I'd been feeling tired and depressed even though I'd finally been able to get Erika and my father out of my house. He whined and lied, saying he didn't have the money to move. He had all the cash he'd been able to stash away in the Swiss banks after Senator Truman intervened.

Finally, they settled into the upscale Bellerive Hotel and began to reacquaint themselves with old friends and rebuild their lives.

Last week Sybil and I met at Wolferman's tearoom downtown. As we sat idly chatting and picking at our Russian salads, Sybil said, "It's hell to get old. Remember when we used to come here and order those turkey sandwiches smothered in mayonnaise? Those days are gone forever. This," she said, shaking a forked piece of lettuce at me, "is God's inhumanity to woman."

I looked at her chunky figure and laughed. "You haven't changed in a decade," I fibbed.

"Liar. I know I've gotten a little *zaftig*." She moved her hands in the shape of an hourglass, "But Herb likes me this way."

I drove myself home that afternoon, went straight to my room, undressed, and stood naked in front of my mirror. Breasts? Not cute little ski slopes like they'd used to be, but not too bad, considering. Waist? Definitely needed some work. Butt? Shapely, but a bit saggy. Exercise would fix that.

I wrapped myself in my silk robe and sat at my dressing table. I squinted at the tiny lines at the corners of my eyes and mouth, the beginnings of wrinkles. My complexion looked muddy and dull. I parted my hair down the middle and gasped. Wiry strands of gray sprouted like weeds in a garden.

I burst into tears, which served to make my eyes red and puffy. "What a mess," I said aloud, and then the humor of it struck me. I began to laugh.

Drying my tears, I picked up the telephone and made an appointment at The House of Beauty for the following Saturday, my thirty fifth birthday. Next I called my hairdresser and told him I needed a new look.

That day a clear blue sky greeted me. Snow had fallen during the night and lay bright and clean on the ground. I ordered juice and coffee.

Sometimes Stern came home to sleep, and I asked Susie Mae, who'd gotten heavy like her mother, if she'd seen him, but she said, "No ma'am, not for a week."

I arrived for my appointment a few minutes late. A pink smocked beautician met me at the door. Why were they always young and pretty? This girl wore perfect eye makeup, brows plucked, lashes long, skin dewy and fresh, and lips painted fire red. Would I look that good by three o'clock? She directed me to a private dressing room where I undressed and put on a fluffy white robe.

I'd opted for the works: mineral bath, a scrub to remove old skin and revitalize the new, hot oils, and massage. Remy, my hairdresser, assured me he could rid me of the dreaded gray sprigs with his daring new color technique.

"I don't know," I said with a skeptical twist of my lips.

"I thought only floozies and ladies of the night dyed their hair."

He promised no one would be able to tell the difference.

"Trust me, madame. You will look gorgeous."

Luncheon was served as I waited for the color to work: cucumber sandwiches on bread without crusts, dainty mints, and hot tea. Finally, Remy rinsed my hair, cut and set it, and put me under the dryer. A manicurist did my fingers and toes, and feeling a tad naughty, I had her use a sizzling red polish.

The makeup artist tweezed my brows and brushed and painted my face, and then sold me all the products I'd need to replicate the look. Remy combed out my hair, dark, silky brown, in lush, beautiful waves. I surveyed the new me in the mirror. I looked wonderful.

I arrived at Harzfeld's at one. Miss Harrison met me as I got off the elevator and ushered me into my customary large, mirrored dressing room with the blue satin slipper chair. Now began the arduous task of selecting my new wardrobe.

As usual, Miss Harrison had already gathered a collection of couturier gowns she knew suited my taste. I bought several new daytime outfits including a stunning Chantal tweed boucle, an unusual bias cut suit by Lelong, and several Chanels.

For this evening's dinner, I bought a Patou evening gown: soft gold lamé, sleeveless of course, low necked with a delicately feminine bodice that clung to my figure. The back of the dress had a deep cowl that fell gently from my shoulders to just above my waist, and the *pièce de résistance*, was a gold velvet cape trimmed in white fox.

Albert had promised to take me to hear Guy Lombardo and his Royal Canadians. I went home to rest. Emil, who I loved dancing with, and Albert were to meet me at eight.

John Charles drove me to the Muehlebach, and I walked through the lobby and down the steps to the Terrace Grill. The maître d'hôtel showed me to our front row table facing the dance floor. I loved this room with its red walls and mirrors placed so that you could see yourself and your partner when you danced. I knew dinner would be perfect because Albert had arranged it. I wanted to order a drink but decided to wait. Albert was never late. Except tonight.

A waiter came to tell me, as graciously as possible, that my hosts had been unavoidably detained.

"They suggest you order and they'll be here as soon as possible."

I fumed.

The waiter understood my agitation. He leaned a little closer.

"Your birthday? Correct? Heartiest congratulations, Mrs. Adler. Mr. Rapinsky has ordered a bottle of champagne. May I bring it now?"

"That would be lovely," I told him, somewhat mollified. Then I glanced around to see who I knew. I spotted one of my friends from the Young Democrats and her balding husband. She smiled, and I lifted my water glass to her. The waiter returned with a silver ice bucket and the champagne. The band members appeared on stage looking handsome in their white jackets, black pants, and bow ties. Their instruments gleamed under the lights.

I felt a soft touch on my shoulder and looked into the magnetic eyes of Jimmy Galeno. "My goodness," I said, "You show up in the most unexpected places."

"What's a lovely lady like you doing all alone?" he asked, his fingers caressing my neck.

I squirmed away.

"It seems I've been temporarily stood up," I answered, enjoying his touch.

"How about I temporarily join you?" he said in a husky voice.

I hated that he could make my heart race like this.

"Don't you have a date?"

He looked in the direction of his table where a gruff, middle aged man with a droopy eyelid and a scar down his cheek sat with two women. One wore an outrageously low cut red dress and sparkling jewelry while the other swished a large, colorful ostrich fan. Both smoked cigarettes in long holders and sipped on Manhattans.

"Naw. She'll understand. Lucky can handle 'em both. May I?" He pulled out a chair and sat.

"So, finally," he said, and I knew what he meant.

Albert had warned me, but I discounted Albert's concerns, especially now, as Jimmy leaned close, his luscious aftershave scent filling my nostrils.

"You are very beautiful this evening, Rebecca. I can't believe anyone would stand you up."

"I haven't been stood up, as you call it. My companion has been delayed."

"The queer?" he laughed, running his fingers through his hair.

"Jimmy. Please. Don't be uncouth. He's a brilliant pianist."

"Okay. Okay. You're right. Anyway, I'm here on business, my sweet. Strictly business. "

"Who is that?" I asked, eyeing the man at the table.

"Name's Lucky Luciano. He's from New York."

The band began to play. "Sweetest music this side of heaven," Guy Lombardo said into the microphone. The music and the champagne melted me.

"Let's dance," I said.

Jimmy smiled and stood, pulling out my chair and taking me in his arms. The band leader nodded to him. We smiled at each other and danced as the vocalist sang "*Boo Hoo, You've got me crying for you.*"

When the music changed – became slower and more intimate – his hand slipped to my lower back and he pressed my body into his. I heard the words to the song: "*We can share it all beneath a ceiling of blue. We'll spend a heavenly day here where the whispering waters play.*"

I cuddled into him and felt his manhood as he held me tight. I drifted in his arms as if there was no one else in the room. We moved together until the music stopped, and even then, we clung to each other. It was a magical moment which ended abruptly as Albert appeared.

"Excuse me," he said as he tapped Jimmy's shoulder. "My dance now."

Jimmy held me for a fraction more, his eyes locked on mine, and then released me with a bow and returned to his table.

"I'm so sorry, Becka," Albert said as he ushered me back to our table. "Our stupid car broke down. Never mind. We're here now, just in time to rescue you from that hoodlum. I see you got your champagne. Isn't the music divine? Emil is dying to dance with you. You must be starving."

We sat and Albert ordered dinner. "Who are those floozies Galeno is with?" he asked,"

"The man is someone named Luciano," I answered. "Visiting from New York."

Albert's eyes popped open. "Oh my God, no. Not Lucky Luciano?"

"What about him?" I asked.

"Don't you ever read the papers, my dear? He's that big time racketeer that everyone is talking about."

"I guess I should pay more attention," I said, wondering why I should care. After all, prohibition had ended a couple of years ago.

The band returned from their break, and Mr. Lombardo declared the next number, "Jazz Baby," sung by his new vocalist. I didn't catch her name but she came on stage in a slinky, sequined gown that sparkled when she moved.

My daddy was a rag-time trombone player.
My mammy was a rag-time cabaret-er
They met one day at a tango tea.
There was a syncopated wedding
And then came me.

Albert leaned close and spoke so no one else could hear.

"That song reminds me of us."

"Really?" I leaned back, confused.

"Dance, wedding, Stern," he whispered, smiling. "I guess you're my Jazz Baby."

"You are an inveterate romantic," I laughed.

The rest of the evening went by quickly. Emil spun me around the dance floor, and the three of us drank more champagne. Jimmy danced with the lady in red, and Lucky Luciano grinned lecherously as he patted the bottoms of passing waitresses.

When they got up to go, Jimmy stopped by our table, bent over, and whispered in my ear. The band played on and I followed him out with my eyes.

"What did he say?" Albert asked.

"Nothing," I answered with a shake of my head.

At midnight, the band played "Auld Lang Syne." Albert reached into his pocket and withdrew a small jewelry box. "I decided you should have this and Emil agrees. An heirloom," he said, "to celebrate your birthday."

"Oh, Bertie," I exclaimed, unwrapping the Jaccard's Jewelry box. "You shouldn't have. I popped open the lid and gasped. Isn't this your mother's engagement ring?"

He nodded.

"I want you to have it." He slipped it out of the box and placed it on the third finger of my right hand.

"When the time is right, maybe you'll give it to Stern. There's a little note inside."

I turned my hand this way and that, the diamond ring sparkling under the lights from the crystal chandeliers.

"It's more beautiful than I remember. Shall I read the note now?"

"No, no. It can wait."

That night as I got ready for bed, I took off the ring and placed it in its box. I looked at the note, a simply drawn heart with the word Stern inside. It was Albert's deeply touching way of claiming his son.

I opened the safe behind the Matisse and put the box inside. Then, I slipped between my satin sheets, my thoughts flitting to what Jimmy had whispered in my ear. "Later."

# CHAPTER THIRTY SIX

## KANSAS CITY, MISSOURI
## 1935
### PATCH

We both knew Margene had been usin' but I when saw her lyin' there in that hospital bed, so sick and pale, my heart broke. She promised Pete she'd quit if we'd just get her out of there. Still, she had a lot of explainin' to do.

We brought her back with us, her and her kid that her mama had been lookin' after. Pete's mother said they couldn't stay at Oakbridge, not that I blame her. Margene was a mess and her little girl, seven year old Darlene, was a handful. Pete found an apartment on Gillham Road, and the three of them moved in together along with an old upright piano he bought off a down'n outer.

Whale got us a job at The Crystal Jungle, a nightclub owned by Virgil Aronson just down the street from the jumpingest place in K.C, Club Reno. Both allowed a fella to shoot craps, get drunk, and get laid, all in one place.

We played from eight 'til closin, just the two of us and a drummer named Four Eyes who specialized in brushes. He called himself a percussionist, but we liked him anyways. We set up close to the bar and provided background music until Margene joined us. Then, a miracle happened.

At first Pete brought her along to get her out a bit, but after awhile, she began to sing with us, and let me tell you, when she did that all hell broke loose. That woman had a voice, deep and throaty. She made a song come alive. Pete played and she sang, and it felt like they melded together.

Soon The Jungle started fillin' up. Night after night she'd open her mouth and the room would go still. Everyone thought she was singin' directly to them. She bought herself some sexy clothes and got her hair done, all blond and pretty. She'd lean against the piano or move behind Pete, the spotlight on them both, and she'd make love to everyone in that room.

She had a way of caressin' words like, "Let me call you sweetheart, I'm in love with you," . . . or. . . "Ev'ry body loves a baby, that's why I'm in love with you," and "If you were the only girl in the world," only she substituted "boy" for "girl." All the while, Four Eyes helped her with breath breaks and Pete would be teasin' the piano keys to optimize her voice.

Club Reno wanted to hire us, but Virgil knew a good thing when he saw it. He offered Pete and Margene enough money so's they couldn't leave. Me and Four Eyes was a different story, but Pete said he had to pay us extra too or no one would stay.

People started buyin' us drinks so's we'd play requests, and Margene and Pete smiled, took a sip or two, and set the glasses down. I guess Margene had learned her lesson, but while Four Eyes and I quenched our thirst a little now and then, Pete began throwin' down straight shots.

Sometimes they'd bring Darlene in with them. Pretty little thing, blond like her mama, but before long, Pete and Margene realized they couldn't raise a child this way. One weekend they drove the girl back to Little Rock and left her with Margene's mama. It's not what they wanted, but you do the best you can.

A week or two later, I came in early to collect my pay. While Pete didn't mind gettin' paid with checks, they were hard for me to cash. Virgil's door stood open, and I heard him talkin' to Jimmy

Galeno, one of the Mafia bosses who'd taken over after John Lazia's murder. I sat down to wait 'til he left.

"To what do I owe this honor?" Virgil grunted.

Jimmy pulled up a chair and had a seat. My ears perked up when I heard him say, "Your new singer is quite a looker. Where'd you find her?"

"Came with the group. Sit down. Have a cigar."

Galeno reached into a humidor and pull out a large black stogie. He fetched a small tool out of his pocket and cut off a piece of one end and put a hole in the other. He saw me watchin' and winked at me. He took out a silver lighter and stuck the cigar in his mouth. I could smell the smoke as it came through the door.

"How's business?" he asked Virgil.

"Doin' okay; well, not as well as I'd like, but okay."

"Remember, Virg," Galeno said, kinda sugary sweet, "a couple a years ago, when we cut the deal about this place, we said we didn't want any problems. You said you'd buy it and turn it into a first class nightclub if the boss'd keep the town wide open and we'd guarantee no raids. Remember that? So now, what've we got? I'll tell you what. There isn't any place in the U.S.A. where you can find it any better. We got classy places like yours here in K.C. Right?"

"Right," Virgil said. "So?"

Galeno's voice sobered.

"We've kept our end of the bargain, haven't we, Virgie? We never let anyone bother you, have we? Not the cops or the Feds? Except that one time when you first opened?"

"Yes, well, what's all this got to do with The Jungle?" Virgil said, whiny like.

"We're starting to have our doubts about The Crystal Jungle."

Virgil sat straight up. "What do you mean?" he cried in a shrill voice.

Galeno didn't move, not his head or nothin'.

"My guys tell me you been holding out on me. Would you do that, Virgie? 'Cause if I thought you would, we just might have to do something about that."

Virgil began to fidget. "I don't know what you're talking about, Jimmy. We've been friends for a long time. I'd never hold out on you. I've always paid you your ten percent, just like we said at the beginning."

"I understand this blond broad you got singing has doubled your business, Virgie. You counting that in?" Galeno asked, a crooked smile crossing his face.

"Of course I am. What you think?"

"'Cause it sure doesn't seem to add up that way. See, I'm hearing these funny rumors, so us being good friends and all, I thought I'd take a chance on coming here and talking to you about it, face to face."

"Well sure . . ."

"Which reminds me, the boss said to tell you he was a little worried also because The Jungle didn't seem to be selling as much liquor in the last few months as before, especially since you got yourself a headliner. Thought maybe you wouldn't mind looking into that."

Galeno stood up and walked toward the desk. He stuck out his hand and said, "You say there's nothing going on, I believe you. We just gotta be sure you keep it that way."

"Yeah, yeah, right," Virgil said. He shook Galeno's hand. "I get it."

"No hard feelings, Virgie?"

"No hard feelings."

As Galeno sauntered out of the office, he winked at me again and two-fingered me a sawbuck. When he stopped to talk to one of the tall blond waitresses, I looked outside and saw Big Benny Blando, Galeno's bodyguard, leanin' against Galeno's black car. Everyone knew not to mess with Big Benny. He ate way too much and it showed, and he packed a lot of hardware and that showed too.

After Galeno left, Virgil came barrelin' out of his office.

"Son of a bitch. Did you hear that?" he yelled. "I bet he's paying off that God damn bartender. One of these days, he'll go to God damn hell."

He called for his manager. "Howard? Get in here."

A bouncer lookin' type with big muscles and a small head showed up pronto.

"Double your order of whisky, understand? I don't care what it costs. Do it. And Howard, when Galeno's boys come in, give 'em something extra. Tell them it's from me. Got it?"

I decided to vamoose. I picked up my pay and my horn and hightailed it over to Club Reno hopin' to do a little jammin' with Benny Goodman's band. It was early yet and I didn't expect anyone to be there, but Benny and Fletcher Henderson, who did arrangin' now and then, were reworkin' some melodies that caught my ear. They sounded a lot like the stuff Pete did, jazzy but sweet. Goodman picked up his clarinet and started to play "One O'clock Jump." I grabbed up my horn and joined him.

He grinned real big and offered me a job. Funny how things turn out.

# CHAPTER THIRTY SEVEN

## LITTLE ROCK, ARKANSAS
## 1937
### MARGENE

I was twenty-one years old that night in Little Rock when I first laid eyes on Pete Adler. I'd lost my job, I had no boyfriend, and the authorities took my baby away from me and gave her to my mother to raise. It was the drugs but I couldn't seem to quit. I had no money. My rent was due. I hadn't eaten all day. I needed a fix. I'd gone to listen to the jazz band because I knew some musicians used drugs too.

But then I heard Pete play. He made music magic, especially considering the rinky-dink piano he had to use. When they started to play "Jazz Baby," I jumped up and grabbed the mike. I loved that song.

Little Rock is a small town, and I saw faces in the crowd that I recognized, boys I'd gone to school with. They yelled and hooted and danced as I sang. Everyone seemed to have a real good time. Pete bounced around on his stool tapping his feet on the pedals, his beautiful hair shining in the spotlight's glare. That's when someone started a ruckus. The way I remember it, one of the boys I knew called out, "Margene. How come you're singing with a bunch of niggers? That redhead a nigger too?"

At first I kept on singing, hoping that the crowd would pay him no mind, but then things got nasty, so I grabbed the young piano player and lit out. My place, more like a room than an apartment, was just a few blocks away. Dodging the cops, we sprinted up three flights of stairs, threw open the door, rushed in, and slammed out the rest of the world.

Safe, we fell into each other's arms, laughing, and stayed there until morning. He gave me a couple of reds that he said the band used to keep up their energy. They saw me through 'til morning when I hoped I could get some real stuff. I didn't tell him I'd been married and had a baby, and he didn't tell me he was just sixteen.

That night he made love to me, tenderly, slowly bringing me to the verge of fulfillment and then teasing me with sweet, little touches and kisses. He used his tongue in unimaginable ways. I'd never felt his kind of passion before. The next morning we showered together and then dressed and went down the street to a cafe. He bought breakfast and watched, grinning, as I downed a big plate of bacon and eggs, grits, toast, and coffee. His eyes, the bluest I'd ever seen, devoured me. I knew I could get clean for him and I told him so. "Don't worry," he told me. "We'll work on it together."

When he looked at his watch, his expression changed from tenderness to alarm. He jumped up, threw money on the table, grabbed my hand, and ran out into the street. "The bus," he shouted. "We've got to get to the bus."

I knew in my head I couldn't travel through the south with a Negro band, but I hated the band leader and sobbed when they drove away. Then I went back to my life.

I struggled along for three more years. Then, the day before Pete and Patch found me, I couldn't take it anymore. I tried to kill myself.

The boys signed me out of the hospital. We went and got Darlene and they drove me, sick and shaking, to Kansas City. It was the beginning of my new life.

I had never known people could be so kind. Pete found us an apartment and stayed with me. He held my head when I threw up and covered me in blankets when I got the chills. It took a couple of weeks, but somehow I made it.

Meanwhile, dear, kind Patch got his mother to look after Darlene. When Bertha had to work, Susie Mae or John Charles took over. My daughter grew to love them, and when the time came for us to take her back to her grandmother, she cried and begged to stay, but of course that would never have worked.

Pete's mother was another story. I didn't blame her for not taking us in. I must have looked ghastly, and her own parents arrived from Germany and came to live with her. But when it became apparent that Pete and I would work together and later wanted to get married, Rebecca refused to meet me. Even that didn't bother me, particularly at first. I looked horrible, thin and pale. After I recovered Pete took me shopping, and I got my hair done like Joan Crawford. I listened over and over again to records by a newcomer, Billie Holliday, and tried to sound like her. She liked to sing with just a piano accompanying her. I did too.

We had been playing at The Jungle for a year. The club filled up every night. People seemed to love us. Pete and I practiced at home – songs like:

*There's a rainbow 'round my shoulder*
*And a sky of blue above*
*Oh the sun shines bright, the world's all right*
*'Cause I'm in love.*
*There's a rainbow 'round my shoulder*
*And it fits me like a glove*
*Let it blow and storm, I'll be warm*
*'Cause I'm in love.*

Then we'd bring it out and the crowd would cheer.

Pete began to talk about a wedding, so I decided to swallow my pride and ask Mrs. Adler to lunch. Given her already visible animosity, I admit she surprised me a little when she took my call.

"Yes. I think it is time we get to know one another," she said. "Come here for lunch on Tuesday."

Maybe I made a mistake, meeting on her turf, but I'd only been to Oakbridge once before, the night we arrived in Kansas City from Little Rock. Pete had driven across the bridge, up the driveway, and stopped the car at the front door. I was barely conscious and my daughter slept in Patch's arms. Pete ran up the steps and banged on the front door. It was late, ten o'clock, but the houseman opened the door. "Hurry, John Charles. My friend's pretty sick. Help us get her in the house."

"Who is it, John Charles?" Mrs. Adler called.

"It's Massah Stern, Miss Rebecca. Come with Patch and a sick friend."

I raised my head to peer out of the window and saw an apparition, a woman in a long white dressing gown standing in the doorway. She spoke a few words to Pete. With raised voice, he said, "She needs to rest. We have nowhere else to go."

She floated down the steps and peered into the car where I lay, dirty and shivering.

"Ramsey," she said. "I didn't know you had a child."

"She aint mine, ma'am. She's Margene's." He nodded toward me, huddled in the back seat.

"I see," the ghostly figure said, peering at me. She turned and walked back up the steps and I heard her say, "She can't stay here."

"Please, Mother. Where can we go?"

"She needs to be in a hospital, Stern. Take her to General."

Furious, Pete got back in the car, slammed the door, and mashed his foot on the accelerator.

"My mama will put her up for tonight," Patch whispered. "We'll find her another place tomorrow."

Pete nodded.

I barely remember being carried into a tiny house that smelled of cooked hambone. They laid me on a bed and put Darlene next to me. I drifted off. I had not been back to Oakbridge since.

Tuesday arrived, a cloudless, warm May day. I dressed carefully in a blue cotton frock with a white bib front and puffy long sleeves. I tied the bow carefully at my waist and pinned my small, straw hat on my head. I drove the car over the old oak bridge, smelling the lovely scent of lilacs that lined the driveway.

John Charles opened the door and ushered me through the spacious front hall. A full length portrait of a breathtakingly beautiful girl hung on the wall of the winding staircase. She wore a beaded bridal gown and a diamond and emerald necklace.

"Miss Rebecca," John Charles said when he saw me staring at it. He led me past the parlor and the book-lined library onto the screened-in porch. The table had been set with sterling and crystal. A pitcher of lemonade sat nearby.

A large, old elm tree in back had begun to leaf out, getting ready to shade the porch. The water in the wading pool sparkled, and the gardens danced with daffodils and tulips.

I didn't expect Pete's mother to be so beautiful or so young. She allowed me to enjoy the view for a few minutes before making her appearance. She wore a navy and white striped knit sweater and a navy skirt.

She leaned against the doorway looking at me, her hands in her skirt pockets. I glanced down at my blue cotton dress and felt cheap.

"So," she said, "We finally meet. You are a trifle older than I expected."

"And you a trifle younger," I managed to reply.

She smiled and poured herself a glass of lemonade. "Would you like some, or would you prefer something stronger?"

"Lemonade is fine."

She sat at the table across from me.

"Tell me about yourself. Stern says you sing quite well."

"It's just that he makes me sound good," I said. "He's a wonderful pianist."

"Yes, he is. I had hoped he would make something of himself." She frowned, and I saw the tiny age lines that she'd carefully hidden with makeup.

"He has made something of himself. He plays and writes beautiful music."

"Yes – he and his little band. There are four of you, aren't there?"

I swallowed. "Actually, our drummer is sick and Patch is out of town, so right now there's just Pete and I."

"Me," she corrected, her eyebrows going up.

"Me," I echoed, embarrassed. "Anyway, we've decided to become an independent group – Peas in a Pod," I babbled on. "We'll perform in nightclubs, here and in places like Chicago and New York. We think it will work for us."

She took a tiny bite of salad. "I see. You plan to travel?"

I smiled, happy she'd asked.

"We have a gig coming up next week in Chicago at the Swingland Cafe." I dug into my salad. "It's a very classy place."

"Classy," she said. "I see. How nice."

Our eyes met, hers cold and appraising. A heavy silence filled the air, and I, sitting there grinning at her like I didn't have the sense God gave a gopher, slowly allowed the smile to fade from my lips.

"Well. Let's get down to brass tacks, shall we? Do you and Stern plan to marry?"

I pursed my lips. "We've talked about it."

"You must know, it is totally impossible."

My chin went up. "And why is that?"

She inhaled deeply.

"Surely you can see for yourself, my dear." She waved her glass at me. "You are not our kind of people."

I set my fork down, straightened my spine, and leaned toward her.

"And just what is 'your kind of people,' Rebecca?"

"Mrs. Adler," she corrected. "Jewish, for one thing. I don't guess you are that, are you?"

"No, but Pete says that doesn't matter."

"He's wrong. It matters a great deal. Besides, you come from an entirely different culture than he does. You would never fit in."

Later I thought of a million things I should have said, but at the time I felt the blood rush to my face and my heart pound with indignation.

"But . . . " I stammered.

"I think we've said all we need to say to one another," she said. "I have a meeting of the hospital board this afternoon, so you'll have to excuse me. Please feel free to stay as long as you like. Enjoy your lunch. Good day."

She swept past me, leaving me tongue-tied and mortified.

I sat motionless, tears welling up in my eyes. John Charles came to clear the plates. He looked at me and said, "Never you mind, Miss Margene." He handed me one of the lacey napkins.

"Here now. You just dry your eyes. Go on. After you feel better, I'll show you out."

On the drive home, a taxi leaped out in front of my car and I almost hit him. That only added to my distress. I crept into our tiny apartment and threw myself on the bed, not even bothering to remove my straw hat. I lay there for the longest time wondering if she was right, and if it might not be better if I got on a train and went back to Little Rock. Pete had gone up to Chicago to sign the contract and wouldn't be home until Thursday. By then, I could be packed and long gone.

I wandered aimlessly around the apartment trying to think. I picked up a book, but the words blurred through my tears. I stared out the window at the garbage-filled alley below. The beautiful day had turned cloudy and cold. I thought about eating something, but the chicken in the icebox only reminded me of the disastrous lunch.

I missed Patch something fierce. He and Pete decided Patch should go with Benny Goodman and check out Hollywood. Might be some recording opportunities there, but Patch said the band wasn't doing so well.

Then they did a run at the Palomar Ballroom in L.A. Patch said Goodman's music caught on and it sounded just like Pete's. We should come on out. But we had no money and few prospects. I shook my head.

If I went to The Jungle, I could get a drink and maybe a hit. Finally, I went to bed and fell into a fitful sleep. When I awoke, angry bile filled my throat. *We'll show her,* I thought, *Pete and me.*

The day after they got home, the three of us went out drinking. I told Pete I was tired of living in sin. He'd had a few too many when he said, "So why don't we go get married?"

Patch said, "I know a preacher in Oklahoma."

Laughing and hooting, the three of us hopped in the car and drove to Oklahoma. We found Patch's preacher, woke him up, and just like that, Pete and I were married.

# CHAPTER THIRTY EIGHT

## KANSAS CITY, MISSOURI
## 1937

### REBECCA

Since Kurt's death I have continued to establish myself as a community leader. I give generously of my time and money to the Nelson Gallery, serve on its board of directors, and am even became a docent. I have opened my beautiful home and gardens to benefits and fundraisers, having discovered that I have a talent for planning parties and directing florists and caterers. And in recognition of my deceased husband's deep commitments, I have kept my position on the hospital board.

My private life is my own. I keep it separate from my social life because Jimmy Galeno is not exactly the type of person with whom I wish to be seen. He is, after all, a member of the Mafia, a *don*, I think they call him. He comes here for dinner once a week, and we have been sleeping together for the past couple of years. That arrangement suits us perfectly.

I think men get more handsome as they age. Jimmy exemplifies that. His swarthy good looks and thick, ebony hair give him a sturdy, distinctive look. I admit his masculinity makes my heart flutter. I prefer the tough, burly type to – say Albert – whom I adore, but in a much different way.

Jimmy commands respect. He doesn't have to raise his voice, though I have heard him do so, which terrifies and excites me, in a quivery sort of way. I love how he moves his body, the way in which he lights his cigarette or leans on one foot in the doorway, arms crossed. He dominates me completely, understands me totally, and ignores my tantrums. I love that about him and hate it, too.

He makes up for all the years of unsatisfying sex I endured with Kurt. His touch is firm but gentle, his voice soft but commanding, and he wrings from me every drop of pulsating, vibrating pleasure that for years I've kept locked inside. At last, I know the meaning of fulfillment.

Meanwhile, Albert is the perfect escort. He shepherds me to dinners and parties. His schedule is heavy, but he and Emil manage to get home every week or so, and always for the big affairs.

Sybil constantly asks me why I don't marry him. I tell her it's because he hasn't asked me. If I told her the truth, she would be shocked and disgusted, yet she never questions his relationship with Emil, I guess because he, too, is an artist.

I haven't spoken to Stern in days. Albert told me he gave Stern money for a small apartment.

"Why did you do that?" I asked, shocked and angry.

"The poor woman needed a place to recuperate, Rebecca."

"But she's obviously trash," I said.

"That's unkind and not like you," he answered. "It's true that she's older than Stern and has had a hard time of it, but she sings like a lark, and he loves her. They deserve a chance."

Stern and his floozy, Margene, traveled upon occasion to engagements in New York and Chicago, but today he called me, and what he told me came as a bolt from the blue. Benny Goodman has asked that he and Margene join him for a performance at Carnegie Hall.

Stunned, I cried, "Benny Goodman, the band leader? Why would he ask you?"

"Because we're good," he replied.

"But Stern. You must be mistaken. Bands like Benny Goodman's don't play at Carnegie Hall."

"I guess they do," he said. "He's booked on the sixteenth of January. He wants me to do an arrangement or two, and he wants Margene to sing."

"Really?"

He snuffed and coughed into the phone. "We're not the only ones. He's asked others also."

"And Margene?" I couldn't help myself. "Why her? She's such a little nothing."

He slammed the phone down in my ear.

I called Albert. "How can that be?" I asked.

"She's actually quite good, and Pete is extremely gifted."

"Don't call him that," I exploded.

"You might as well get used to it, Becka. That's his name now."

"But why Benny Goodman? And at the most famous concert hall in the world?"

"Why not?" he said in a flip manner. Then more seriously, he asked, "Have you heard the girl sing?"

"No, and I don't want to."

"You really should, you know. You might be surprised."

The Christmas season arrived. Sybil called to tell me she and Herbert would pick me up for our crowd's annual Christmas party at The Rendezvous. Everyone would be there, the Rosens and Kate Roth who invited her neighbor Tim Bash, the sheriff, and of course, Kurt's partner Sam and his wife Serena. As usual, Albert and Emil spent the holidays abroad.

We arrived after nine, and the place hummed. The rooms glowed with lighted Christmas trees and poinsettias on every table. Ben Rosen checked our mink coats, and we gathered around our table. Just as the waiter brought our drinks, my son seated himself at the piano. A young man with slick, black hair and dark framed thick glasses arranged himself at the drums. They both looked nice with white shirts, red vests, and black bow ties.

He began by playing a familiar Gershwin number. His beautiful, long fingers, exactly like Albert's, danced across the keyboard. The crowd smiled and continued talking. Someone brought him a tall drink, and I saw him play with one hand while he held the glass to his lips with the other. He spotted me and his eyes opened wide with surprise. Then he smiled and raised his glass to me.

Herbert leaned across the table. "Wonderful, isn't he? We all knew he would be."

"Benny Goodman thinks so too," I informed him. "He's asked my son to arrange songs for his concert at Carnegie Hall." I didn't mention Margene.

"By golly. That's terrific," Sam Seligson said.

Stern switched melodies, the lights dimmed, and then Margene walked out. She took her place by the piano.

"I should have known you'd do this," I said to Sybil, the eternal prankster. Flushed with anger, I picked up my purse and prepared to leave.

"Sit down, Becka," she demanded. "Don't make a scene."

Margene stepped into the spotlight wearing a low-cut green satin gown. She stood with her back against the piano, her position relaxed, elbows comfortably resting on the wood. She had finger-waved her hair.

*Come to me, my melancholy baby,*
*Cuddle up and don't be blue;*

she began singing,

*All your fears are foolish fancy, may be.*
*You know, dear, that I am strong for you.*

Her voice resonated deep and throaty, inviting, and daring.

*Ev'ry cloud must have a silver lining,*
*Wait until the sun shines through,*
*Smile, my honey dear, while I kiss away each tear,*
*Or else I shall be melancholy too.*

Little by little, people stopped talking, and a hush fell over the room.

"Wow," Ben whispered. "She's something."

*Birds in the trees, whispering breeze,*
*Should not fail to lull you into peaceful dreams.*
*So tell me why, sadly you sigh,*
*Sitting at the window when the pale moon beams. You shouldn't*
*grieve, try and believe*
*Life is always sunshine when the heart beats true;*
*Be of good cheer, smile thro' your tears,*
*When you're sad it makes me feel the same as you.*

I couldn't believe my eyes. I'm no expert, but she shocked even me. Far from being the frumpy, small town girl I remembered, she seemed confident and charming.

When she finished, the room erupted in wild applause. She bowed and threw kisses and then honored Stern with an extended hand. He smiled and waved. Sybil leaned over and murmured, "Aren't they cute?"

Stern played a jazzy number I didn't recognize and later learned he'd written. His hands pounded the keys, his foot bounced on the floor. Then with Stern accompanying him, the drummer did a solo that brought people to their feet. It had been a long time since I'd heard my son play, and I must say my heart filled with pride.

Margene sang two or three more songs, all in her husky, sexy voice. Loud applause followed each, and cries for more continued until, at last, the lights came up. Hand in hand, the two walked to our table and greeted me and my friends.

"Mother Adler," Margene said. "How nice to see you."

I could have slapped her. Mother Adler indeed.

Stern kissed me and then took her around the table, introducing her to all my friends. When he came to the Seligsohns, Sam jumped up and hugged him.

"I've known this boy since he was born," he said to Margene. "I hope he's treating you well. If not, you come see me." Everyone laughed. "Won't you join us?"

They sat for awhile, and a waiter brought them each a drink. Margene ordered a soda, trying to impress me no doubt, but Stern got scotch with a beer chaser. He laughed louder and talked more shrilly than anyone at the table, but no one else seemed to notice. We stayed until well past midnight, dining, drinking, and listening to my son, Margene, and the odd-looking little drummer. "She's really quite lovely," Sybil said on the way home. "We should make more of an effort to get to know her."

"We'll see," I said.

As Herbert navigated the car across our bridge, I saw a car sitting in the dark shadows of the oak trees, lights out. I stepped from Herbert's Buick, and Sybil couldn't resist one final shot.

"Good night, *Mother Adler*," she said, giggling. I thanked them with a sour grunt, wondering to myself why I put up with her. Then I went inside to wait for Jimmy.

# CHAPTER THIRTY NINE

## NEW YORK, NEW YORK
## 1938
### ALBERT

The Goodman concert at Carnegie Hall changed the public's perception of jazz. What Pete had been doing all along, combining the different styles of music, Goodman accomplished in just one concert. That night we heard jazz, swing, blues, and classics, some done with riffs and improvisations. What a thrill. Emil and I wouldn't have missed it.

When we plied Rebecca with promises of shopping at Bergdorf's and dinner at Twenty One, she decided to join us. How we got out of town with all her luggage intact, I'll never know.

At the last minute, Pete threw a monkey wrench into the whole thing. Patch already knew Goodman and even occasionally played trumpet in his band, but Four Eyes still played backup for Pete and Margene.

A percussionist could make or break a vocalist. He needed to be familiar with her style so that he could signal key changes, set up breaks, and figure out when she needed to take a breath. Margene was used to singing with Four Eyes, and Pete wanted him to back her when she sang at Carnegie Hall.

Phone calls flew back and forth, and for awhile it looked like Margene might get cancelled. Goodman had a vocalist of his own, a cute little Texas-born girl named Martha Tilton. He figured he didn't need to add to his troubles by having to switch drummers and vocalists mid-stream.

Maybe I stuck my nose in where it didn't belong, but I called Benny on the sly. We good Jewish boys knew how to stick together. I promised him tickets and dinner to my next concert, and he finally gave in.

"Okay," he said, "but for just her one number."

What a glorious night it was. Everyone dressed for the occasion, ladies in their beautiful gowns and gentlemen in top hats and tails. The hall vibrated with excitement. I'd pulled some strings and obtained fabulous seats. Rebecca sat between Emil and me, looking her usual gorgeous self.

The show made musical history. To everyone's surprise, even the snobbiest New Yorkers loved it. Fletcher Henderson did the arranging for Benny, and when the band played the number Pete had arranged, his hot-swing style went over quite well.

People who'd never heard Negro and white musicians playing together saw an integrated group of musicians: Count Basie, guitarist Freddie Green, trumpeters Harry James and Patch Patterson, all on the same stage together.

When Margene's turn came, I held my breath. The on-stage drummer changed places with Four Eyes. She sang her heart out and brought loud acclaim from the audience with her deep, throaty Billie Holiday style, even though Martha Tilton wowed them at the end.

People were tapping and clapping, grinning and cheering, and when Goodman, Harry James, and saxophonist Babe Russin played the finale, "Sing, Sing, Sing," backed by drummer Gene Krupa, the crowd went crazy.

We had dinner reservations at Twenty One after the show. Patch didn't come, saying he wanted to go out with the band. Maybe so, or perhaps he thought the club, like so many others, had a "No Negroes" policy.

New York columnist Lou Harvey sat at a table across from us at dinner. He waved at me, but when he spotted Becka, he hurried over to introduce himself. He pulled up a chair and chatted with her, his eyes devouring her, until his party arrived.

He seemed reluctant to leave, ultimately returning to his own table, but not before he promised Becka he'd write about Pete and Margene in his paper. After that, when people stopped by to visit with him, he quickly sent them over to meet the "new up 'n comers."

Becka glowed every time someone asked Pete or Margene for an autograph, and she even seemed to make an effort to get along with Margene. They sat across from each other, and after Lou Harvey left I saw the two of them talking. I tried to listen in but heard nothing important until Becka leaned forward and said, "Can I ask a favor of you, my dear?"

Margene glance sideways at Pete but said, "Of course."

Becka cleared her throat. "Would you *please* stop calling me Mother Adler?"

Margene blushed. "What shall I call you then?"

"Rebecca will do nicely."

Margene gave her a charming smile and said, "Rebecca it is."

It looked to me like the beginning of an alliance, if not a friendship.

Pete was in a state of euphoria. At the time, it looked like excitement. Now, I'm not so sure. Emil picked out a delicious wine, but Pete downed a few scotches even before we ordered. When he signaled for his fourth drink, Margene rested her hand lightly on his arm. He shrugged her off. Even I suggested he go easy, but he laughed and said not to worry. I noticed with surprise that he had a tooth missing.

"Somebody hit you?" I joked.

"You should see the other guy," Pete answered, wiping his nose with his sleeve. Margene handed him her hanky.

We ordered salads made tableside, and steaks which Pete barely touched. I suggested crepes for dessert, but Margene pointed to Pete's drooping eyes and said she'd better take him back to the hotel. Emil helped her load him into a cab, and we all returned to our suites at The Plaza Hotel. What had been an exquisite evening had ended in a rather dismal manner.

Emil's experience with musicians and artists at the Sorbonne caused him to recognize warning signs in Pete long before I did: the highs and lows, the runny nose, the missing teeth. He urged me to talk to Rebecca, but I hesitated, not sure what to say. Emil kept insisting, so when we got back to Kansas City, I called Rebecca.

I asked her to meet me for dinner at the Continental Hotel. Emil and I belonged to the KCAC, the Kansas City Athletic Club, located on the top floor of the hotel. After New York and the long airplane ride home, I desperately needed a good workout, a long, lovely swim, and a relaxing massage. Maybe that would prepare me for my talk with Becka.

I saw her sitting in the dining room next to the window, sipping a martini and staring outside at the gently falling snow. She was casually dressed in a handsome gray wool suit, her short, dark hair done in soft waves.

I stood and stared at her for a time, admiring her grace and youthful beauty. How could she have a grown son? She saw me and beckoned. I adjusted my ascot and walked down the steps to join her. I bent to kiss her cheek. She breathed deeply of my cologne and I of her delicious scent.

I ordered a martini for each of us. She gushed about New York and thanked me again and again for persuading her to go. Then she told me of her many upcoming engagements; luncheon dates, gallery tours, and meetings at Menorah, the hospital built by the town's wealthy Jews.

Dinner arrived and we ate heartily, unembarrassed to chew and talk at the same time. After all, she is my oldest and dearest friend. We have a child together. We have no secrets. So why am I finding it so hard to talk to her?

"Becka," I began, but she stopped me.

"Please, Bertie. Not tonight. We are having such a lovely time."

I took her hand in mine. "But we must talk about this, my dear. Our son needs us."

She lowered her head and sat silent, her hands folded in her lap. Finally, she whispered, "I know."

"He's in big trouble. He drinks way too much, and I think maybe he's gotten himself involved with drugs."

"Did Margene do this to him?" she asked. "She's a drug addict, isn't she? Didn't he bring her home? Didn't she convince him to marry her? Aren't they both addicts? What am I supposed to do about all that?"

I scowled at her.

"Stop it, Rebecca. It's not Margene. She doesn't drink or do drugs anymore."

"And just how do you know that?"

"I have contacts. The thing is, Pete – our son – needs you. He should be in treatment somewhere, Menninger's in Topeka perhaps. He needs help with his addiction. He won't do it if I tell him, but maybe if you do, or you and Margene together . . . "

I drew in a breath, "You have enough money, and you must do this for him."

She hunched her shoulders. "Isn't Menninger's for people who are mentally ill?"

"Yes, but . . ."

"Why won't a hospital do just as well?

"Any place is better than nothing."

She curled her lip. "So? You have money too, and you're his father. Why don't you do it?"

"And take the chance that someone might find out?" I asked. "Is that what you really want?"

She sat back in her chair and rolled her eyes. "No. Of course not. "

"Then you'll try? You'll call him and try?"

She exhaled. "I guess," she said. "But what if he won't listen to me? Then what?"

"We'll cross that bridge when we come to it."

We ordered crème de menthes to settle our stomachs and leaned back in our chairs to make a plan. I would call Menninger's, and she would have a talk with our son and try to convince him to admit himself somewhere.

"Maybe it would be better to ask Margene for help. Perhaps she could persuade him better than you."

"Don't be ridiculous. You think he won't listen to his mother?"

I raised my eyebrows.

"I'll do it," she said, and swallowed the rest of her drink in one big gulp.

So it was arranged. Rebecca would make the call as soon as Pete and Margene returned from New York. I had a big concert of my own coming up, one with the symphony in San Francisco, so I spent hours at the piano, but I made time to get hold of Whale Parker.

I told him I needed to talk with him about a very confidential matter and could he meet me someplace discrete. He suggested his church on Harrison. He still played there on Sundays, and after the service, it would be empty.

"What time should I be there?" I asked.

"Well, let's see. We usually start around ten."

"And what time do you end?"

"Usually around one."

I should have paid more attention to his use of the word, "usually."

I arrived at twelve thirty to find the church still crowded. People milled about. Someone made an announcement from the podium. Children ran up and down the aisles. The service had not even begun. I decided to leave, but a heavy colored lady in a dressy pink outfit with a big, matching hat took my arm and escorted me to a seat.

"Now you just sit right there, honey. You'll be fine."

A child in a fancy white dress sat next to me. Someone had done up her hair in three chunky braids. One, perched on top of her head, seemed to leaned frontward and flop toward her face. I smiled at her. She glared at me. I waited. Someone else made an announcement. The lady in pink came by, bent down, and said I shouldn't worry. Wouldn't be too long now.

I admit I'm not much of a church or temple goer. I try to find time to attend my faith's high holiday services. I love the Kol Nidre sung on Yom Kippur. Some years ago, I couldn't resist going to B'nai Jehudah to hear Rabbi Mayerberg rant about Tom Pendergast and his political machine, but then the board of directors made him stop, and that ended my interest in his sermons. Still, Friday night services began at seven thirty and ended at nine. Everyone sat still except the children who squirmed and counted the ceiling lights. There was no jumping up and down. People rose when the name of God was invoked or for the Kaddish, when we mourn the dead. That's it.

This had a whole different feel.

At last  the preacher walked up to the podium high above the congregation, and I thought the service got under way. I couldn't be sure because people frequently interrupted the minister, stood up, waved their hands to the ceiling, shouted, hummed, and nodded their heads.

Normally, I don't feel ill at ease among colored folks. I've played with many Negro musicians and knew them to be respectful to me and one another. Today, however, I fidgeted uncomfortably. I wished I hadn't come. Whale's idea of a private place didn't match mine.

The musician had gotten noticeably heavier. The bench groaned when he sat at the organ, an old wood instrument with buttons and knobs, and two worn foot pedals. Somehow he wrung amazingly beautiful music from that pile of junk.

Two dozen members of the choir dressed in maroon robes sang soulful melodies and songs with more zest and swing than I'd heard at the Benny Goodman concert. I closed my eyes and listened to the words.

*I'm living on the mountain, underneath a cloudless sky.*
*I'm drinking at the fountain that never shall run dry.*
*Oh Yes. I'm feasting on the manna from a bountiful supply,*
*For I am dwelling in Beulah Land.*

I found it a deeply moving and enjoyable experience.

The choir changed hymns and suddenly, the little girl sitting next to me poked me and said, "You 'sposed to stand up when they sing this song." I jumped to my feet and after that did what she did. When in Rome . . .

It was four o'clock before the church finally emptied out. Whale came to get me. We went down front and sat in the first pew. He apologized.

"You're just never quite sure when these things start," he said.

"To tell the truth, it's my first time in a Baptist church, let alone a Negro one," I said, "and I wouldn't have missed it for the world. Tell me. Where is Beulah Land?"

"Heaven, suh. Beulah Land is Heaven."

"Such beautiful songs."

"It's where my kind of music all began, ain't it?" Whale said, grinning. "Now, what can I do for you?"

"I've come about Pete." I told him my concerns involving Pete's use of liquor and drugs.

"Alls I know is I got him that job at The Jungle Club," he said, "and he did right well, him and Patch. Then the girl joined them, and I thought they had it made. He and Margene been doin' gigs all over town, some paid, some not."

"Did you know he was using drugs and smoking marijuana?"

"Everyone smokes marijuana, Albert."

"I don't," I said.

"You should. Makes your music sound better, not that it don't sound great already."

"And what about the girl. Does she do it too?"

"Nah. Never seen her so much as take a puff. She learned her lesson, but that don't mean it ain't easy to get – that and junk too." He stood up and stretched.

"Are we still bein' confidential?" he asked.

"Yes. Of course."

The lights in the church had been turned off, and the January darkness came on fast. There was a little lamp sitting on the organ. It had a green glass shade, and when he turned it on, it cast an eerie shadow around the sanctuary.

He lowered himself to the bench and said, "I seen his mama once or twice at The Jungle shooting craps."

"So?" I didn't see anything strange about that. Everyone went downtown now and gambled. Even Emil and me.

"She's goes there with the big cheese."

I jerked my head up. "Pendergast?"

"Naw. Not him. His hit man, Galeno."

I frowned and rubbed my forehead in disappointment. Ever since our youth, she'd carried a torch for that guy.

"So what are you thinking?"

He hemmed and hawed, breathing deep, not wanting to look at me. Finally he said, "I think she's the one you oughta be worried about."

"Yeah. Well . . . " I didn't know what to say.

He slapped the organ, and it shook like it was going to fall apart.

"Oh well," he said, his voice brightening. "I probably shouldn't have said anything. Why don't you come with me tonight? I'll play my gig, and then we'll find some boys and do a little jammin'. Take your mind off your troubles. What do you say?"

I shook my head. "You go ahead."

I thanked him for talking to me and told him I wouldn't say a word to Rebecca. I asked him to keep his eyes open for Pete.

"Let me know if you hear anything."

We shook on it. As I walked out into the brisk night air, I wondered if I ought to look up Jimmy Galeno.

# CHAPTER FORTY

## CHICAGO, ILLINOIS
## 1938
### MARGENE

Pete upchucked in the elevator of our hotel the night of the Benny Goodman concert. Then he had a horrible nosebleed, and I didn't think I'd ever get it to stop. After using reams of toilet paper and all the towels in the bathroom, I somehow got him cleaned up and into bed, unconscious and snoring.

By then, I had blood in my hair and smelled of vomit. I showered and turned on the water as hot as I could stand it. I meant to wash my hair and body. Instead, I slid down the wall of the shower, covered my face with my hands, and sobbed. What had happened to us?

Not so long ago, I'd been in exactly the same mess. I remember opening my brain-fogged eyes in that dingy little hospital for the indigent and seeing a vision. I imagined a haloed, redheaded Jesus. He lifted me out of my bed and carried all eighty pounds of me to a horseless carriage with a Negro chauffeur.

In my stupor, I managed to beg for my little Darlene. My next memory was of her curled up next to me in the backseat of the car, my head in the redhead's lap.

They told me later, as gently as possible, that my mother had no problem getting rid of me, but that she fought for Darlene.

"Look at her," she cried. "She can't take care of herself, let alone a seven-year-old child."

But Pete loved me and would have done anything to make me happy, so he promised we would take care of her. Only later did he discover that he couldn't do that.

My memories of the next weeks are dim: blankets to stop the shivering, ice to cool me down, blinds pulled against the nightmares, spoonfuls of soup. Little by little, he nursed me back to health. He found an old upright piano that would hold its pitch, and he and Patch hauled it up to our tiny apartment: just a living room, a tiny kitchen with a nook that looked out on a brick wall, and a bath with a leaky toilet. When we pulled the Murphy bed down, there was no place to sit except the piano bench and a rickety old chair.

Sometimes he would play familiar tunes, soft, sad little songs like "Mood Indigo." Other times, he would sing out loud, "*Daisy, Daisy, give me you answer true,*" and substitute my name for hers. He'd wake me with Gershwin and put me to sleep with Chopin.

Slowly I got better, and before long he suggested I join him in singing songs I already knew.

Who would not love such a man?

Then one day, He played "Jazz Baby," and I sang it just like I'd remembered. *"Cause I'm a Jazz Baby. I wanna be jazzin' all the time,"* and I knew that's what I was meant to do. I begged Pete to take me with him, to let me sing at the club.

"I get the heebie-jeebies sitting around this apartment all day. Please," I begged. "No giggle water, no grass. Just water and a little soda once in awhile."

Darlene came to live with us. We dropped her off at Bertha's on our way to the club at night and picked her up early the next morning, a crazy schedule that didn't work for anyone except Pete. He came to love her. There were a few good times, the Barnum and Bailey Circus, picnics in the park, ice cream for breakfast, but she hated being cooped up indoors while we slept.

I locked the door and hid the key, but one afternoon, she found it and sneaked outside to play. We woke to someone banging on our door, Officer O'Toole, the local beat policeman, with Darlene sobbing in his arms. She had chased her ball into the street and had almost been hit by a car. Unless we took better care of her, he would have to call the authorities. We took Darlene to Bertha's house. Pete and I needed to talk.

He sat on the rickety chair and asked, "Who's her father?" He'd never seemed to care before.

"A boy I knew in high school, just a one night stand. We'd been to a party, got drunk, and boom, baby on the way."

"Did he offer to marry you?"

"I never told him," I confessed. "I didn't know myself until my mother commented on my weight. Good Christian folks, her and my Dad. They went to church every Sunday, said grace over dinner, read the Bible like a novel at night. We talked about adoption, but Mama wouldn't hear of it. My father patted my hand and told me we'd work it out.

"I had Darlene and went back to school. But everyone at school ridiculed me, and the church kicked us out. When my dad died, I dropped out of school, got a nickel and dime job at a dry cleaning place, and began to sing at the local honky-tonk. I even hoofed a little. They liked me. That's where I learned about liquor and grass. I earned enough to get my own apartment. My mother took care of the baby while I worked. Right about then, you and Dusty Miller came to town."

I stood up and went to the icebox to get a soda. "Want one?" I asked.

He shook his head.

"I'd never met anyone like you before. After that night, I would have gone anywhere with you, but you know what happened. I thought you felt the same way as I did, but months went by and I didn't hear from you. I struggled to spend time with

Darlene and help my mother pay her bills. Someone at work taught me about drugs.

"The first time I used heroin, it was in a warehouse. I'd gone there with some friends, young and dumb as me. Their boyfriends knew where to get the stuff. It scared me to death but one of them showed me how to make the vein in my arm pop up and gave me my first shot. I thought my head would explode, but then I lay back and drifted into the most beautiful world I'd ever seen. All my troubles melted away. Everyone loved me, you most of all. I never wanted to leave that place, and after that, I never did. I spent every penny on drugs and gave myself shots in the privacy of my own apartment."

I paused and stared off into space. "Until I couldn't pay the rent anymore. Then I had nowhere to go, nothing to eat, nobody who cared. I wanted to die."

Pete sighed heavily and said, "I know the feeling."

I looked up in surprise. "You do?"

"That's why I brought you back here. . . and just so you know, I never stopped thinking about you."

"Oh, Pete," I said and went to hug him. I sat on his lap, and the rickety chair gave way tumbling us onto the floor. We untangled ourselves and laughed.

He bent to me, his kiss as sweet as that first time way back in Little Rock. He ran his long fingers lightly up and down my breasts, my nipples, my neck. Oblivious to the dust bunnies curled in the corners, he drew pretend circles around my eyes and then touched my ears and lifted my chin to meet his lips. His eyes filled with longing, he raised my sweater over my head. No longer laughing, I helped him remove my clothes and then his.

He offered to lower the Murphy bed, but, afraid to break the mood, I shook my head and touched his bare skin with my tongue in places he'd taught me felt good. At that moment I wanted nothing more than to please him. He moaned. His eyelids fluttered, and he moved over my body.

I raised my hips to meet him, but his mouth sought me out, and before long I moaned, begging him to stop. At long last, we merged together, the sweetest union ever, and I knew no matter what, I'd never stop loving him.

The next day we drove Darlene to Little Rock and dropped her off with my mother. She was glad to have her back and agreed we could see her whenever we wished. We made plans for the following summer and drove away knowing we'd done the right thing.

After the Goodman concert, we were much in demand, thanks in part to Pete's mother who made a good impression on the guy from *The New York Times*. He ran a story and said he planned to run another.

A *Times* staffer called.

"Are you from Kansas City?" he wanted to know.

"Yes."

"What is your husband's full name?"

"Pete Adler."

"No middle initial?" he asked.

That sort of threw me but then I said, "Oh, I see what you mean. Actually, Pete is his middle name. Stern Peter Adler is his full name, but I don't know whether he'd want you to print that. He hasn't used his first name for a long time."

"Got it," the man said. "Does he arrange for anyone else?"

"Not yet," I said.

"Do you have anything in the works?" he asked.

"Sorry. That's confidential."

Pete stood in the bedroom doorway. He looked awful –sleep creases on his face, red eyelids and a prickly red beard. "Who was that?"

"Just a reporter from *The New York Times*," I bragged.

"Oh Pete. We've been getting calls all morning. Go shower and shave. We'll have breakfast, and then you can get busy."

Pete was still in the bathroom when the next call came through. Long distance from Chicago.

"This is Jules Stein," the voice said. "Is Mr. Adler in?"

"Jules Stein?" I repeated, my ears perking up. Must be a practical joke. "Sorry," I said. "He's indisposed."

"Is this Mrs. Adler?"

"Yes, but if you're kidding, I'm going to hang up."

He laughed. "No kidding, Margene. I just talked to a friend of mine at *The New York Times*. I'm calling to inquire if Pete Adler could possibly be the son of my good friend who died several years ago; Kurt Adler of Kansas City."

I was stunned. "Why yes. He is."

"Wonderful," the man said. "I think I have good news for you both, but I want to visit with you in person. Could I interest you in coming to Chicago? I'll pay."

"No, no. That's not necessary. I mean, yes. We can come. We have an engagement there day after tomorrow."

"Do you know who I am?"

I could hear the smile in his voice.

"Unless I'm wrong, you're Mister Music Corporation of America," I said, hardly able to believe my own words.

"Correct. You're not only a beautiful vocalist, you're a smart young lady too. Come by my office Thursday at noon. I'd love to take you and Pete to lunch. We have much to talk about. By the way, I heard Pete's mother attended the concert. Is she still in New York?"

"No. She went back to Kansas City today."

"Too bad. I always liked her. Well, never mind. See you Thursday."

I was sitting on the bed, still stunned, when Pete came out of the bathroom. He took one look at me and said, "Why are you looking like that?"

"You're not going to believe it." I told him about Jules Stein.

"I remember him," my husband said. "He was a doctor. Eyes or something. Used to come by our house now and then. Played in a band. Sax maybe. My dad didn't think much of him."

"Well he owns Music Corporation of America now. You know, MCA? The big booking agency? And he wants to see us."

"What for?"

"I don't know, but maybe it's something to do with being our agent."

"MarGENE," Pete groused. "Don't get excited. We're small potatoes to a guy like him."

That got my hackles up, and I jumped up to face him. "Maybe not," I said. "He even called me a vocalist."

Pete laughed. "Okay. Okay. We'll have lunch with him. Can't hurt anything. That's for sure. Now scram so I can get dressed."

"Hurry up," I called as I left him and went downstairs to the dining room.

I smiled to myself, thinking how much better he looked, all dewy fresh and clean. He'd put on a clean white shirt but still had the towel wrapped around his slender waist. What made him think he could hide the needle marks in his arms from me? After all, wasn't I an old pro? But maybe now he'd quit the drinking and the drugs.

I hopped on the elevator, full of excitement and hope. *Today, we'll start anew,* I told myself. *We're really going places.*

# CHAPTER FORTY ONE

## KANSAS CITY, MISSOURI
## 1938
### PETE

We walked into Jules Stein's office at MCA. He jumped to his feet and hurried around the desk to greet me. "Stern Adler. Yes sir, my boy. I'd know you anywhere. Still the same red hair. Come in. Come in."

He looked vaguely familiar. "I remember you although it has been a long time. Meet my wife, Margene."

Smiling, she modestly extended her hand, but he pushed it away and instead, pulled her to him for a hug. She beamed.

"You're as pretty as they say, my dear." he said. "Have a seat. Coffee? Tea?"

We shook our heads.

"I'm sorry I couldn't make it to New York. Goodman is a client of mine, but we're moving our offices to Hollywood, so I had to stay here and supervise. I would have loved to see your mother. Tell me about her."

"She's well," I answered.

"My friend, Lou Harvey at the *Times*, told me how beautiful she is."

He leaned back in his chair. "I always envied your father, you know. I must tell you, I felt awful when I heard he'd died, Stern. . .

or is it Pete now? Someone said you were on the plane, too. It must have been a terrible experience."

I stopped breathing and let the words hang in the air. Finally, I said, "I think about it every day."

Margene turned toward me, a surprised look on her face.

"You do?"

"There are some things you can never get out of your head," I told her.

"Of course," Jules said, popping his chair upright. "But come on, you two. You must be starved. I'm going to take you to the best German restaurant in Chicago."

I wanted to get out of there all right, but not for food. I desperately needed a hit.

Dark, heavy wood chairs and tables filled the space. No curtains hung at the windows because the place needed all the light it could get. A big coat of arms hung on the wall, a black eagle with red claws painted on a gold shield. The owner greeted our host affectionately and showed us to our table.

A pitcher of black beer magically appeared, and the waitress, dressed in a skirt and blouse costume, filled each stein to the brim. Jules ordered schnitzel smothered in mushroom gravy, crusted potatoes, and spiced carrots. It brought back memories of my childhood when Hilda prepared such dishes. I guzzled the beer, fending off the shakes, and Jules began to tell us a little about himself.

"At your age," he said, "I played in a band, saxophone mostly, though I loved my violin. Sometimes we traveled by train, and of course I took the opportunity to talk with all the attractive women on their way to and from their colleges in the East. One girl in particular caught my attention. She and her companion were on their way home to Kansas City from Smith College. I admit to being instantly smitten. She promised to come hear me play at the Muehlebach.

"A week later, the girl showed up with her parents and yours in tow. None of them thought me an appropriate suitor." He laughed.

"Nevertheless, Kurt Adler and I found we had common ground. I told him I financed my attendance at Rush Medical College by playing in the band, and he invited me out to Oakbridge for dinner."

I urgently needed something stronger than beer.

"You were just a little tyke, but I remember that flaming red hair. Your mother overwhelmed me with her beauty and graciousness, while your father tried to talk me into becoming a surgeon like himself instead of an ophthalmologist."

I excused myself for the restroom. Sweat poured off my brow. I relieved myself, washed my hands and face with cold water, and got back to our table just as our lunch arrived. The waitress immediately returned with another pitcher of beer, my mug having long since been emptied. She asked if she could get us anything else.

Whisky, I thought, but didn't ask.

I picked up my fork. Jules dug in and continued talking. "I had only met your mother at the Muehlebach that one time, and at first I thought she was Kurt's daughter, but that evening at dinner she wanted to know all about my band, and if I'd stopped practicing medicine. I told her I might."

"So did you?" I asked.

He laughed and said, "Simply put, I had a lot more fun playing in a band than taking care of people's eyes. I remember your mother poking your father and saying something like, 'See? He can do both.' I had no idea what she meant."

"From the day I was born, he wanted me to study medicine," I explained.

"Oh." He nodded. "Mine did too, and you can see how far that got him." His smile lit up the room.

"At any rate, over time I met other Kansas City Jews, one of them a young divorcée. I fell madly in love with her, married her, and decided to move to New York and become a booking agent. Just couldn't get the music out of my soul." He took a huge bite of meat, chewed it vigorously, wiped his mouth, and said, "So . . . now . . . what about you."

Margene told him I used my middle name, Peter, Pete for short, that we'd met in Little Rock, discovered we liked singing and playing together, and apparently other people liked us, too. We had to scrounge our own gigs, but the Benny Goodman thing would probably help.

"And that's about it," she said with a shrug.

I motioned the waitress for more beer. "Damn, this stuff is good," I said.

"Well," Mr. Stein said, pushing his plate away, "this is your lucky day. From now on, I will be your agent. I will book all your engagements, maybe even move you to Hollywood. I predict you will be an overnight success. Personal appearances, recording sessions. We'll see how it goes. We take out our regular commission. You keep up the quality of your work, your worries are over. Deal?"

Margene let out a whoop.

"Oh, Pete. This is the answer to our dreams. There is nothing to think about."

She turned to Jules and said, "We're in."

Maybe he sensed my reluctance, or perhaps he already knew I had a problem.

"Don't you think you two should talk?"

"No," she said, firmly. Then her voice softened.

"It has been really hard for us."

She told him we'd missed some good offers. Our gigs had been fewer and farther in between, and I hadn't felt well. She turned to me.

"Come on, Pete. What do you say?"

JAZZ TOWN

I saw the excitement in her beaming face and did what I had to do. I took a deep breath, nodded, and said, "Sounds great."

I sucked in my first lung full of marijuana at the age of fourteen, the same age I had my first taste of scotch. By the time I left Miss Sissy's, I was addicted to both. Patch could take it or leave it, but not me. I craved both but managed to keep it under control, at least until after my father died.

When people asked me what happened the night the plane crashed, I couldn't tell them. I guess I'll never know. Maybe if I hadn't been high on grass and a little drunk, things would have been different. Maybe I could have saved his life.

We arrived home from Chicago on Monday, and Tuesday my mother called. I hated the way she treated Margene, but things had seemed to get better in New York. At least they were speaking to one another. Besides, I desperately wanted my mother to be proud of me. I wanted to tell her about Jules Stein myself.

"Come for lunch and we'll talk," she said. Her all too charming manner should have alerted me, but it didn't.

I rang the bell, and John Charles opened the door. "How do, Mr. Pete," he said. He took my coat and hat.

"Hello, John Charles," I said, impressed that he used my professional name.

"You're looking well," *and older,* I thought. "How's Susie Mae?"

"She's doing good. Got two little ones of her own."

"Is that so?"

"Oh, yessuh. She's in the kitchen making lunch. Hilda is getting on, you know. Needs a little help now and then."

"She must be older than God," I laughed.

"Not quite," he answered, smiling. "Your mother is waiting for you in the library, suh."

I followed him past the parlor, noting my handsomely polished baby grand with the lid shut. The power of the ache in my heart startled me as did the thickness that arose in my throat. I wondered if anyone had opened it since my father slammed it shut.

Mother greeted me at the door.

"Come sit down. Would you like something to drink? A cola perhaps?"

What I really wanted was a good strong scotch, but I said, "Cola will be fine."

John Charles went to the bar, fixed the drinks, and handed us each a glass. Then he withdrew. Silence reigned.

"Well," my mother finally said. "Are you feeling better than the last time I saw you?"

"Much," I said, although I felt like shit. Either sickness or icy January temperatures had me shivering, even as a fire crackled in the fireplace.

My mother looked particularly lovely. I liked her best when she dressed casually in cashmere sweaters and wool skirts. Today, she wore purple, the color of her eyes, and a strand of pearls at her neck.

"I wanted you to know how happy I am that I decided to go to New York. Otherwise I would have never known how really talented you are."

Her words overwhelmed me.

"And Margene, too," she continued. "I must admit, she has a nice voice."

High praise from my mother. I stared at her, open-mouthed. "Well, thanks," I managed to say.

She stared out the window, hesitant and a bit off-putting; not at all her style. Finally, she cleared her throat.

"I guess," she said with a self-conscious little cough, "you are wondering why I called this meeting."

"A meeting?" I said, smiling at her. "Relax, mother. Just spit it out."

"I'm concerned about your drinking, Stern."

"My what?"

"Your drinking. That and other things. I hear you use drugs."

She took me by surprise.

"Who told you that? Margene, the little devil."

"I might agree with your terminology but, no, not your wife. Your father."

Every nerve in my body tingled.

"My father is dead, " I said. "I killed him. Remember?"

She looked shocked.

"Why would you say such a thing?"

"Because it's true, isn't it? That's what everyone thinks? If I'd gone for help that day, he'd be alive."

She came and sat beside me.

"No. That's not true at all. When the plane crashed, Kurt's head hit the windshield. The doctors said he never could have survived."

"But John Charles heard him speak," I said.

"No. John Charles heard a dying groan. That you and the woman survived was a miracle."

I had trouble making sense of her words. "But . . ."

She took my hand in hers.

"There is something else I must tell you. It's about your father."

"What more could there be?"

"His name," she answered. "It's Albert Rapinsky."

I heard what she said, but it sounded like an explosion coming out of her mouth.

"Albert?"

She nodded.

"How can that be? He's a homosexual."

"Yes, but it happened."

She pulled away from me and buried her face in her hands.

My thoughts raced.

"All these years I thought . . ."

She raised her head, eyes dry, and in a firm tone said, "I did what I could. I married Kurt. I couldn't explain you to him, much less to the rest of the world. Besides, he had everything we needed – money, family, position, a place in society. What do you think people would have said about me had they known I'd had a liaison with Albert before I married Kurt Adler."

"Are you sure?" I asked, slowly shaking my head in disbelief.

"Positive. You are Albert Rapinsky's son."

I stood and went to the bar.

"I need a drink," I declared.

"No, you don't. That's why I asked you here, to try and convince you to seek treatment. Albert thinks you should go to Menningers."

"Why there? I'm not crazy, you know."

"You must admit yourself somewhere. General Hospital, perhaps. No one will know you there."

"You're nuts," I said. I'd never spoken to my mother that way before. She looked shocked and hurt, her eyes blazing purple. I softened my tone.

"You don't know how hard it is. No one does unless they've been through it. Margene knows."

I poured three fingers of scotch into a glass, downed it, and poured some more.

"Stop. You see? You need to do what I suggest, for yourself, your wife, and me, especially for me."

I turned so fast some of the liquor sloshed over the rim of my glass.

"And why is that?" I scoffed.

"Because" . . . she stammered . . . "I promised Albert you would do as I ask. Don't disappoint me."

"Why must you always think only of yourself, Mother?"

"Well this time, I'm thinking of you," she answered. "You have the makings of a great musician. Don't waste your talent this way."

"Now you sound like Father, or who I thought was my father. According to him, I already have wasted away."

I turned and walked out.

She came running after me.

"Stern. Stop. Can't we talk about this? We haven't even had lunch yet."

I grabbed my hat and coat.

"I love you, Mother. I'll do what you ask. Don't worry. Everything will be all right."

But I knew everything would not be all right. Once again, I'd let everyone down. I'd hit rock bottom. All those unwritten songs whirling in my head would never come out.

I went to Smoky's, my favorite bar, a place Margene and I frequented. They had a nice little piano, so we loved to go there after work, have a drink, and sing our old favorites. It was only two in the afternoon, but I got a bottle and took it to the piano. I had to think. My fingers roamed the keys.

I liked Albert. I think I always knew about the homosexual part, especially after meeting Emil. It didn't matter to me. Maybe I got my lack of courage from him. I thought about Patch getting shot; I'd been afraid of that gun, but I could have stopped it. I thought about Louie beating me up and my father threatening his father. I thought about the night in the lineman's shack, terrified of being alone, and that gig in Little Rock when Margene saved me from getting killed. I put my head on the keyboard and sobbed uncontrollably, remembering the plane crash. Was it all my fault?

And what about our future, Margene and mine? I'd never even gotten around to telling my mother our great news. We could buy a house, a new car. We could bring Darlene up from Little Rock to live with us, take her with us when we traveled or hire a nanny to stay with her at home so she wouldn't miss any school.

My mother was right. I had to admit myself to a hospital, get clean so all those dreams could come true. I'd go to General where no one knew me. I'd sign in under a false name. I took time to think of a good one. John Smith, I decided, and laughed.

My head felt like it would split open. I reached into my pocket and pulled out a bottle of pills, something I'd bought on the street. I poured a few of them into my hand and shoved them into my mouth. Then I chased them with the rest of my booze. I left money on the table, put on my hat and coat, and stumbled out.

I knew a shortcut to the hospital. I knew all the shortcuts. Patch had taught me the shortcuts long ago. I stumbled down an alley, tripped, and fell. The leaves felt soft and smelled good. My hat tipped to one side cradling my head. *I am so tired,* I thought. *I'll just rest here for a moment. Then I'll get up and go on to the hospital.*

# CHAPTER FORTY TWO

## KANSAS CITY, MISSOURI
## 1938
### REBECCA

I stood on the front steps in the freezing cold and watched Stern drive away. Our little talk hadn't gone exactly as I'd planned, but he did say he'd do as I asked. Shivering, I wrapped my arms around myself, and hurried back inside. Susie Mae stood in the hall, her lower lip jutting out.

"What is it?" I asked, annoyed by her look.

"He gone?" she asked.

"Who? Stern? Yes. He's gone. Go back to the kitchen and tell Hilda he won't be staying for lunch."

Her face drooped."Yes'um," she said. She went down the hall mumbling to herself.

"Susie Mae," I called after her.

"Yes'um?"

"I know you wanted to see him, but he'll be back."

I don't know why I felt the need to explain to the maid, but I did.

"We had a little spat, but it will blow over."

"Yes'um," she said, brightening.

I went to the library to call Albert, but before I could dial, the phone rang. I picked it up. Jimmy's voice sounded strange, tight.

"Will I see you tonight?" I asked.

"Yes, but not at your house. I've made other arrangements."

My inner alarm went off, and with a furrowed brow I asked, "What's going on?"

"Nothing for you to be concerned about. There are some guys in from Chicago. I'll take care of it. Pick you up at eight."

Before I could respond, he hung up.

I stood for a minute staring at the phone, then set it gently in its cradle. It seemed he always had something going on. He told me almost nothing about his life, what he did during the day, the people he knew.

Of course, I knew he had a wife and two children, a boy and a girl, but we kept our private affairs separate from our personal liaisons. We both liked it that way, just a weekly interlude in our busy lives.

I called Albert and told him what occurred between Stern and me.

"I tried. I really did," I said. "He became unreasonable and stormed out, but I believe he will accede to my wishes. He won't go to Menninger's but I think he'll admit himself to the hospital. I suggested General."

"Did you tell him about us?" he asked.

"Yes, Albert. I did. He finally knows."

"How did he take it?" I heard a quaver in his voice.

"Much as you'd expect. At first he didn't believe me, but then he seemed to accept it. I imagine once he thinks about all this, he'll understand."

I could hear Albert letting out his breath.

"Good," he said.

"I'm sure we'll hear from him later."

Albert promised me that after Stern got well, he'd help him find a new course for his musical talents.

"And one other thing," he said before we hung up. "Make friends with her, Rebecca. "

I knew who he meant.

That evening I dressed carefully, wanting the night to be special. Maybe it was because Jimmy sounded so stressed on the phone or maybe I needed a little tenderness. I bathed and applied generous amounts of sweet smelling almond lotion. I powdered carefully and stepped into lacy black panties with long elastic garters.

I ran my hands through each sheer black stocking, checking for runs. I hunted through my drawer and found a low cut black bra, skimpy and revealing. Jimmy didn't seem to mind my sagging breasts; in fact, quite the contrary.

I didn't know where he planned to take me, but I felt sure it would be no place we'd be recognized. I decided to dress casually in a one-piece black knit. Then I applied my makeup and surveyed myself in the full length mirror. I liked what I saw but needed something sparkly to perk things up.

I searched my jewelry box for just the right thing but came up with nothing I liked. Then, a thought occurred to me. I went to the wall safe and pulled out my diamond and emerald necklace. I tried it on in front of the mirror. Perfect. The tiny diamonds and the green stones glittered and danced under my dressing room lights.

I laughed when I thought how the original owner of the necklace, Kurt's straight-laced, old fashioned mother, would have felt had she known I would wear it to an assignation.

Jimmy was late as usual. When he did arrive, he looked worn out and harried. I told John Charles not to wait up but reminded him to leave the yard lights on.

Jimmy helped me into my fur coat. I grabbed my purse and we walked down the steps to the car. I scooted over in the back seat, and he crawled in next to me. Big Benny, Jimmy's bodyguard, drove. As we crossed the oak bridge I said, "Why so glum?"

He stared out the window, silent, his gloved hands opening and closing.

"Jimmy? What's going on?"

He turned to me, his lips tightly pursed, anxiety on his face. I'd never seen him like this before.

"Some out-of-town guys are trying to take over my territory." He forced a grin. "But I got it covered."

He didn't say, "I think I've got it covered," but I could tell that's what he meant.

"Of course you do. You're way too powerful to let that happen. After all, you own Kansas City. This is your town, not theirs."

His eyes bored into mine. Finally he said, "You're good for me, baby. Really good. We're two of a kind. And you're absolutely right. This is my town."

He straightened his shoulders, smiled, and took my hand. "Anyway, me and my boys will take care of it tonight. Right, Benny?"

The driver nodded. "Right, boss," he said in his deep, raspy voice.

"You and the boys?" I asked, thinking all my trouble dressing and smelling nice had gone for naught.

"They don't need me. They know what to do. You and me are gonna have a good time, so you don't need to bother your pretty little head about it anymore."

He took a deep breath and leaned back into the seat, brushing his hand down my mink sleeve.

"You're looking swanky tonight, doll."

I hated it when he called me doll. It made me sound like his moll.

"You look tired. Are you sure you're up to an evening with me?"

I heard Benny chuckle, and Jimmy said, "Try me."

We pulled up in front of The President Hotel.

"Is this where we're going?" I asked, eyes wide with alarm. "Someone might see us."

"That's my hope," he said. "Listen, baby. I need to do this. It's a Tuesday night. Some kids that no one has ever heard of are playing, so none of your hoity toity friends are going to be here. It'll be all right. Trust me."

"But why, Jimmy? You didn't tell me. I'm not dressed for nightclubbing."

"You look spiffy, sweetheart, and I gotta do this so that if something bad happens, I have an alibi. Understand?"

"Yes," I said, not at all sure I did.

Benny came around and opened the door. I slipped out, and Jimmy escorted me into the Drum Room. It's one of the nicest places in town, with a red and black drum shaped bar, and subdued lighting. I took a quick look around – a few couples, but no one I knew.

We sat at a back table and ordered drinks. Three skinny Negro kids played piano, drums, and a sax, but no one paid any attention. I began to relax as we chatted nonchalantly.

Halfway through dinner, I saw Jimmy look toward the door, and the muscles in his face tightened. A couple of strangers had entered and made their way to the bar. I could tell he recognized them by the way his back stiffened, but he gave them no sign and turned back to me.

Benny slipped in and leaned against the wall not ten feet away. Two more men, people I'd seen in the elevator at Tom Pendergast's building, took a table near us. They both wore heavy overcoats that did nothing to conceal the long, black guns they carried.

The men at the bar ordered drinks, talked among themselves, and shot furtive glances our way. Finally they sauntered over.

One of them, a heavyset, dark-complexioned man with a pock-marked face and puffed bags under his eyes, nodded to me.

The other, slimmer, more neatly dressed, looked down and said, "I thought you'd be holed up, Jimmy, my boy."

Jimmy laughed. "Why would I do that?"

"I don't know. Just a rumor."

He leaned in so close I could smell garlic on his breath.

"We heard the big boys are in town."

I recoiled from the garlic, and Jimmy waved his hand in front of our faces.

"I know all about 'em. You can tell 'em for me to get lost. I don't pay attention to their comings and goings. Now if you gents will excuse us, my date and I would like to enjoy the music."

He pointed his cigarette at the combo.

"Don't say we didn't warn you," the fat man said. "Come on, Birdy. We got better things to do."

Benny relaxed, and when I looked again, he'd disappeared.

"Who are they?" I asked, frankly afraid.

"Just some minor nuisances," he said. "They'd love to see me gone, but they needed to know I'm not easily scared off. They'll pass the word around we got our eye on them."

We stayed awhile longer before Jimmy whispered, "Let's vamoose."

He steered me out the door and into the car. Benny drove, and to my surprise, we circled the block, ending at the rear of the President Hotel. He watched us enter the back door, then pulled ahead and parked.

We found the freight elevator and rode to the top floor. Jimmy kissed me and felt for my body under my coat.

"I've been wanting to do that all evening," he said. "That dress is a teaser."

I laughed and pushed his hand away.

"Later," I said. "I'll give you the whole routine."

When the elevator stopped, we got off and went to our room. The lights were on, curtains drawn, and the bed turned down. A bottle of champagne sat icing in a silver wine cooler.

"How do you manage these things?" I asked, tossing my coat and purse on the chair by the door, and kicking off my shoes.

He lit a cigarette and watched me, arms folded.

"You are some looker, baby. Come here."

I smiled. He grabbed me and held me close, pressing against me so that I could feel his excitement.

"Can you tell how much I want you?" he kidded. Dropping his cigarette into an ashtray, he took off his coat and picked up the bottle.

"Champagne?"

"Sure."

He popped the cork and poured. Fizz dripped over the rims. We clinked glasses. I started to sit, but he took my hand and pulled me close. I felt his lips on my cheeks, just little pecks, and then on my eyes and my forehead.

He found my mouth with a long, deep, exploring kiss, his lips moist and sensual on mine. This is what I had come for, these glorious moments of raw emotion.

"That's not all I want," I said, loosening his tie.

"Me, either," he whispered, unzipping my dress. It slipped off my shoulders and fell to the floor.

"And we'd better take this off," he said, unclasping my necklace. He laid it on top of the bureau. Then he sat on the bed. I stood in front of him and brought my leg up. I put my foot on the covers next to him, undid the garter, and slowly rolled down my black silk stocking. Slipping it off my foot, I held it up with two fingers, and with a little smile, dropped it.

His warm hands stroked my body. I lowered my foot and raised the other one, placing it on his knee. His eyes followed my actions as I loosened the garter and leisurely slipped off the stocking. He reached under my panties and pulled me to him, inhaling my scent. We collapsed together onto the bed where we did hungry, longingly unspeakable things to each other.

Our lovemaking soared. Much later, he turned out the lights and I curled up in his arms and sank into a deep, dreamless sleep.

Something woke me, and naked, I went into the bathroom. I didn't turn on the light, but I heard the bathtub faucet leaking. When I finished, I flushed the toilet, and began making my way back to bed.

Suddenly, without warning, the bedroom door crashed open. I saw fiery flashes of light and heard the rat-a-tat-tat bursts of explosions. Then . . . blackness.

# CHAPTER FORTY THREE

## KANSAS CITY, MISSOURI
## 1938
### MARGENE

By the time we got home from Chicago even Pete was excited. Being represented by MCA meant the difference between two-bit gigs here and there and steady work with real money; two young people on the brink of success.

Patch went bananas when Pete called him from Chicago to tell him the news. He agreed to come home so that we could have a big going away party, one where the boys could jam all night with their best buddies. Patch hoped maybe Mr. Stein might be able to get engagements for the four of us again; him, Four Eyes, Pete, and me.

Pete's mother called and invited him to lunch. He worried about what she had on her mind, but he went anyway, wanting to tell her about Jules Stein in person.

Ever since the Goodman concert, her attitude toward me seemed different. That night at Twenty One, when she'd asked me to call her Rebecca instead of Mother Adler, I suddenly realized how offensive that must have sounded to her, given the narrow age difference between us. If only for Pete's sake, I would try to be more cordial.

Yet, looking back now, I should have gone to Oakbridge with him. Instead, I dropped him off and went to The Jungle to find Virgil.

I told him our good news and that we wouldn't leave him in the lurch. Mr. Stein gave us time to get our affairs in order. He wanted us to move to Los Angeles where opportunities flourished, but he knew we had to give notice and find a new place to live.

I arrived at our apartment around six, but Pete wasn't there. I thought he had probably gone off to tell his friends. I fussed about wondering what to do about dinner. Maybe we'd go out, get a beer and a sandwich at the deli.

I plumped pillows and straightened the magazines on the coffee table. I picked up a copy of Revue and flipped through it. Damn him. Why didn't he call? He had a habit of getting involved in something and forgetting about me. I looked at my watch every five minutes.

Where was he? I started calling around, first Virgil to see if he'd shown up there, then a couple of the bars where I knew he might go. I understood facing his mother might be difficult, and he might need a drink or two afterwards. He must have caught a cab to Smoky's because they remembered seeing him but didn't know what time he left.

So where was he?

Maybe he'd gone downtown, found someplace warm and forgotten the time. . . or . . . gotten drunk. I'd kill him. By eight o'clock an icy film blanketed the streets. I wrapped myself in my coat, pulled a scarf over my head and went to find him.

I had a nagging feeling in the pit of my stomach. I hit the Club Reno and the Hey Hay Club. Not there. I swung by Miss Sissy's, but she'd gone to Omaha to visit her sick sister, and the ladies said he hadn't been there in weeks.

By the time I got home, I found myself brushing at panicky tears. I slipped on the icy steps and cut my knee. Blood dripped down my leg as I limped up the stairs praying, *Please let him be there, even if he's passed out on the couch.*

That's what I hoped, but the place was empty. I put a bandage on my knee, then sat at the kitchen table in the dark, staring into space. I turned on a light and thumbed through another magazine. Finally I lay down and dozed.

It was well past two in the morning when I awoke. I called Patch. After ten rings, he answered. I told him Pete hadn't come home, that I just knew something had happened to him. He said he'd be right over.

I didn't want to ask Rebecca for help, especially at this hour, but by now I'd reached the panic stage. Maybe she had some idea where he might be. Finally I called Oakbridge. To my utter amazement, she answered the phone. She sounded out of breath.

Stupid me. When I heard her voice, I broke into tears.

"He hasn't come home," I sobbed.

"Margene? Is that you?"

"And I don't know where he is." I could barely control my words.

There was a long pause, and then she said, "Do you mean Pete?"

"Yes, of course I mean Pete. Where could he be?"

"I'll wake John Charles and we'll come for you. Don't worry. We'll find him." She hung up.

# CHAPTER FORTY FOUR

## KANSAS CITY, MISSOURI
## 1938
### REBECCA

Just as I unlocked the door I heard the phone ring. I rushed to pick it up, hoping to hear Jimmy's voice.

What happened? I remembered the firecracker sounds – gunshots. Terrified, I slid to the floor, eyes shut, hands clasped across my mouth.

"That ought to do it," someone said.

Another round of shots and the door slammed shut. I heard footsteps running in the hall outside our room, then silence except for the steady drip, drip of the leaky faucet.

I lay there naked, not daring to move. What if they came back? I whimpered, sat up, dizzy and disoriented. After all that noise, you'd have thought someone would come. No one did.

A white light shone in through the window – the moon, big and round. I could see the bed clothing scattered in tuffs and tatters, Jimmy sprawled amongst them. Spurred into action, I grabbed my under things off the floor, and my dress and shoes, and threw them on. My purse. Where was my purse? Ah, yes, on the chair by my coat. *Get out*, I thought. *Get out of this room.*

I cracked the door. The hallway was dimly lit, empty. I found an elevator, not the one we'd used, and punched the button. I heard it coming. My heart raced. The door opened. Empty. I stepped inside and pushed number one.

No one was in the lobby. I walked out into the night. Where was Benny? Where were the other men? I didn't care. I desperately wanted to be away from this place. The yellow light of a cab appeared. I held up my hand. It stopped and I got in.

"Thank God," I said, grateful for enough mad money to get me home.

As John Charles drove to Pete and Margene's apartment, I realized I wore no stockings. No one would notice. I smoothed my hair and straightened my dress, drew in a deep breath, and composed myself. And then – my hand flew to my throat. My necklace? Where was my emerald necklace? I remembered. On the dresser in that damned hotel room.

I had to think this through. A ten thousand dollar necklace, a priceless heirloom gone, but except for Jimmy, no one would ever connect it to me.

Ramsey stood at the curb with Margene. He got in the front seat with John Charles, and Margene crawled in back. She sobbed out the story, and we sat with the heater running trying to figure out what to do next.

"I've been to every club I can think of," she said. "No one has seen him since he left Smoky's."

"Miss Sissy's?" asked Ramsey.

"Not there. Did he say anything to you?" Margene asked me.

"We talked about his drinking," I confessed. "I suggested he admit himself to General Hospital. He promised he would."

"So let's go back to Smoky's and start from there."

Outside Smoky's, the red neon light blinked on and off, but the place was closed.

"If he tried to get to the hospital, how might he go?" John Charles asked Ramsey.

"Well, he'd head down Main Street and cut through the alleys," he said. "That's how we got around."

I never realized how quiet a town could be so early in the morning. A straggling few wandered about, but we saw no streetcars and few autos. Margene shivered beside me as I snuggled inside my fur coat and then I did something strange. I wrapped my arms around her.

"Turn down here," Ramsey told John Charles, pointing to a narrow lane between two buildings.

Trashcans and papers were everywhere, and leaves, piles of leaves. We inched along through one alley after another. Two more and I could see the hospital.

"He's not here, Ramsey," I said, thinking this whole thing a fiasco.

"It's Patch now, ma'am," he reminded me.

Margene sat straight up and cried out, "Stop. Isn't that his hat?"

How she spotted it in the dimming moonlight remains a mystery to this day.

Patch jumped out and ran over to the mound of leaves. He picked up the hat and then I heard him yell, "He's here. It's him. It's Pete. I'd know that coat anywhere. Hurry up."

We tumbled out of the car and frantically began brushing away at the refuse. Pete lay with his face resting on his hand.

"Is he breathing?" Margene cried.

Patch and John Charles rolled him over.

"I think so. Barely. We gotta get him to the hospital."

John Charles pick him up and put him in the back seat. Margene cradled him in her arms as we sped to the hospital. When we got there, Patch jumped out and ran for help.

Things became a blur. I saw Pete placed on a gurney and wheeled away. Someone steered us to a waiting area. Margene sat next to me, trembling. Patch and John Charles leaned against a wall nearby. I looked at myself and thought, *What a mess,* but somehow it didn't seem to matter.

After what seemed hours, a nurse came and got us. Margene rushed ahead. Pete lay on a bed, half-covered by a white sheet. He looked ghostly pale, his red hair a sharp contrast to his skin. Tubes came out of his mouth and arms.

"What's his name?" the doctor asked.

"Pete." "Stern," Margene and I both said together, and then I said, "Pete."

The doctor smiled and said, "Well I'm glad you both agree on that. Are you his wife?" he asked Margene

She took Pete's hand in hers and nodded.

"And I'm his mother," I said.

"I see. I'm Doctor Greenberg. I assure you both, we're doing all we can to save this boy's life."

I stared at Pete's face, his slack mouth, his closed eyes. I reached up and brushed at a leaf tangled in his hair.

"What happened to him?"

"Looks like a combination of too much alcohol and too many pills. We've pumped his stomach. That black stuff you see around his mouth is charcoal. Helps to absorb the drugs." The doctor rested his hand on Margene's shoulder.

"I think we got to him in time. He's a lucky man. If you hadn't found him when you did" . . . he shrugged . . ."What's your name, dear?"

"Margene," she said, never taking her eyes off her husband.

"Well, Margene, he's not out of the woods yet, but I believe he'll make it. He's in a coma right now. We'll just have to wait and see, but he's young. We're going to keep him here and watch him. You can stay, but when we move him upstairs, you'll have to leave. Hospital regulations."

First she smiled, and then she broke down in tears.

"There, there," Doctor Greenberg said. "God willing, he'll get through this."

Patch and Margene stayed with Pete, her fingers curled around Pete's. John Charles took me home.

I made my way up the winding staircase to my suite and collapsed on the bed, exhausted. The terror of the previous night roused me from sleep. Once, I sat up straight up in bed, certain I'd heard the sounds of gunfire. Middle-of-the-night worries clouded my brain. *What if someone had seen me?*

I turned on my bedside lamp. Comforted by the sight of my own surroundings, I lay back only to struggle with the images of Jimmy's bullet-riddled body. Not until morning did I learn what had happened. **"Gangland Killing,"** the newspaper said. No mention of who did it or why, and thankfully, no mention of me.

Shocked and sickened, I mourned the loss of my lover, but at the same time, I breathed a sigh of relief.

Late that afternoon the doorbell rang. I looked out my bedroom window and saw a sheriff's car. My heart leaped to my throat. *What should I do? Where can I go? Calm down,* I told myself. *They can't know anything.*

John Charles came to announce the visitor.

"Sheriff Bash," I said, following John Charles down the stairs. "How nice to see you."

"Hello, Rebecca," he said. As he took off his cowboy hat I saw him staring at my portrait on the wall.

John Charles vanished into the kitchen.

"Won't you come in?" I said.

"I can't stay. I just dropped by to bring you something I think belongs to you. Let me explain. I happened to be only a few blocks away from a murder scene last night, so I answered the call. It was a bloody mess. Policemen everywhere. A gangster named Jimmy Galeno had been shot."

"How awful," I said, struggling to keep my breathing regular.

"The officers figured he'd most likely been with a prostitute. They found some silk stockings but she got away. In the melee, I saw something I'd seen before. I picked it up and put it in my pocket. I believe it's yours."

He held out my diamond and emerald necklace.

Taken aback, my brain whirled. "Well for goodness sakes," I said, thinking quickly. "I discovered it missing only today and was about to call the police. Thank goodness you found it."

He smiled.

"Better not leave it lying around, Rebecca. It's probably worth a lot of money."

"You're right, of course. I must be more careful."

"Have you any idea . . . " he began.

"No. None whatsoever. I can hardly remember the last time I wore it. How can I ever thank you?"

He stared at me for a moment, his eyes thoughtful and appraising. Then he turned to leave.

"No need," he said.

I saw him out and stood for a moment with my back against the door, my heartbeat returning to normal. Then I walked upstairs, removed the Matisse from the wall, spun the dial, and returned the necklace to the safe.

# CHAPTER FORTY FIVE

## KANSAS CITY, MISSOURI
## 1938

### MARGENE

Once Pete came around, I knew what I had to do. Rebecca wanted him to stay in the hospital, but I begged to take him home where I could help him through the awful days to come.

"All right then," she said, "but we must take him to Oakbridge."

I won't describe those awful days, but every time he said he couldn't do it, I reminded him of where he found me in Little Rock.

"If I can get through it, so can you," I told him – over and over again.

I guess he got sick of hearing me because he finally stopped complaining. He just huddled under blankets or curled up in a corner on the floor, shivering, moaning, and sobbing into his hands. At long last, the tremors went away and we began to talk of the future.

"Stein won't want us anymore," he said.

"Let's just get you well and then we'll see," I told him.

"It won't be any good, Margene. I guess we can always go back to The Jungle."

I didn't want to go back to The Jungle. I had Hollywood on my mind.

Rebecca left us alone, though she saw to our personal comforts and meals.

One day she came to Pete's room and knocked softly on the door. "Would you have lunch with me?" she asked.

"I don't think so," I said, remembering the last time.

"We won't be long," she told Pete." Just a quick bite at Wolferman's."

"Go on," he said. "I'll be fine."

She waited until we ordered and then said, "It may not always have seemed like it, but I love my son. I have always wanted what's best for him. I admit, I didn't think you filled the bill, but a few weeks ago you proved me wrong."

She paused and looked down at her hands.

"I have no doubt you've saved his life, and for that I am very grateful. I will find a way to prove that to you."

"You don't have to do that," I said, thinking how I would have felt had it been Darlene.

"I do and I will," she said. "I think I have misjudged you, Margene. Perhaps we can find a way to get along."

"I'd like that, " I said.

"Any suggestions?" she asked.

I thought for a minute and then I had an idea. "Well for one thing, you could teach me how to buy the right clothes. I have awful taste, and you always look like you stepped out of *Vogue* magazine."

She laughed in a merry, charming way I'd never seen before.

"I'd love to do that."

She stood up. "I need to find a telephone."

Our lunch arrived just as she returned to our table.

"I've taken care of everything," she said, a broad smile lighting up her face. "My saleslady at Harzfeld's will be waiting for us. Let's hurry and eat. Then, Margene,  you and I are going shopping."

# CHAPTER FORTY SIX

## KANSAS CITY, MISSOURI
## 1938

### PETE

Over time, I watched my wife and my mother become friends. Don't ask me how that happened. It just did. Margene gave up the apartment and came to live at Oakbridge. My mother stayed away from me until I stopped feeling so bad. She's not good around sick people.

She had Hilda make her famous get well soup and John Charles brought it to me, bowl after bowl. I remember him taking soup to my grandfather right before he died. I wondered if that would happen to me, but instead, Margene kept spooning it into my mouth, and day by day, I got stronger.

Albert Rapinsky came often. We talked of his family, how his father died and his mother taught piano lessons, his career, his and Emil's life, and mine.

I'll never think of him as my father. Kurt Adler was that, but I know that Albert will always be there for me.

Patch came every day – with his horn. He could hardly wait to get back to business. The day came when Margene said, "Time to go downstairs and do a little jammin'."

I had to laugh. I could barely walk upright and they wanted to jam, but hanging onto the banister with John Charles steadying me,

I got down to the parlor, and there stood my piano, in its old place, lid open.

Weak and unsteady, I sat down and placed my fingers on the keys: a beginning. We laughed when Susie Mae brought milk and cookies for us all.

Every day, I got better, but I cringed when Margene brought up the future. One evening, Mother, Margene, Patch, and I sat in the library playing Monopoly, a new board game Patch had found.

Margene said, "You know Pete, you're almost well. Why don't you call Jules Stein and ask if the offer still holds?"

"What offer?" my mother asked.

"Before Pete got sick, Mr. Stein told us he'd be our agent. He wanted us to move to Hollywood," Margene said.

"So call him," Mother said.

I shook my head. "I can't. He won't want us now. Anyway, I'm too embarrassed. I've made such a mess of things."

"Well, for heaven's sake. I'll call him," my mother said. "I've known Jules Stein for twenty years."

She reached for the phone. "Anyone have his number?" she asked.

Margene handed her his card.

"Jules Stein, please. Rebecca Adler. Yes. I'll wait."

The three of us stared at her, paralyzed.

"Jules? Is that you? Rebecca Adler here, Kurt's wife. Yes, it has been a long time. How's Doris? Wonderful. Looking for a house in California? What fun. Kurt's death? Yes. It was a tragedy, but fortunately, Pete survived, and speaking of Pete, I guess you know he's been ill? Well, thank you. He's doing fine now. He and Margene fully expect to come to Hollywood soon. When would you like them?"

She listened for a long time, nodding and smiling.

We dared to breathe.

"In June?" she said. "All of them in June? I'm sure that will be perfect for them. Pete will get back with you in the next day or two. In the meantime, give Doris my regards and tell her I'm looking forward to coming to visit you when you find a place in Hollywood. Love to you, too. Bye."

She turned to us. "Now that wasn't so hard, was it?"

We burst out laughing.

"What did he say?" I asked. "What was that about all of us."

"He wants you to form a band. Find ten or twelve quality musicians here in Kansas City, get organized, arrange some songs and be out there in June, ready to go. He'll arrange the gig, whatever that is."

Margene and I fell into each other's arms, relief flooding us both.

"Does that mean me too?" Patch asked.

"Of course," I said. "You and Four Eyes and eight or ten more. You need to get out of here and go find us a band: sax and trombone players, trumpets, guitar, bass."

He said, "It won't be hard. The clubs ain't doin' so good. A lot of guys lost their jobs. I see them hangin' out at the Union."

"Be choosy, Patch. Pick the best ones. We'll try them out here. If they're good enough, they stay. If not . . . ." I pointed my thumb toward the door. "I'll get busy writing and arranging, and Margene can start warming up her voice. Hollywood, here we come."

# CHAPTER FORTY SEVEN

## KANSAS CITY, MISSOURI
## 1938
### SUSIE MAE

The day they brought Mastah Pete home, he looked more dead than alive. John Charles carried him up the stairs to his old room. I'd put clean sheets on the bed but he done throwed up on 'em afore John Charles even set him down.

Miss Margene wanted us all to stay out but I couldn't do that. I brought fresh water to wash him and blankets to stop the chills. Miss Margene, she knew how to talk to him, what to say. She never left his side, but I knew best how to clean him up.

Hilda made him her good soup, but for the longest time, he couldn't keep it down. Miss Rebecca, not good with sickness, stayed away, but I knowed she cared. I'd see her sitting alone in the library staring out the window, a sadness in her eyes.

Sometimes she'd get up and close the door trying to shut out Mastah Pete's wailing. Other times, she'd come into the kitchen and sit at the table – wouldn't talk or nothin – just sit. Made us all a little itchy.

Finally the day came when Miss Margene brought Mastah Pete down to the parlor. 'Course, everyone called him Pete by now, even me. Seeing him sit hisself at the piano and begin to play gave me goosebumps. Before long he and Patch banged out music just like the old days. And then, all manner of music people toting their instruments began wandering in and out of the house. Good thing we had no close neighbors to complain.

At night I'd go home to my two chillin, and the next morning there I'd be back at Oakbridge. Me, John Charles, and Hilda went back to doing what we'd been doing for the past twenty years. Life goes on, don't it?

# CHAPTER FORTY EIGHT

## KANSAS CITY, MISSOURI
## 1939
### REBECCA

He decided to call the band Pete Adler and his Peas in a Pod. MCA liked it. By the end of May, they were ready to leave Kansas City. I hated to see them go. Over the past few months, I'd found I like Margene although two 'ladies of the house' in one dwelling can be thorny.

Because of Pete our relationship was at once endearing and difficult. Nevertheless, she has a way of handling herself that I admire. I befriended her as I never expected to do and thanks to me, she acquired a lovely new wardrobe.

Her daughter Darlene arrived on Decoration Day, all excited about moving to California. She's a sweet little thing, twelve, I believe, and in need of socializing. I'll be up to the task when she visits.

I gave much thought to a proper gift for my daughter-in-law. The day before they left, I invited her into my suite. I took down the Matisse and opened the safe.

"I want you to have this," I said, withdrawing my dowry money. "My father gave my husband a good deal of money to take me off his hands. Though it's a ridiculous old tradition, I've learned it has some value. It provided a valuable safety net for me though I had to wrest it away from my husband. Now I'm gifting it to you with full confidence that you will know what to do with it."

Margene began to cry. She threw her arms around me and I patted her back, surprised at how good she made me feel.

I withdrew the little jewelry box from the lockbox and put it in my pocket. Then I closed the safe, my emerald necklace safe inside.

When Albert came to say goodbye, I gave him the Jaccard's jewelry box. "Perhaps you'd like to do the honors," I said.

He opened the case and momentarily gazed at the ring before he handed it to Pete.

"This belonged to my mother," Albert told his son. "I want you to have it."

Pete stared down at the diamond nestled snuggly amongst the sapphires, his mouth slightly open. Then he burst into smiles and threw his arms around Albert.

"You know," he said, "I couldn't afford a ring for Margene." He went to her and slipped it on her finger. She, too, hugged Albert and I saw tears in her eyes.

I still live at Oakbridge. Pete, Margene, and Darlene visit when they can. Hilda finally retired so I've hired a new cook, a colored girl Bertha recommended. She's not as good as Hilda, but I'll train her. John Charles and Susie Mae have remained at Oakbridge, and a good thing, too. The next time Pete and his family come, my new grandchild will be with them. An heir is on the way.

The End

# Beth Lyon Barnett

About the Author

Beth and her husband live in Prairie Village Kansas, a suburb of

 Kansas City, Missouri with their dog, "Too Tall" Looie who they rescued from life in a cage. Beth's work has appeared in numerous magazines and periodicals including *The Kansas City Star*. She is a graduate of Mills College in Oakland CA. As a registered X-Ray Technologist, she directed a large hospital radiology department and later worked for the French company, CGR Medical Corporation, selling high-end and special procedures diagnostic X-ray equipment. She is a founding member of the local Court Appointed Special Advocates (CASA) projects. Beth is a member of the Kansas City Writer's Group, an original member of the amazing e-pub group, Write Brain Trust, and the board of directors and copy editor of Whispering Prairie Press, publishers of *Kansas City Voices,* a periodical of writing and art.

Visit Beth at:  http://www.bethlyonbarnett.com

# Beth Lyon Barnett